THE WINDWARD KING

K.T. IVANREST

INK DRAKE PRESS

THE WINDWARD KING

Cover design by Damonza.com

ISBN: 978-1-956675-01-6

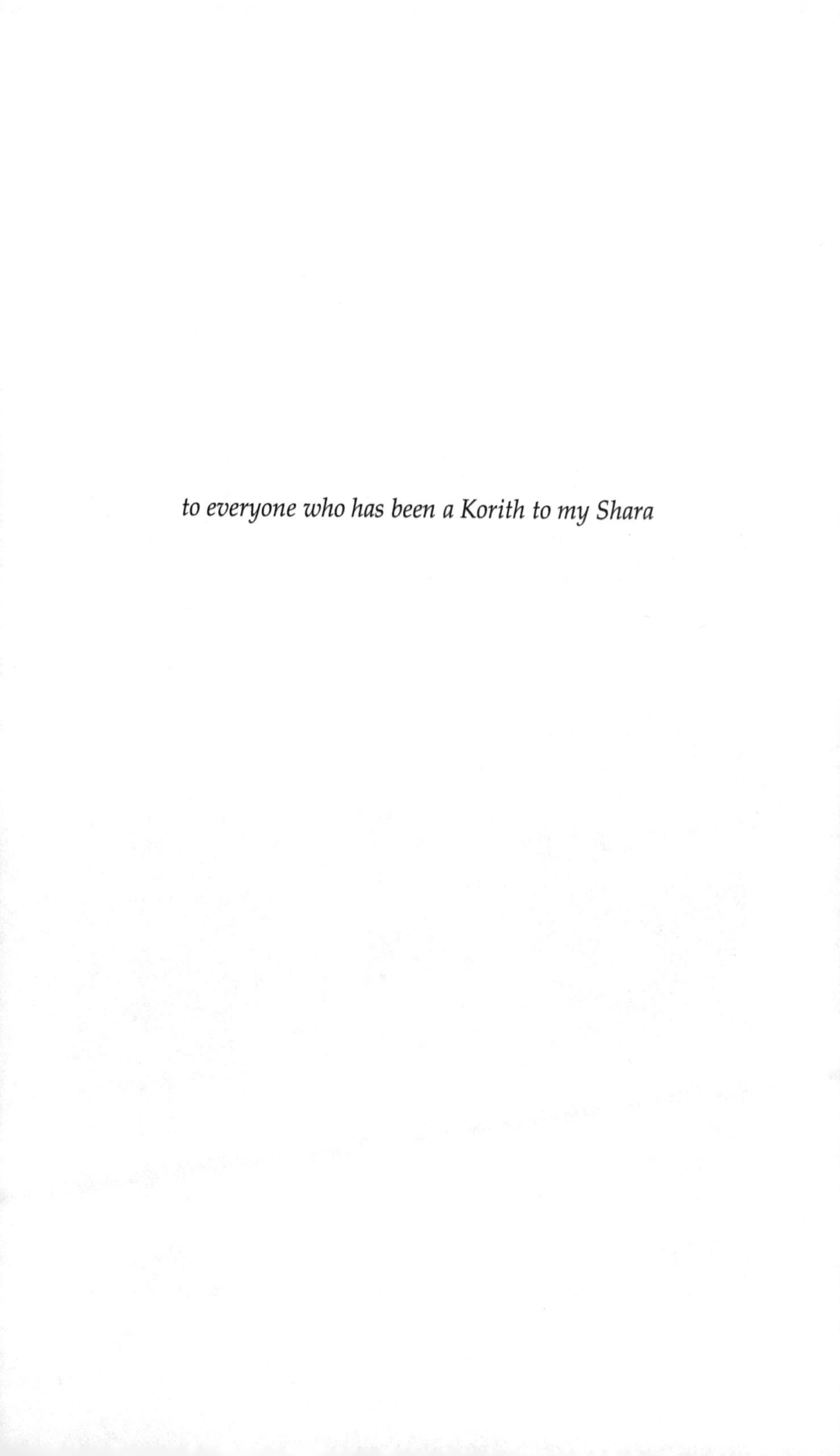

to everyone who has been a Korith to my Shara

BARATH
N
S
Shor Kal
SOMETH
FARNA

NORTH TO
Alvithi Territory
Shor Sprinta
Delgar
Pannel
FARNA
Tel Aveth
WOLF'S NOSE
THE TALONS
SEA

CONTENTS

THE WINDWARD KING

K.T. IVANREST

Chapter 1

Teveth

By the time Shara realized he shouldn't have jumped, it was too late.

He'd spent all morning on the mountain ledge, shifting to dragon form and back, building confidence and determination until he'd finally convinced himself he was ready. A shift midair.

He hadn't been ready.

Cold spring wind slapped his face as if some invisible hand were trying to startle him from sleep. But the nightmare kept coming—the dark cliffs flashing past, the grasping trees reaching up to meet him, the bright disc of the lake throwing sunlight into his watery eyes.

Dragon, dragon, dragon!

Power thrummed through his limbs but refused to obey. Always uncooperative, always sluggish, but of course it would give up on him *now*, a hundred dragon-lengths above the springtide festival. Now, when he needed everything, just once, to go right.

And instead his carefully woven plans were unravelling even faster than his abilities.

Dragon. Claws and wings and—

A roar split the clouds, and his stomach lurched. Not that. Even hitting the ground would be better than *that*.

His clan-brother pelted toward him in a flash of rich brown scales, his laughing bellow searing across the sky. Pulse racing, Shara squeezed his eyes shut, stretched his arms further, splayed his fingers in a desperate attempt at wings. He was *not* going to let Lethir catch him, not after he'd spent the last month preparing for today.

Was anyone watching? Family members, clan mates, festival guests? What if they'd all paused their merriment to see whether he—

Focus. His sister Rathen claimed that this exercise sharpened one's focus. But focus on what? The pathetic tingling in his limbs? The wind tearing at his clothing and hair and horns, the persistent beat of Lethir's wings growing ever louder . . .

Dragon, Shara! Come on, you stupid teveth!

His body thrilled, and his breath hitched. There! He could still do it. Draw out the scales and wings, smother the burning humiliation, ignore that the sun had gone out—

The massive shadow overhead materialized, and with a laughing roar, Lethir plucked him from the sky and banked toward the lake.

Shara didn't bother trying to escape. It never worked.

The lakeshore teemed with visitors from every clan—earth, fire, and water alvithi, all gathered to renew old relationships and forge new ones amidst a celebration of spring. Cubs and kits romped in the shallows while older children challenged each other to shifting games. A wolf and a sea dragon sunned themselves atop a pile of broad rocks, watching the children and avoiding the loud greetings and conversations rippling up and down the shore. Lumpy piles of wood marked the sites of future bonfires, some rigged with pots and spits, others bare. One already burned from a low corner, and a man hastily tossed sand over it as a woman scolded a small dragon.

If there was one thing Shara was good for, it was serving as an entertaining cautionary tale to alvithi children about the dangers of being inadequate. Lethir flew a low, leisurely lap around the lake before dropping Shara amid a cluster of young men and women. Snickers and whispers crackled around him.

Lethir landed in a spray of sand and gave his wings a dramatic flick before shifting. Shara shoved himself upright and brushed himself off, trying not to stare. Watching Lethir shift was like watching waves roll along the seashore—seamless, graceful, and powerful, a swirling eddy of push balanced perfectly against pull. To have toresh like that . . .

Lethir paused in his human form and dropped his guard, but Shara wasn't fool enough to take such obvious bait, and with a careless shrug, Lethir shifted the rest of the way into his true form. Pine-branch horns arced back from his forehead, and scales of the same rough brown patterned themselves over his arms and along his cheekbones. Like some of the other young alvithi, he added wings in honor of today's festivities.

Because nothing said "pompous pine tree" like a pair of wings.

"All right there, teveth?" Lethir raked a lazy hand through his hair and over his horns.

"I'm fine," Shara muttered, picking grains of sand from between the birch scales on his forearm. Somewhere in the world, *fine* meant *boiling in humiliation,* right?

"*Are* you, though?" asked a young woman whose curly hair had been shifted bright blue to match her scales. "Why didn't you shift?"

Shara's clan-mates exchanged subtle glances, rustling their wings as if in preparation for a collective escape. Maki and

Pela bit their lips in their usual method of restraining laughter, but no one else seemed ready to embarrass Shara in front of so many visitors.

Bless the Eagle for small things, anyway.

Giving up on cleaning his scales, Shara shrugged and brushed at his tangled curls. "Did you really think I wasn't going to?"

It was a cowardly reply, but better to let her think he'd planned a sensational last-minute shift than to lie outright.

"Lethir!" The blue-haired girl prodded Lethir's arm. "Why did you interrupt him?"

Lethir growled and narrowed his eyes at Shara, who hunched and retreated a step, breath catching in his throat. *Burrs!* He knew better than to challenge Lethir, even with words.

His clan-brother listed his head, wolf-like, and his lips parted into a sharp-toothed sneer. "You know what? You're right. Let's give him another try."

He shifted as he moved, body curving forward into the powerful tree dragon. Shara staggered back with a squawk, tripped on someone's foot, and toppled over.

Lethir pounced.

Hissing sand and grasping claws. Lethir launched upward, dragging Shara into the sky. The world spun, someone shouted, Shara's insides turned to stone and then lava, and suddenly he was falling, falling—

Frigid water enveloped him, and the world fell mercifully silent. The drapes of his surcoat swirled around him, and he let himself float, suspended and still, for as long as his breath would last.

Lethir and his friends were still laughing when he surfaced.

"See you, teveth!" Lethir shouted, tossing a jaunty wave over his head as the group moved off down the shore.

Shivering, Shara pulled himself toward the shore and

crawled, dripping, onto the sand. Gazes swept over him like the brush of feathers from a passing bird. Half-relieved at the disinterest, he shifted into a lynx and back into his true form. Awkward, slow, embarrassing, but at least now he was dry.

Teveth.

Humiliation curdled into a determined sludge in his stomach. He would *not* spend the rest of his life as teveth.

It's just a word, Shara. All it means is you're still learning. There's nothing wrong with that.

Scoffing, he shoved his father's words away and climbed to his feet. It was just a word when you went on your first hunt or entered into an apprenticeship, or when all eight of your siblings wanted to affectionately remind you that you were youngest. It wasn't just a word when you were twenty-two and still being passed around the clan like a spare tool because you weren't good enough for anything more.

Swallowing hard, he raised his eyes and began searching in earnest for his eldest brother, Clan Han's leader. He had a question to ask, and if everything went well—and it would; it *had* to—then *teveth* would finally be just a word again.

And not a word for Shara.

CHAPTER 2

LESS SHARA

Alanthas ko Han stood a head taller than everyone else and accentuated it with perfect posture. In human form, he could have passed for nobility, or so said those who'd met nobility. Shara shared his brother's birch features, but without them, he'd have been lucky to pass for a servant.

Drawing a breath, he inched closer to Alanthas and the other clan leaders.

"... too young to visit the humans ..."

"... the Barathi king, yes, a few weeks ago in his sleep ..."

"... *another* band of pirates; that's the third ..."

"Alanthas?"

His brother pivoted, the catkins on his spring-budded horns swaying with the motion; his expression crushed the last of Shara's hope that Alanthas hadn't seen the whole thing. Excusing himself from the group, he ushered Shara to an empty patch of beach and gave him a cursory sniff. "You're all right, then?"

Shara's toes curled, dragging through the sand. "I'm fine." Embarrassed, disappointed in himself, and looking over his shoulder for Lethir, but what else was new? "I thought it would be good . . . That is, Rathen said . . ."

His brother arched his eyebrows. "And is your name Rathen?"

Shara's face flooded with heat. Just because Alanthas was twice his age didn't mean he had to go and use their father's old admonitions. "That's not what I meant."

His toes dug deeper, and he plucked a yellow leaf from his autumn horns and shredded it. This was all wrong. The plan had been to leap from the cliffside, shift with all the toresh he could muster, soar gracefully to the shore, find his brother, and ask—

"Can I join the hunt?"

Raucous laughter exploded down the shore—his sister Fansha, already several rounds into the day's drinks and convinced she was hilarious.

Alanthas threw an exasperated smile in her direction, then turned to Shara. The smile faded. "You wish to hunt, Ishara?"

His shoulders slumped. As a child, he'd been intimidated by Alanthas's constant formality, but now that extra syllable felt like another weight he couldn't carry. "I know I'm not good at—"

"That isn't what I meant." He regarded Shara seriously, looming like a disapproving tree. "You know this isn't about hunting prowess."

No, it wasn't. It wasn't so much a hunt as a cooperative performance. Every hunter had to be ready to shift at the slightest notice, to change color or form or both with finesse, to improvise as an individual or as part of a team depending on what was needed.

Power and instinct, talent and toresh, confidence and decisive action.

All the things Shara lacked.

Even so, he rolled his shoulders back and tried to look enthusiastic and not like he wished he were playing malir in his cave or inventing riddles for his five-year-old niece.

"I know," he said. "But I want to try."

He didn't have to distinguish himself—there was no chance of that. But if he could just keep up. If he could, for once, not be the one struggling and falling behind.

Alanthas folded his arms, and his eyes swept over Shara, lingering on his sea-blue surcoat. One of their mother's last creations, left as a gift for her youngest son. Would she have cared that Shara had been unable to shift until he was nearly four? Comforted him after his coming-of-age ritual or cringed with everyone else? With eight other children, would she have noticed him at all?

Was she watching him now from the Eagle's realm, waiting to see him hunt? Waiting in anticipation—or dread?

The determined sludge in his stomach solidified. "You know, never min—"

"Very well."

The hum of voices intensified as Shara's senses flared. "What?"

"I'll see you're given a place in the hunt. Earth, sea, or sky?"

"Earth." The odds of him plummeting to the ground again or drowning midshift were too great for anything else.

"What's this?" Something very loud and vibrantly green barrelled into Shara and wrapped him in a choke-hold. "Causing problems again, baby brother?"

Shore and water and sky blurred together as Rathen yanked back and forth on Shara's horns, scattering autumn-yellow leaves to the ground around them. Just when Shara feared he'd have to spend the rest of the day with bare horns, his sister dove for Alanthas, who sidestepped her neatly, never losing his poise.

"Wetwings." She kicked sand at him with a grin. "Anyway, what'd I miss?"

You told me to jump off a cliff, and I was fool enough to try it.

"Ishara is joining the hunt this year."

Rathen burst into laughter but cut herself off when neither of them joined her. "Wait, you're serious? Shara? This Shara?"

"This Shara." Irritation crept into Alanthas's usually even voice.

She raised her hands, then slapped Shara's shoulder. "Well, I . . . well! Good for you."

"Thanks," Shara mumbled, but he knew his sister's tone all too well. *Give it a try, Shara, but don't be disappointed if you fail.*

Too many memories echoed with that sentiment.

"Well." He faked a smile. "I'll just . . . go . . . for now." He'd finish off the last of the winter's dried fruit, then find Thia and his other little nieces and nephews and distract himself weaving riddles.

Alanthas nodded. "Be at the Speaking Rock when it's time."

Shara fled as if Lethir were bearing down on him again, but he'd not gone a dozen paces when he heard his name. He knew that tone, too—the one that told him to walk faster, because he wasn't going to like what he heard.

But he stopped anyway.

"He asked," Alanthas was saying.

"Yes, but are you sure it's wise to trust Shara on the hunt? He's fair under normal circumstances, but today is different."

"I know. But he seemed determined. And to be honest, I'm pleased to see him trying to be a little less . . ."

A pause. At last Rathen offered, "Shara?"

"Precisely."

A pair of bear cubs collided with Shara's legs, toppled over onto the sand, and sprang back into their true forms, laughing in delight. Shara shook himself and hurried on.

A little less Shara.

His fists clenched. He could do that. He *had* done it. He'd asked. He was going to join the hunt.

Mishala's horns, what had he been thinking?

CHAPTER 3

THE SPRINGTIDE HUNT

Shara had barely wrestled down his nausea when Alanthas began announcing the hunting parties—and appointed Shara and Lethir co-leaders of their group.

From the look on Lethir's face, it was difficult to say who was more horrified by this arrangement.

The only other thing Shara remembered from the Speaking Rock was the prayer to the Eagle, and when he came out of his haze, he found himself flying along the mountain ridges to his party's appointed meeting place. Another, smaller lake was nestled amidst a sea of green, its little stretch of rocky shore rising almost immediately into dense forest. It would be good hunting.

Unless Lethir decided they'd be hunting Shara.

Emotions churning, he touched down alongside the other four hunters, clenching his claws around the rocks to steady his nerves before shifting into his true form to match the rest of them.

Pine and earth and the unfamiliar scents of his fellow hunters spiced the cool spring air. Shara had drawn only two soothing breaths when Lethir went breezing past. He threw his wings wide, clipping Shara's shoulder, and planted himself before the group.

"Let's get started. I'm Alethir ko Han." He pointed at the blue-haired girl. "This is—"

"Ashi." She chirruped and offered the group a cheerful wave instead of a clan name. Typical water alvithi.

"Ashi. And you two?"

They were sisters, Epalith and Omatha, with the distinct red-black scales and spiralling horns of the westernmost fire clan.

"And you?" Epalith asked Shara when Lethir showed no intention of introducing or acknowledging him.

"That's Shara." Lethir waved a careless hand, but a faint bite iced his tone. "Anyway, we'll be taking the area here"—he flicked a wing behind him—"keeping between these two peaks. Game should be plentiful, but steer clear of mothers with young."

He continued the speech, rehearsing clean kills and bird signals and other things they'd all known since before their first hunts—even Omatha, who was young enough to be a proper teveth.

"Any questions?"

Epalith faked a yawn, hissing a slender trail of smoke. "Yes, are we camping here tonight, or is the hunt actually going to begin anytime soon?"

Omatha clapped a hand over her mouth and giggled, and Ashi grinned. Shara swallowed his snicker. No need to give Lethir another reason to trounce him.

Lethir bristled and then sleeked. "We'll go in two groups. Ashi and I will start as hawks. You two go in as deer and scent out the ground. Signal if you find anything promising. And watch out for neeka, especially—"

"We know how to hunt, tree-head."

Shara bit down another grin; Epalith would make the hunt bearable. "And me?"

Lethir's eyes glinted. "Stay out of the way and try not to burr anything up."

The eager mood splintered into stunned silence, broken by the soft teasing of little waves against the rocks. Omatha shook herself, shifted, and bounded toward the trees as if she couldn't escape the tension quickly enough. Lethir and Ashi followed in a flutter of wings.

Shara closed his eyes to shift, but a hand caught his arm.

"Are you going to take that?" Epalith's coal-dark gaze bored into him.

Telling her that he heard "stay out of the way" several times a day would do nothing for his reputation. Nor would pointing out that Lethir was a better leader—a better every-thing. "He's just trying to bait me."

"But you were appointed co-leader, and even if you hadn't been . . ."

His face flushed, but he shook his head. "I'm not going to divide us or delay the hunt by challenging him over something stupid."

But he'd hunt no matter what Lethir said. Let *that* be his challenge.

She stared so hard she might have been trying to light Shara on fire with nothing but will. At last she scoffed, smoke curling around her sneer. "Molting coward."

A blur of reddish-brown and the tapping of doe hooves on stone, and Shara stood alone on the shore. Swallowing a growl, he squeezed his eyes shut again and focused on shifting.

Despite Epalith's jabs at Lethir, the team worked well together—and perfectly well without Shara.

As soon as Lethir had realized that someone would need to deliver their kills to the lake, he'd appointed Shara to the task. "Find us again when you're done. You're always falling behind anyway, so you have plenty of tracking experience."

The first time, Shara did as ordered, but as he deposited the second kill at the alvithi gathering and Alanthas's gaze burned into his back, he began to wonder whether he ought to challenge Lethir after all. He'd lose, but he'd be doing something.

He took his time returning to their hunting area, letting the wind carry him at its own pace while he rolled possibilities through his mind. Not that he'd ever go through with them. For another alvithi, maybe. For Thia when older children picked on her. But not for himself.

A frustrated keen scratched at his throat, and he banked south. If he flew on, he'd eventually catch sight of the northernmost islands of the human nation of Barath. His people traded in the city of Shor Kal occasionally, though Shara had gone only once, when a harsh winter had prevented supply ships from reaching the city and hunting had been poor. He still had some of the human gifts, including a book of myths and legends containing hilariously incorrect assumptions about the alvithi.

The memory made him snort, jolting his attention back to the hunt. His claws tightened, and he was tucking his wings for a dive when a scent wafted through the air, strong and pungent.

Boar.

His better judgment fought a brief battle with his predatory instincts. He wouldn't risk taking on a den of boar alone, not even as a dragon—contrary to what the human book said, al-vithi dragons were not much larger than horses. But he could lead the team to the den, and this time, he wouldn't let Lethir send him away.

He flew a quick loop, sealing the place in his memory. As he banked overhead, something sharp swiped at his nostrils, a new tinge of unpleasant odor he couldn't place, mingled with the heady rush of boar. Not rot or death, but—

Gone.

He wheeled and breathed deeply, trying to catch it again, then chided himself. He knew better than to chase phantom scents, especially after so many failed childhood hunts.

Not this time. Loosing a determined cry, he turned his course toward the lake.

On the western shore, the yellows and browns of the un-derbrush were giving way to green spring buds. A neat pile of quail steamed in the blood-splattered grass near the edge of the water, guarded by three foxes and a russet-feathered ea-gle.

Shara circled overhead, heart hammering, and made sev-eral short, high calls. He didn't dare land or shift. If he told Lethir the den's location, his clan-brother would bully him into taking the quail and leaving the boar to the rest of them.

Coward.

But he remained aloft anyway, circling and signalling twice more before peeling off toward the den. For agonizing mo-ments, the sky remained empty except for clouds, but at long last, four dragons rose into the air. One soared away with the quail; the other three fell in line behind Shara. His heart leapt, and he quickly shook himself sober. The real test lay ahead, and Lethir's mood would be more sour than ever.

They touched down a safe distance from the den and shifted their scales to match the deep browns and greens of their surroundings. At a disgruntled snarl from Lethir, Shara led the way, letting the gentle pricks of pine needles against his claws steady him. It was almost cold here, the dense, full evergreens blocking out all but faint threads of sunlight.

Not teveth, his mind whispered with each quiet step, each chirp of birdsong overhead. *Not teveth.*

The scent grew stronger, sharper. Ashi's tail lashed, and Omatha nuzzled Shara, half-bouncing with eagerness. Even Lethir's ears pricked in begrudging interest.

A dark hollow reached into the hillside ahead, draped with brush, a fallen spruce bough sprawled alongside the entrance. But though the scent swirled around them, there was no sign of the boar.

No sign of anything, in fact. The birdsong had stilled, and not a single squirrel-dragon moved in the trees.

Shara shook himself as his scales rippled with unease. He was overreacting. The boars were probably out foraging, and—

A growl thrummed in his throat. The unfamiliar odor had returned, not so much a scent as a faint stinging in his eyes. Like an onion, or—

His blood chilled, and he'd barely opened his mouth to hiss in warning when three massive shapes erupted from the cave.

Chapter 4

Enough

The first neeka collided with Ashi before Shara knew what was happening. Her howl of pain raked through him like claws as he hurled himself out of the second neeka's path, heart racing.

Ashi rolled to her feet and scrambled backward, swiping viciously with her claws despite the deep, bloody gashes in her shoulder. Somewhere nearby, Lethir's distinctive bellow answered another warning screech.

With a terrified whine, Omatha sprinted into the trees, and as the third neeka made to follow, Shara dove and tore into its hind leg. It whirled, quick as an alvithi, and he bounded back, snarling a challenge through his fear.

Never engage a neeka! came the oft-repeated warning. *Get out of their territory as fast as you can.*

It leapt, and he bolted.

It matched his pace like an evil shadow, all dark scales and powerful wings, reptilian movements and unearthly shrieks. He hurtled through the dense trees, their branches too thick— he couldn't take flight here without risking injury. For now, he'd have to outrun it. If he was lucky, it'd be satisfied with merely driving him off its land.

When was he ever lucky?

Gulping for air, he threw himself forward with yet more speed. The underbrush reached out with grasping fingers, and he pressed his wings tightly to his sides. No time to look back, but the neeka was there—its looming menace, its stinging stench. A scent he should have known all along.

And instead he'd followed a wisp of smoke straight into the fire.

Lethir, Omatha, Ashi . . . It was the only prayer he had the time or presence of mind to muster.

Leaping at the nearest tree, he propelled himself off its thick trunk and changed course. A scrambling hiss, but the neeka somehow kept pace.

Panic pressed at the corners of his mind. This had been foolish. He couldn't—

His stride faltered, and needle claws dragged over his tail. Howling, he staggered, ricocheted off a tree, awkwardly leapt a half-rotted log. The neeka's hold came loose, and he slashed his tail at its snout without looking back.

Run, run, run!

Sunlight filtered through the thinning trees ahead, and new energy spiked through him. Lungs burning, he threw his throbbing wings wide, galloped into a patch of light, and sprang into the air. Branches scratched his limbs as he shot through the trees, but it was enough to—

He streaked past a fire-gold dragon. Omatha.

Stomach heaving, he wheeled to put himself between her and the neeka—just in time to see it break through the trees and crash directly into her.

Startled shrieks rent the air and swelled into a high, fierce ringing in Shara's ears. In a flurry of claws, Omatha spiralled away, one wing flared, the other hanging twisted and limp. For a moment she seemed to float, and then, with a keen, she dropped.

He dove after her, scrambling through the branches with his claws outstretched, but it was too late. Omatha hit a fallen tree and slid to the ground with a whimper.

Shara slammed to the earth and almost fell into his true form. Gasping for breath, he hurried to kneel beside her. Deep, bloody gashes marked her flank, and a blood-streaked branch jutted through her torso. "Omatha!"

Overhead, a scream cut off abruptly. The neeka's body broke through the trees and hit the ground. It didn't move, not even when a birch-scaled dragon plummeted on top of it.

Alanthas waited five endless heartbeats before shifting and jogging to Omatha's side.

Shara's mind spun, the terror and adrenaline of the chase finally giving way to horror and guilt. "Why were you—"

"Just flying over." Without warning or pause, he seized the branch and pulled it from Omatha's body. Her roar shook the trees, but Alanthas nodded and patted her slender snout gently. "It's all right. You'll be fine. Don't try— No, don't—"

But with another howl, Omatha shifted into her true form, perhaps unable to stop herself. Tears poured down her cheeks, and her body trembled violently against the pain and the venom of the neeka's claws.

"It's all right," Alanthas repeated, peeling off his coat and turning to look at Shara. "What happened?"

Shara stared numbly, and before he could make his voice work, Omatha sobbed, "Thought . . . thought it was a boar's . . . Shara, I'm sorry I . . ."

"It was a mistake. There's no cause for shame." Alanthas tucked his bunched coat beneath Omatha's head. "You lie still. Ishara, where are the others?"

Shara pointed a shaking hand the way he'd come, Omatha's needless apology and his own guilty silence ringing in his ears.

Alanthas shoved to his feet, all stern authority again. "Fly back to the lake. We need a healer and at least half a dozen warriors. And *stay there*, Ishara. Don't come back here."

"But shouldn't I—"

"You've done enough," Alanthas snapped. "Now go." In a swirl of scales and wings, he darted off into the trees before Shara could argue.

It didn't matter. No argument came. No thoughts, no words.

You've done enough.

His gaze fell to his feet. To the dead neeka. To Omatha's quivering body, her bloody wounds, her tear-streaked face.

Sucking in a rasping breath, he closed his eyes to shift, but the images remained as clear as before.

Shara returned to the shore and alerted the other alvithi, and as activity burst to life around him, he found himself taking flight again. In the sky, he could do what he did best—stay out of the way.

He flew wide, slow circles over the lake. Past the caves. Around the main camp. Back again to the lake, where his eyes fixed on the Speaking Rock. His throat closed. As soon as the truth came out—that Shara, not Omatha, had led them all to the neeka den—he'd have to make the slow climb atop the rock and apologize for his ill judgment.

For himself.

Shame pushed him higher and further than any current of

wind could have done, and when he finally looked over his shoulder, he no longer saw any sign of his home amid the mountains.

He kept flying.

He flew until his wings ached, then flew further. The sparkling band of the sea appeared far ahead and off to his right, but it wasn't until the last golden streaks of sunlight faded into night that he reached Shor Kal.

Grateful for the darkness, he sank to the ground behind a hill outside the city and rolled onto his side, huffing with exhaustion. Almost against his will, his body shifted to his true form, and he curled into a ball and let the prickle of the grass against his skin anchor him to the world. Wisps of night wind brushed at his sweat-soaked face. For long, silent minutes, he lay still, reminding himself how it felt to breathe deeply without his chest aching.

Not physically aching, anyway.

He might have slept, for the next thing he knew, a squirrel-dragon was skittering over his foot and up his pant leg. Shooing it away, he shoved himself upright and stared down at his hands. Even to his eyes, they were faint in the darkness, but he watched intently as he shifted away his alvithi features. The claws blunted to fingernails, the birch scales disappeared. His scalp tingled as his horns vanished, and the cold wind sent prickles shooting up his suddenly bare back. His mother's coat provided no protection, its artful drape hanging open to his waist to display the scales and leaves that trailed down his spine in true form.

Human in appearance, he climbed shakily to his feet, and when a new sense of balance had settled over his exhausted limbs, he set off toward the city. What he would do there, he had no idea. A few imarth lived in Shor Kal, the half-blood children of alvithi and humans, but he had no desire to seek them out. No desire to be near anyone at all.

You've done enough.

His shoulders slumped. Distantly, he knew that beneath the sharp, urgent tone, Alanthas had meant it to be reassuring. But either way, it was true. He'd done enough. Not only today, but every day. Enough to prove he would never be enough.

Teveth.

Shivering in the nighttime cold, he reached back awkwardly and drew the drape of fabric over his head like a hood, praying his mother wasn't watching. Watching like Alanthas, who'd been flying over their hunt site.

Eyes stinging, Shara swallowed and began the descent down the hill toward the city. There would be no one in Shor Kal to check on him. No one to ensure he didn't make a mess of things and let a poor injured girl take the blame.

Shara, I'm sorry.

Like any part of that had been her fault.

With nothing else to do and too many heavy thoughts dragging his mind beneath the earth, he muttered half-hearted prayers as he trudged through the fields and onto a gravel path.

Omatha.

Lethir and the other hunters.

His brothers and sisters. Alanthas in particular, who would now have to take Shara's place at the Speaking Rock.

Only when houses dotted the path and lantern lights hovered over the street did the pain cut through his daze. Human feet were not designed to walk on gravel. But his heart twinged at the thought of shifting even the soles of his feet, so he strayed off the path into the scraggly spring grass.

His thoughts wandered as well, slipping from one person to another until he was mumbling a litany of names in time with his sluggish footsteps and the angry growling of his stomach. Not so much prayers as apologies.

The grass stopped abruptly, and he looked up to find himself at the edge of a maze of docks. Ships clustered together like schools of hungry fish, large and small and everything in between, some with sails and others bare, a few crawling with people but most empty and still.

The nearest rose before him like a mountain, the word *Myriad* emblazoned across its back in letters as tall as Shara. Three masts jutted into the night sky—an image of Omatha floated over his vision, and he pushed it away and tried to count the sails wrapped neatly around the many crossbeams. The number increased every time he started over, and in the light of dozens of gently swinging lanterns, the whole scene shifted endlessly.

A man hurried by, and Shara ducked nearer to the ship, swaying with hunger and thirst and fatigue. The docks raged with the odors of humans and fish, of wooden crates and whatever was packed inside them, of water and wind and salt. Senses reeling, he leaned against a post wound with thick rope.

Shift. Hunt. The idea made his insides writhe worse than ever.

"'Bout time!"

Shara squawked, shied, and toppled over, barely landing on the dock instead of in the water.

"Oh, drunk, is he?" A stocky woman stepped into the lantern light and scowled. "That's great."

Head spinning, he hauled himself upright. He never should have stopped walking—his body weighed so much more now.

"You're Lord Ainsith's boy, aren't yeh?" She jerked her thumb at the ship. "What, you stop at a tavern or three on your way here? We've been expecting you for hours. Now hurry up and get on board and hope I don't tell his lordship that his servant's a lazy drunkard."

Without waiting for an answer, she shuffled up a broad ramp leading onto the *Myriad*'s main deck. There was something familiar about her clothing, but focusing too hard on anything made him dizzy.

"Hurry up!"

"Wait!" he croaked. "I'm not . . ."

The words died in his parched throat. What did it matter? If there was one thing he was good at, it was being nobody. He could get on the ship and disappear. When Lord Ainsith's servant did arrive, Shara would already be someone else, forgotten. And when his limitations inevitably caught up with him again, he could be yet another nobody. For the rest of his life, if he had to.

"Well?" the woman grumbled.

He opened his mouth to ask where the ship was going, but what did that matter, either? With wavering steps, he followed her up the ramp.

CHAPTER 5

THE STOWAWAY

Once, when Shara had been mired in a particularly deep mud hole of self-pity, he'd made a list of all the things the Eagle had put on earth to torment him. Lethir, of course. Rathen most of the time. Burrs. Damp fur. Tasteless food. Overcooked food. Mice. Tangled wefts. Swirly handwriting.

Ships topped them all.

But even worse, as it turned out, were navy ships, where the officers took offense at people sneaking aboard by pretending to be servants to important noble passengers.

"Hurry up." The officer's hand pressed between his shoulder blades as he lingered at the base of the stairs.

Shara made it three steps before the monstrous floating box gave another lurch. He staggered, nearly knocking his head against the wall, and growled. Why was he still here? He'd spent a cold, sleepless night in a hammock in human form, then a miserable morning growing more and more nauseated as the ship left the docks and pressed further out to sea.

All he had to do was shift. Fly away or dive overboard and disappear. But every time he thought about it, an illness that had nothing to do with the pitching ship swept over him. He didn't want to shift.

Not that he wanted to be thrown into a Barathi prison, either.

Stomach swirling, he resumed climbing, his escort close behind. Men and women in the practical clothing of Barathi sailors moved about the *Myriad*'s deck with ease, dedicated to their tasks and apparently unaware that the ship was trying to throw them into the sea. The exceptions were two men wrapped in layers of fine clothing, both gripping the ship's rail and clearly trying to appear unbothered by its constant motion.

"Ridiculous," the older of the two was saying. "Forty percent? I might as well go into business with pirates. Besides, if you marry my daughter, you'll receive all the privileges extended to the nobility, and that will more than . . ."

The thundering wind swept the rest of their words away.

"Might as well be a pirate already," muttered Shara's captor, guiding him toward a pair of doors at the rear end of the ship. With a rap of his knuckles against the wood, he pushed the door open.

The rush of water and hollow drumming of wind faded into the strict stillness of the cabin, and only their footsteps remained as they approached the desk at its center. A woman sat behind it, watching their entrance.

"My apologies, Admiral Thosena, but—"

"I've told you, lieutenant, never apologize for coming between me and paperwork." She dropped her stylus and leaned back in her chair. "Our guests are settling in, I trust?"

"Not even properly out to sea and they're already bargaining," the man grumbled.

She managed to give the impression of rolling her eyes without actually doing it. "Ainsith offer up his daughter yet?"

Despite the situation, Shara bit down a snicker.

But not well enough, for her attention moved to him. "And who is this?"

He nearly shifted out of habit but caught himself at the last second. A human wouldn't think him rude for not greeting her in his true form.

"Stowaway, ma'am. Came on board last night claiming to be Ainsith's manservant."

No, she probably thought him worse than rude.

"Hmm." Thosena brushed a hand through her white hair. A testament to Drasan ancestry, not age—she couldn't be much older than fifty. "Thank you, lieutenant. You're dismissed."

Shara cringed. He hadn't relished the idea of being interrogated on the deck of the ship, or wherever its equivalent of the Speaking Rock was, but facing the admiral privately wasn't a much better alternative.

The lieutenant closed the door on his way out, and in place of hackles, the hairs on the back of Shara's neck prickled. The giant floating box had been bad enough; now he was trapped in a small one.

Thosena prodded at the stylus like a child out of sight of a stern parent. "That true, what he said?"

He dragged his toes over the worn wooden floor. "Someone thought I was Lord Ainsith's servant. I, uh, didn't correct her."

It sounded a lot more dishonest now that he wasn't distraught and delirious.

"Ah." Without looking down, she absently rearranged the documents on the desk. "And who are you really?"

He shrugged. "Nobody."

"Nobody." Chuckling, she pushed herself out of her chair with easy grace. How long did it take to acquire such comfort at sea? "Everyone's somebody." She pivoted at the end of the room, silhouetted against a broad stretch of paned glass windows that offered a blurred view of the sea beyond. "Let me guess: big family, lots of siblings, always overlooked. Decided you wanted to make something of yourself. Travel to the capital, distinguish yourself, earn a noble title and all the rest. But you've got no money, so you thought you'd climb aboard the next ship headed to Farna and hope to make it unnoticed."

"Um . . ." Take out the grand aspirations and put in "vanish into obscurity," and she wasn't far off. The big-family-always-overlooked part certainly rang true.

"I've seen it before."

Not sure how to respond, Shara let his gaze fall to the desk, where several official-looking documents had been stacked beneath a small cube. From the bottom of the pile jutted a paper cut along one edge with an intricate pattern of notches and grooves, the design vaguely reminiscent of overlapping feathers. The only things on the paper apart from a stray ink blot were a large, artfully scribbled signature and an oblong seal of green wax swinging almost cheerfully from the last letter of the name.

It was nothing but a fancy piece of paper, but somehow it reminded him exactly how clueless and overwhelmed he was. Some foolish part of him had believed that all he had to do to be human was not shift. Humans and alvithi shared common roots, after all—language, religion, even ancestry, or so said the legends.

But Shara was so far from those roots that he might as well have been perched on the highest branch. How would he pass as human if even *paper* was confusing?

Thosena's boots sounded on the wood, and Shara retreated hastily. "Sorry, I—"

"It's fine. Not every day you see a locking order, is it?"

He shook his head and pretended he knew what that meant.

"Now then." She folded her arms and studied him. "I ought to dump you over the edge, but I'd lose sleep over that, and I like sleep. You have some sailing experience?"

"No." And after he got off this boat, he would never have any ever again.

"No?"

"We lived . . . further inland. I only rowed on the river."

"Ah. Any wind or water sense?"

"No." His face flushed, though there was no reason he should feel embarrassed for not possessing the subtle human magic. Nor should he be worried that his lack would give him away—most humans didn't have it, either.

"Well then, what *can* you do?"

Nothing came to mind, especially with that paper mocking him from the desk, but she was trying to help. He scanned the room, eyes landing unhelpfully on a belt laden with a sword and a pistol.

What could he do? Rathen had called him diplomatic once, but she'd meant it as a gibe. His fingers brushed over the corner of his sleeve, where his mother had embroidered his name in silver thread. "I . . . I'm not bad at weaving." Not as good as his parents and brother Alopar, as he'd often been reminded, but not a disaster.

To his relief, she perked up. "Weaving. All right then, *Nobody*. Weather holding and no delays in ports along the way, we'll be in Farna in about a week. You're going to spend that time mending anything that rips—clothing, nets, hammocks, you name it. It's not weaving, but it's the closest I've got. You do as you're told and stay out of the way, and I won't feed you to the sea dragons. Fair?"

A week stuck on this ship did not seem fair at all, but that was his own fault. Maybe in a few days, the thought of shifting wouldn't make his throat constrict.

"Yes," he said. "Thank you. And I'm sorry about stowing away."

Swirling with sea-scent, she stepped around her desk and guided him toward the door. "Sometimes you make it work, and sometimes you leave it all behind and start over. I know how that goes."

He doubted that, but he thanked her again anyway and left the room, leaning against the doorframe as she called the lieutenant back inside.

Leave it all behind and start over. He wrapped his arms around his torso and drew a calming breath. He'd done the first half without thinking. Now he had to survive the second.

Chapter 6

Being Human

Shara staggered from the ship, swelled with relief, took a step—and nearly fell off the dock.

The sturdy wooden boards felt uncomfortably immobile beneath his feet. Too solid, too still. No rocking or swaying or cruel attempts to toss him into the water. Every step he took fell too hard, like the docks were leaping up to meet his footfalls.

But he'd made it. Six days of nausea and tasteless food, the faint bite of wind and water magic sizzling on his tongue, and sailors who sang out of tune, pried as much as Shara's cave-brothers, and snored even worse. Now the city of Farna spread before him, tucked into the grassy hills rolling along the shore and guarded by the jagged, rocky slopes jutting up behind and around it.

His new home.

Before he could take it in, the chaos of Farna's military docks swallowed him and ushered him away from the *Myriad*. Sailors rushed back and forth, some working silently, others competing to see who could shout the loudest and longest.

Dockworkers and ropes groaned together under the weight of crates or the pull of ships. Sails fluttered and snapped. An official-looking woman consulted a sheet of paper while a pair of sailors waited to board a nearby vessel.

After a week with an assigned task on the ship, Shara once again found himself the only one with no purpose.

He took a final glance at the *Myriad* and pressed into the crowd, careful not to bump into anyone. Almost all Barathi military officers were nobles, and he had no desire to start his time in Farna by offending someone who held both military power and high social rank. Especially not after observing the behavior of Ainsith and his companion all week. Whatever had compelled Thosena to let them on board, it hadn't been a sense of noble camaraderie—though that might have kept her from throwing them overboard when she clearly wanted to.

A grin tugged at the edges of his mouth, and for a ridiculous second, he wrestled with the urge to return to the ship and ask to join the Barathi navy. It might not be so bad. He could spend the rest of his life taking orders and mending things, couldn't he? Surely he'd grow accustomed to life on the sea eventually.

He rounded a corner and glanced down into the water, letting sense settle back over him. He did *not* want to join the navy, but despite a week of thinking, he hadn't come up with anything better. Nothing appropriate for a talentless alvithi, anyway. Yet now he planned to walk into Farna and . . . what?

He sagged against a nearby post and sighed. All week, Thosena's words had played in his mind. *Leave it all behind and start over.* But start over with what? What was the point of resetting the game if you had only half the pieces? Of weaving on a rotting loom? What in all the skies had made him think he'd succeed at being human when he'd never been anything but teveth as an alvithi?

He didn't want to start over.

Stuffing his shaking hands into his coat pockets, he stared at the murky water. He could shift and swim away. Stay down there, give up being Shara. A few months from now, humans would be sharing the legend of the sea creature that inhabited the bay. Children would brag about spotting or touching it. Others would toss food into the water, hoping to lure it to the surface.

"Shara!"

His heart leapt into his throat, barring most of his startled squawk as a member of Thosena's crew trotted to his side. Huffing, the man pressed something into Shara's hand. "Almost missed you. Here."

The contents of the small cloth bag clinked, and Shara's jaw dropped. "This is—"

"It's not much." He rocked back on his heels. "But we didn't want you to wander off into the city with nothing. Good luck, eh?"

Without waiting for a coherent reply, he slapped Shara on the back and vanished into the crowd with a wave.

The weight on Shara's heart seeped down his arm and into his trembling hand, and the dull throb from a week of gripping a needle faded as his fingers twitched around the bag. The crew had collected money for him. Wished luck to the awkward boy who'd stowed away on their ship.

Swallowing down a lump, he tucked the bag into his coat. *Just get to the city. Start with that.*

It wasn't much of a plan, but at least he could be sure he wouldn't end up in a den of neeka this time.

Shopkeepers and job hunting were worse than neeka.

Loosing a heavy sigh, Shara slouched into his chair, squinting his eyes against the setting sun. Humans, he'd learned on the ship, ate meals at fixed times of day rather than whenever they were hungry, and The Dragon's Beard eating house bustled with so much activity that he feared the weight would crush the stilts holding the building above the water.

The young woman who'd shown him to his little table had disappeared, looking faintly amused at his request for "whatever you have that isn't burnt." She was lucky he hadn't asked for what he really wanted, which was something raw and bloody.

Good job, Shara. You'll be human in no time.

Letting his eyes half close, he traced his finger along the table's wood grain as if mapping out his long, exhausting path through the city. Every shop he'd stopped in, every person he'd talked to, had felt like approaching Alanthas all over again, like all the weeks he'd spent convincing himself that joining the hunt would solve all his problems.

"Here you are." The woman set a plate before Shara, grinning. "Not burnt in the least."

His face bubbled with heat, though not as badly as when he'd asked the farrier for a job. The request that he be good with animals had seemed promising—right up until he'd learned what a farrier actually did.

Why would anyone *nail metal* to a horse's hooves?

Humans were odd.

Then again, they also believed dragons had beards.

"Thanks," he said as she placed a bowl of berries and a cup of mead next to the plate, where three rolled flatbreads oozed with lumps of fish in a brownish-red sauce. It smelled incredible.

"That'll be eleven tonas. Anything else you need?"

"Um . . ." He wrenched his nose away from the food. One more, and if she said no, he'd give up and start again tomorrow. "I'm trying to find a job. I don't suppose you need help?"

Say no, say no. The same shameful words he'd been praying all day.

"Oh, I don't know. I'll ask my father." She glanced over her shoulder as a crowd of sailors shoved through the door. "It might be a while, though; sorry."

"No problem." He handed her the little coins and turned hurriedly to the food. If he ate fast enough, he could escape before she brought him the answer.

Eating quickly wasn't a problem—the food tasted even better than it smelled, though there was something discomfiting about eating something he hadn't helped capture or prepare. On the other hand, if they gave him a job here, he'd be preparing plenty of food—and he'd learn the recipes for the creamy pepper sauce and thick, salty flatbreads.

It was a comforting thought until a man with a white ponytail sidled his way past a group arguing about the prince's upcoming coronation and stopped at Shara's table. "I hear you're looking for work."

Shara shoved his hands into his lap and pretended to be a well-behaved human who hadn't been about to lick sauce from his fingers. "Yes."

The man folded his thick arms, picking at the twisted leather cord around his bicep as he surveyed Shara. "I've got plenty of servers and cooks, but I do need someone here first thing in the morning to receive deliveries and supervise the stock boys. Pretty straightforward, just need to be good with money and not let a pack of stingy merchants and lazy kids walk all over you. Oh, and be here by five bells every morning. Got any experience?"

Being walked all over? Plenty.

Shara forced a smile past the memories and the writhing in his gut. "Only the early hours."

The man laughed. "That's the part that scared everyone else away. I've got to get back up front, but come find me if you're interested and we'll talk, eh?"

He hurried away. Shara licked his fingers clean. The sauce no longer tasted good.

He waited until the man disappeared into the kitchen before slinking quickly from his table and out into the evening. The door clacked shut behind him, sealing the warmth and laughter and music within.

Flashes of white pulled his attention skyward, where two figures breezed past on gliders marked with official-looking insignia. With easy grace, they banked and soared directly overhead, swirls of air tousling Shara's hair. The faintest tang of wind magic pricked at his tongue.

Maybe the patrol would hire a shapeshifter. He wouldn't need wind sense or even a glider.

Sighing, he drew his coat more tightly around him and made his way off the dock and onto the street, paying little attention to where he was going. Apart from the Guide's church just up the hill, everything looked the same, especially as the bitter wind and looming storm clouds drove the last of the sunlight below the horizon and draped the city in darkness. He would have to find somewhere to stay before the weather turned foul, but he couldn't stomach the thought of being locked in a room with nothing to do but craft new ways of saying no when shopkeepers offered him work.

". . . get the banner taken down," came a voice as he shuffled along. A woman ushered a boy through a door and handed him a long, hooked pole. "Rain's coming."

"Nobody else takes theirs down," grumbled the boy as he prodded at the banner—the same dark fabric and snowy white fox emblem Shara had seen throughout the city.

"Then no one else respects the king."

The boy waited until his mother disappeared into the house before muttering, "What does he care? He's dead."

"His soul isn't!"

Shara chuckled. Even human mothers had perfect hearing.

He followed the stone-paved road out of the city and south along the rocky shore. Away from Farna, he could smell the storm clearly on the salty air, yet every step led him forward instead of back. He could shift when it was time and fly to the city quickly, or else remain here and find shelter beneath one of the light towers dotting the shoreline.

He left the path and wandered along the water's edge, shifting his feet for more protection. Scooping up a handful of rocks, he tossed them one after the next into the sea, enjoying the quiet plunk, the growl of the waves, the hiss of the first misty rain. The wind seized his coat and yanked it against his legs, pulling him toward the water until the frigid waves stung his toes.

When the rocks were gone, he stopped walking and drew his hands within the coat's drape, but it did little good—everything was damp now, from the hair plastered against his neck to the sandy cuffs of his pant legs dragging along the shore.

Not for the first time, his thoughts strayed to his cave-brothers. Soon they'd be bedding down for the night, each in his preferred form. Inori as a fox, Bathar as a wolf . . . A dozen fluffy alvithi all piled together, warm and secure no matter what weather reached the mountains. What would they say about his sleeping alone for the last week, cramped in the little hammock on Thosena's ship?

Did they miss him? Even care that he was gone?

He raised his eyes to the mountains stretching up from the

island across the bay as though he might see all the way back to the clan. Instead he glimpsed motion in the sky—a little white speck wavering violently in the harsh wind while the pilot struggled to maneuver his glider over the water.

Shara's breath caught. No amount of skill or wind sense could correct that glider's flight. He spun, peering around the shore though he knew he was alone. No better help would come.

He squeezed his eyes shut, summoning his dragon form, building it around himself with infuriating slowness. If he didn't reach the pilot in time . . .

His body sizzled, and he sank to all fours and opened his eyes to see the glider lurch sideways, twist midair, and plummet into the churning sea.

CHAPTER 7

KORITH

No! Bounding forward, Shara threw his wings wide and leapt into the darkness. The angry winds struck him like a massive hand, and he careened off course, wingtip brushing the icy waves. Snarling, he flapped harder, climbed higher, then trained his eyes on the dark water.

The pilot's white hair and the pale fabric of the ruined glider stood out like soaked stars in the black waves of night. Shara banked sharply, still wobbling in the erratic winds, and maneuvered closer to the flailing figure. Hovering as best he could, he lined up his course, watched the approaching wave . . . The moment it passed, he dove, spread his claws, and grabbed.

The human was heavier than he'd expected, and Shara's momentum nearly sent them both skipping over the water like rocks. Cold panic shot through his limbs and seized his muscles, and only habit kept his straining, rain-soaked wings beating, beating, until finally he heaved the human from the water with a grunting squawk. The pilot's flailing ceased, and Shara felt an arm wrap securely around his leg.

At least only one of them was panicking.

The shore seemed impossibly far, but as the first flash of lightning cut through the sky behind him, Shara dropped the human on the rocks at the nearest light tower's base and tumbled after him in a panting heap. Again his true form surfaced as if of its own will, and he shifted himself human before crawling to where the drenched pilot crouched, coughing and shivering.

"Are you all right?" Shara pulled his coat off and leaned forward, holding it out—it wasn't much, but it was drier than anything the young man was wearing. "Is anything broken?"

To his shock, the human laughed. "No more than usual." He didn't take the coat—one hand supported his other arm, which hung awkwardly at the shoulder. Despite the pained set of his features and the blood dripping from his temple, however, his eyes brightened as he regarded Shara in the dim tower light. "You're alvithi."

His voice was rich with awe that Shara didn't deserve.

"I . . . Well, yes, I suppose." More or less, anyway.

The pilot's face spread into a smile. "Th-that was amazing. Rescued by a d-dragon!"

Cheeks burning, Shara withdrew the unclaimed coat and climbed to his feet; his knees ground into the rocks as he moved, the pain driving away his lingering panic. Thunder rumbled overhead, and he held out a hand. "You need to get somewhere warm and dry. And see a doctor."

"Oh, no need." And with no other warning, the pilot gripped his dislocated arm just below the shoulder and drew it gently but firmly down, forward, and back up. Even in the storm, the faint pop of the joint resetting was audible.

Shara gaped.

The human chuckled. "I've put myself back together plenty of times before. I'm used to it. W-well . . ." Teeth chattering, he let Shara guide him to his feet; the contents of a bag slung over his chest clunked as he swayed. "Not the plummeting to my untimely death part. Speaking of which, I don't s-suppose you saved my glider, did you?"

Shara stared. The man had just reset a dislocated shoulder as if it were nothing. He could have drowned, he was bleeding, he might still get freezing sickness, and he wanted to know about his glider? "Uh, no. I . . . sorry."

"Figures. Six months of modifications and now th-this." Together, he and Shara tied the coat into a sling. "Did I at least look good and dramatic when I crashed?"

Make that injuries plus a jostled brain. "Um, sure. Do you, uh, remember your name?"

Another laugh. "I'm fine, really. And it's Korith. And you're . . . Shara?" He nodded at the sleeve they'd tied, where Shara's name glittered silver.

"Yes." He nearly shifted to greet Korith properly, but he didn't need more undeserved admiration.

"Well, thank you, Shara. I owe you."

Shara squirmed. "It wasn't really . . . I nearly fell in after you."

Korith grinned and brushed dripping white hair back from his forehead. "Then I'd've been saved by a sea dragon instead. Equally amazing. We'll do that next time."

The easy confidence in his words cut sharper and deeper than the weather. Shara's muscles seized, rooting him to the spot while an animal desire to flee shot through him.

"You all right?" Korith squinted at him.

He drew a shaky breath and swallowed the urge. He couldn't abandon a drenched, shivering, bleeding human on the shore in the middle of an oncoming storm. And anyway, Korith was delusional, or ignorant, or easily impressed. Possibly all three. He had no way of knowing the truth about his rescuer.

Korith wouldn't know what proper toresh looked like, either, and with that reassurance in mind, Shara let his eyes unfocus. He pictured a horse, trailing invisible fingers over its mane, along its nose, down its legs.

Korith's delighted laughter announced that the shift was complete, but when Shara turned to look at him, his expression grew serious. "Are you sure? You don't mind?"

Shara butted him with his nose and clopped to a large rock, and after a cautious climb, Korith slid onto his back. Not a pleasant sensation, having a human on your back, but Korith sat still and balanced, wobbling only when he shivered. Suppressing a shake of his own, Shara picked his way back to the road and glanced left, then right. He didn't care where they went so long as it was dry.

After an awkward, rain-soaked pause, Korith said, "Uh, left. Back to the city. Can you understand me?"

Could he—? Shara snorted and gave a gentle buck.

A quivering laugh. "Well, how was I to know? You're the first alvithi I've ever met."

And the last if Shara didn't get him somewhere warm. Another peal of thunder rolled across the sky, and he moved off toward Farna as quickly as he dared.

Korith lived in a garden.

Dried plants hung from ropes strung across the rafters; live ones blossomed in pots of various sizes spread around the front of the room. Here early spring flowers, there a variety of herbs, and in one corner, a small collection of plants that should not have been alive at all this early in the spring. Shara squinted in the dim lantern light, sniffed, and gave up.

"What—"

"Not here," Korith whispered. "Come on, up the stairs before—"

"Lord Aman!"

Korith cringed. "Before that." A guilty grin spread over his drawn, rain-streaked face, and he turned to the woman illuminated in the door behind them. "Evening, Na Mithel."

"What did you—? No, you don't even have to tell me." Her gazed flitted over him, from the hair dripping water into his eyes down to the puddle he was leaving on the floor. "Soaked through, bleeding, arm injured *again*, and no sign of that glider of yours. I told you a storm was coming—"

"But did I listen?"

"—but did you—" Her eyes narrowed, but humor tugged at her lips. "Very well, be difficult. Now hurry upstairs and dry off; I'll send up tea. Honestly . . ."

She disappeared into the back room, and Korith chuckled and nudged Shara toward the narrow staircase running along the side of the room.

Three steps up, something nearly knocked Shara over the edge. *Lord Aman.* "So you're . . . noble?"

Korith laughed. "In name, anyway."

After a week with Lord Ainsith, Shara swelled with relief at the easy humor in his voice. "And you live above a garden?"

"It's an herbary. Mostly plants for medicine and cooking. But yes, some flowers, too."

"Why would you buy flowers?"

Korith frowned over his shoulder. "Why wouldn't you buy flowers?"

Other than the plethora of plants growing in the hills, free to anyone who bothered to find and admire and pick them? Other than the ability of anyone with a basic knowledge of seeds and soil to grow their own flowers?

Humans were odd.

"And this is *your* herbary?"

"Yes and no. I own the building. Na Mithel and her family rent the lower floor. They live in the back and sell out the front."

Korith unlocked the door at the top of the stairs, and Shara nearly fell down the stairs a second time. Dozens of faces stared at him from the opposite wall, people of every age and size and appearance, all of them black and white and grey. Faces sketched in vivid detail and a startling variety of emotions—anger, sorrow, joy, contentment, embarrassment, disgust, confusion, excitement, pride … An entire wall of portraits.

"Did you draw all of these?"

"Mm-hmm," came Korith's muffled voice from within a large bureau.

"They're beautiful." His chest warmed—there was Na Mithel wearing that exasperated smile, like she'd faded into charcoal and stepped onto the page. "You're incredible."

"Yes I am. Good on you for noticing." Korith reemerged wearing a broad grin and passed half the clothing in his arms to Shara. "For you. I'm going to clean this up"—he indicated his red-streaked temple—"and change. Make yourself at home."

He disappeared into the next room, leaving Shara in the sudden silence of the first human dwelling he'd ever been in.

Though his loose undershirt and trousers were dry thanks to his shift outside, they were hardly clean, and he peeled them off and pulled on the fresh garments. Noble clothing. It was an odd thought, as was the entire concept of nobility. Honoring certain people because of their parentage. At least Shara deserved his distinction, though being teveth was hardly an honor.

Footsteps on the stairs interrupted his thoughts, and a little girl appeared bearing a tray laden with a large pot and three cups, one of which was inexplicably full of piko seeds. Her portrait, too, hung on the wall.

"Momma says to tell Lord Aman to drink *all* of it," she said importantly.

Shara gave her his best no-nonsense nod and pretended not to notice when she flinched at a crack of thunder. "I will do that. Thank you."

He carried the tray to a desk heaped with books and drawing supplies. Behind it, an arched opening in the stone wall housed the remains of a fire. Careful not to dirty his host's clothing, Shara hefted an armful of logs from a small pile in the corner and set to work.

The fire was blazing when a clean, dry Korith reappeared and caught Shara examining a large black-and-white-striped vase full of fancy sticks.

"Walking canes," Korith explained. "My shoulders aren't the only things that don't stay where they belong."

"Oh." Good thing he hadn't used them for kindling, then.

"Speaking of which, I hung your coat in the bathing room to dry. Thank you for that." His gaze swept past Shara and landed on the fire, and he beamed and headed toward it. "And for this."

Two padded chairs sat before the fire, one considerably more worn than the other. Korith moved the tea tray to a small table between them and poured two cups of tea, spooning in generous portions of piko seeds for no reason Shara could imagine. "So," he began, gesturing for Shara to sit and handing him a cup of seed tea, "what's an alvithi doing in Farna?"

Shara slumped into his chair. The distraction of Korith's fall, the weather's frigid embrace, the heady scents of flowers and fire and Korith and tea—all of it vanished like a blanket pulled from his shoulders. Drawing his legs to his chest, he cupped the hot mug in his hands. Thunder rolled through the sky, and rain rattled against the windows. It would have been cozy if not for his inner chill.

"I . . . I thought I was starting over, but I think I'm just making a mistake. Another mistake." He gazed into the flames and swallowed thickly. "At least I'm consistent."

For a few minutes on the ride back to Farna, he'd thought he could fool Korith completely. Leave him at his door, disappear into the night, and in Korith's mind, Shara would always be the amazing alvithi who'd saved his life. Nothing more—and nothing less.

Claws constricted around his chest. To have even one person think of him that way . . .

"Listen, I—" He set the tea aside and pushed to his feet. Maybe it wasn't too late, despite his confession. "I should go."

He made it two steps before his conviction fled and left him with the raindrops skipping over the roof, the entirety of the unfamiliar human city beyond these walls, the ache at the idea of being alone again.

In the end, even being teveth was better than that.

"Unless . . . unless you need help with anything?"

Say yes.

With a single sweep of Korith's eyes, a single studied look, Shara understood why all the portraits looked so real, all those people so *seen*. It was enough to make him want to flee all over again, but then Korith's face spread into a smile.

"Actually, now that you mention it, there are a few things . . ."

CHAPTER 8

THE CAPTAIN OF THE GUARD

Two weeks later, Korith still had not run out of things, and at this point, Shara was certain he was inventing them.

Folding his seagull wings, he dove for the familiar alley next to Korith's favorite eating house, where he alighted on a trash barrel and gave his wings an extra-birdlike ruffle.

But as usual, no one noticed him amid the early-morning bustle. Humans, it turned out, were not solitary and unsociable as he'd grown up believing. The locked windows and closed doors of their homes served more to make them feel safe than to actually divide them, and no matter the hour, the streets and shops of Farna thrummed with activity. Between the continuous chatter and the fact that seagulls were ubiquitous, Shara was invisible.

He hopped to the ground behind the barrel for another slow shift, then slipped out onto the main street. Gliders dotted the clear sky like flower petals on the wind, and the buildings stretched like endless rows of neatly arranged caves, greeting him with their doors thrown open despite the spring chill. No endlessly stretching mountains and mirror-glass lakes, no soothing aromas of pine and earth and warm fur, but when he stood still and let Farna swallow him with all its sounds and scents and movement and people, he almost felt warm inside.

He pushed into the eating house and wove his familiar way to the counter. Korith had openly admitted that he hadn't the first idea how to use his kitchen or anything in it. Shara knew enough not to poison anyone or burn Korith's house down, but since Korith had objected, loudly and with much squirming, to Shara bringing dead rabbits into his apartment, Shara fetched breakfast for both of them every morning—and ate rabbits when Korith wasn't looking.

Scooping up the waiting package of food, he smiled gratefully at the young woman behind the counter and hurried away when she looked like she might speak to him. Another well-established ritual.

Humans preferred hawks for deliveries, and back in the alley, he clasped the package's ties in raptor talons and shoved into the air. The city shone brighter than usual today, for the mourning banners in honor of King Isith had at last been taken down. In about a month, Prince Regent Iliath would be crowned the new king. Korith had promised—threatened—to take Shara to the coronation.

The thought drew his eyes to the Barathi palace, which sat atop the highest hill, looking like an alvithi who had shifted into two creatures at once and rectified the mistake by adding six more appendages and a signal tower for a tail. A wooden building sat at the center, its roof shingled in an undulating pattern like waves. Most everything else was white stone, some areas the same height as the wooden portion, others taller, with balconies overlooking the sea. An odd building, and nothing like some of the seaside fortresses Thosena had scoffed at on the journey south.

Taking a last look and a final draught of sea air, he angled through Korith's open window and deposited their neatly wrapped breakfast on the floor. Already the room felt familiar, almost welcoming—Korith's bed piled high with an absurd mound of pillows, the wardrobe that was always half open, the desk buried beneath art supplies, the half-empty shelf waiting for the return of all the books Korith had loaned out, the giant vase stuffed with Korith's canes.

No Korith, though, so Shara spent a minute preening his feathers simply for the enjoyment. Humans did not preen. They also didn't preen each other, a fact Shara had learned rather abruptly after trying to groom Korith. His new cave-brother didn't mind Shara shifting into a lynx and sleeping curled on the bed, but "I draw the line at hair chewing. Even when you're a giant furball."

Someone knocked on the door.

A loud clatter and a muffled curse wafted from the next room, followed by sloshing water. By the time Shara had shifted, Korith was glancing around the doorframe, his hair still dripping and his chest bare, a small puddle at his feet. "Could you answer that?" he whispered, already ducking back out of sight.

Whoever was outside knocked again. Not one of the Mithels, then, who were all too polite for that, and who didn't need to come upstairs given how often Korith went down to check on them.

Perhaps it was Thania, who visited regularly to ask Korith to lunch, only to receive an apology and an excuse every time. At first Shara had thought his cave-brother was avoiding her, but no, Korith's expressions of regret were genuine—as was the way he turned bright red and forgot how to form a complete sentence whenever she visited.

Biting down a grin, Shara set the breakfast on the single

bare corner of the desk and unlatched the door. Why humans locked themselves inside their homes during the *day* . . .

"Good morning, Lady Beth—"

His breath hitched. The tall, annoyed-looking military officer was most certainly not Thania Bethen.

"Er, good morning," he repeated, brushing at his clothing as if to wipe away traces of hawk.

Today would have been a good day to start wearing those shoes Korith had bought him.

"Si!" Half-dressed and still damp, Korith reappeared in the doorframe. His eyes fell on the yellow flowers in the officer's arms. "Are those to apologize for making me get up at this absurd hour?"

The woman rolled her eyes, a soft brown beneath her spectacles, and shoved the flowers at him. She smelled faintly of dirty dog; perhaps she'd stopped to pet a stray on her way here. "Your tenants seem to think my office needs brightening with something that will make me sneeze."

Korith grinned. "You mean something that'll ruin your eye makeup."

"Also that." She brushed her flower-tainted hands on her pant legs. "So, did you finish them all?"

"I did. But first." He caught Shara's arm, stalling his attempt to flee. "Si, this is a friend of mine, Shara. Shara, this is my sister—"

"Half-sister."

Korith's good humor flickered so quickly that Shara might have imagined it. "Sira Tishel, captain of the royal guard."

Tishel's elegantly dark-rimmed eyes swept over Shara. Once, twice, three times. "Of course."

Shara peered down at himself—he didn't know what her words meant and probably didn't want to, but that much pitying dismissal had probably turned him invisible.

"So do you have them or not?" Tishel asked Korith.

"Yes, yes. Hills, you're impatient." He ambled toward the desk.

The aroma of flowers wafted beneath Shara's nose, and after a moment of awkward hesitation, he inched after Korith and set to unwrapping their breakfast.

"So," Korith asked, moving aside another cane and pulling open a drawer, "how's coronation preparation going?"

To Shara's surprise, the tension in Tishel's limbs lessened. She removed her spectacles and brushed them against a corner of her coat, then held them up to the light. "About how you'd imagine. The Tethamari have confirmed that Princess Nashai will be coming to represent the royal family."

"And the peace treaty?" Korith kept riffling through the contents of the drawer, but his attention rested wholly on his sister.

"Nashai and her entourage will remain after the coronation to begin the peace talks. His Highness has been working non-stop since receiving the news."

Korith tapped a stack of portraits on the table and snatched up the length of twine Shara had discarded. "A chance for peace with Tethamar, an opportunity to spend hours alone with his books, *and* a politically acceptable excuse to avoid all the nobles scrambling to court his favor before he becomes king. He may never leave his study again."

The corner of Tishel's mouth lifted, and belatedly Shara recognized her as yet another member of Korith's portrait family. "His advisors are ensuring he eats, anyway. I can't speak to anything else."

The bundle tied, Korith handed it to her. "Here you are. That last one . . . I did the best I could based on the description, but I don't think I got the nose right."

"Then we'll have to capture him so he can do a portrait sitting in prison."

"Sounds excellent. Stay for breakfast? I've got some ideas about your—"

"As much as I enjoy your constant unsolicited advice, I have responsibilities to attend to." She brushed at her hair, as dark and impeccable as her eye makeup. "And this way you won't have to pretend you have clean platters and then distract me while you wipe off a dirty one."

Korith grinned, unabashed. "I can clean when I'm dead. I've got better things to do."

"Like lose horribly at malir?" She nodded at the game board on the little circular table by the fire.

He beamed. "Shara is spectacular at malir."

Unwrapping berries did not make enough noise for Shara to pretend he hadn't heard this remark. "I've made some really terrible plays this round," he protested over the rush of heat flooding his face. "And Korith bit his tail off three moves in, and—"

And humans didn't have tails.

Next time someone knocked on the door, he was going to shift into a housecat and pretend to be napping on the bed. Or better, *actually* be napping on the bed.

"Hills, we need to teach you to accept a compliment. You say that every time you win," Korith scolded. "Which is every time we play."

"And yet losing repeatedly hasn't made you any humbler," Tishel observed.

He ruffled a hand through his snowy hair. "Give it time."

"I'll come back in a few decades, then." She fluttered the portraits like a fan and turned to go. "Thank you for these, as always."

"Happy to help." Korith followed her to the landing,

waved her down the stairs, and, to Shara's dismay, closed and latched the door again. Tishel's footfalls echoed on the stairs, and Korith patted the shrine beside the door in time with the sound. The little wooden Guide figurine wobbled, and the eagle on its shoulder seemed to stretch its wings further as if to take flight.

"So, she was . . ." Shara bit his tongue.

"Terrifying?" Korith laughed and disappeared into the kitchen. "You don't get to be captain of the guard at thirty-five without being a little terrifying. Not to mention—ha! Terrifying but wrong: we have *six* clean . . . Wait, did you clean these?"

"You asked me to."

"Really?" He reemerged with platters and eating sticks and set them amidst the food. "I have no memory of that."

Not surprising—Korith frequently forgot things, and asking Shara to clean dishes was undoubtedly not important enough to have gone on his meticulously kept list of appointments and activities. Not that the list mattered much, either, since Korith seemed thrilled to ignore it at the first opportunity to help someone, sit in a tavern for four hours straight, or do both at once.

"Sorry about that, then," Korith said, indicating the clean dishes. His chair scraped loudly against the floor and creaked as he sprawled into it. "Awfully menial. Especially for an alvithi."

Shara perched on his own chair—why did humans find these things comfortable?—and reached for an egg. "It's fine. Alvithi clean things, too."

"Yes, I suppose that—wait. You cleaned them as a human, right? Not a furball?" He narrowed his eyes at his platter and tilted his head as though he might discern tongue-streaks in the proper light.

Shara piled a heap of berries on his platter and left the answer to Korith's imagination.

He'd meant his first reply, though—it *was* fine. He and Korith had reached a mostly unspoken agreement that Korith would teach Shara how not to make a fool of himself in front of humans, and in exchange, Shara would help Korith with whatever he needed. What did it matter that Korith needed simple things? For the first time, Shara was neither disappointing everyone at every turn nor confirming their unspoken belief that he would fail.

And with food steaming before him and the now-familiar scents of his new home and unusual cave-brother blanketing him, even his lingering anxiety about learning to be a proper human felt insignificant.

He skewered a berry with his eating stick and closed his eyes to savor it.

CHAPTER 9

MISTAKES AND MISGIVINGS

The Crown and Raven eating house didn't skimp on breakfast, and Shara and Korith left the apartment full and satisfied, greeting Na Mithel and her daughter on their way out. Shara's feet rubbed in his new shoes, their insides lined with thick, squashy wool that welcomed his toes as he curled them through it. Not the worst thing humans had invented.

Not the best, either. That honor went to sunspots: balls of mashed fruit wrapped in a thin layer of dough, fried, drizzled with honey, and speared on sticks. Shara's stomach would have uncomfortable words with him later about the dough, but it would be worth it.

"So, the portraits you gave your sister," he said as they left the cart with several sticks each—apple for Shara, rhubarb for Korith.

"Wanted criminals, for the most part. They print posters and hang them around the city to let people know to be on the lookout."

Shara's hand stalled midway to his mouth, the sunspot stick wobbling as he walked. "Oh. Well, that's . . ." It was something, certainly. "And in return, she shares all the news from the palace?"

Korith chuckled and pointed his cane around a corner to North Shore Street, which was odd, because Shara had been certain they were already on North Shore. Farna made more sense from the sky. Most things did.

"Honestly, I knew all of that already. If there's one thing I'm excellent at, it's—"

"Everything?"

"Well, there is that, of course." He swung the cane playfully at Shara's legs and threw him a rakish grin. "But I was going to say gossip."

"Gossip?"

"Mm." He wilted slightly, as though overwhelmed by his own sunlight. "But if we don't talk about the kingdom's affairs, we don't talk about anything."

They lapsed back into silence. Shara focused on his sunspots, and Korith tapped out a beat against the cobblestones—and occasionally Shara.

It was typical Korith behavior, which was almost comforting when not everything about Korith was predictable. He always smelled and looked the same, but he never moved the same, and not just because some days he walked with a cane. His body seemed to be held together with knots that slipped loose without warning—yesterday Shara had watched him pop his knee back into place as if the action and accompanying pain were completely commonplace. Other days there were no visible injuries at all, only the inconsistent movements that spoke of constant pain which flared whenever it pleased.

But Korith walked smoothly today, so his uncharacteristic silence apparently had another cause. Previously, he'd kept up a steady stream of explanations—what the symbols on the shop signs meant, what some of the objects for sale did, how to recognize a noble and what to do if approached by one, what was and wasn't acceptable when bartering for goods, how to avoid giving offense or accidentally flirting. The basics of being human in a large city.

Now, however, he watched Shara's reactions to the city, studying him like he wanted to draw a portrait but couldn't make out the details. He probably thought he was being subtle, but humans were about as subtle as wings on a cat.

"So have you learned her name yet?" Korith asked after several streets of silence.

"Who?"

"The girl at the Crown and Raven." He waved at the eating house on their right and quirked an eyebrow.

Shara ducked instinctively and forced his face not to turn red, an alvithi trick he had no intention of ever revealing to his companion. "I said two sentences to your sister and mentioned tails. If I asked the server's name, I'd have to talk to her, too, and that's another mud hole of mistakes I don't want to roll in."

"Well, sure, but mistakes are how we learn." Korith chomped on a sunspot like it was a mistake full of nutritious lessons.

Something that wasn't food soured in Shara's throat, tainting his mood. *Learn to accept a compliment, Shara. Mistakes are how we learn.* He sank his teeth rather viciously into the gooey dough, fruit oozing down his chin.

Something pricked his arm, and he jumped to see Korith wielding an empty stick like a miniature sword. "So the tail-biting I understand, but what do alvithi have against mud?"

He grimaced and scratched at his arms. "It gets under your scales and it crusts and it's uncomfortable and itchy."

"Huh. Can't say I've ever had that problem."

Shara flushed. "What would a human say?"

Korith took another bite and considered while he chewed. "Mm . . . sea I don't want to swim in, maybe. A wind I don't want to sail into. A hill I don't want to climb. Or if you're feeling straightforward, a lot of mistakes I don't want to make."

Alvithi, too, had many ways of expressing the same sentiment, but Shara swelled with exasperation anyway and took another too-violent bite. "And which will make me sound the most human?"

Another laugh, another teasing cane-prod. "How about the one that will make you sound the most you?"

He snorted midswallow and nearly choked, and a fit of coughing almost jolted him into a passerby. *The most you.* The cough twisted into a derisive snort.

"Sorry," came Korith's voice. "I didn't—ah, here!"

With cautious grace, Korith wove his way across the street. He tossed his empty sticks into an alley refuse barrel and pushed into a shop. Coughing once more, Shara shoved against his darkening thoughts and followed. He swung open the handsome wooden door and stepped into—

"Books."

An entire store full of books. Books on shelves, books on tables. Half-assembled books in one corner and ancient, half-disintegrated books in another. And a smell—not leather but something else—that made Shara's nose twitch with the desire to sneeze.

"Books." Korith ducked behind a tall shelf.

Shara trailed after him, moving carefully. Something about this place seemed to sleep, and if he made a wrong move, he might wake the books and set them all reciting their contents at once like a thousand rival storytellers.

Behind the shelf, Korith was burying a little cart beneath a pile of books, some alarmingly thick.

"You know," Shara observed, "if you didn't keep heaping

books on people who came to visit you, you wouldn't need to replace them."

Korith chuckled. "I'll get those back someday. Or I won't; if they're helping someone else, I don't mind the loss. Anyway, *these* are for you." He pried a book from between two others, scanned its cover, and shoved it back onto the shelf. "Hills, they're still making copies of that?"

For several uncomfortable seconds, Shara watched him pile book after book onto the cart, a weight settling in his stomach while uncomfortable suspicion crept into his mind.

"Why?"

"Like I said, I"—a book thudded onto the mound—"feel bad asking you to wash my dishes and make my deliveries and all that. Now that you've been here a few weeks and have a better grasp of things, I thought I'd help you start a real life. Something more . . . more Shara, you know? And it's completely up to you what you do, of course, but between you being alvithi and me being noble, I did have"—he strained for a book on the highest shelf—"a few ideas that I think you'd be excellent at, and—"

"No." The word rushed out with more force than Shara had intended. Flushing, he scuffed the floor with the toe of his shoe. "I mean . . . You don't have to do that. I'm fine, really."

But inwardly he cursed himself. He ought to have seen this coming given the way Korith had been watching him so closely, gauging his interests.

"Fine?" Korith raised an eyebrow. "You hardly do anything; aren't you bored?"

Shara shrugged. "Not really. Not so long as you keep dirtying dishes and making a mess of your clothing and forgetting how to use a broom—"

"Yes, and maybe tomorrow I'll drop a pencil, and you can spend the afternoon picking it up!" Without turning his smirking gaze from Shara, he made an exaggerated show of drawing a book off the shelf and setting it atop the growing mountain.

Shara's muscles tightened, and feline ears he didn't have slid back to pin against his head.

But there was a chance he could still salvage this. Better to admit the truth now than spend the next month slowly disappointing Korith day by day. "Korith, listen . . . I appreciate what you're doing, but there's no point. You're wasting your time."

"Wasting . . ." Korith's good humor vanished. "Wasting my time on—"

"On me." Sighing, he dragged a hand through his hair, realizing too late that his fingers were sticky with honey. "Whatever ideas you have, there's no point wasting them on a teveth."

Korith's serious expression faded into confusion. "You've lost me."

Disappointment boiled into faint anger as Shara sought the words to explain. Why couldn't Korith let him be? He'd been happy, content . . . "Look, it's—"

A clatter across the room drew his eyes to the storekeeper, who bent to retrieve a slender ivory tool from the ground. The man didn't so much as glance their way, but Shara slunk from the shop anyway, not sure whether he wanted Korith to follow.

But follow he did, down the street to a small terrace bordered on the far side by a waist-high wall. Two children toddled along it, arms outstretched, bragging to their watching parents about their balancing prowess. Shara halted at the other end of the wall, shifting out claws and scraping them over the stone. For a moment he felt calmer. Then he felt like a molting idiot.

You just ran away from books.

But it had not been merely books. Memories flooded through him, and his claws dug deeper as Korith perched on the wall beside him. They stared out at the water. Ships and gliders ferried people around the little islands that made up the rest of Farna, like a half-submerged sea dragon curled within the bay's embrace.

After several futile attempts, Korith gave up brushing hair out of his eyes. He scooped up a rock and slowly lifted and lowered it in some sort of exercise for his shoulder. "Teveth, was it?"

How strange that there were people in the world who did not know that word.

"It's . . ." He sighed. "I told you that unbonded alvithi sleep together in groups. The teveth sleeps closest to the cave opening—literally the word just means wind-side. Windward. But since the teveth is generally the youngest or least-experienced group member, it also gets used for new apprentices, young hunters, younger siblings. The person who gets all the least-pleasant tasks." He thought of Thosena and Tishel. "Like a new recruit, but not so official."

"Hmm." Up and down went the rock, lilting in rhythm with the church bells as they sounded the hour. "So the teveth is the strong, trustworthy, reliable one."

"What?" Had Korith been listening at all?

"You said the teveth sleeps closest to the cave entrance— that means it's the person bearing the brunt of the wind and weather *and* the first person to face any threats that come through, right?"

Annoyance raged through him. "Oh *please;* it's—"

"And it's the person everyone relies on to do all the necessary tasks that keep your clan—"

"Korith!" The intended snarl erupted instead as a frustrated squawk, so loud that the children paused in their wall-walking game to look over. It worked, though: Korith's smug expression faded, and Shara pressed on. "This isn't a joke. It means I'm untalented and . . . and not good enough for anything, and whatever you think I can help you with or whatever you want me to be . . . and all the books . . . Well, I can't." He wasn't going through all that again. He leaned heavily against the wall, suddenly exhausted. "I'm so tired of failing."

He hadn't meant to say it aloud, and now he prayed human hearing was as bad as he'd always believed.

If Korith *did* hear it, he didn't respond. Instead he pushed off the wall and stood directly beside Shara. His fingers twirled around the silver chain he always wore tucked beneath his shirt. "Is that why you left your clan?" He paused. "Or did they . . ."

Heat bubbled through him at the suggestion; thank the Eagle he had not endured *that* shame. "I left. I . . ." He wasn't ready to explain. "I left. I'm sure they don't miss me."

His shoulders sagged, and only then did he realize he'd been watching for them, closely observing the motions of both people and animals, waiting and wondering. But no one would have come after him. Not Shara.

He swallowed past the wad of fur lodged in his throat.

"Well, *I'd* miss you." Korith prodded him with the rock. "Even if you do eat raw meat and chew on my flowers when you think I'm not looking and leave my door open to the whole world. So you'll stay, won't you? If I promise not to offend your alvithi sensibilities with too many books?"

Embarrassment and surprise spun a slow dance in Shara's chest, and he puffed out a long breath. "I . . . You're sure? You don't mind that I'm . . ."

Korith's arrogant grin spread over his face again. "I'm always sure. It's part of my charm. And no, I don't mind that you're the strong, trustworthy, re—"

Shara whirled and strode away, too relieved to be truly annoyed. Laughter echoed behind him, and Korith drew abreast and shoved against him.

"Come on," he said, directing them left—away from the book shop, thank goodness. "You may be teveth, but I know you can fly. Let's see if my new glider is ready for testing."

Chapter 10

The Sketch

"Stop!"

Shara obeyed so abruptly that the teacup slid the length of his little platter and toppled over the edge, shattering in a scorching puddle over his bare feet. Hissing, he leapt back and wiped his toes hastily against his pant legs.

From his position on the bed, Korith winced. "Sorry. The light was perfect." He fluttered his sketchbook.

Dark, rain-soaked skies stretched over Farna. "What light?"

"The dramatic kind. Just stand there a bit."

Shara rolled his eyes but did as asked. Korith regularly drew from memory, but he had Shara now, an infinite number of models all in one person, and he'd been taking advantage of it as often as Shara would allow. This was the first time, though, that he'd drawn Shara himself.

It wasn't a pleasant sensation.

"Korith, your tea?"

"It can wait." His arm moved in broad strokes, his eyes darting between Shara and the paper. "Turn a little to the left."

The wall of portraits greeted him. Tishel and Na Mithel; Lady Bethen, who'd still not managed to catch Korith on a favorable day; Nareni, the girl at the Crown and Raven. Lower on the wall hung new portraits, all of them Shara. An angry young man with dark hair and a fierce scar over one eye scowled out at the apartment. Beside him beamed a portly old man stroking a pointed beard, wisdom in his eyes that Shara himself certainly didn't possess. Even that was more Shara, though, than the curly-haired woman and her teasing, secretive smile.

"There. Thank you."

Shara's gut tightened in anticipation, but Korith kept sketching, so he scooped up the shards of shattered teacup and ducked into the kitchen to prepare another cup of tea.

Grimacing, he pushed aside a bottle of mead and pulled down the little ceramic canister bearing the alsum, which he'd hoped not to touch again for several hours. He clamped his mouth shut, scrunched up his nose, and twisted his head as far as his neck would allow, then spooned a tiny dose of the reddish powder into the teacup.

He'd given up trying to talk Korith out of taking the poison—his cave-brother assured him that it was fine in small doses, that humans took it all the time to dull pain or anxiety, that there was nothing dangerous about putting it in a tea blend already intended to bring about sleep. Whether true or not, Shara wasn't the one in the middle of a pain flare, so it didn't matter what he thought.

When the lerian-root tea was steeping, he tossed a small bunch of piko seeds into the cup and padded back into the main room.

"Here you are. A delicious cup of poisonous, sleep-inducing, crunchy tea."

Mishala's horns, humans were odd.

Accepting the cup carefully, Korith toasted him with a strained smile and downed the entire thing with a long sip.

"Is there anything else I can get you? More pillows?" He hated that Korith had days like this, but after a month in his company, Shara had learned that all he could do was offer his help and make jabs at Korith's pillow collection. It felt so insignificant, but then again, that was fitting for Shara. "Less rain?"

Korith chuckled and adjusted the pillow beneath his left knee. "It's not the rain. Well, it might be in part. That's the fun—I never know. I crash into the sea in a storm and dislodge my arm and feel normal the following day, and yesterday I attend Lady Pachel's birthday celebration and now this."

Absolutely nothing about that sounded fun. "Fewer nobles, then?"

"Or birthdays." He grinned weakly and lolled his head to the side to peer out the rain-streaked window. Shara snuck a glance at the sketch, but it looked the same as all the rest from this angle. After a silence, whatever thought Korith was chasing seemed to elude him, and his eyes focused again on Shara. "Can you bring me that pencil off the desk?"

Several dozen pencils littered the desk, but only one was *that* pencil. Shara picked it up, hesitated, and glanced at the books.

He hadn't completely convinced Korith to leave him alone or bury the ridiculous teveth redefinition, but Korith had assured him that the small collection of books would better educate him on humans—specifically, nobles. "If you're going to be helping me, you'll need to know some of this eventually."

Exactly what help some of these books were going to be, Shara still wasn't sure. Did anyone really have a use for *A History of the Noble Houses of Barath from the Ascendance of His Most*

Royal Majesty King Inthar to This Present Time, Researched and Compiled by Lord F. A. Manthas and His Daughter, Her Ladyship Etharia Manthas?

He'd made it through the title, anyway.

L. Roald's *History of Barath* was surprisingly interesting, but today he picked up the book on speechmaking and climbed carefully onto the end of the bed. Korith accepted the pencil, and they fell into familiar silence.

Shara stuffed a pillow behind his back and opened the book in his lap. He trailed his fingers over the smooth paper while his eyes and mind adjusted to the cramped letters and dark, intimidating paragraphs. Intimidating yet fascinating, and somehow the discussions of rhetorical techniques always left him thinking of nights spent weaving riddles for Thia and her friends.

His fingers tightened around the book; he'd not said good-bye to her. He hadn't said goodbye to anyone, but Thia might actually miss him.

Eventually a flutter of paper pulled his attention from its wanderings. Korith set his sketch and pencil on the table beside the bed, looking half-asleep already. His jaw clenched as he lowered himself onto his back and brushed clumps of hair from his damp forehead. He mumbled something too incoherent for Shara to make out, then faded into silence. Only the rain and the soft crackling of the fire remained.

Even with the tea, Korith slept fitfully, if at all. He passed only minutes in stillness before shifting, twisting, tucking pillows and blankets here and there.

Shara's reading went no better, and after a quarter of an hour, he gave up and wandered to the kitchen. He nibbled at the sweet, dark slab of what Korith had called chocolate—not as good as fresh fruit, but not bad—but the kitchen itself needed no attention. He'd cleaned the bathing room yesterday, and the

Guide's shrine was dusted. He dared not touch Korith's desk except to eat a wilting flower.

His search for occupation paused beside the bed, and after assuring himself that Korith was asleep, he slipped the drawing from the table.

The face was Shara's—the slant of the jaw, the slope of the nose, the mess of dark curls. Yet sketch-Shara's gaze was direct and sure. His eyes shone bright and proud. His chin jutted out confidently, and his lips parted in a cocky smile.

Shara's face, someone else's soul. Invisible hackles lifted at the disconnect.

"What do you think?"

Korith's voice nearly sent him leaping through the rafters. His fingers spasmed around the sketch, wrinkling its edges, and he shoved it hurriedly back on the table.

If only he could so easily push the image from his mind.

"It's nice." Rain lashed against the window, and he swallowed down his roiling emotions and turned away to stoke the fire. "You have a vivid imagination."

The rain passed into a bleak, windy afternoon, and after a brief flight to occupy his restless mind and body, Shara shifted into a lynx and curled up purring beside Korith.

He awoke to evening shadows and the familiar *shf* of pencil across paper. Stretching, he folded his paws more comfortably over Korith's legs, and a heavy hand settled on his head and scratched between his ears.

"Evening, furball."

It was worth being called *furball* to have a cave-brother he could nestle against, but even so, he gave a disgruntled yowl and pushed out his claws to prick Korith's leg.

The scratching ceased, and a flutter of wind magic ruffled his fur in all the wrong directions. Shara hissed, though with no real malice, and Korith hissed back. Either that or he was gasping for breath and dying horribly—it was difficult to tell the difference.

Rolling away, Shara leapt off the bed, stretched again, and shifted. As always, a chill shot up his suddenly furless limbs, and, as had become habit, he pulled the drape of his mother's coat over his head in a makeshift hood. Behind him, the bed creaked as Korith slowly slid his legs over the side and planted his feet on the floor.

"Are you feeling better?"

Grimacing, Korith reached for his cane and pushed himself standing, and Shara could see the answer in his movements before he spoke. "Not as better as I'd like. Not that I expected any different, but . . ."

"But?"

"Never mind." He raked a hand through his tousled hair, nearly obscuring the frustration that flashed over his features. "Is it supper time yet?"

Shara let the obvious subject-change pass. "Fresh mountain goat tonight?"

Korith's face twisted, but he disappeared into the kitchen without the usual retort.

Extra sunspots instead, then.

Shara pushed the window open enough to fly out. Cold air rushed over him, sweet with lingering rain. Across the bay, a light flickered, but he'd only learned enough of the light signals to discern a few letters. They didn't spell *Tethamari*, anyway, and apart from the coronation, Princess Nashai's impending arrival was all anyone talked about—some more enthusiastically than others.

He was about to shift into a seabird when his gaze caught on the portrait. The air grew stifling as sketch-Shara's eyes met his, and suddenly he felt . . . broken. Korith had captured so many people in his drawings. Bared so many souls. Shara had watched him do it—Korith was always honest.

But not with Shara. That gaze, that smile . . . None of it was Shara.

There was nothing in Shara worth capturing.

His fingers trailed over the paper's rough edge. After a quick glance over his shoulder, he snatched it from the table and stuffed it into his coat pocket.

Korith said nothing about the missing portrait. He might not have noticed its absence at all, for he kept glancing out the window while they ate, and his attention returned regularly to the timekeeper on his desk and the church bells sounding out the evening hours. With each chime, he talked less and fidgeted more, and at the end of the meal, most of his food remained untouched.

"Is something wrong?" Shara finally asked when Korith began prodding at a pillow with a pair of eating sticks.

The sticks clicked out a quiet, intense rhythm. Korith's unfocused eyes followed their twitching movements, open and closed and open and closed, until they stopped abruptly and he looked up. "I need a favor."

Shara didn't like the sound of that, but he wrapped his arms around his torso and waited.

"I'm supposed to visit the palace tonight. The Guide obviously has other plans for me, so I need you to go as my representative."

"Me? Go to the *palace*?" He was still working out being a proper human in the Crown and Raven. "I don't think that's a good idea."

"Excuse me, I thought of it, so it's a brilliant idea."

"Not all your ideas are brilliant." He folded his arms and forced his face not to break out in scales. "Look, why don't you ride instead? I can be a horse again."

Korith was already shaking his head. "Not like this. By the time I arrived, I'd be in no state to meet with His Highness, and—"

"His Highness?" Shara squawked so loudly that the shop downstairs fell briefly silent. "You want me to go to the *prince*?"

"Prince regent, and yes. There's a gifting ceremony—it's tradition for a new ruler to present each of the nobles of the court with a token gift, and for the nobles to reciprocate."

"That's a lot of nobles," Shara said, grasping at grass. "I'm sure he won't notice if—"

"If my gift is the only one left unclaimed at the end of the evening?" His fist tightened around the eating sticks, and he glanced toward the timekeeper again. "No. I'm not going to lose my standing at court or have my future king think I'm unreliable because my body chose today to laugh at me."

"And has it occurred to you," Shara managed after several incoherent moments, "what might happen to your court standing if you send *me*?"

"You'll be fine." A hint of urgency tinged his voice. "Trust me, it's a simple, formal exchange. You give him the gift, offer him House Aman's best wishes on his upcoming coronation, and accept his gift on my behalf. That's it. It's a perfect opportunity for you to meet him."

"But—"

"I'll tell you exactly what to say. It's not long, and anyway, you've been reading that book on rhetoric, haven't you?"

Burrs. He was going to burn that book as soon as this conversation ended.

"Shara, you'll be *fine*, honestly. You're smart and resourceful and I trust you completely."

Shara's stomach wrenched. "I didn't realize drinking alsum caused delusions."

"See, and you're funny, too."

They fought a silent battle with their gazes, and in the end, Korith set aside the eating sticks and rose. Shara held his breath. Maybe he'd changed his mind. Realized how foolish it would be to send someone like Shara on so important an errand. Someone who wasn't even worth drawing.

Korith moved slowly around the desk and pulled a small package from within one of the drawers. He pushed it across the desk and looked up at Shara, his features tight. "Shara, it's bad enough that I have to send someone in my place. I can't neglect this entirely. Please?"

Shara's jaw clenched, and he stared at the wall so he wouldn't have to watch Korith eye the timekeeper and the window, wouldn't have to see the tightness in his jaw, the creased forehead, the fidgeting. He could argue with boisterous, confident Korith, but not with vulnerable Korith. Worried, doubting Korith.

Not in a month had he seen his cave-brother like this. This ceremony must truly be important.

All the more reason for Shara not to go—and all the more reason he had to.

I'm not going to lose my standing at court . . .

Shara chewed his lip. He didn't know what that would entail, but if it was anything like being teveth among the nobility . . . He wouldn't condemn anyone to that fate, especially his cave-brother.

Sighing, he glanced at the Guide's shrine. Korith had offered to buy an Eagle figurine to place inside as well, but Shara had declined—they were the same creator in the end, wor-shipped in different earthly guises. Now, however, he wished he'd taken Korith up on the offer, if only for the comfort of familiarity.

Instead he shed his mother's coat, and the last of the familiar comfort vanished in a wave of nerves and nausea.

"Fine," he grumbled, turning toward the wardrobe. "Tell me what to do."

CHAPTER 11

THE GIFTING

The Barathi royal palace loomed ahead, the largest human structure Shara had yet seen. It must have been built with some sort of sorcery, for every time he took even the smallest step forward, it grew exponentially larger—and closer.

He'd opted to walk the whole way rather than shift and fly. Korith had sent him off with an abundance of time to spare, and Shara had hoped to spend it practicing his little speech and growing accustomed to the fine clothing Korith had lent him—an assortment of pieces that were supposed to mark him as more than a servant but less than a noble.

But now he stood a hundred paces from the main gate, and if he'd actually done any of that practicing or accustoming along the way, he couldn't remember a single moment of it.

Pulse quickening, he ducked beneath one of the trees lining the road, checked for passersby, and cleared his throat.

"Your Highness," he began, bowing to the tree, "on behalf of the House of Aman, I am pleased to accept—"

No, not accept. Offer first, then accept.

His face warmed. He couldn't even exchange gifts with a molting *tree*.

With a moan, he buried his face in his hands. He shouldn't have agreed to this. True, he *was* bored cleaning dishes and fetching meals and helping Korith help the Mithels with their flowers. But a vast gulf stretched between *dishes* and *prince*, and Shara stood firmly on one side of it with no wings to carry him safely across.

But Korith had sent him anyway.

You're smart and resourceful and I trust you completely.

He stifled a strangled laugh. At least if this exchange erupted in disaster, Korith would finally realize the truth.

It wasn't much consolation.

Squirrel-dragons wrestling in his stomach, he shuffled back to the road. His hands knotted in the sash angling across his chest, an elegant strip of cloth designating him an official representative of House Aman. So far, the thing had done nothing but rub against his neck and earn him scowls from the few passing nobles who'd bothered to notice him. It seemed that Korith's warnings and Admiral Thosena's mutterings about the rivalries among the Barathi nobility had been accurate.

Just what he needed—people who'd be pleased to see him humiliate himself, and Korith, in front of the prince.

"Your Highness, on behalf of the House Aman—no, House of Aman. On behalf of . . ."

Sea-cursed humans and their ridiculous rituals. Like a prince needed gifts anyway. Was it too late to turn and—

"Sir?"

He squawked and leapt back, and the two handsomely dressed guards at the main gate raised their eyebrows in unison.

"Sorry. I was . . ." How long had he been standing there muttering under his breath? "Sorry."

He hurried into the courtyard and immediately missed the shelter of the trees. The shadow of a glider slid over the stone ahead, and he checked his urge to duck or run or glance into the sky. The patrol wasn't going to swoop down and eat him.

But he quickened his pace all the same, and then it truly was too late to retreat, for two more guards nodded him unceremoniously into the palace.

The palace.

His boots tapped against the stone floor, and he swallowed his heart back into place. It was just a cave. A giant cave adorned with bright lanterns and paintings full of colorful geometric shapes, but a cave nevertheless.

Drawing a steadying breath, he pulled out the paper on which Korith had written directions to the reception room and set off down the hall.

A left, three corridors down, a right.

"Your Highness, on behalf of . . ."

Another right, then up a staircase. Larger-than-life statues frowned down from their plinths, and fluffy cats peered up from mouse-free corners.

A second staircase and a long, wide hall. Murmured conversations floated out of nearby rooms while servants slipped quietly past. If the prince paid him as little mind as the staff, the gifting might not be so awful after all.

Just one more corner, and . . .

His footsteps faltered. The reception room should have been straight ahead behind a pair of double doors that Korith had described in somewhat excessive detail. Instead the corridor came to an abrupt halt at a simple wooden door more fit for a closet than a ceremony.

He spun, searching. More doors lined the hall in this direction, but they too suggested servants rather than royalty.

Heart in his throat, he moved back up the corridor, looking

left and right at each new hall he came to, praying he'd gone only a little too far. But nothing looked anything like the doors he sought, and at last he consulted Korith's instructions again, trying to match each step to one of the places he'd passed, one of the turns he'd made.

Useless—his memory had already begun to blur into a mass of white stone and flickering lanterns, endless staircases and rows of doors. Before his eyes, Korith's handwriting began to swirl as well. He reached out and steadied himself against the wall.

Breathe, Shara.

Yes, he was lost, but it wasn't over yet. If he could find a servant—

The idea melted as quickly as snow in sudden spring. He couldn't ask for help while wearing the sash. He'd only shame Korith and Tishel and whoever else belonged to House Aman. But if he took it off, he'd be a nobody wandering around the palace, as likely to be thrown out as sent in the right direction.

Then again, being thrown out might not be bad. He could put the sash back on and start over.

His heart leapt. He didn't need a servant, he needed a *window*. He'd fly back to the courtyard and begin the maze of the palace again, paying closer attention this time.

Bolstered, he pressed on, trying to keep himself going in roughly the same direction despite the constant lefts and rights. It didn't matter where he ended up—if he kept going, he'd hit one of the outer walls eventually.

He would, wouldn't he?

Somewhere in the far distance, bells began to sound the hour, and he increased his pace to match his heartbeat. Half an hour remaining. Never mind that he was lost; he'd still not got the speech correct, and he wouldn't be able to practice it while navigating the palace a second time.

He shook his head, trying to bury the rising panic, but something about the unnatural hush in this hallway had laid hold of his senses, and—

Voices ahead. Hardly thinking, he rounded a corner, yanked open the first door he came to, and shut it hastily behind him. Almost immediately, he felt stupid for the overreaction.

Calm down. You're lost, not a fugitive.

Resting his forehead against the door, he drew a deep breath—and froze.

A sharpness to the air, a scent both familiar and frighteningly out of place.

Blood.

Human blood.

Don't turn around. Don't turn around.

He gripped the doorknob, ready to burst back into the hall regardless of who might be passing by. What did it matter if he made a fool of himself in the middle of the royal palace?

The royal palace—the last place he should be smelling blood.

Sparks shot up his spine, and he whirled before he could stop himself.

Two figures in the uniforms of palace guards lay crumpled on the floor, one in the middle of the room, the other at the base of a finely carved desk. Dark blood soaked the thick rug beneath them, the tangy scent mingling with the odor of recent death.

He flailed behind him for the doorknob while his gaze darted about the richly adorned room, but whoever had done this had vanished, and—his heart sank—they hadn't gone out the window. An intricate metal grate covered the glass panes, leaving openings large enough for a sparrow, but not a murderer.

And not Shara, either. Lethir could have done the shift easily. Alanthas, Rathen . . . Any of them.

But not Shara.

On his left, the door to an inner room hung open a crack, emitting the faint orange of dying firelight. He took a wavering step toward it—was there any chance the window in that room would be unprotected?—and a glint of light on the floor caught his eye. Almost desperate for the distraction, he changed course and moved toward the object, a golden circle of some sort . . .

He scooped it up, and his blood chilled. A circlet.

Cold metal trembling in his hands, he examined the room again, but he hadn't far to look. The double doors he'd come through were carved and painted with the distinctive white fox crest he'd seen so often on the king's mourning banners.

Hardly able to breathe, he hurried toward the second room and pushed the door open. "Prince Il—"

A horrible, sickly, *wrong* stench burned his nostrils and fired in his throat. Gagging, he clapped his hand over his mouth and squeezed his stinging eyes shut. Claws speared from his fingers as his body fought to shift into something bigger, stronger, faster. He knew that scent—he'd spent all day avoiding it while spooning little portions of reddish powder into Korith's tea.

Whatever had happened here, someone had used much, much more than a spoon's worth.

Swallowing hard, he rubbed tears from his eyes and pried them open, then dragged in a shallow breath. "Your Highness?"

No answer, and no unconscious prince anywhere in the

room. Only ruins—a chair on its side next to the fire, shattered ceramic and trails of dark liquid along the floor, a rug bunched and twisted by scuffling feet. A gust of wind rattled the grated window, and the smoldering fire flickered in response. On the edge of the hearth hung something white, and he crouched and reached for it.

A damp, sticky piece of fabric.

He'd raised it only halfway to his nose before it became too much. With a choking cough, he flung the fabric away and retreated through the door, his feather of calm vanishing completely in the poisoned air. He cast a final look at the two guards and fled back to the corridor.

Cool air rushed over him, soothing him long enough for a hint of sense to touch his distress. He had to tell Korith. Find an uncovered window and shift and—

Footsteps.

Stifling a panicked squawk, he quickened his pace. *Get home. Tell Korith. Don't stop. Find Korith.*

His body rippled around him in a shift he couldn't prevent, so he didn't bother trying. Step after step carried him down the hall, faster and faster. A corridor flashed by on his left, a figure approaching down its length.

"Lord Aman?" called a voice.

Abandoning caution, Shara sprinted to the end of the hall, careened around the corner, and dove for the nearest window.

CHAPTER 12

GUILTY

Shara sailed through Korith's window and all but collapsed with a relieved screech. The unoffered gift skidded across the floor and bumped against the wall. Familiar scents engulfed him, and he breathed deeply, allowing his heartbeat to settle before he shifted.

He was halfway into his human form when he sensed the unfamiliar presence across the room.

"Tishel." He swayed, seized by a powerful urge to leap forward and embrace her. The person he needed, the person best able to deal with this, already here and . . .

A shiver ran over his limbs. Already here.

She stood frozen in the doorframe, a worn-looking Korith beside her with one hand still on the knob. Her eyebrows reached for her hairline, and slowly she stepped into the apartment and shut the door.

"Shara?" Korith frowned and eyed the timekeeper as he followed Tishel into the room. "What happened? What're you doing back already?"

Before Shara could form a reply, Tishel's hand settled on

her sword hilt. "Close the window."

Shara obeyed without thinking, wincing at the sounds of the hinges and wooden frame sealing him into the room's simmering tension.

"Your timing is impeccable," Tishel continued, nodding slightly before turning to Korith and drawing her sword. She levelled the tip at his throat, and though her hand was steady, her voice cut like the blade. "I'm only going to ask this once. Where is Iliath?"

Korith's eyes flew wide, and he stumbled back a step, catching himself on the desk. "What? What do you mean, where—"

"I asked you a question." She followed his motion. "Lieutenant Mereth saw Lord Aman hurrying from Iliath's quarters right before two of my own were discovered murdered in the middle of his office. Iliath himself is missing."

Korith stilled; his knuckles whitened as he gripped his cane. "I wasn't—"

"I received Mereth's wind message just a few minutes ago, and I was only down the street from here. You could have flown from the palace in that time, I suppose, but when I saw you in this state, I assumed he'd made a mistake." Her eyes slid to Shara. "And yet here stands your friend, your *alvithi* friend, just returned from some errand and wearing your clothing."

Shara's shoulders drooped under the sudden weight of the noble garb. Impeccable timing indeed. He'd flown several wide loops over the city to shake off the animal panic and gather his thoughts. If he'd come straight here, Korith would have had warning, and if he'd stayed away longer, Tishel would believe Korith innocent.

And if he hadn't lost control and shifted into Korith in the first place . . .

"And that proves what?" Korith's words cut into his gloom. "I sent Shara to the gifting as my representative, and he needed proper clothing. Do you really think I'd be so foolish as to send him to abduct Iliath while disguised as me? When he could look like anyone?"

Tishel's lips bunched. "Fair point." She whirled, and before Shara had time to blink, she'd backed him against the wall and set the blade at his neck. "And you?"

"Sira!" Korith snapped.

She ignored him. "Well, alvithi?"

Shara made to shake his head and stopped before he sawed his throat open. "I had nothing to do with it, I swear. I got lost in the palace and wound up at the prince's rooms. The two guards were dead, and I smelled . . ."

"Smelled?"

"Alsum. A lot of it. I . . . I panicked and ran, and I was focused on coming back here to tell Korith, and I shifted into him without thinking." He forced himself to look past Tishel, though he'd have preferred holding her fierce stare to meeting Korith's eyes. "I'm sorry."

"Why? Did you make me look bad?" He flashed a brief grin, then sobered. "It's all right, Shara. *I'm* sorry you walked into such a mess. And are being *blamed for it.*"

Scowling, Tishel scoffed and sidestepped, blocking Shara's view of his cave-brother. Her eyes bored into his, as if she hoped to frighten him into honesty. It would have worked, too, if he'd been inclined to lie.

Finally she lowered her sword and sheathed it. Shara fought to keep himself from sliding to the floor. Out of all the fears he'd entertained about tonight—

Tishel seized his arm and clapped something cold over his wrist.

The world went black. He floated in endless darkness, his

senses grasping for sensations that no longer existed. Cut off from everything, hollow and dull and . . .

Arms encircled him and hauled him upright. Someone called his name through the muddling darkness. Korith. Korith was the voice.

"What was that?" He staggered as Tishel released him, and the world spun back into focus.

"Binding cuffs." She nodded at the metal around his wrists, chaining them together—and preventing him from shifting. "Wasn't sure they'd work on an alvithi. Now then, you're coming with me."

He had no strength to fight back as she pulled him toward the door. "But—"

"Si, wait." For the first time, Korith's voice thrummed with fear.

She neither stopped nor turned. Tugging the door open, she pushed Shara through and shut it behind them.

"Wait!" came Korith's voice from the other side. "Shara!"

CHAPTER 13

ANOTHER FORM

For the second time that evening, Shara trudged toward the palace. This time, he spent the walk trapped in his ever-darkening thoughts. Did Tishel truly believe he'd kidnapped Iliath and killed the guards? What was she going to do to him? Throw him in prison? Torture him until he confessed?

But when he emerged from his daze, they were entering the palace itself. Down a corridor . . . past a distinctive painting . . . around a corner . . . up a staircase . . .

With a quick "Lieutenant" at the man guarding the door, Tishel steered Shara into the last place he wanted to be.

An empty room and a red-stained rug greeted him, the color vivid now that more lanterns had been lit. Without pause, Tishel led him into the second room, its air still soaked in the stench of alsum. She ignored his shudder and surveyed the room like she expected Iliath to climb from a hidden compartment in the wall and announce that everything was fine.

Please, please climb out of a hidden compartment in the wall.

"Good enough." She pulled Shara to the fireplace and unlocked one of his shackles, looped it through a metal ring embedded in the stone, and refastened it about Shara's trembling wrist.

"Captain, please, what—"

"I'll be back." She strode through the door and shut it behind her.

Shara swayed. He tugged on the chains securing him to the wall, then tried to shift. Another storm of darkness threatened to swallow him, and the chains clinked loudly as he shook harder than ever.

Silence smothered the room. Tishel did not return. Half of him prayed she wouldn't.

Desperate for relief, he extended a leg and hooked his foot around one of Iliath's chairs. The simple wood was far heavier than it looked, but not even the horrible scraping brought anyone to the door. When he'd pulled it near enough, he collapsed into it and gazed numbly at the coals, watching little tendrils of heat flare and fade. Anything to distract himself from thinking about why he was here, what would happen to him when Tishel did return, how long he could last with that miasma gnawing his senses raw.

He tried to focus on the room's other scents. The strongest had to be Iliath, and the rest would be people the prince had met with recently. One seemed familiar, but every time he breathed deeply, the alsum threw him into a fit of coughing. If only he could reach the window.

Somewhere in the room, a timekeeper ticked out his lengthening isolation. Slowly, slowly, his heart rate calmed and his body stopped shaking. He was ready to slide to the floor and try to sleep when footsteps sounded outside. Several sets, all of them heavy. Soldiers?

The door swung open, and Tishel filed in alongside two unfamiliar figures—a stocky woman with a steady gait and easy poise, and an angular man wearing large, round spectacles and a dubious expression. Though both were red-faced and breathing heavily, they exuded authority and importance, or maybe that was because Shara was chained to a wall.

"Shara, these are Prince Iliath's advisors, Erith Malothi and Vel Gepar. My lady, my lord, this is . . . Shara."

Gepar peered at him like Shara was on display in a shop window. "Really, Captain?" he said, his voice even more skeptical than his expression. "*Him?*"

"Do you know any other alvithi, Lord Gepar?" asked Malothi mildly, smoothing her dishevelled grey hair.

"He's practically a child!" Gepar retorted, flourishing a hand at Shara. "This is ridiculous. Captain, when you said you had a plan—"

"It's no more ridiculous than anything else we've been able to devise." Despite Malothi's firm tone, she gave Shara a small smile that was probably meant to assure him he wasn't ridiculous. "And Captain Tishel is correct—we need to act *now* before the rumors begin to spread. We'll have to make do."

Shara's stomach roiled worse than when he'd thought he was being arrested. He drew a long breath, and the familiar scent caught again in his nose. "Thosena."

They frowned in unison.

"What?" Tishel asked.

"I . . ." Embarrassment mingled with sudden worry. Surely the admiral wouldn't have . . . "The scent. I can smell Admiral Thosena."

Malothi's eyebrows shot up, and she opened the book she was carrying and flipped through it. "Admiral Thosena met with Iliath earlier this evening, yes."

Shara huffed in relief.

"You can *smell* her?" Gepar's features pinched in revulsion. Something about his narrow face, constantly moving hands, and lilting tone reminded Shara of children's tales about bad-tempered sorcerers.

"I . . ." His face flushed. "I'm alvithi." It was more an apology than an explanation.

"Yes, you are." Tishel fixed Shara in a cool stare, her eyes hard and so unlike Korith's. "An alvithi in Barath."

Warning laced her voice, a subtle invitation for Shara to imagine all the things they could do to him—or Korith—if he refused to cooperate.

He could imagine a lot. Everything but a way out of this.

At length, Gepar shrugged stiffly. "It seems we have no alternative. Captain?"

Tishel pulled a key from her belt and took hold of Shara's wrist. "Given that you did such a fine job impersonating Lord Aman, you're going to take another form for us."

Another form. Shara's throat worked, and he licked his lips and fought another urge to be ill. "Who do you want me to be?" he managed, though he knew the answer.

Sure enough, Tishel nodded around the ruined room. "Prince Iliath."

Shara sat in the again-silent room. Still chained to the wall, still unable to shift.

Still Shara.

Beyond the closed door, Tishel and the two nobles argued. First over how to receive the Tethamari delegation when Tethamar could very well be behind this. Then over exactly how terrible this idea was and whether there might be other options.

Shara prayed for other options. Despite Tishel's implied

threats, he'd tried to refuse, tried to tell them how unsuitable he was, but none of them had listened. In the end, he'd stalled by asking for a portrait of the prince to use as a reference. Now he waited, Korith's noble clothing dragging him into a deeper slouch with every passing minute.

If he refused, he was doomed.

If he agreed, all Barath was doomed.

Gepar was grumbling that his young son had more political experience than Shara when a loud *thud* silenced one argument and started a new one.

"—depart this—"

"—not going anywhere; where is he?"

Shara nearly fell off the chair. It was Korith.

"Lord Aman, I'm afraid this is—"

"You needn't lie, Lady Malothi; I already know."

"You already . . . Captain, you told him?"

"I had little choice." Tishel's voice was tight. "Go home, my lord."

"I'm not leaving. Where is Shara?"

A scuffle, a hiss. The door burst open and Korith staggered inside, determination burning in his eyes. With wavering steps, he crossed the room and sank against Shara in a heavy, one-armed embrace. Sweat soaked his body, but Shara didn't care.

"Korith." Never had he been so happy to see his cave-brother. Swallowing the urge to nuzzle him—humans did not nuzzle—he drew several long, calming breaths, grounding himself in Korith's scent.

"All right, furball?"

"I . . ." Better to simply not answer. "What are you doing here? How did you get here?"

"Friend with a carriage owed me a favor. And I'm here to rescue you." He lolled his head to offer Shara a guilty smile.

"Oh. Right."

"Shut up. It's a rescue in progress." He lowered himself shakily into the second chair and closed his eyes. Wiping a hand over his brow, he sucked in a deep breath and held it, and just when it seemed he'd forgotten how to breathe, he blew out a heavy puff of air. "So it's true? He's really missing?"

Shara reclaimed his own seat, inching it as close to Korith's as he could. "Yes. They . . ." Nerves surged through him, and he buried his spinning head in his hands. "They're going to make me take his place."

A grim chuckle. "I expected as much."

"*Me*, Korith. They . . ."A low moan swallowed the rest of his misery, and for a heartbeat, he regretted having ever saved Korith from drowning. Just as quickly, he batted the thought away. Korith had endured pain and fever and exhaustion and who knew what else to reach him. Korith was all he had.

And for once, Korith didn't heap encouragement onto him—he simply sat and waited. Shara swelled with guilty gratitude, but he didn't want to try again, and they fell into silence. The flames flickered slowly, as listless as Shara. Beyond the door, someone paced. Korith tapped his fingers against his knee. The scent of alsum refused to fade.

Finally, Shara couldn't contain his fear any longer. "Korith, I can't—"

"You can and you must." Tishel hefted a portrait into the room, dragging the door shut with her foot, though not before the two nobles frowned in at Shara. She propped the painting against the wall and adjusted her spectacles. "I'm certain you've heard that Iliath was—is—to be crowned king in less than a week. Guests are arriving from across the country, not to mention the princess from Tethamar. Iliath hoped his first act as king would be to sign a peace treaty with the Tethamari, and I'm sure it goes without saying that they won't be pleased if they arrive and discover he's vanished—assuming they aren't behind it."

Like they could blame Iliath for his own kidnapping. "And you want me to sign a treaty in his place?"

"With luck, we'll have found him before they arrive."

A glimmer of hope pushed Shara to his feet. "Then why do you need me at all? Surely there's someone else who could rule until you find him? A relative?"

He ought to have read that book on noble houses after all.

Korith snorted. "There are a few too many, unfortunately, and none with a particularly strong claim. Remember what I told you about all the rivalries and alliances between the Barathi noble houses? If Iliath were to suddenly die, there'd be a war *here*, never mind the Tethamari." He lowered his voice and nodded toward the door. "I expect those two are already working out how they'll seize control if Iliath's not found. Hills, there are some who'd be happy to help him stay lost if they thought it would improve their own chances at power."

Tishel nodded. "Better no one else knows he's missing. We realize this is far from ideal, but frankly, you're our only option, and we'll make the best of it. The next week will mostly be coronation preparations anyway. You'll have the assistance of Malothi and Gepar and myself, and as Lord Aman is incapable of staying out of a situation when he could be meddling instead, I expect he'll insist on being involved as well."

Korith nodded, somehow both supportive and smug. "Of course he will."

Shara's mind reeled, and he grasped for friendly words and ideas. Less than a week, if he was lucky. No signing treaties or negotiating with the Tethamari. Mostly coronation preparations.

Just pretend to be Iliath and prevent a war—possibly two.

None of it made him feel even a feather better. He was a failure, after all. A teveth. The last person anyone should rely on. Tishel had said it herself—they'd only picked him because he was their only option.

Ishara ko Han, a fake prince.

He could practically hear Lethir laughing.

"I . . ."

Korith's chair creaked as he slowly sat forward. "You can do this, Shara."

Quick as a falcon, all his earlier relief at seeing Korith vanished. His anxiety shifted into annoyance, even anger. Anger at Tishel and Malothi and Gepar, at Iliath, at Barath and all its nobles and rules, at his own cowardice preventing him from fighting his fate. But mostly at Korith, sitting there with that determined glint in his eyes, like that day in the bookshop. Like he'd organized this entire fiasco just for Shara.

"Fine," he growled, and before he could stop himself, "but when this is over, I'm done."

"Done?"

"Done." The rashly spoken word solidified into determination. "Done letting you shove 'opportunities' at me when I'm guaranteed to burr them up. Done with all the books and the nobility and whatever plan you think you have for me just because I'm alvithi." He thought of the sketch and nearly snarled. "Done and . . . and *gone*."

Korith flinched like he'd been slapped, then set his jaw as though he might argue. Shara almost wished he would—arguing with Korith would distract him from what lay ahead.

But in the end, his cave-brother's expression closed. "Very well," he said, rather thickly.

Tishel removed a key from her belt and unlocked Shara's shackles, and a lightness soared through him, an energy so blissful that he forgot to be angry or afraid or guilty.

Then she grabbed the painting and held it up. "Well? Let's see it."

CHAPTER 14

PRINCE LESSONS

No matter how many expressions Shara molded onto his face, the unfamiliar man in the mirror continued to look miserable, uncertain, and decidedly unprincely.

He jutted his chin up the way Korith did and went cross-eyed staring down his new nose. Looped his hands behind himself, thrust his shoulders back, and pinched a muscle between his shoulder blades. Gave the prince's white hair a dramatic toss and sent himself staggering off-balance.

Somewhere in Barath, the real Iliath waited to be found. Dirty and unkempt, hungry and exhausted, tied up and even beaten—and still more dignified than Shara.

Groaning, he climbed into the window alcove and rested his head against the elaborate metal lattice. Daylight nosed its way into the bedroom like an eavesdropper, and Korith would be arriving soon to resume Shara's prince lessons. And after that would come others, people who expected Iliath. And instead they'd get Shara.

Just Shara.

Another urge to flee spiked through him, and the binding

cuff secured around his ankle seemed to constrict. Tishel hadn't taken any chances.

Whimpering, he yanked the worn cushion out from beneath himself and hugged it. It smelled strongly of Iliath, who must have spent a great deal of time here, peering out over the bay. The alcove was, so far, the only comfortable aspect of Iliath. Everything else was more—more height, more breadth, more power, more grandeur. Eight years more age and a lifetime of experience as a prince, a Barathi, a human.

A soft knock at the outer door startled him to his feet.

"Your Highness?"

He looked about the room and flushed. *He* was Your Highness.

Leaving the bedroom—"Never meet with anyone in this room!"—he crossed into the study and pushed open the door.

On the other side stood a frowning Korith. "No. You don't open the door. Tell me to come in and make me do it myself."

"But you're—"

Korith shut the door in his face. And knocked again.

Shara rolled his eyes. "Come in."

"Better." He secured the door and surveyed Shara, then shook his head.

"Is there still something wrong?" He'd made dozens of minor adjustments before they'd all agreed that he matched Iliath exactly in both looks and voice.

"No, not at all. But it's odd, you know? Seeing him and knowing it's you."

Like last night, Korith seemed determined not to mention Shara's accusations, for which Shara was grateful. It was himself he'd been angry at more than Korith, and though he'd meant every word, he could have spoken less harshly. Korith was, after all, his only friend.

"How are you faring?" Korith asked. "I missed you last

night—I forgot how quiet the place is without a giant cat snoring at the end of the bed."

. . . his only friend, but still obnoxious.

He jerked a shrug. He'd spent the night anxious and lonely and uncomfortable, but he doubted he could make a prince's body say any of that. "I've been better."

Korith made a sympathetic noise and helped himself to a roll from the breakfast tray. He moved more smoothly today, and the cane seemed present more out of habit than necessity. He lifted the bread to his mouth, but his eyes never quite left Shara, and a strange expression lingered on his face.

Shara gestured to his ankle. "I can't—"

"No, I know. I'll get used to it. Right before they find him, probably, and then I'll accidentally call him *furball*."

Shara snickered, his first laugh as Iliath, and the smile pulled some of the tension from his tired limbs.

It all came rushing back as Korith's expression turned businesslike. "Shall we?"

Last night they'd gone over the most basic information. First, Iliath's personality and defining characteristics, which had quickly transformed into Korith's personal "Ode to Iliath." Amidst a fulsome list of examples and a torrent of words like *honest, intelligent,* and *driven,* only *reserved* had come as a relief—Shara couldn't have faked exuberant confidence like Korith's for longer than a few minutes.

Next had come the names and roles of people Shara would likely encounter in the next few days, such as the young man who served as Iliath's secretary and the eight men and women who made up the council.

"His advisors aren't on the council, though; they're more like glorified secretaries," Korith had clarified. "Gepar primarily manages the treasury and other financial affairs, and Malothi writes speeches and edicts and the like."

Today the lessons resumed with cups of cloudberry tea and a list of things Shara wasn't allowed to do himself, including opening the door (which was ridiculous), making his own tea (also ridiculous), and readying his private ship (fine, because Shara had no intention of going anywhere near it).

Dressing himself wasn't on the list, thank the Eagle, and Korith segued into a lecture on the contents of Iliath's massive closet and ended it with a test that left Shara looking, if not feeling, more royal.

Last night's gifting had been rescheduled, so after clothes came a review of the ceremony, this time from the prince's perspective. Despite the fact that all the responses were formulaic, Korith still managed to work in plenty of practice speaking like Iliath. Not that his critiques of "Fewer pauses, more big words!" and "Rounder tones!" were in any way helpful.

Then came a lesson on posture—mostly Korith shoving Shara's chin up to an uncomfortable and rudely high angle.

"It's not rude, it's regal. You'll get used to it."

He said "You'll get used to it" almost as often as he said "You're doing fine." If there was one thing Korith excelled at other than gossip, it was platitudes.

Korith was recounting how Princess Nashai had lost her hearing when a sharp rap at the door sent Shara leaping. Tea splattered over his hand and slopped onto Iliath's shirt.

"Your Highness?"

Just Tishel. He slumped and blew out a sigh. "Come in."

She ignored Korith's bright "Morning, Si!" and planted herself in front of Shara, who wrung out his shirt and rose reluctantly and scrambled for what to do next. Something about shoulders up and chin back, or shoulders back and chin up, and eyes . . . somewhere . . .

Her gaze swept over him, less frightening than usual owing

to the dark shadows pooling like smeared makeup beneath her eyes. Had she slept at all last night?

Just when he was sure he'd failed some unspoken test, Tishel bowed. "Your Highness."

Bowing at people had been on the list, so he simply nodded and said, "Captain." Before he could stop himself, he added, "I don't suppose you found him?"

Tishel snorted and pulled a small flask from her hip. "No, but we've quelled the rumors. We told those who came for the gifting last night that you were attacked but managed to flee and hide." She took a sip from the flask, and Shara's nostrils flared—was she *drinking* chocolate? "I'm sure *that* rumor will spread, but it's better than the truth. I'd suggest looking wary and a bit jumpy today, but . . ."

The vague flick of her hand at him said the rest. He scrunched his toes in the thick wool of Iliath's boots.

"Now then. Gepar and—"

The scrape of a chair against stone and a shrill female voice sent them all whirling to face the door. Tishel's hand leapt to her sword, but her expression twitched quickly from concern to distaste as the voice outside continued its tirade.

"—come all this way!"

"I'm sorry," came a much softer voice that must have been Amesal, Iliath's young secretary, "but I really must—"

"You are not going to keep me out when you just admitted that half-breed whore—"

A door banged open, and the argument grew louder. Growling, Tishel pushed her way into the outer room, and before Shara could decide whether to follow and rescue poor Amesal or hide and rescue himself, the angry woman caught sight of him.

"Your Highness!"

She swept into an exaggerated bow, flicking the skirt of her long coat to the side in a flourish he'd seen Korith and other nobles use. In Shara's head, a little Korith voice lectured about her garments: how her coat's artfully draping sleeves were cut in the latest fashion, how the deep green color was both popular and appropriate for the season.

"Lady Pareth," Korith whispered with a hint of acidity.

"Lady Pareth," Shara repeated. His voice wavered over even those simple words. *Breathe, Shara.* He'd been over this with Korith not ten minutes ago. He couldn't have forgotten it already. "What can I do for you?"

Lady Pareth straightened and brushed at her garments, sending the scent of roses wisping across the room. "Your Highness, I do apologize for the fuss, but I'd only just disembarked when I heard the news of the attack, and I simply had to come straightaway to reassure myself that you were well and express my deepest concern over this horrific incident."

Dropping her chin slightly, she twirled a finger around her loose hair and fluttered her eyelashes.

Shara stared. Was she expressing supposed concern over Iliath's near death or hinting she wanted to mate with him?

Humans were odd.

Nobles were worse.

Korith's subtle kick startled him from his discomfort, and he started to bow before catching himself. "Thank you for your kind words, Lady Pareth. I'm"—disturbed? bothered?—"honored by your concern for his—er, my well-being."

"But of course. To think that our beloved prince could be attacked within the royal palace, within his very rooms!"

Her expression of exaggerated horror shifted into a scathing glance at Tishel and then back into her simpering smile so quickly that Shara's alvithi senses reeled.

"Indeed," Korith agreed earnestly. "It is most fortunate

that the royal guard are trained so well and possess such dedication to our future king."

Tishel went violently red, and her jaw clenched.

Lady Pareth somehow turned a scowl into another eyelash flutter. "As I'm certain you're aware, my prince, I will be formally representing my house at the gifting, but in the meantime, please know that House Pareth is, as always, at your service."

Shara's mind spiralled into a dive after a proper response. He couldn't recite the formulaic words Korith had taught him, but a mere "thank you" seemed insufficient. What would a prince say? "I'm . . . pleased to hear that your house will continue to, uh . . . be loyal."

Well, now he knew what a prince *wouldn't* say.

Whether Lady Pareth was oblivious or too sycophantic to care, she merely smiled and bowed again. "Thank you for seeing me, my prince."

She nodded politely at Korith, scowled at Tishel, and departed. Shara almost threw the bolt behind her, and only the binding cuff prevented him from dissolving into a kitten.

"Only just disembarked." Korith snorted. "She's been here three days."

"Your Highness, I'm so sorry." Amesal wrung his hands. "I told her you were unavailable, but she—"

"It's fine. I know how—" He bit his tongue. Iliath didn't know what it felt like to be pushed around. "That is, don't worry about it, Amesal."

He gave the young man an encouraging smile and felt a feather of fondness for Iliath when Amesal smiled back, apparently unsurprised at his prince's behavior. Dipping his head, Amesal stole back into the corridor, and Shara fled to the study and sank into the nearest chair with a low keen.

"Are they all going to do that?" he muttered, scrunching

his nose to banish the lingering rose scent. "Tell me they're sorry and loyal and then—"

"Flirt?" Korith rolled his eyes.

The disdain was clearly for Lady Pareth, but even so, Shara slouched so deeply that he nearly slid off the chair.

"Shara, you did—"

"Fine, I know."

"Yes, fine." Korith's shadow hovered above him. "Look, you've taken on an impossible task, and you won't do everything right. There's no shame in that. We'll help you as much as we can, but we won't be able to tell you every single thing to do and say. You need to trust yourself as well—your heart and your instincts."

His heart and his instincts. White stars danced over his vision, and his head spun.

He'd been right last night—they were all doomed.

". . . didn't he, Si?" Korith's voice cut into Shara's vision of impending disaster. "Sira?"

Tishel jerked her attention from the door. "What?"

"Didn't Shara do fine out there?"

She scowled and shrugged. "He held a basic, polite conversation. If there was concern about his ability to do that, then I pray we find Iliath sooner rather than later. Until then, whatever you're teaching him, do it faster. And don't forget his meeting with Malothi and Gepar in an hour. Excuse me."

She stalked to the door, and Korith jumped into her path. "Don't worry about her, Si. Listen, why don't you—"

Tishel shoved past her brother and shut the door firmly, leaving Korith staring after her and Shara wishing he could be anywhere else.

CHAPTER 15

GEPAR'S COUNSEL

Even safe behind several locked doors, Shara could hear Amesal scrambling to turn away other nobles, all loudly demanding to see Iliath and reassure themselves that their beloved almost-king was well. As much as the voices rubbed his scales the wrong way, at least he had Korith, who kept up a running commentary on the voices he recognized.

"Watch out for her, she'll be trying to marry off her daughter to you."

"Oh hills, if he's here it means he's in debt *again*."

"This one actually burned down a rival's warehouse a few months back. Inquiries and hearings and all these witnesses summoned to testify; it was a mess."

At the end of the hour, they escaped Iliath's chambers and ambled toward the room where Shara would meet his advisors. Despite the guards trailing them and the increased likelihood of encountering demanding nobles, Shara relished the change—another hour caged by ever-shrinking walls and plagued by the lingering sting of alsum, and he would have gone mad.

As they neared their destination, the stone halls gave way to quietly creaking floorboards and wood-panelled walls.

"It was originally the royal family's summer retreat," Korith explained, quietly enough that the guards wouldn't hear him lecturing the prince on basic history. "After the capital was destroyed in the civil war, they fled here and expanded it into a proper palace."

Though darker than the stone corridors, the halls exuded warmth and comfort. Shara might have sought refuge here, too, if he hadn't been so desperate to escape.

The desperation only increased when they reached the council room: thick, sound-swallowing carpets, stifling air, and not a single window. At Korith's nod, he settled awkwardly into the straight-backed chair at the head of the table. Malothi, Gepar, and Korith sat as well. Tishel paced. No one spoke.

At last, Malothi smoothed the pile of papers she'd brought. Clearing her throat, she frowned at Korith. "I hope it goes without saying, Lord Aman, that everything pertaining to this ordeal is to be held under the strictest confidence, both now and after. You may be important to our 'king,' but any indication that you've abused your quite unexpected and frankly inconvenient involvement in this affair, and I will personally strap you to the mast of a sinking ship."

Her tone never changed, and faint wrinkles of humor lined her eyes, yet the underlying threat burned as fiercely as seawater on a wound.

"Relax," Korith drawled, waving a hand and smiling guilelessly. "I won't say a word." He leaned over to Shara and, in a dramatic undertone, whispered, "You'll save me, right?"

Refusing to indulge him, Malothi gestured at Shara. "Now that we have the immediate problem in hand, we need to focus our attention on the coronation and the Tethamari."

Korith twitched upright. "We need to focus our attention on finding Iliath."

"No." Tishel pivoted. "*I* need to find Prince Iliath."

"You most certainly do, *Captain*," Gepar said, wringing his hands, "as it was you and your guard who failed to prevent his abduction."

Tishel stiffened. Her shoulders drooped and her head ducked, but her voice remained sure. "And it is we who will recover him."

"And what do you plan to do?" Korith pressed, flashing a brief glower at Gepar before fixing his sister in a look of exaggerated interest. "How do you hope to find him when you can't tell anyone he's missing?"

It was so obvious an invitation to boast that Shara couldn't blame Tishel for scowling. "I have some ideas, but with respect, Lord Aman, we are here on Shara's behalf to discuss *his* role."

"But—"

"Lady Malothi?"

Korith huffed in defeat and returned to his sketchbook, no doubt already watching for his next opportunity to put his sister on a pillar. How many such pillars had Tishel shoved over and used to build her wall?

Malothi slid a small pile of papers to Shara, all covered in line after line of swirling script in a deep blueish-purple ink. "This is your schedule for the week," she told him, chuckling sympathetically when his jaw fell.

"All of this?" His vision blurred, then focused too sharply. There had to be a hundred things on this list. Audiences, meetings, dinners, garment fittings, rehearsals, a parade—on and on, each line a new opportunity to say the wrong thing, make the wrong move, lose his wind and plummet from the sky. The word *Tethamari* stuck out here and there alongside dozens of other unfamiliar names and places and . . .

He sat back, heart pounding. "I can't do this."

"You will," Malothi said.

Gepar twirled his hands with a sort of nervous elegance, and his nose wrinkled like he could scent fear and didn't care for it. "Unless you want the kingdom to erupt into chaos."

Shara's stomach had already erupted into chaos. Closing his eyes, he rubbed another sky of flashing stars from his vision, but that cleared the way for an image of the list.

"I understand it's overwhelming," Malothi said, "but bear in mind that many—most, in fact—of the people on this list are coming to Farna from other islands and have rarely spoken with Prince Iliath. Some have never met him. We've also cancelled anything that isn't a formality or coronation preparation, so you needn't worry about audiences of actual import apart from the Tethamari, nor about meeting with the council. The prince's relative youth will also give you considerable leeway so long as you maintain proper royal demeanor. Lord Aman can assist you in that."

Gepar scoffed. Korith scribbled a giant mustache onto his sketch of Gepar.

They spent what felt like an hour perusing the list. Again and again, Shara's body tried to shift out claws, and not even the cuff could stop his fingernails from piercing deeper into the padded arm of his chair with every reminder of how little he knew. These people were mad to believe he could impersonate their prince.

Drawing a slow breath, he traced a shaking finger over the edge of the page, curling it into a gentle fold as if making the paper look less official would make its contents less intimidating. Sad that the coronation itself now seemed the simplest of all.

The conversation stalled after the coronation—no one wanted to discuss what might happen if Iliath still hadn't been found, nor acknowledge that if the Tethamari *were* behind the abduction, none of this planning had any point.

Shara leaned back in the uncomfortable chair, starved for sunlight and fresh air and a giant bowl of fruit. "All right," he said, trying to sound marginally authoritative. "What else?"

Malothi twirled a loose strand of hair around her finger. "You will go nowhere without your guards, not even within the palace. The added benefit of your presence as Iliath is that it will have ruined whatever immediate plans the kidnappers had, and it's entirely possible that they will try again. We must not give them the opportunity."

Shara wasn't sure he agreed—with his week now laid before him, being kidnapped didn't sound entirely awful.

"Captain Tishel has already increased the guard around your rooms, and after this morning's visit from Lady Pareth, I will see to replacing your secretary as wel—"

"What? No!" The words burst forth without consulting his mind.

Malothi pursed her lips, and Tishel stopped pacing. Gepar, who seemed to waver constantly between nervousness and disapproval, finally settled on disapproval. Only Korith smiled.

"I . . ." Shara ducked his head. "I'm sorry. I . . . I like him. And it wasn't his fault. Please don't . . ."

The idea of Amesal being sent away stung deeply, personally. All for a single mistake.

Gradually, the room came to life again. Tishel took a drink from her flask and resumed wearing a road into the carpet, and Malothi and Gepar exchanged a few hushed words.

Swivelling to face Shara, Malothi nodded. "Very well. But if we hear of further incidents—"

"Of course." Shara nodded hastily.

"Only one thing more, then." Gepar slid two papers along the table and set a stylus on top. "The first of these is a model of Prince Iliath's signature. Sign the second."

Shara's nerves faded beneath the urge to roll his eyes. Any of them could have done this, but the task fell to him because *he* looked like Iliath. He skimmed the second document, all swirling handwriting he could hardly read. "What is it?"

Gepar huffed. "That, like your secretary, is none of your concern. Please recall that you are not here to have an opinion."

Heat surged through Shara's face. "Yes. I mean, no. I understand."

Korith kicked him beneath the table.

"If it will ease your conscience," Malothi told him, "it's merely a note to the treasury authorizing payment for coronation decorations."

"And you're being cheated at that price," added Korith, craning his neck for a better view.

Not even the thick carpet could obscure Tishel's footfalls now.

Shara's signature looked like a pile of tangled yarn, but he doubted anyone would care so long as the decorator got paid.

"Good," Malothi said as Gepar reclaimed the papers. "As you're now aware, *Your Highness*, you have an appointment with the tailor shortly. Lord Aman will accompany you, and Lieutenant Mereth will be present as well. If the rest of you would stay behind, please."

Shara nearly bolted, and to his surprise, Korith followed him from the room without protest or other commentary. They set off down the hall, and Shara was about to heave a sigh of relief when Korith flapped a hand at the guards and subtly steered him into the next room.

"Korith, what—"

Shushing him, Korith closed the door, then made for the wall that divided the two rooms. A large painting of a fox hung there, and with silent, practiced ease, he lifted it off the wall, set it aside, and removed the panelling beneath. A narrow gap of darkness greeted them, just wide enough for a person.

"Do this often, do you?" Shara muttered, but he stepped closer anyway.

". . . legitimate question," came Malothi's voice. "How *do* you intend to find him when we cannot admit he's missing?"

Tishel's pacing ceased. "As I said, I have ideas, but first, I *would* like to include a few others in—"

"Absolutely not."

Shara pictured Tishel collecting herself. "With respect, this search is going to be difficult as it is. With additional—"

"No." Malothi's regret crept through the panelling. "I'm sorry, Captain, but the risk is too great. Lord Aman's presence has already complicated matters."

"Lord Aman is not a soldier, nor in a position to do anything to find Iliath," Tishel responded stiffly.

Shara glanced at Korith, but neither his expression nor his posture changed.

"If I might?" Gepar's chair creaked over his voice. "As was mentioned, replacing Iliath will have interrupted the kidnapper's plans. I suggest we wait a day before attempting any search in order to give the kidnapper time to react and, perhaps, to make a mistake out of surprise. This will also give our *esteemed* Captain time to better orchestrate a search."

In the ringing silence that followed, Korith's hand strayed to his throat and dragged on the silver chain. "*Nothing.*" His voice could have melted iron. "He wants to do *nothing.*"

In this opinion, Tishel and her brother were alike. "Someone overpowers and kills two of my guards, abducts the prince regent, and leaves us with a woefully inadequate replacement, and you wish to do nothing. Forgive me, Lord Gepar, but if I didn't—"

"I hope, Captain, you don't intend to accuse me, a noble of the court, of sympathy with our prince's kidnappers—or worse."

Tishel coughed. "I merely—"

"Enough," Malothi interjected. "We have a young, uneducated, frightened alvithi disguised as Prince Iliath, the true prince to find, a Tethamari delegation arriving any day, and a coronation to manage. This is not the time for division."

But Gepar hadn't finished. "Iliath was abducted, not murdered. That suggests the kidnappers want something. It may be they hoped to stop the coronation or influence it somehow. If we wait even briefly, we might entice them to make their demands clear."

A whirl of brown, and the panelling nearly crushed Shara's fingers—Korith had apparently heard all he could take. Face twisted in disgust, he replaced the painting with a sort of savage silence before spinning and striding from the room. He didn't speak for several hallways except to growl "Nothing."

"Korith? Lord Aman?" What would Iliath call Korith? That had probably been somewhere in the lecture this morning, along with what to do when your painfully optimistic cave-brother had his scales raked the wrong way.

Korith grew more coherent, if not more cheerful, the further they walked. "Nothing" became "This is unacceptable" and "What if the kidnapper retaliates?" He punctuated all of his complaints with cane thwacks against the walls.

Outside a large room filled with padded chairs and beautiful paintings stood a man who must have been Lieutenant Mereth.

"Your Highness." He bowed and smiled broadly.

Shara tried not to stare at the man's unexpected cheer. Why couldn't Mereth have been captain of the guard?

"The tailor should arrive shortly." Korith rammed his

hands into his coat pockets and flapped its skirt restlessly. "If you'll excuse me, Your Highness, I need to—" He bit off the rest, his eyes roving the walls frantically like he might find the remaining words engraved in the stone.

And before Shara could question or protest or even think, Korith bowed stiffly and stalked off down the hall, muttering to himself—and leaving Shara alone.

CHAPTER 16

SAILOR'S BLOOD

Even after Korith's disappearance, the garment fitting might not have been so bad—but then the nobles started arriving.

Exactly what appeal there was to standing around a room drinking and gossiping and watching someone else have a robe hemmed, Shara couldn't fathom. Yet within minutes, men and women dressed in finery began filtering into the parlor. A servant announced their names as they passed, and Shara paid as much attention as he could while standing before a mirror and sweating in four layers of beautifully crafted coronation garments.

Na Fanshe, the tailor, seemed to feed on the room's simmering energy. She practically danced around him, making small adjustments here and there, bouncing on the balls of her feet, and raising her hands in silent applause every time she paused to examine the effect.

"Lovely. Oh, excellent." She pinched Shara's collar and beamed. "Eleth?"

Her young apprentice handed her a little ball of pins, and

she bounded around Shara's back. With all that movement, she might accidentally stab him, and then he wouldn't have to greet every noble who came gliding past. And he could ignore Lady Pareth, who'd settled at a nearby table and kept trying to catch his eye.

His coat rustled, and he seized on the distraction and glanced down at Eleth. "How are you liking your apprenticeship?"

Eleth started. "Very much, Your Highness," he answered, wobbling into a bow. "Na Fanshe is very knowledgeable."

"I'm glad to hear it. And see it." He flicked a hand enough to indicate the garments without disturbing their careful placement. He'd learned enough from his parents to recognize skill. "You both do beautiful work."

"Thank you, Your Highness." Eleth sank into a crouch at Shara's hem, ears red.

"He has quite a natural talent," Fanshe's cheerful voice said from behind Shara. "Even Lord Verta had no complaints about his work."

Perhaps Lord Verta was related to Tishel. Or Gepar. Korith could have told him, but—his hands balled into fists—Korith had abandoned him.

Another pack of nobles drifted past, offering more greetings and compliments and exclamations of eager anticipation for the coronation. Along the eastern wall, a small group argued economics. Korith's friend Lady Bethen sat in a secluded corner, poring over a book with another young woman.

No one seemed interested in having a real conversation with Iliath, which struck him as both an immense relief and unusual. And sad. Did the prince not have any friends?

He was casting about for something else to say to Eleth and Fanshe, mostly to avoid Lady Pareth, when a man came breezing through the doors.

The servant cleared his throat, eyes a bit wide. "Lord—"

"Yes, yes, he knows who I am."

The room froze, and the hairs on the back of Shara's neck stood on end. Every eye followed Lord Whoever-He-Was as he prowled across the hall, all grace and beauty and power. No one greeted him, and his eyes never left Shara—bright, hungry eyes that gauged the distance between them as though the man were preparing to leap and bring him down in a single bound.

If neeka could shapeshift . . . Throat closing, Shara sucked in a breath through his nose and buried the thought. Just another noble. Another arrogant, deadly hunter, and he'd known plenty of those.

But that thought brought no comfort, especially when the man sprawled into a chair beside the mirror, tossed one leg over the other, and lounged back without greeting or bow.

Like wind hissing through grass, the nobles fell into a whispering hush. Their gazes burned into Shara. Waiting.

Not daring to speak, he dipped his head politely. The newcomer's eyes glinted, and when he returned the gesture, it was not a bow but the patronizing nod of someone acknowledging a subordinate's deference. Familiar humiliation scorched through Shara's body, and he jerked his gaze to the mirror, cursing himself. He'd misjudged the man—this was a predator who liked to play with his food.

He'd known plenty of *those*, too.

A servant hastened to the man's side and bowed. "May I fetch you anything, my lord?"

Eyes still on Shara, he bared his teeth in a feral grin. "Sailor's Blood."

Shara twitched, and the man's sneer widened. Like he *knew* Shara was teveth, knew—

His stomach lurched. The man couldn't possibly know the truth.

Unless he was the kidnapper.

Fanshe sidled into Shara's view, more subdued. "Would you like us to leave you, Your—"

"No." The word tumbled out too quickly, but he didn't care. He had no desire to be alone with that man, especially surrounded by an audience. "Please continue."

A true professional, Fanshe did not acknowledge the waver in his voice, only flapped a hand at Eleth. The boy stared at the noble a moment more before resuming his work on Shara's hem, but his eyes kept darting to the chair.

Shara couldn't blame him, especially when the servant returned with a glass of something nearly black. The man raised it in toast and swirled it methodically before taking a long, slow sip.

Icy fingers twisted around Shara's spine. His vision darkened, and his body throbbed as it fought uselessly to shift despite the binding magic. Iliath stared out from the mirror like a desperate prisoner, eyes too wide, breaths too quick. Korith would have scolded him, but Korith—

Shara bit that thought off before it could sting him worse, but at least the sharp prick of betrayal was enough to distract him from his mounting fear. He drew a long breath, and the battle in his limbs subsided.

Eleth's white head bobbed into view. Clearing his throat, the boy rolled his shoulders back and held up two scarves. In a voice that suggested he'd been practicing for this moment, he asked, "Does His Highness prefer the blue or the gold?"

In a blink, Shara forgot the noble. Was this a riddle? He could recognize weaving skill, but he knew nothing about Barathi fashion. More to the point, both scarves looked black, identical but for a gentle sheen when the sunlight hit them just right.

As he squinted and tried to look thoughtful, Fanshe settled

a hand on Eleth's shoulder. "I do apologize, my prince, that I was unable to acquire the trim for the scarf. It seems another dispute over shipping rights has arisen around Pannel, though I'm certain my prince has heard already."

"Oh, uh . . . yes."

Did Barathi squabble over everything? Not that his people were much better, boasting over who had the biggest catch, who could fly the furthest, who had the most toresh.

"A shame, that," said the stranger, his cultured voice as silken as the fabrics. He pushed himself lazily from the chair and strolled toward Shara, wine sloshing against the sides of his glass. "But of course our young prince is well aware of the complexities of trade."

Shara didn't have time to be insulted by a jab he didn't understand. He forced his attention back to the scarves and was about to choose one arbitrarily when the man snatched them from Eleth's hands.

"Give those—" The demand lodged in Shara's throat as the man's eyes snapped to his.

"Yes?" the noble purred. He thrust his wine glass at Fanshe and made a show of comparing the scarves while Eleth backed helplessly away.

Throat full of fur, Shara wrestled down another painful urge to shift, trembling with fear and anger. Korith's bright voice rang in his mind, telling him to speak, to act. But what was he supposed to do, a teveth in a prince's body? Even if he challenged the man, he was nobody, and he had a horrible feeling that this man could tell, and all those nobles were watching . . .

His gaze jumped to Eleth, and something kicked in his stomach.

A hiss of fabric. Still twirling the scarves, the man prowled a slow circle around Shara, trailing the bite of sea air, the bitter sweetness of wine, a hint of sulfur. The nobles fell silent again, and Lieutenant Mereth crossed the room, no longer smiling.

Do something! But what? Alanthas would coolly stand his ground. Rathen and Lethir would challenge. Korith would say something lighthearted to smooth everyone's scales. And Iliath . . .

Shara had no idea.

Then the man was before him again with those mocking green eyes and that malicious smile. He draped the gold scarf over his own neck and held up the blue one like a garrote. "This one, wouldn't you say, my prince?"

With frightening delicacy, he settled it around Shara's neck, fingers crawling like industrious spiders as they smoothed its folds. Shara held his breath, waiting—for a cutting taunt, a whispered threat, a tightened knot.

But the man drew back and rested his chin in his hand, surveying Shara like his next meal. "Splendid."

And without another word, he turned and sauntered from the room.

CHAPTER 17

THE KING'S TEARS

Shara fled from the garment fitting with every intention of collapsing on Iliath's bed and sleeping forever—but his rooms were already occupied.

He froze just inside the office. Behind the closed study door ahead, shuffling footsteps halted abruptly.

Silence.

Drawing a soundless breath, he crept forward, ears straining. A soft rustle of fabric cut off abruptly in a faint hiss. Then silence again. Whoever was inside must have realized there was no escape.

The thought threw him forward and through the door with almost physical force. If he caught the kidnapper, if he found Iliath, he could give all this up and—

"Korith?"

He staggered to a halt and almost laughed with relief, but relief wouldn't come. A guarded expression shadowed Korith's face, and his body quivered in the unbalanced posture of someone who'd frozen midstep. Something white hung from his fist.

Shara's eyes went wide. "Is that . . . ?"

The piece of poison-soaked cloth Shara had pulled from the fire last night.

This time, the panicked urge to shift was too much. Pain seared through his limbs, and the cuff seemed to burn around his ankle as the world spiralled into darkness. He pitched sideways, tried to catch himself on a chair, and dragged it down with him. It cracked against his skull, throwing white stars over his vision while he strained for the cuff.

"Shara!"

Heavy footsteps, then a thud. Korith seized his foot and twisted it, and before Shara could summon the energy to fight, a metallic *click* tapped at his ears.

The cuff fell away and the pain vanished, and Shara's true form erupted all at once. With a strangled shout, Korith bolted for the door. Shara flailed for his leg as he passed, but rather than flee, Korith slammed the door shut and spun to lean heavily against it. Cautiously, as if afraid of startling a wild animal, he lifted a hand. "Shara."

Panting, Shara braced himself against the chair and shoved himself standing. He flexed his claws, revelling in the sensation until he remembered why he'd hit the floor in the first place. If Korith was involved in this . . .

"What are you doing here?"

Korith's expression closed, and his hand tightened around the fabric. From beyond the window, laughter filtered into the room like a bright but useless assault on an army of suspicion and fear. Neither of them moved.

"Look," Korith sighed at last, pushing himself cautiously from the door and moving to close the window shutters. "I owe you an apology. Several. And an explanation."

"Explanation first."

"All right. But first, can you not look like you're going to eat me?"

Shara scoffed. "This is how I really look, you know. And we don't eat humans."

"Well, you look like you might. And are those tree branches growing out of your head?"

"They're horns."

"Are you sure? Because they have leaves and—"

"I could stab you with one if you'd like to find out."

"All right, all right." A glimmer of his familiar amusement shone through now. "Keep your hair on. Or"—he flapped a hand—"your horns, I suppose."

Too exhausted, irritable, and unnerved to care what that was supposed to mean, Shara shot him a hard look and shifted himself bald.

Korith pitched forward, clutching his stomach and dissolving into sputtering laughter. Despite himself, Shara grinned, and some of the tension faded from his limbs as his hair regrew. But he didn't shed his form, and when Korith finally emerged from his snickering cocoon, it was all Shara could do to keep his breathing steady.

"Explanation?"

"Explanation, right." With a final, breathy laugh, Korith lowered himself into one of the chairs by the fireplace. He set a key, the fabric, and a few scraps of burnt paper on the table, then drummed his fingers restlessly against it. With every beat, the stifling air grew warmer and Shara grew colder, until—

"I'm a spy."

A spy.

For several heartbeats, he didn't know what to say or even think.

Korith, a spy.

"For the Tethamari?"

"Wha—? No, fur-brain. For Iliath."

Shara's knees gave way, and he sagged against the wall and slid to the floor, lightheaded. Korith wasn't a traitor. Shara's only friend . . .

Leaning forward, Korith rested his elbows on his knees and folded his hands. "I don't know what you've heard about King Isith, but there's merit to the complaints that he wasn't particularly interested in what was going on beyond his own shore. Iliath wanted to be better informed. A few years ago, he secretly assembled a small group of people to gather information for him about, well, everything. Tethamari and Barathi affairs, the pirate fleet up near Delgar, Kana Faresh, the crime syndicate operating out of Shor Sprinta . . ." He reached into his shirt and drew out the silver chain, from which hung a tear-shaped pendant. "There's a legend that an ancient Barathi monarch called his inner circle the King's Tears, because they were the only people he trusted to see his true emotions."

Shara recalled how none of the nobles at the garment fitting had seemed at all close to Iliath. "And he chose you."

"Well." Korith seized his cane and twirled it. "In a way, I'd been doing it on my own for years. Talking. Listening. Sitting in taverns pretending I was a spoiled, lazy—don't give me that look, furball." He smirked. "Anyway, it turned out several Tears had already been getting information from me, and about a year ago, Iliath formally invited me to join them." He puffed with pride, though the quick duck of his head and the flush of color over his cheeks suggested how truly humbled he was. "Told you I was good at gossip."

Gossip and binding cuff key theft. Shara gave a wispy laugh. Muscles loosening, he rubbed his thumb along the scales on the back of his hand and, for the first time that day, closed his eyes without fear.

Korith's chair creaked, and his feet shuffled over the rug. He settled himself beside Shara, radiating a comforting warmth. A quiet stillness wrapped itself around them, and they sat without moving or speaking. Another bout of laughter echoed beyond the closed window shutters.

Korith sighed. "And now that we've had the explanation . . . I'm sorry I ran off. I'd already informed the Tears of Iliath's disappearance, but after what Gepar said about waiting, I couldn't stomach the thought of doing nothing."

A wry smile tugged at Shara's mouth despite the lingering sting of betrayal. "You drop whatever you're doing the moment anyone asks. You visit the Mithels six times a day to make sure they don't need anything. You can never stomach the thought of doing nothing."

"Yes, well, your questionable counting skills aside"—Korith elbowed him gently—"in this case I truly couldn't do anything. Not for Iliath. But I could have helped you, and I should have. Especially since it's my fault you're in this situation in the first place."

Shara snorted. "You asked me to go, but I got lost and shifted into you all on my own. Your only fault was trusting a teveth."

"And I'd do it again in a heartbeat." Korith smiled. "The smart, trustworthy, windwardly, directionally challenged one."

Shara shot him a look. Better teveth than delusional.

Maybe.

Korith's gaze fell to the floor. His hands twisted, and a shadow passed over his face. He pursed his lips, apparently searching for words.

Shara tensed. It was either bad news or another lecture about Shara's potential, and he didn't have the appetite for either. "So!" He shifted away his alvithi features as he grasped for another topic. "So you came in here to search for clues. Did you find anything?"

"Nothing useful." Korith ruffled a hand through his snowy

hair. "Just those scraps, and all that's on the papers is dates. I'm almost certain he has information hidden here somewhere, but I was interrupted by a grumpy alvithi before I could find it."

Shara rolled his eyes. "You'd be grumpy too if—oh!"

The source of his original anxiety came rushing back, and he sprang to his feet. Closing his eyes, he pictured the strange noble—those eyes, that infuriating smile, that predator's bearing. "Korith, who—?"

Korith yelped and recoiled, his face screwing up in revulsion. "*Hills*, Shara."

Shara threw off the form like it was a slimy, mud-soaked blanket. "Sorry."

"What I get for teasing you about your horns." Still a bit wide-eyed, Korith let Shara pull him to his feet, then jabbed him with the cane. "That was uncalled for."

It was a small comfort knowing Shara wasn't the only one unnerved by the man. "Yes, well, if you'd come to the garment fitting, you'd have been stuck seeing him in person. Who is he?"

"At the—" Korith's expression darkened. "What was he doing there?"

"Flaunting his horribleness? I don't know." He yanked back the shutters and threw the window open, sucking in a gulp of sweet spring air. A clear blue sky beckoned, dotted with seabirds and gliders.

Sighing, he turned away from the view. Little though he wanted to remember any of the garment fitting, he gave Korith as much detail as he could recall—until he reached the scarves. Skin crawling with shame as he pictured Eleth's face, he skimmed over the specifics, making it sound like he'd deemed it more appropriate to Iliath's personality not to respond to the man's cruel challenge.

At the end of his narrative, he received a brief, unasked-for lesson in Barathi profanity while a pacing Korith brought himself under control.

"So who is he?"

More swearing, more pacing.

"Korith?"

Korith stopped abruptly. "The peace treaty." Cursing again, he spun and struck his cane against the wall. "Hills, I can't believe I didn't—"

"*Korith.*"

Korith jumped. "Right. Sorry. His name's Kana Faresh. He's a Tethamari royal who was . . . well, simply put, he fled Tethamar about six years ago and sought political asylum here."

It did nothing for Shara's nerves to remember that the name Kana Faresh had been on the list of things Iliath was collecting information about—right between pirates and a crime syndicate. "Royal?"

"He's the reigning king's uncle. And—" Korith wobbled and caught himself, hissing. His face twisted in pain, and he eased his way to a chair and dragged his pant leg up to expose the worn brace beneath, like cloth armor fitted around his knee. "And that peace treaty with Tethamar? Part of the agreement is that Faresh will be returned to Tethamari custody." He slid his fingers amidst a series of laces and loosened them before prodding at his knee with a grimace. "Should've worn the new one."

Shara stared into the fire. A Tethamari royal—a traitor, from the sound of it—here in Barath and being used as a pawn in their negotiations. "Does he know about the terms?"

Korith jabbed a congratulatory finger at him. "I didn't think so. But with Iliath suddenly missing and Faresh visiting you today, I'd say there's a very good chance he does."

Shara's heart sank. "So he was either there to confront Iliath about the treaty or there because he kidnapped him and wanted to see me. And I—"

"You did brilliantly. No, honestly. Baiting Iliath is one of Faresh's favorite pastimes, and I've seen Iliath snap at him more than once. The man's enough to make anyone lose his composure. Your reaction probably wasn't what Iliath would have done, but I'd say it was wiser. Either Faresh is disappointed that he failed to get a reaction this time, or he knows he can't bully the fake Iliath." Pride shone through his strain. "I'm impressed."

Boiling with shame, Shara whipped around before Korith could see his reaction. Impressed. He'd done nothing, *nothing,* to deserve that. And he'd lied to Korith to make himself sound more capable.

He curved a finger around the metal grating and stared out the window. The binding cuff was off. He ought to go before he made any more mistakes or let anyone else down. He'd barely managed a conversation with Lady Pareth. He'd only stood up for Amesal on accident, and he'd done nothing at all for poor Eleth. Now he was hiding the truth from Korith.

And Iliath. This morning the prince had been little more than an inconveniently missing royal, the source of all Shara's discomfort. But now that Korith had mentioned the Tears, Iliath felt like *someone.* Someone Korith and others respected, who cared about his country and people. Someone else Shara could disappoint.

He glanced at Korith and back into the sky, and his stomach twisted. If he left now, disappointment was guaranteed.

He sighed heavily. Apparently guilt was every bit as effective as binding magic.

A familiar pop and another hiss announced Korith's victory over his loose knee. "Shara?"

He forced his face into something resembling neutrality, and after waiting a few breaths to make sure the expression stuck, he turned. "So what now?"

From the look in Korith's eyes, he wasn't fooled, but he didn't press. "We— No, not if you can't . . . not without . . . unless . . ." He nimbly retied the laces while the mumbling continued, until finally he asked, "What's the last thing you have to do today?"

"I'm reviewing the coronation vows with Walker Galthi in the chapel."

"Fine." He shoved his pant leg back into place and pushed himself cautiously to his feet, testing his weight. "Assuming none of the rest of my body mutinies, I'll meet you here after that."

His sudden energy made Shara wonder exactly how long he could stretch his meeting with the priest. "And then?"

"We pay Faresh a visit."

CHAPTER 18

ACCOMPLICE

It turned out that in addition to being a rogue Tethamari royal, Kana Faresh was also something of a pirate. And to prove it, or rub everyone's faces in it, he lived on a ship anchored in the bay. Apparently he claimed this arrangement had something to do with laws about land and sea, but after Shara got his first look at the ship—unabashedly named the *Accomplice*—he was fairly certain it was just ostentation.

A rush of wind swept beneath his seabird wings, and he began another slow circle of the ship, tracking the approach of Korith's glider and screeching his frustration into the night. Nothing he'd said had been able to change his cave-brother's mind, and when Shara had foolishly suggested they follow Gepar's lead and wait for Faresh to act, that had been the end of it. So now here they were, visiting a Tethamari exile with even more money than arrogance and far too many hands in the Barathi economy.

"Half the country's had dealings with him," as Korith had put it, "and half the country's loudly decrying anyone who's had dealings with him. And that's the same half, by the way."

In a flutter of white, Korith landed on the deck. Shara banked. Last chance to relieve himself directly over his cave-brother's head and have done with this ridiculous plan.

Instead he alighted on a railing at the far end of the ship. Drawing deep, soothing breaths, he fluffed his feathers and stretched the tension from his coiled muscles. Everything would be fine. Korith had been here before, and Shara would be spending most of this escapade as a cat. All he had to do was keep to the plan without coughing up any hairballs.

Korith had no need to announce his presence: the door to Faresh's private quarters opened, and warm, golden lantern light spilled through.

"Lord Aman. Good evening." The cool silk of Faresh's greeting seemed to strangle the warmth from the light.

But Korith strode forward with a smile, confident as ever, and the two disappeared into the room. Stillness settled over the ship, broken by a whisper of wind and muffled voices from below.

Shara fluffed again. One breath, then another.

At last he hopped to the deck and shifted, slowly compacting himself into the small form. Fortunately Korith hadn't suggested an even smaller animal during their planning—no need for Shara to dredge up memories of failing to become a mouse and a butterfly.

Shaking off an echo of tittering laughter, he slunk across the deck and down a staircase. The ship swallowed him like a neeka's maw.

The *Accomplice* was built for speed, smaller and sleeker than the *Myriad*, but now that Shara was a cat, both the ship and the sensation of being aboard seemed larger than ever. Footfalls vibrated the floorboards, ropes swayed overhead, and every gentle roll threatened to send him tumbling tail over paws. The clumsiest cat in the world.

"... another casket of Sailor's Blood," came a voice.

"Another?" Gruff laughter. "That's the third this week."

Teeth grinding, Shara pictured Faresh sitting in a finely decorated room, sipping the dark wine while Korith pretended to be a carefree noble in search of the best price on something or another, no questions asked. How Korith would tease secrets about a missing prince out of *that* conversation, Shara had no idea, but that was Korith's problem.

His was finding Iliath.

Gradually he developed balance and speed. He sniffed at every corner, at the crack of every door, even at a pile of soiled laundry. Dirt and salt, roasting fish, damp fabric, a sharp blend of herbs. The stench of cheap alcohol mingling with the sweetness of fine wine. And everywhere humans—but no trace of Iliath.

The kitchen, sleeping quarters, and mess area all turned up empty. He gave the four cannons and several barrels of firing powder a wide berth. Down he moved, scouring one level after the next, until the thrum of water pulsed in his ears and the air tightened around him, reeking faintly of sealant. Crate after crate loomed in the darkness, packed with whatever Faresh was shipping or storing.

Or hiding.

In the darkest corner, he shifted into his true form and let his heightened senses lace through the room. No voices, no movement, no prince scents. After steadying himself on two legs, he set off amidst the crates.

Row after row he searched, ducking into every empty space, craning his neck to look behind and around the boxes. When that brought up nothing, he began again. This time he brushed his hands over the rough wood and sniffed at cracks. He even tapped each crate lightly so someone trapped inside would hear.

But surely not even Faresh would seal a prisoner inside a box. And yet how likely was it that he'd locked Iliath in a cabin?

An image filled Shara's mind—Iliath tied to a stately chair while hulking thugs beat him and Kana Faresh watched, that sneering smile twisting his aristocratic face. Biting down a snarl, Shara withdrew his hand from crate GV1 before his claws did any more damage to its label.

Six casks of Sailor's Blood, probably.

But no prince. Nor any signs of hidden doors or other compartments where someone might hide a prince. Only pitch and pine, salt and stale air.

Which meant it was time for the final part of Korith's plan.

The foolish, dangerous part.

He shifted back into a cat and loped to the upper levels, still sniffing and hoping. Once he caught a soap scent that he associated with Gepar, and his thoughts darted to the palace. He'd not considered what Iliath's advisors would say if they found out about this. And after Malothi had threatened to drown Korith, too.

Warm lantern light and cool air greeted him as he rose. Several leaps brought him to a narrow ledge running just below the ceiling, and he padded slowly along, whiskers quivering.

Footsteps sounded on the stairs, and a dark shadow stretched down the hall. A woman stepped into the light.

Shara bit down a yowl.

She might have walked straight out of Korith's sketch—dark hair swept neatly into a low ponytail, sharp eyes and elegant cheekbones, full lips pressed into a frown. Faresh's lieutenant, Darai. The woman Korith had told Shara to impersonate for the next part of the plan.

She wasn't supposed to be here tonight.

Slipping along the ledge, he studied her movements until

she disappeared into her quarters. A mattress creaked, Darai groaned, and something heavy thudded on the floor. The hall fell silent.

Shara settled against the rough wood, mind spinning as the noiseless minutes stretched on. Korith had told him to follow through with the plan if he didn't find Iliath. But Korith hadn't counted on Darai's presence; surely borrowing her form and trying to trick Faresh and his crew into revealing the prince's location was now a pointless risk? Especially since Shara's senses had failed to detect Iliath aboard the ship.

Like they did such a good job detecting those neeka?

His whiskers drooped, and his certainty wavered in the lengthening silence. Iliath's absence didn't mean Faresh hadn't orchestrated his abduction. The prince might be a prisoner elsewhere under Faresh's orders. So long as Darai stayed in her room, the plan could still work. And if success meant Shara would be free, he had to try.

Besides, what good had ever come from Shara making his own plans?

His resolve hardened, and before he could change his mind, he crept back the way he'd come. After the springtide hunt, after this morning . . . He wasn't going to mud this up too.

Safely away from Darai's room, he climbed down and ducked into another cargo area. The shift took several painstaking minutes, for he had to create not only Darai's form but also her clothing and weapons. Not something he or any alvithi liked doing. Not something he should ever have told Korith about.

At last the only change to make was wiping the discomfort and unease from his expression. Ignoring the bubbling in his stomach, he breezed down the hall, chin high, shoulders back. Like being Iliath or Korith or Alanthas. All these people with their perfect confidence, their steady assurance. The act must have worked, for a young serving boy squeaked at the sight of him and ducked hurriedly away.

Night air and silver moonlight greeted him at the top of the stairs, and he tucked himself into yet another dark corner to wait. If he could catch Korith's attention as his cave-brother left Faresh's room, he could tell him about Darai.

Scant minutes passed before the door opened. Korith emerged in a billow of golden lantern light, as jovial as ever. "A thousand thanks," he called over his shoulder as he crossed the ship to unfurl his glider.

A thousand thanks. Their agreed words for *continue the plan,* an indication that Korith hadn't dug Iliath's location out of Faresh.

Pulse racing, Shara half stumbled forward. Did he call out to Korith and pretend to have business with him? Keep to patches of darkness and sneak his way across the deck?

The glider snapped into position, and wind sense sizzled in the air. Shara's pace quickened with his heartbeat.

"Lieutenant."

The hated voice dragged him to a halt, and his gaze darted to where Faresh stood silhouetted in the doorframe.

"Sir."

Swallowing his heart back into place, he made his way across the deck. He feigned smoothing his hair and chanced a look toward Korith, but the taste of magic had faded, and he already knew what he'd see. He was alone.

He paused just inside the room, unable to make himself go further, and the garment fitting unfolded before him again: Faresh lounging in a chair, one leg propped over the other, the stem of an elegant wine glass threaded through his fingers. Shara gulped down something halfway between a snarl and a whimper.

"I was under the impression you'd left for the evening," Faresh said.

Shara scowled, no acting required. "So was I."

"Hmm." He gave the glass a slow twirl, and his eyes narrowed in amusement. "Is our esteemed guest giving you difficulties already, Lieutenant?"

Shara's jaw dropped. *Our esteemed guest.* Did that mean—? Was it possible this might actually—?

"Lieutenant?"

Frantically he twisted his expression back into a scowl. "He's demanding to speak with you."

Faresh tilted his head toward the timepiece on the wall, and his mouth pitched into a smirk. "Held off for almost an hour. I'm impressed."

Uncertainty prickled down Shara's spine. Iliath would have been here a day by now. Unless they'd moved him to the ship only recently?

There was nothing for it but to press on. "I told him you had better things to do."

"Well, perhaps he needs a *reminder*." His voice cooled. "And while you're at it, you can tell that spoiled—"

Hurried footfalls thudded over the deck. Shara spun—and nearly impaled himself on the real Darai's sword.

Yelping, he jumped backward into the room, pursued by a wide-eyed Darai. Faresh leapt to his feet with a startled curse; the table wobbled and the decanter crashed to the floor.

For a heartbeat of silence, no one moved. Then Faresh ran for the door, and Darai lunged at Shara. He ducked and scrambled backward until he collided with the bureau running along the wall. Cabinet knobs and decorative trim ground into his back. His claws shot out, and before Darai could attack again, he propelled himself off the bureau and dove for her waist. Snarling, she stumbled back, then down.

They hit the floor in a grunting heap, and as she tried to roll and pin him down, Shara raked his claws over her arm and crawled free. His hands and knees met something wet—then daggers of broken glass.

He reeled back with a howl and struggled to his feet, vision blurring with tears. Bloody hands throbbing, he bolted for the door. He had to get off this ship.

He burst onto the deck, and something erupted like thunder in the darkness. Shara whirled, disoriented, and—

"Watch out!" came Korith's voice.

He spun just in time to dodge a blow from an oncoming crew member. The man careened past, unbalanced, and Shara ran for the railing, ears pounding with angry shouts and thundering footsteps and another crack of pistol-fire. The shot streaked past his shoulder, and wooden splinters exploded from the nearby mast.

The barest glance from Korith told him to flee, and before he had time to wonder whether Korith would be safe, another shot echoed behind him.

Gritting his teeth, he sprinted to the edge of the ship and launched himself into the sea.

He was Shara again, and fully healed, by the time a winded Korith landed in the shallows. Heaving a sigh of relief, Shara hurried to help him. "Are you all right?"

Korith sloshed toward the shore, limping slightly and wobbling on the uneven rocks. His half-folded glider trailed behind him like an anchor that might drag him back into the sea. "Are *you*? You were bleeding, I—"

"I'm fine." Guilt made the words sharper than he'd intended, and he stepped away from Korith once they reached the shore. After all the problems he'd caused tonight, he didn't need Korith's concern weighing his wings down too.

You don't have wings, you molting idiot. You're supposed to be human.

Like he was any better as a human.

They trudged up the shore in silence. The dull hiss of the rocks under their feet seemed to scream into the night, and Shara glanced inadvertently toward the *Accomplice*. It sat as still as ever, pale light spilling from its windows and portholes.

Claws gripped his chest—he'd left someone on that ship. Iliath or some other prisoner. And now that he'd revealed himself as alvithi, Faresh would be on guard. Their one chance, and Shara had ruined it.

The rocks gave way to a grassy rise cut by a path. Wrapping his arms around his torso, he fixed his eyes on the paving stones and forced every feather of concentration into counting them.

One . . . two . . .

The scent of rain spiced the air, fresh and clean after the confines of the ship, the heavy odors of sweat and wine—

Nineteen . . . twenty . . .

The wings of Korith's glider fluttered feebly with every stride, like a halfhearted flag, a mourning banner for the king, the father of Iliath, the—

Thirty-one . . . thirty-two . . .

At forty-eight, they reached a crossroads, and he peered down the road leading from the city. Somewhere along that empty stretch, he'd rescued Korith. The only thing he'd done right since arriving in Barath.

Fifty-six . . . fifty-seven . . .

"Well." Korith's tone was light, but his voice split the inky silence like another round of gunfire, and this time it went straight through Shara's heart. "That could have been worse." But after a pause, even Korith seemed unable to swallow his own optimism. "Then again, it could have been better."

"It was a disaster." Shara sighed and drew his coat more tightly around himself, willing the thick human garment to protect him from the night's events as well as the spring chill. "I'm sorry."

"*You're* sorry?" Korith kicked a stone across the path. "I'm the one who nearly ruined my cover."

Little though Shara wanted to discuss it, he asked hopefully, "*Nearly* ruined?"

"He doesn't have any proof we were together. I told him I'd returned for a scarf I left behind, and I said I shouted because I couldn't tell which Darai was the real one." Shara was about to be relieved when Korith added, "But given that he practically threw me off the ship, I'm not sure he believed me." He shrugged a bit too carelessly. "Then again, if all goes well, he won't be our problem after the treaty, so there's still hope."

But his free hand twirled his silver chain into knots, and Shara's shoulders sagged. Would this affect Korith's place among the Tears? His standing in Iliath's eyes?

"Does Faresh know? About the treaty?"

A sudden, intense energy burned in the darkness. "Oh, he absolutely knows. So we still have that, even if Iliath wasn't on board." He glanced at Shara.

"I . . ." He told Korith about his search and repeated his conversation with Faresh. "The way he said *already* and *almost an hour* . . . Maybe they'd only just moved Iliath onto the ship, but I couldn't sense anything." He hugged himself. "Not that my instincts are worth anything."

"Shara." Korith paused, leaving a deeper silence where their footsteps had been.

"Sorry."

Korith rolled his eyes, his exasperated smile illuminated by the faint moonlight. "Stop with the apologizing, furball. It's giving me a headache, and I have plenty of other aches to deal with after today. It wasn't your fault, and we're not giving up, and between Faresh knowing there's an alvithi in Barath and thinking I'm more than I seem on the one hand and you being dead on the other, I'd rather you not be dead. You couldn't have known Darai would be there. I told you she wouldn't be. You went through with the plan like we discussed, and . . . what?"

No explanation was necessary—his expression said it all.

Korith gaped, his blue eyes stark in the moonlight. "You knew?" As quickly as it had come, the encouragement vanished into disbelief. Betrayal.

Shara shrugged helplessly. "I saw her on my way up from the cargo hold."

"You knew and—"

"She went into her quarters, and I heard her bed creaking and then nothing, so I thought she was asleep. And you said that if I didn't find Iliath, I should—"

"I said—" He cut himself off with a frustrated growl and gestured wildly at Shara; the glider clattered to the path. "So now it's my fault you can't think for yourself?"

Shara stumbled back. "It was your plan! I didn't want to ruin it by—"

"By using common sense instead of blindly following orders like a . . . a *teveth*?"

"That's what I am!" Shara snarled through the sting, aware that Korith looked stricken, that he was opening his mouth to form an apology Shara didn't want to hear. "I told you, but you— This is what you do, isn't it? All the nudging and shoving and interfering. This is why you let me stay with you in the first place. You wanted someone you could drag into *this*."

"I wanted an *ally*! Someone I could trust to have my back!"

Shara's throat closed. Waves hissed against the shore, and a lone gull cried mournfully. His gaze wandered to the ship, the palace, his feet, but what did it matter where he looked?

Blinking hard, he rolled his shoulders back and made himself meet Korith's eyes. "I'm glad I'm not dead," he managed thickly. "Thank you for that. Even if it was a waste."

He shifted, hating the sluggish process more than ever before, and launched into the midst of a flock of seabirds, joining their chorus and pretending he couldn't hear Korith shouting after him.

CHAPTER 19

SAYING HELLO

The last thing Shara wanted to see the following morning was another ship, but no one cared what Shara wanted. Certainly not the Tethamari, who had been sighted rounding the Wolf's Nose just before dawn.

Some ancient Barathi custom stated that all visiting dignitaries must be greeted as they entered the bay. Whether this was politeness or precaution or some sort of nautical posturing, Shara wasn't sure. In the end, every explanation landed him in the same place: back on a ship.

In the palace courtyard, Malothi surveyed his garments, adjusted his slender circlet, and nodded approvingly. Gepar yawned and complained of the early hour and glanced repeatedly toward the bay. Tishel straightened her uniform and checked the ammunition in her pistol. No one acknowledged Korith's absence. Shara tried not to think about it.

They climbed into a carriage, and with Tishel and some of the royal guard flanking the vehicle on all sides, they made their way out of the courtyard. Shara gripped the edge of his seat as the carriage began its descent into the city. He'd been told that walking to the docks was unprincely, but apparently lurching back and forth, knocking his head against the wall, and repeatedly biting his tongue were acceptably royal?

At least the window curtains blocked the view of the bay—and a certain ship anchored at its center.

After a few minutes, though, he wanted to claw them to shreds. This stifling carriage, the morass of his tangled thoughts—too many prisons. Drawing aside the thick fabric, he trained his eyes on the city. Brown and grey buildings flickered past, window boxes overflowing with cheerful spring flowers, doorframes decorated with intricately twisted sea plants and vines. Here and there, vendors took advantage of the morning chill and grey skies to offer hot drinks and steaming breakfast foods.

A strange fondness swelled in Shara's chest, then a pang of longing. To disappear into those streets again, be nobody again . . .

They'll find him. He fought down a squirm. *They'll find him, and I'll be free.*

They rattled past a familiar cart loaded with sunspots, and Shara's hands tightened around his seat cushion. Was Korith still angry with him? Lying in bed after yesterday's strain? Or had Faresh taken more extreme measures, and Korith was—

He sucked in a sharp breath and swallowed the rest of that thought. Forcing his hands to release their hold, he lifted one to the window and returned a young girl's wave. Gepar tsked. Shara clenched his jaw and waved more enthusiastically.

No one spoke—they'd reviewed this meeting to death already—and at last the sloping hills levelled and the docks spread before them. Practically leaping from the carriage, Shara waded into a familiar rush of energy and the riot of seaside scents. How was it possible that only a month ago he'd stumbled off Admiral Thosena's ship and onto these docks, fretting about finding a job and passing as human?

Now he was passing as a prince. It might have been comical if it hadn't been so pathetic.

Sailors paused as Shara and his retinue passed, trading their shouted orders and jests for respectful greetings and well wishes. Others carried on unloading supplies, tying up ships, folding sails.

"Were all these ships here yesterday?" he asked.

"Commander Hannathi's squadron arrived early this morning from Tel Aveth." Tishel dipped her head at the nearest ship.

Shara linked his hands behind his back and tried to look nonchalant. "Ahead of the Tethamari's arrival."

Malothi made an approving sound. "Perceptive."

Color rose in his cheeks, though it had hardly been a difficult connection to make.

They rounded yet one more corner to see a familiar figure standing before a small, graceful ship.

"Admiral Thosena." Shara swallowed an over-friendly greeting and smiled politely; Thosena wouldn't—couldn't—recognize him as the stowaway she'd allowed on her ship. "I wasn't aware you would be joining us this morning."

Her mouth pitched into a grin. "Nor was I, Your Highness, but an inconveniently large stack of paperwork arrived on my desk this morning that simply begged to be ignored."

Shara chuckled before he had time to consider how Iliath would have reacted to such blatant dereliction on the part of one of the kingdom's highest-ranking officers. Then again, if Thosena preferred jokes to insincere obeisance or subtle challenges to his nonexistent authority, he certainly wouldn't complain.

The ship had already been prepared for launch, and as soon as Shara and his escorts were on board, Thosena began calling orders to the crew. An efficient bustle erupted around him, and he climbed to the upper deck to keep out of the way. The helmsman dipped his head, but his hands and expression remained steady despite Shara's presence. That was some relief, especially once they left the dock and the ship started trying to throw them off.

Well, Shara, anyway. Everyone else walked as steadily as before.

Tottering to the railing, he gripped the polished wood and stared up at the gliders speckling the sky and skimming over the water. The mountainous arms of the island cupped around the bay like hands, sheltering Farna and its collection of little islands.

He let out a breath. Just to the other end of the bay. No massive, rolling waves like last time. He could make it.

In a flutter of tawny wings, a squirrel-dragon wheeled over his head and alighted beside his hand. Chittering and thrashing its long tail, it scampered up his arm and settled on his shoulder as though they were old friends. Several sailors paused in their work, and the helmsman smiled as the squirrel-dragon fluttered its wings, batting Shara's cheek.

Shara chirruped softly. "Good morning, little—"

A hand raked through the air. Startled into flight, the squirrel-dragon gave an affronted squawk and swooped away.

"Get out of here," Tishel snapped, flapping her hand again before scowling at Shara. Like it was his fault the squirrel-dragon could sense the truth when an entire ship of humans could not.

"It wasn't going to hurt me."

"No, it was talking to you." She rolled her eyes. "Royalty don't talk to animals, Your Highness."

"They should," Shara muttered. He dragged a hand through his hair and caught his fingers on the circlet, nearly flinging it into the water. Tishel rolled her eyes again, and her longsuffering sigh annoyed Shara into his next words. "I'm sorry your *brother* was unable to join us today."

She stiffened. "Asking a member of one of the noble houses to attend you would have shown undue favor. Lord Aman knows that. I'm sure he's making *fine* use of his time elsewhere."

Shara clenched his teeth against the urge to tell her the truth. "I'm sure he is," he answered fervently—though Korith was probably off drowning Shara's latest disaster in a mug of mead. More to distract himself from that thought than because his argument had any weight, he grumbled, "So it's acceptable for Malothi and Gepar and Thosena and you to be here, but not Korith."

Tishel's artfully lined eyes widened, then narrowed. A strange look stole over her face as she stared out over the water, and one hand spasmed around the railing. A long, windy silence passed. "He didn't tell you."

"Didn't tell me?"

For the briefest moment, Shara thought her shoulders drooped, but then the ship crested another vessel's wake and threw them both off balance, and when he looked again, her features had fallen into their practiced neutrality. She met his eye and turned resolutely away, focusing too hard on picking dirt from beneath her fingernails.

"I'm not noble."

Shara stared. "What? But Korith—"

"Is my half-brother," she snapped. "His mother was noble. Mine wasn't."

That half-breed whore. Lady Pareth's words leapt through the rattling winds.

"... oh."

He could think of nothing else to say. She'd throw him off

the ship if he tried to comfort her, and she'd scoff if he pointed out that she was imperious enough to be two nobles at once. No point telling her he knew how she felt, either, not when he deserved his status and she had proved herself capable despite hers.

He traced a finger along the wood grain. "I'm . . . sorry."

Tishel shrugged, though it was jerky and halfhearted. She grabbed her flask and took a long sip.

A glider shot past in a flash of ivory, and Shara tried again. "He's proud of you, you know. Korith."

Her face twisted with derision. "Oh yes? And that's why every time I see him, he has some new idea about how I can be better?"

Shara winced. "I know he's overzealous, but—"

"I don't need his pride. Or his help. Stay away from the squirrel-dragons, all right?" She pivoted and strode away.

Shara stared after her. *I don't need his pride.* The warm scent of chocolate swirled with the bitter words and cold wind. *Or his help.*

Something burned in his chest, searing deeper with every heartbeat. He whipped around and gripped the railing, scowling into the sea so he wouldn't look back, wouldn't turn and shout out all the reasons she was lucky to have a brother who cared about her and wanted her to succeed and . . . and believed in her and—

"Your Highness?"

He jolted, a scream stopping just short of his teeth.

"Pardon me, Prince Iliath." Admiral Thosena's mouth twitched in a suppressed smile. "The Tethamari ship is in sight."

Sure enough, the narrowed entrance to the bay spread before them, guarded by a few more small islands and dozens of people who'd gathered on the rocky shores to watch. Beyond fluttered the sails of the Tethamari ship.

Shara drew a breath and released it slowly. "Thank you."

Even the Tethamari would make an acceptable distraction right now.

Another Barathi tradition required that the Barathi monarch board the visiting dignitary's ship and sail into Farna aboard it. Something about a show of trust.

Trust along with Tishel and a generous portion of guards.

The *Rosette* was painted with elegant green stripes, and each of its three sails bore a symbol that reminded Shara of a dragon scale split down the middle. Despite its delicate name, it towered over Iliath's graceful ship like a wolf over her cub, and Shara squirmed as he crossed to its massive deck. More people to see him, more ship to rock beneath his feet, more things for him to trip over. More sails casting dramatic shadows over this crucial event.

"Remember to look at her while you speak," Malothi whispered for the sixth time, "and if she asks you to repeat yourself, don't get flustered."

"And don't try to make conversation," Gepar warned.

Tishel said nothing, but her expression evoked Lethir so perfectly that Shara could hear his clan-brother's voice in the wind. *Stay out of the way and try not to burr anything up.*

A desperate laugh snagged in his throat. Burring things up was practically guaranteed, but staying out of the way was no longer an option.

Movement ceased, from the crowds on the nearby islands to the sailors and guards spread across the deck to the five finely dressed people preparing to greet him. Even the ship itself stilled, held in place by magic that pricked at the tip of Shara's tongue. Tension thrummed like the wind in the sails.

His eyes settled on Nashai, and after a deep bow, he swept his hands in the sign language word of welcome Malothi had taught him. The draping sleeves of his coat swished about him, a much more stately effect than the hanks of hair blowing into his mouth.

"Welcome to Farna, Your Highness." He accepted and kissed her outstretched hand, then raised his head and smiled through the urge to linger over her scent. "I am deeply honored by your prescent—er, presence."

Brilliant, Shara.

Fortunately, Nashai caught his meaning. She inclined her head, the braids in her dark hair draping over her shoulder. "And I by your invitation." She had a smooth, cultured voice, like swirly handwriting that was actually legible. "I only regret that the coronation of a new ruler must follow upon another's death; please accept my family's condolences over the loss of your father."

"Thank you, Princess."

Nashai stepped to the side, gracefully extracting her hand from Shara's hold and kindly ignoring that he'd forgotten to let go. "May I introduce my entourage: Lady Satha Oshari and Lord Dai Fethan, my father's advisors. Tir Sothal, the captain of my guard. And you'll remember Lady Teren Masar, my interpreter."

Shara gave them a collective bow. "Welcome to you all. I look forward to speaking with you at length about the relationship between our countries. I feel this peace between us is long overdue."

The two advisors nodded politely while Captain Sothal, who clearly thought Shara would be ignoring him, rolled his eyes. Exactly what Shara needed—another guard captain scoffing at him. At least he could count on Tishel not to be planning to assassinate him.

Probably.

He waited another few heartbeats before gesturing toward his own entourage and beginning a second set of introductions. Lady Masar, who looked about Shara's age and every bit as sea-strained as he felt, spelled out the names with her fingers. It took all his willpower not to watch—there was something mesmerizing, something alvithi, about speaking with movements.

"Thank you all," Nashai said when he'd finished, "for coming to welcome us."

Only one thing more. Shara nodded toward his ship, which had already turned and begun its journey back toward the harbor. "Please allow us to escort you to the city."

Activity burst to life around them, and the sting of magic faded. With an enthusiastic lurch, the *Rosette* ploughed toward Farna.

Princess Nashai climbed the stairs to stand by her helmsman, but as Shara made to follow, a hand settled briefly on his arm.

"Well done," Malothi said, smiling.

"Yes," Tishel agreed, and Shara was about to be shocked when she added, "You said *hello* properly. Surely nothing can go wrong now."

CHAPTER 20

BETTER MISTAKES

The best thing that could be said about the return journey was that Shara had not started a war by the end of it. On the other hand, he might have accidentally flirted. Repeatedly. If Nashai didn't consider him completely obnoxious, she no doubt thought him an awkward, rambling fool. Which was still better than her suspecting Iliath of plotting something sinister against Tethamar.

Probably.

He left Nashai with an invitation to a private dinner—the royal sort of private: Shara and his advisors, Nashai and hers—and escaped to Iliath's rooms. More than a dozen tasks stood between now and tonight, enough to distract him from endlessly picking apart everything he'd said and done during his first meeting with Nashai. Iliath's schedule might even have been invigorating if not for the accompanying terror of knowing that an entire kingdom now depended on whether he signed the wrong document, displeased the wrong noble, or wore the wrong color.

"Your Highness." Amesal rose from his desk beside the

outer doors and bowed. "Lord Aman came to see you."

Speaking of the wrong noble. "Did he say what he wanted?"

"He's still here, my lord. He said he'd wait."

Burrs.

Doing his best to smile, Shara thanked Amesal and pulled open the doors, a knot tightening in his chest with every step toward the inner rooms.

But the study sat empty. Swelling with relief, Shara seized a bowl of fruit off the table and chomped so loudly on an apple that the sound nearly obscured the clattering beyond the bedroom door.

Well, that explained the missing Korith.

And sure enough, when he opened the door, there sat Korith amid a snowy meadow of paper. Dark circles shadowed his eyes, and a sling hung around his neck, though his arm wasn't actually in it.

Shara lifted his chin and peered down at him, trying to look dignified while clutching a bowl and a half-eaten apple.

Korith's mouth twitched. "You're getting good at that."

"It's easier when you're on the floor. How did you get in here? I thought I locked this door."

"Oh, you did."

Molting obnoxious human. "And does your sling match your clothing on purpose, or was that a coincidence?"

A wolfish grin. "What do you think?"

Shara rolled his eyes, closed and locked the door behind him, and dropped into his own human form. He peeled off Iliath's heavy coat and kicked away the shoes, but no matter how slowly he moved, he couldn't think of anything to say to fill the silence.

Nor, for once, could Korith. They stared at one another over the disaster spreading across the floor while Shara picked his way through the papers and settled himself on the bed. Pulling his knees to his chest in unprincely fashion, he chomped again on the apple. Outside, the rain he'd smelled last night finally tapped curiously at the window panes like a gossip drawn to the tension within.

A crackling sound, a flash of white, and then a ball of paper bounced off Shara's forehead.

"Look," Korith said, already crumpling a second sheet, "what do you say we agree we were both idiots who made bad choices and said things we shouldn't have and . . . well, that part was mostly me—"

"And the bad choices were mostly me," Shara finished, puffing a breath of relief despite the shame of admitting it aloud. "So the game's even."

"We both made mistakes." He set aside the wadded paper and leaned back on one arm, chewing his lip as his gaze strayed across the floor. Slowly, a strained expression twisted over his face. "But I wouldn't say we're entirely even."

Shara tensed, and the hairs on the back of his neck rose. Extracting his claws from the half-eaten apple, he adjusted the fruit bowl in his lap to give himself a moment to prepare. "Oh?"

"What you said last night about me shoving people into things . . ."

Shara cringed. "That was—"

"True. Truer than you know."

True? Then this was an apology, not an accusation. "How so?"

Korith drew a deep breath and rubbed the back of his neck. "The other night, when I sent you here for the gifting? It's, ah, possible I exaggerated how crucial it was that you be there. In fact, it's possible you didn't have to go at all, and I sent you only because I hoped it'd increase your confidence."

A gust of wind threw a rainy curtain against the window, sending faint wisps of storm and sea air swirling into the room. Shara took a long breath and a loud bite of apple, oddly calm after his tense anticipation. Maybe he'd suspected it from the beginning. Maybe he'd simply spent so long last night railing at his cave-brother in his mind that he had no anger left, nor any desire to prolong his estrangement from his only friend.

Whatever the case, all he could muster was a mildly exasperated chirrup. "Of course."

Korith gave a huffy laugh. "That predictable, am I?"

"Well, between all the ridiculous books and the 'I have some ideas about your new life in Barath, Shara' and you redefining *teveth* to suit your delusions about me, it's not exactly a surprise. Like I said yesterday, you hate doing nothing—you always want to be the gryphon."

"I— Sorry, what?"

Shara flushed. Of course humans wouldn't be familiar with that legend. "It means—"

"No, no, don't tell me. I'll work it out. Besides, I'd much rather you call me a delusional gryphon than threaten me with the, uh . . ." He waved his hand above his head. "Angry yellow leaves of terror."

Shara snorted a laugh despite himself and shifted out his horns. "Next time, I'm shifting into you and giving you a beak and talons."

Amusement and aversion warred over Korith's face. "I would deserve it and will do everything I can to avoid that particular horror." His expression softened. "I really am sorry, though. When you looked at that portrait I drew of you and said I had a vivid imagination, I . . ." He paused, opened his mouth to continue, and instead swallowed down the words with a shake of his head. "But I never should have tricked or manipulated you. I'm a gossip and a spy and apparently a gryphon, but I don't want to be a liar."

Shara tossed the apple core gently at Korith and missed horribly. "A good actor is what you are. I should have known all that worry over your reputation and reliability was just scales on a mouse."

Korith gave a weak laugh. "Yes," he said softly, but his hand strayed to the chain around his neck before falling back to his lap. "Anyway, I'm sorry. And, well, what I did was wrong regardless of the outcome, but I'm also sorry for landing you in this situation."

Shara rolled his eyes. "You keep saying that, but I'm still the one who muddied it up when it mattered."

Always right when it mattered . . .

"As I said, we both made mistakes. Then and last night." He scanned the paper garden he'd planted around himself with a satisfied nod. "We'll make even better mistakes next time."

And there went the last of vulnerable, relatable Korith. Sighing, Shara shifted away his horns and slumped back against the wall. "You don't fail very often, do you?"

"Every day and twice in the last hour. But if you trip crossing a room but still make it to the other side, is it really a failure?"

"I don't know—why don't you walk across the room, and I'll stick my leg out, and we'll find out?"

Korith snickered and threw another wad of paper at him. "Look, last night was a disaster, but we're only halfway across the room. Let's not shift the failures out of proportion before we get to the other side."

"That's not how shapeshifting works."

"It is when I'm making a brilliant point."

Shara tossed the paper back. "I thought you were making

a brilliant mess. What're you doing, anyway?"

Excited energy rolled from the floor. "I found Iliath's files."

Shara jolted upright, annoyance vanishing. He half slid, half fell off the bed to settle on a patch of uncovered floor. Dozens of papers littered the rugs, covered in an equal variety of hands and colors of ink, some creased with old folds, many full of the holes and slits that would once have had ribbons woven through them to hold the letters shut.

He picked up the nearest sheet and scanned it. Unfamiliar names, unfamiliar places. Nothing new there. "And?"

Korith tucked his arm back into its sling. "And this"—a pile to his right, neater than the rest—"is what he's had us collecting lately. It's mostly about plants, medicines, things like that. I haven't been through it yet because, well, it's about plants. I've taken every drug in the country; I don't need to read about them too. This"—the papers strewn about them—"is everything he has on Faresh."

Shara's stomach flopped. "That's—"

"Not a lot, considering." At Shara's raised eyebrows, he chuckled. "I told you, half the country's dealt with him. No one wants to admit it, of course, especially when all the noble and merchant rivalries make Faresh's operations look efficient and legitimate in comparison."

"And what have you found?"

Korith lifted a sheet from his lap and flourished it with surprising energy for someone with shadows beneath his eyes and needles where his joints should have been. "I'm still reading it—and not remembering a lot at the moment, frankly—but this is what I was hoping for. It's a list of every warehouse he's ever used in Farna and the people who own them. There are several names on here that I *know* would be happy to hide an abducted prince."

"For the right price, I imagine," Shara grumbled.

"Exactly." He produced a pencil from somewhere and scribbled a note in the notebook tucked beside him. "I'm going to take this all home and get through as much as I can, and I'll contact the Tears and see if anything—"

A knock at the study door sent them both scrambling. Shara hurried to his feet and rebuilt Iliath's form around himself, then grabbed at the prince's clothing while Korith collected the papers into messy piles.

"Stay here," Shara whispered as he wrestled his feet into the shoes. Not that he particularly wanted to face his visitors alone. If it was Princess Nashai . . . or another of the Tethamari . . . or virtually anyone in Barath . . .

But Korith couldn't help him this time, and his friend ushered him into the study and closed the bedroom door behind him with a hushed "Good luck. Here if you need me."

Swallowing hard, he gave himself a last once-over and called, "Come in."

"Your Highness." Malothi's voice was as stiff as her bow. "Might we have a word?"

Shara feigned calm while his mind flew through everything he'd said and done so far today. "Of course."

She, Gepar, and Tishel filed into the study, and Tishel had no sooner thrown the bolt than Malothi rounded on Shara. Neither her expression nor her tone held their usual forgiveness. "It has come to our attention that one Korith Aman paid a visit to Kana Faresh last night."

Oh. That.

"Rumor also has it that their meeting was interrupted by an alvithi." She folded her arms and peered down her nose at him; Korith would have been proud, especially since she was a head shorter than Iliath. "Given Lord Aman's passionate insistence at our council yesterday that we find Iliath as soon as possible, I must assume the two of you went there in search of him. Do you care to deny it?"

Yes, but he didn't dare try, not when Malothi seemed likely to shift into a neeka at any moment. "No."

A storm of huffs and sighs blasted through the room, timed perfectly with a low rumble of thunder beyond the window. The rain fell harder, and the angry stares grew stonier. The timekeeper on the mantel ticked away, oblivious.

Finally, Malothi brushed a hand over her face, and some of the anger faded. When she spoke, she sounded more like a stern master lecturing an errant apprentice. "Perhaps we did not make your purpose clear. You are here to stand in Iliath's place. You are not here to find him, and you are certainly not here to assist Lord Aman in whatever delusions he has about doing so."

Shara bristled through the chastisement. True, he'd used the same word not minutes ago, but she needn't have said it like *that*. "He's not del—"

"He is an inconvenience at best and a liability at worst, particularly now that he fancies himself some sort of hero."

"An inconvenience?" The word stung, too close to another word, one Malothi didn't know. Hands fisting, he stood straighter and returned her down-the-nose stare. "He's nothing of the sort. Just because he's not a royal advisor or a guard captain . . . If it weren't for him—"

"If it weren't for him, we would not be having this conversation." Her voice hardened once more. "He is here only by unfortunate circumstance. It would be a shame if another were to remove him from the equation."

His jaw dropped. "You can't—"

"Don't presume to tell us what we can and cannot do."

"And don't presume you'll still have a fake prince after threatening my friend!"

Thunder rolled over the sudden silence. Shara's body trembled, but he held her gaze. No matter what Korith had done so far in his misguided quest, Shara wouldn't let anyone hurt him, or take him, or call him *inconvenient*.

After long moments of pursed lips and shared looks with Gepar, Malothi gave Shara a conciliatory nod. "I apologize for the rather extreme suggestion. This situation must not go any further off course than it already has. So long as Lord Aman respects that, he has nothing to fear. But I must insist that until Iliath is found, you answer to *us*, not Lord Aman. That goes for use of your shapeshifting as well, since it seems our efforts on that score were ill-advised." She glanced toward Shara's ankle, but to his relief, she didn't blame Korith this time. "Am I understood?"

His heart still hammered, but he nodded stiffly.

"Good. Now then, I don't suppose you'd care to explain why the two of you thought Faresh might be involved in this?"

He hesitated, choosing his words carefully; after his accidental outburst, he didn't want to draw attention to Korith. "Faresh knows about the terms of the peace treaty."

Malothi stilled. Gepar's nervous finger-tapping ceased, and Tishel's lips pressed into a thin line. The three glanced at one another, all narrowed eyes and taut muscles.

Malothi gestured at Tishel. "Captain, speak with Admiral Thosena immediately about having that ship watched. Do *not* let him out of the bay under any circumstances."

Tishel bowed crisply and turned, and Malothi gave Shara an appraising look and a rather begrudging nod. "Thank you for bringing this to our attention."

She and Gepar made to follow Tishel, and something snagged in Shara's memory. "Wait. There was someone else aboard the ship. Some other prisoner."

Halfway to opening the door, Gepar made a jerking motion that slammed it shut again. Malothi, however, looked unimpressed. "And?"

And? "And Faresh was threatening to ... well, I don't know, but he sounded angry."

"And you think this prisoner has some tie to Iliath?"

"No, not necessarily, but—"

"Then how is this relevant?" Tishel cut in.

He glanced from one indifferent face to the next. Did they not understand? "He's holding someone prisoner! You can't let him— You need to do something!"

Three sets of eyebrows lifted. Malothi's came down into a cool, piercing stare. "Are you giving us orders?"

"No, but—"

"Do you not remember what I just told you?"

"Yes, but—"

"Our sole concern with regard to Kana Faresh is ensuring he does not flee Farna before the peace treaty is signed. If we tried to rescue every fool who fell into debt and couldn't pay, we'd never do anything else. You will kindly refrain from telling us what we *need* to do about things you do not understand and focus instead on doing as you're told. Am I understood?"

His jaw worked, but his certainty wavered. Had he overreacted? Was he worried about some spoiled noble who couldn't pay back a loan? Had it been a prisoner at all? Faresh had said *our esteemed guest*, after all, but his tone had suggested—

"Well?"

"Yes." The word burst out before he had time to think, and the tightness in his chest twisted like a hot knife. Shoulders bunching, he stared down at his feet. ". . . yes, of course. I'm sorry."

Gepar sighed as though he'd truly feared Shara might continue to argue, or else play the no-fake-prince piece again.

Malothi cleared her throat. "Very well. Now fix your coat and come along; we have but a few minutes until your next audience."

"And stop slouching," Gepar grumbled as he twisted the doorknob. "You're a *prince*, after all."

Shara's fingers faltered on the buttons.

No, I look like a prince.

With a single glance toward the bedroom, he followed them out, almost relieved to have an excuse to avoid his haven. Korith would want to discuss the conversation, would praise him for arguing and tell him he should have kept going. Either that, or he'd confirm Malothi's remarks about debtors and make Shara feel worse about having spoken at all.

A soft cough dragged him into the present, where Tishel strode beside him. Malothi and Gepar were already halfway up the corridor.

"I'll look into it," she said curtly.

Shara almost tripped. "You mean . . . ? Tishel, thank—"

"Don't thank me. Lady Malothi is right, and I'm only doing this to keep you and Lord Aman from doing something stupid. Again. You're too valuable, and he . . ."

Her cheeks went faintly pink, and Shara pretended not to notice. "Well, thank you anyway."

After a few silent strides down the hall, she grabbed her flask and swirled its contents. "I almost liked him better when he was young and self-absorbed. Now he thinks he has to help everyone he meets. And it's rubbing off on you." Something bubbled in Shara's stomach, but before he could identify it, Tishel shot him a hard look. "And that's not a compliment."

CHAPTER 21

NASHAI'S REQUEST

The space beneath Iliath's bed was unnaturally clean. Shara knew this because he was hiding there, curled in a fluffy lynx-ball and dragging a claw along the stone to mark out another day as Prince Iliath. Someday, someone would move this bed and be utterly baffled to find a little tally on the floor.

A laugh rumbled in his chest until he wondered how many more marks he'd have to make. Whatever Gepar and Tishel had said, he was not a prince and he was not Korith, and the three little scratch marks failed to convey how long those days had dragged.

He'd spent hours at the rescheduled gifting ceremony, receiving expensive pledges from noble families puffed up with their own importance. Unfortunately, quite a few of those same nobles were staying at the palace, which grew rapidly fuller with every passing hour.

He'd met the families of the two guards killed during Iliath's abduction, a somber audience free of formality and full of tears.

He and Gepar had spoken to a squat, bespectacled man at the treasury about some duplicate receipts—surely His Highness hadn't really authorized payment to the metalsmith twice?

When not trapped in meetings, he distracted himself by reading Iliath's peace treaty notes and chapters of helpful-looking tomes from the prince's shelves or palace library. So far the primary effect had been to emphasize how little he knew, but at least the books didn't simper or giggle, ask him to sign official documents, or bow obsequiously.

Kkkk . . . Dawn had barely prodded its way through the clouds and misty rain, but he began clawing out day four. Perhaps marking it in advance would make it go faster.

It did—right up until nobles started swarming into the palace to welcome the Tethamari.

Dressed in yet more royal finery, Shara followed Tishel to the reception hall, bracing himself for an entire afternoon of saying and doing the wrong things.

So of course Tishel chose that moment to mention the rampant speculation that Iliath and Nashai intended to strengthen the peace treaty with a marriage alliance, so Shara had better not do anything to encourage those rumors.

"But don't dispel them, either," she added. "In case he truly is planning something."

"So, don't do anything. Or say anything. Or . . . anything."

She nodded and adjusted her spectacles. "Just be yourself."

He led Nashai around all afternoon. Malothi and Gepar took turns accompanying him and introducing Nashai to guests. Lady Masar spelled names and signed conversations, transforming with alvithi-like speed from a graceful and expressive interpreter to a self-conscious attendant every time her skills weren't needed. Shara focused on neither dispelling nor encouraging rumors. The jealous expressions on some faces and faintly scandalized looks on others suggested he was failing miserably on both counts.

They halted at last beside a window and accepted drinks

from a passing servant. Nashai balanced a glass of pale purple wine in her palm, and though she'd been perfectly polite and even friendly since her arrival, her posture so closely mirrored Faresh's that Shara had to look elsewhere.

He glanced instead at Lady Masar, who'd disappeared again behind her veil of thick, white hair. Nevertheless, she caught him looking, and they both turned hurriedly away. The prince watching Nashai's interpreter would certainly quell the rumors—and start new ones.

"Tell me, Your Highness." Nashai's gaze drifted along the wall to their right, where Malothi conversed with an unfamiliar noble. "Are your advisors always so careful of you, or only since my arrival?"

She smiled teasingly behind her glass as hot blood rushed across Shara's face.

Sipping at whatever golden liquid was in his glass, he tried to look as though he found her question amusing. "Only since your arrival. Perhaps they're afraid of the effect you'll have on me." Was that flirting? Had he accidentally flirted again? "Too much Tethamari influence, you know."

. . . yes, suggesting that he didn't want too much involvement with a would-be ally was *much* better than flirting.

She eyed him with skepticism and—was that disappointment? Neither expression was new. She'd worn them both plenty of times throughout their dinner the other night and again during their awkward walk in the gardens yesterday.

At least she likes squirrel-dragons. Tishel could insist that royalty didn't talk to animals, but Nashai and Lady Masar had been delighted by the visit of a second squirrel-dragon and several birds.

But there were no animals here, only a pair of women who glided over and showered Nashai with a flurry of compliments.

Shara politely excused himself and fled.

He sought Korith as he moved through the crowd. His cave-brother slouched in a far corner, deftly juggling sips of wine and a cheerful conversation with an unfamiliar couple.

Was Korith investigating as a Tear or drinking with friends? The man and woman smiled far too genuinely to be kidnappers, but Shara could hope for underlying menace anyway.

"...one ship, Admiral Thosena," came a voice from his other side. "That's all I'm asking."

"You're asking to exploit the navy's resources for your own benefit."

He glanced toward Thosena's conversation, and his steps faltered briefly. He didn't know enough about navy resources to even pretend to aid her, but he tried for an imperious frown when her interlocutor looked his way.

Rather than wait to see if it had any effect, he hurried from the hall and up the corridor. Right, left, left again, enough twists to prevent Tishel or anyone else from following. When he'd rounded yet another corner and found himself alongside the gardens, he leaned wearily against a wall and drew a long, steadying breath. Though the clouds gave the day a dreary look, the temperature had risen, and the windows overlooking the gardens hung open. Gradually the pounding in his head diminished, replaced with a gentle swirl of cedar and the comforting aromas of spring.

On the breeze came voices, quiet but insistent, both familiar. Shara inched sideways and peered around an arched doorway.

"...not be here." Gepar stood beneath the budding branches of a thick maple, rolling his hands.

Kana Faresh leaned against the tree trunk. "I was under the impression the gardens were open to anyone. I do grow weary on occasion of life aboard my ship, you know. There's only so many times I can admire the many possessions in my cargo hold, after all."

"So plant a tree on the deck," Gepar snapped.

Faresh stroked his chin. "I'll consider that. Now if you'll excuse me, Lord Gepar, I was—"

"Leaving." Gepar jerked his head toward the bay. "Before Her Highness or any of the rest of them see you. They might think you're eager to return home after all, Faresh, and—"

Footsteps sounded behind Shara, and he spun, ready for a lecture from Tishel or Malothi. Instead, Princess Nashai stalked toward him, Lady Masar in her wake.

"What," Nashai seethed, "is *he* doing here?"

"Uh, well—"

"Am I to understand, Iliath, that my uncle not only lives in your country, he also frequents your palace?"

He took a breath and tried for a calm expression; Nashai couldn't hear his desperation, but she could see it. "I can't deny he's here from time to time, but I promise he's not a frequent guest. And he certainly isn't here by my invitation." He gestured into the gardens. "Lord Gepar is telling him he's not welcome."

Nashai scoffed and glanced around Shara, and he took an instinctive step to block her path. "I promise you, Your Highness," he went on, "I'll make sure you don't see him again while you're here."

"No."

No? "Your Highness?"

"No," she repeated. "I would prefer he be where I can watch him." Her ferocity melted into a wheedling smile, and her tone sweetened. "Would you be so kind, Your Highness, as to extend him an invitation to stay in the palace for the duration of my visit?"

Just thinking about that made Shara want to claw a hole in something—preferably Faresh himself. Not that he could argue with Nashai's line of thinking. Within the palace, Faresh would be much easier to watch and far less able to flee if he sensed things weren't going his way. And if he *was* involved in Iliath's abduction, perhaps Shara or Korith could learn something.

None of which made the idea of his presence any more palatable.

Reluctantly, Shara nodded. "If that's what you want, Your Highness, then I'll see he's invited. In fact"—might as well get it over with—"I'll ask him right now."

He turned toward the gardens and nearly collided with Gepar, who bounded through the archway, face blotched red.

"Your Highness." His eyes widened. "Princess Nashai."

"Has he gone?" Shara asked with poorly concealed hope.

Gepar brushed at his garments. "He has. I sincerely apologize, Princess, that you had to see him here."

Rather than answer, Nashai looked expectantly at Shara.

He cleared his throat, and as Lady Masar moved so Nashai could better see her, he scrambled for a way to make the request sound palatable. "Lord Gepar, Her Highness has asked that we invite Lord Faresh to stay in the palace while she's here. I was—"

"What?" Gepar frowned over his shoulder, then dipped his head at Nashai with a sort of fatherly concern. "Your Highness, surely you do not wish to sully your visit with his presence."

"I assure you I do, my lord. His Highness agreed to honor my request." She crooked an eyebrow at Shara.

He fixed his gaze on a tree in the gardens, the only friendly object he could find. "Yes, I did," he told it.

Nashai's eyebrow lifted higher. Lips pursing, she turned back to Gepar. "Perhaps you would convey your prince's request to my uncle."

Shara could guess at only a few of Lady Masar's signs, but

Gepar's rolling hands left no room for misinterpretation. "Your Highness, I'm perfectly aware of your concerns regarding Kana Faresh, but given the presence of so many guests here for the coronation, I'm not certain this would be wise."

"If you're aware of my concerns, you should understand why I wish to keep him close." She folded her arms. "I discussed this matter with my entourage just this morning, in fact, and my desire is confirmed by seeing how free he feels to present himself wherever he wishes."

Gepar glanced at Shara, who bit his lip and said nothing. He was supposed to do what his advisors told him, but he'd already given Nashai his word. And surely Iliath wouldn't let Gepar tell him what to do?

How did Alanthas make settling disputes look so easy?

At the thought of his brother, an idea sparked in his mind. Maybe there was a third way. Listing his head the way Alanthas always did, he let his gaze stray along the wall and pretended to deliberate. "Lord Gepar's concern is valid," he began.

Lady Masar's fingers seemed to cringe. Shara faltered, and before he could regain his nerve, Nashai asked, "Are you going back on your word?"

Shara winced. "No, but . . ."

"Then what, precisely?"

He sought for arguments, but all he managed was a croak, and his plan vanished like a sun that had changed its mind midrise.

No one spoke. Nashai frowned, Gepar scowled, Shara fidgeted. The trees rattled in the wind, and a pair of squirreldragons chittered to one another, unburdened by cares like politics and treaties. Slender streaks of sunlight prodded their way through the clouds to watch, and Lady Masar's hands settled with awkward finality at her sides.

After what felt like an hour, Gepar gave the princess a stiff bow. "As you wish, Your Highness. I will see he is invited."

"And ensure he accepts," she added.

The furrows in Gepar's forehead grew deeper than ever, but he echoed, "And ensure he accepts. Pardon me, please."

He shot Shara a fierce scowl before striding back into the trees.

Shara was about to heave a sigh of relief when Nashai pinned her disdainful frown on him. "Thank you *so much,* Your Highness, for your support. Perhaps it is Lord Gepar's signature I should seek upon our treaty, if it happens at all."

Before he could think of a response, she spun and strode away. Lady Masar gave Shara a bow that couldn't make up for the pity in her eyes, then hurried after Nashai.

Groaning, he slumped against the wall and closed his eyes. His traitorous mind painted the scene upon the darkness, and the conversation hissed in the wind. Everything he'd said, hadn't said, should have said.

Molting coward.

He raked a hand through his hair, and this time Iliath's circlet went flying. It clattered across the floor and hit the wall in a mocking song of metal on stone. Sunlight glinted off its surface and danced obliviously over the ground.

He almost left it there. It certainly didn't belong on his head.

CHAPTER 22

MALIR AT MIDNIGHT

The only improvement to Shara's day was learning that Korith's day had also gone poorly. Not that this helped either of them, but it made Korith less obnoxiously positive than usual.

"I really thought . . ." Korith muttered for the fourth time. He crumpled the paper on which he'd been scribbling and tossed it into the fire, where it burst into inappropriately cheerful flames.

"I'm sorry," Shara mumbled, also for the fourth time.

"Stop with the sorry." Another wad of paper arced across the room and landed on the bed beside Shara. Korith huffed. "That was supposed to hit you."

"Sorry."

They shared a loud, hissing sigh. Shara scooped up a handful of dried fruit from the large bowl in his lap—he'd already eaten half its contents and had no intention of stopping. Let the servants think what they would about Iliath's increased appetite.

Korith slouched in his chair. "Nothing from Sira, nothing

from the Tears on Faresh's warehouses, nothing from anyone at the reception. Nothing from Iliath's notes except plants."

"Gepar and Malothi hate me. Nashai thinks I'm a joke. Faresh..." Faresh had positively gloated about being asked to stay at the palace. "If Nashai didn't want him back, I think I'd eat him."

"Ha!" The chair clacked under Korith's triumphant jolt. "You *do* eat humans."

"He'd give me stomach cramps, but..." But right now, stomach cramps seemed a small price to pay for a Faresh-free life.

Snickering, Korith slapped the table and climbed to his feet. Shara squeezed his eyes shut and groaned. There was no mistaking his cave-brother's familiar regroup-and-start-over pose.

"All right," Korith said, and sure enough, new vigor spiced his voice and stride. Something cool and smooth bumped Shara's forehead, and he swatted the cane away and bent protectively over the fruit. Korith prodded him again. "Get up. It's the night before your coronation—"

"Don't remind me."

"—and you're taking me flying."

Shara's eyes betrayed him and opened. "What?"

"You need a distraction, I want a dragon ride, and it's the first properly warm day we've had this spring. So come on." He jabbed Shara again and gestured toward the window. "Let's go."

Flying was far more difficult with a laughing, easily distracted human on your back.

Shara soared southwest, his wings stretched wide to catch the gusty night winds. How he'd missed this, one of his favorite pastimes. Nothing but the stars and sea, the clouds and mountains and silence, and Shara wending his way through them all.

And this time, Korith. Korith and considerably less silence.

They flew and flew. Korith shouted information about the places they passed, occasionally lurching left or right to point out something distinctive. The islands grew rockier, the coastal cities less frequent.

Shara alighted at last atop one of the craggy peaks, where a flat slab of rock afforded a safe place to land and a moonlit view of the surrounding islands and shimmering sea. A quick sniff for signs of threat turned up nothing but birds and mice, so he folded his wings.

Korith slid off, still laughing breathlessly, and gazed out over the islands as Shara shifted. "That was amazing. How is it you don't fly everywhere? If I could spend all day on my glider, I'd never do anything else."

Shara chuckled. "Mostly we do fly everywhere. You can't reach the caves if you can't fly."

And sometimes you *could* fly, given time, but your childhood friends came to your family's cave anyway so they didn't have to wait for you.

His toes curled. He'd not thought of that in years.

Pebbles crunched as Korith settled on the ground and started fishing things from a bag: a malir board, Shara's dried fruit, and a massive basket of sunspot sticks.

Shara watched, still half-enveloped in memory. Korith wouldn't have come to his cave. Not unless it was to encourage him.

Something about that thought made him slip into his true form, and he sat across from his cave-brother and propped his scaled elbows on his knees, the leaves on his horns rustling in the wind. The world sharpened around him — the tang of the air, the sweet aroma of the pastries, the steady firmness of the rocks, the glimmer of the moon and millions of stars soaring overhead. He reached for a piece of fruit, then moved the magician into position on the board.

They played three games in silence — there was too much to say, too much to think on, and it would all be waiting when they returned to Farna. For now, the world held only Shara and Korith and the board between them.

Korith lost so badly each time that Shara began to wonder whether he could see the board properly. As the fourth game began, it became too painful to watch any longer.

"Korith, no." He caught his friend's wrist over the far corner where Korith had been about to place the lady. "You really don't want to put that there."

"I don't?"

"You don't."

Korith glanced several times between the game and Shara, weighing the stone figure in his palm. "You realize we're opponents, right?"

"Trust me, not even your worst enemy would let you make that move. Put it somewhere else. *Anywhere* else." He shook his head. "How are you so bad at this?"

Unabashed, Korith settled the lady on a different square. Still not a particularly smart play, but better. "Thania tried to teach me strategy once, but it seems malir is fated to join the list of things at which I am somewhat less than amazing."

"Like humility?" Shara asked dryly, moving his butterfly opposite Korith's king.

Korith plucked a sunspot-laden stick from the basket and brandished it at him. "Humility doesn't mean dismissing your strengths any more than it means focusing on your weaknesses.

It's simply living in the truth. And the truth is that I—"

"Lost." The red-stone lady made a satisfying *thunk* as Shara pushed it off the board. "Again."

Korith blinked. "Already?"

"Already." He smiled slyly. "Maybe Lady Bethen would give you another lesson if you stopped rebuffing her every time she came by. Shall I shift into her so you can practice?"

A fit of coughing revealed that complete sentences weren't the only things Korith couldn't manage when faced with Lady Bethen. "That—" *Cough.* "That was mean."

Snickering, Shara began resetting the board. "I'm just saying, the *truth* is that she's going to give up on you eventually."

"Oh, *now* who's the gryphon?"

"Still you." He sat up straighter and shifted his horns away as if in preparation. "Come on, it'll be perfect. I'll look like her but still be me, so she'll have all sorts of problems and need a lot of fixing, and that'll finally give you a reason to talk to her."

"Oi, now that's—" Korith stalled and sat back, his feigned offense withering into a defensive frown. The sunspot stick wobbled in his grip, and his troubled gaze slid to the board, the rocks, some scraggly grass, his left knee. With each movement of his eyes, the furrow in his brow deepened.

Shara wilted. He couldn't even make a joke without mudding it up. "I'm sorry, that was unfair."

Korith flapped his hand. "No, it's fine," he said in a light, distracted voice. "It's . . . No, you were only . . ." His lips kept moving, but the words stopped coming. Before Shara could try another apology, though, Korith shook himself and sat up in a flourish of exaggerated energy. "Unfair indeed," he agreed, poking the sunspots at Shara again. "Accusing me and then sinking yourself in the process, knowing I'll be so distracted with you that I'll forget to defend myself."

Shara rolled his eyes, but he had no more desire than

Korith to hover over the uncomfortable subject, so instead he prodded the magician forward and gestured at the board. "That's basically what I've been doing to you all along."

Korith eyed the board. Perhaps he was reliving their past games, for every few seconds, his eyebrows pressed lower and his head tilted further to one side. ". . . huh. Good strategy, that." He grinned triumphantly. "But now you've told me."

"I have others."

"Oh." Chuckling, he made another spectacularly bad play. "Who taught you, anyway? Or did you teach yourself?"

"My father. Malir was the one thing we always did together." He picked up the bull absently, and his eyes unfocused. "You'd have liked him. He was always telling me *teveth* was only a word. Just meant I was still growing."

That had been easy for him to say, with all his skill and self-assurance and toresh. Just like Korith. Easy to tell someone it was all right they couldn't fly when you were the one hovering among the stars.

He huffed softly; so much for leaving his problems in Farna for the night.

"How old were you?" Korith asked gently. "When he died."

"Sixteen. I . . ." He gazed over the mountains, remembering the funeral flight, lighting the Eagle's path home for Ilanthas ko Han. Emotion welled in his throat, and a dragon's weight settled over his chest. "I think I was relieved." His hand spasmed around the bull. He'd never admitted that to anyone. Not even to himself. "I loved him and missed him, but . . . but when he was gone, there was one less person to disappoint. One less person I could never hope to be."

Even as he welled with relief at speaking it all aloud, the dragon weight grew heavier. Had he felt similarly about others who'd died? His mother? His hunting teacher, Ibari? What if he felt the same way when Alanthas died, or Korith?

He half slammed the bull into place, face burning. As if them being gone would make him happier. As if Rathen being less fierce, or Alanthas being less of a leader, or Korith being less confident, less optimistic, less *anything* would make the world better or transform Shara into someone more worthy.

It wasn't *their* fault he couldn't match them.

He raked a hand over his eyes. "It's just as well I gave up trying. Lethir always said all the toresh in my family got used up before I was born."

Korith's prince fell over with a clatter, and he righted it stiffly. "I don't know what toresh is or who Lethir is, but I hope you decked him for that."

Shara couldn't suppress a chuckle, both at the absurdity of the suggestion and at the idea of Korith decking Lethir. "No. He'd have trounced me. And he was right; anyone in the clan would tell you the same."

"Then I hope you decked them all," Korith muttered.

"You don't even know what toresh is," Shara reminded him, advancing the bull toward Korith's unicorn. "Maybe I'm just *living in the truth* of not having any."

"Maybe." Korith gave him a faint smile of acknowledgement. "But it sounds like something alvithi are supposed to have. Something you want."

They stared each other down until Shara gave a jerky shrug. He waited for Korith to invent some ridiculous definition of *toresh*, too, but his cave-brother merely leaned back on his hands and peered at the stars. Shara mirrored him, and for several minutes they forgot the game and stared at the blanket of crystals. Shara's back itched, immaterial wings longing to fly again.

"Is that why you're always apologizing for yourself?"

Shara jolted, dragging his gaze from the heavens. "I don't do that."

"You absolutely do. Even that night you rescued me. I thanked you, and you said something ridiculous like it wasn't that important and you almost fell in after me. Like you hadn't saved my life well enough or something." He jabbed the prince toward Shara. "I'm glad you decided to do it at all, you being so teveth and un-toresh and all."

Shara's insides turned to stone. "That's . . . Of course I . . ." The butterfly's hard edges bit into his palm as he gripped it, but all thoughts of strategy had fled, and his limbs trembled suddenly, as if he were back on that beach and facing Korith's spiralling fall all over again. "Do you really think I'd have let you drown?"

"Hills, of course not. But honestly, when was the last time you accepted a compliment without trying to explain why you don't deserve it? Or focused on what went right instead of what went wrong? When you catch an animal, do you think, 'Oh no, I can't eat its bones, so this hunt was a failure'?"

"Well, actually, sometimes we do eat—"

"Leave my analogy alone. And that's disgusting, by the way." He stuck his tongue out and gagged.

Shara snorted. "You're the one who said mistakes are how we learn. Well, bones are—"

Gagging again, Korith tossed the unicorn at him. He ducked on instinct, and the game piece sailed past, bounced several times over the rock—and tumbled over the edge.

Shara had twisted halfway around to stare after it when he remembered they'd borrowed Iliath's malir board.

He spun back and met a wide-eyed Korith. His cave-brother opened his mouth. Closed it. Glanced toward the sea, then back at Shara. From somewhere far below rose the faintest echo of stone clattering against stone.

"If we save his life," Shara ventured, "he'll forgive us, right?"

"Sure," Korith croaked. "Uh, sure. Yes. That's a fair . . . I can replace that."

"Right. Good."

In silent unison, they backed away from the board.

Shara crawled to the edge of their rock and settled onto his stomach. A slender crack in the stone ran between his hands, and he slid a claw through the narrow gap and picked at it absently. Korith eased down beside him, grabbed a pebble, and tossed it over the side. Then another, and another. Night wrapped itself around them.

They sprawled there for long minutes, and in the silence, Shara tried to focus on anything but what Korith had said. A rock. A wisp of cloud. The moon. Korith shivering. Something dark churning in the water far below.

He squinted intently. A pod of whales?

He puffed out a breath, blowing a stray curl of hair from his face. How easy it would be to leap from the ledge, soar to the water, and disappear with them. No Farna, no coronation . . .

The wind whispered through the sky, brushing like a familiar wingtip, and Korith withdrew his hands into his sleeves and hunched his shoulders. He scooped up yet another pebble and passed it slowly between his sleeve-covered hands, as if this stone were somehow special.

"I don't want to fix you, furball," he said softly. "You or anyone else."

Shara paused in his clawing but didn't dare look at him. "No?"

"No. I knew you thought I was interfering, but I never meant to suggest . . ." The pebble tumbled from his hands. "I just don't want you to hate yourself because all you ever see is what you're not. You're alvithi; you've got keener senses than that."

"I don't—" He frowned at his dirty fingers and tried to rustle wings that weren't there. "I don't hate myself."

He was simply being realistic. But he couldn't say that. Korith would argue—and if Shara tried to argue back, he might ramble himself into discovering that his friend was right.

Shaking his head, he shifted a pair of wings from his back, focusing intently on the transformation and ignoring the guilty kick in his gut that told him he was avoiding the problem. But he had enough problems already, and only one he could fix. He stretched the wings wide and tucked one snugly around Korith. His cave-brother shot him a curious frown.

"You're shivering. It's not—" He bit off the rest; apologizing that wings weren't as good as a blanket would prove Korith's point.

Something twisted uncomfortably in his chest. Did he really do that so often?

Korith's muscles relaxed. "Thanks, furball. Or . . ." He traced a cautious finger over Shara's knobby wing joint, and a grin stole over his face. "Birchball."

"You're hilari—" He tensed, something hovering on the edge of his senses.

Korith went rigid. "What is it?" he whispered.

Tilting his head back, Shara sniffed. The wind smelled the same. The earth rested still and solid beneath him. Moonlight glimmered over the water like a silver road.

"Is it bears?" Korith whispered, burrowing more completely beneath Shara's wing. "Would now be a bad time to admit that I'm terrified of bears?"

"*Bears?*" He choked on a laugh. "Korith, it's . . . ships."

Not a pod of whales after all. He pointed, though Korith wouldn't be able to see the clump of dark little wedges now nestled in a cove like a squirrel's hoard of pinecones.

Korith emerged from the bear-proof shield of Shara's wing. "Out here? How many?"

The distance and darkness strained even Shara's eyes. "I don't know. Half a dozen? More than one or two, anyway."

Korith's brow furrowed. "We're somewhere in the Talons. There's nothing around here to merit that many merchant ships making deliveries—or pirates trying to capture them."

"Navy?"

"Could be." He didn't sound convinced, though. "Come on."

They moved together, Korith to replace the malir board into his bag, Shara to shift. Over the sound of clattering game pieces, his body dissolved slowly into the familiar itching tingle and a swirl of far-off whispers, all his possible forms begging for release at once. When he was a dragon again, Korith climbed onto his back, and Shara leapt silently from the ledge.

Eyes trained on the little pod of ships, he swooped down, banking hard to change their angle—anyone looking up would be sure to see their silhouette against the moon. Korith's legs pinched his wing joints, and his hands tightened in Shara's leafy mane, but he kept silent.

They maneuvered alongside the mountain rising up around the ships in a protective cove. A ledge, an outcropping, a cave . . . somewhere to land. After a minute of silent flight, he found a suitable place, hidden from the moonlight and wreathed in the added shadow of scraggly trees.

Korith slid from Shara's back and crouched, his eyes narrowed as he studied the ships. Furled sails, empty decks—and bands of color painted along the large, sleek body of each vessel. The color was impossible to determine in the dark, but the design was unmistakable.

Not pirates.

"Tethamari," Korith confirmed. "Tethamari navy."

Shara had planned to remain a dragon, but a jolt of nausea practically kicked him back into his true form. "Are you sure?"

"Yes." He raked his hands through his hair, eyes remaining fixed on the ships as though he expected them to vanish. "Eight ships."

"A whole squadron." Despite the situation, satisfaction fluttered through him at the recall of this information.

"Yes." Korith elbowed him, but concern still creased his features. "What in the hills?"

Questions burned at the back of Shara's throat. Was this an act of war? A precaution? Normal but worrying? Some form of tribute honoring Iliath's coronation? Were they in disputed territory? Could these be pirates masquerading as Tethamari?

"Come on," Korith said, pushing to his feet. "We need to get back."

"Back?"

One look revealed that Korith knew what he was thinking. Folding his arms, his cave-brother bit his lip and let out a heavy sigh through his nose, then shook his head. "We don't have time to search eight ships. Especially after last time."

Shara cringed. They couldn't afford another Faresh incident.

"If he is on one of those ships . . . As much as I hate to admit it, Gepar is right: if they kidnapped him, that likely means they want him alive. We'll go back and work out what to do. Tell Admiral Thosena what we saw. Well, we'll tell her something, anyway."

Shara nodded and closed his eyes to shift, but they slit open for a last look. Even if the ships weren't hiding Iliath, he could think of too many other alarming reasons they might be there.

Chapter 23

The Coronation

The weather didn't care that a new Barathi king was being crowned.

Hazy mist clung to the city the next morning, threatening to wrap the coronation cheer in blankets of rain. Gusts of wind rattled the palace windows, and overhead, streaks of cloud gave way to tiny glimpses of blue sky that vanished the moment they were noticed. It was restless, uncertain weather, as if Shara's emotions had spilled into the world.

The weather did nothing to halt the arrival of dozens of ships, everything from tiny rowboats to massive merchant vessels, though fortunately no Tethamari squadrons. Nor did it dampen the celebrations already underway throughout the city. Early in the morning, Shara had ventured onto a balcony and nearly panicked into his true form at the shouts and cheers and applause rippling up to meet him.

At least he'd remembered to wave briefly before fleeing.

Now he paced the length of the chapel opposite the throne room. If he moved quickly enough, loudly enough, he might be able to drown out the incessant murmur of the hundreds of people on the other side of the door, the patter of footsteps, the swish of fabrics, the occasional bursts of laughter.

The sounds faded as he reached the front of the chapel, and he sank again into one of the pews and leaned forward until his forehead rested against the seat in front of him. He was supposed to be praying, but he was doing a terrible job of it. More pleas than prayers, his thoughts as scattered and gloomy as the clouds. Once he'd even begun to apologize, but apologizing for his inadequacy seemed the height of ingratitude and disrespect, as though he were accusing his creator of having made a mistake.

Of course, that left the far more terrifying possibility that the Eagle *hadn't* made a mistake.

He shoved to his feet and resumed pacing, breezing past beautiful wood-panelled walls, paintings of holy men and women, scenes depicting the Guide's time on the earth. It was like watching a rushed play, a story that un-told itself every time he paced the other direction.

The door cracked open, interrupting his sixth prayer that Iliath might miraculously reappear, and Tishel stepped inside. She took one look at him, frozen halfway up the center aisle, and rolled her eyes. "You do realize this is the easy part, don't you?"

He swallowed, tried to answer, and gave up. Three heartbeats ago, he'd thought the same. He'd told himself as much throughout the morning, and Korith had reminded him of the same fact last night.

But now the moment stared him down like a neeka. "Is it . . . ?"

"A few minutes."

Nodding, he lowered himself onto the edge of a pew and brushed at his resplendent coronation garments. By the door, Tishel mirrored his motions, smoothing her dress uniform and plucking a dog hair from her pant leg. Did she ever wear anything but military clothing? Was she allowed to? Did she wish she could?

What would Lady Tishel have worn to the coronation?

A knock rattled the door, and he leapt to his feet as a royal guard spoke quietly to Tishel. Her gaze moved past Shara to the front of the chapel, and her lips moved silently before she nodded to him. "It's time."

His mouth went dry, and like Tishel, he turned to the altar. At its side stood a much larger version of the little statue in Korith's shrine: an old, bearded man with a travelling cloak and walking stick, a magnificent eagle perched on his shoulder with its wings outstretched.

Eagle, shelter me. Guide, lead me. They were ultimately the same, but he'd take as many types of help as he could get.

Drawing a deep breath, he stepped forward, jutting his chin high. "I can do this."

Tishel's lips pursed, but it wasn't a frown. "Since the esteemed Lord Aman isn't here to say it . . . Of course you can."

His nerves settled a fraction, and he threw her a brief smile before stepping into the hall. Guards lined the walls, all standing perfectly straight, each holding a sword crossed over his or her chest. Eyes followed as he passed. Tishel's boots clipped quietly on the stone, and his coat train hissed in his wake.

At the entrance to the throne room stood a little girl, not much older than Thia, holding a basin of water. Shara paused and dipped his hands into it. The chill seeped up his arms and into his chest, steadying him. Water sloshed over his fingers, washing away his past—Iliath's past, Iliath's mistakes.

And his own? Could he do that?

He gave the girl a fleeting smile and continued forward, leaving a gentle trail of water droplets to mark his progress into the sumptuously decorated room. Several hundred people watched from either side of the central aisle, whispering and shifting like a curious ocean.

The common people lucky enough to have been invited stood here in the back. There was Amesal, beaming brightly. There Na Fanshe and Eleth, both bouncing with excitement. Shara barely stopped himself from smiling at the Mithel family—perhaps they had crafted the bouquets of liverleaf and snowdrops, or twined the kingsblossom garlands adorning the walls.

The colors grew increasingly bright as he moved up the aisle, the scents sweeter and headier. Nobles greeted him now, faces he recognized vaguely as the men and women who had been pledging their loyalty over the last however many days. Faresh lurked in their midst, all careless arrogance but for his neeka-sharp eyes. No pledge of loyalty there.

And finally Korith, standing a few rows back from Princess Nashai and her entourage. His face glowed with pride and encouragement. Shara's stomach knotted; even if they did find Iliath—no, *when* they found him—there would be no second coronation. Korith was watching his sovereign and mentor become king as much as he was watching Shara.

Rolling his shoulders back, he took the final steps.

Upon the dais at the front of the room stood Walker Galthi in his simple brown robes, his expression brimming with fondness. Shara knelt on a thick blue cushion at his feet and stared at the floor, which seemed preferable to looking at the throne looming behind Galthi.

Quiet, measured steps brought two young men to the priest's side. One held a large, open book; the other handed over a round object hanging from a chain, its contents smoking and sharply sweet.

As Galthi waved the censer over him and solemnly murmured prayers from the book, Shara fought to keep his eyes from watering. He might have dipped his head in an ocean of incense and drawn a deep breath, so thick was the fog of spicy-sweet smoke that enveloped him.

One of the acolytes gave a quiet, guilty cough, and an equally guilty grin stole over Shara's face. His taut muscles loosened, and the initial overwhelm began to fade. The aroma seeped through him, soothing his nerves.

Galthi passed the censer to the acolyte and turned his attention entirely to the book. He said a prayer of thanks to the Guide, then addressed the crowd, bestowing a blessing upon all who had gathered to witness the coronation of their next king. Then a prayer for Barath's peace and prosperity, one for the king's wisdom, another for . . .

"Prince Iliath, are you willing to take the oath?"

Panic seized him in its talons. *No! Not yet!*

What person in their right mind would do this? What if they never found Iliath, and Shara was doomed to spend the rest of his life impersonating Barath's king? A whole country following a teveth, someone so deep beneath the waves that no form would prevent him from drowning.

Breathe, Shara. He could almost feel Korith poking him in the back, prodding him out of that deep sea. "I am."

He hardly recognized the sure, resonant voice with which he answered. Again and again it left his mouth as if of its own will, making Prince Iliath's vows for him. Vows to rule with justice and fairness . . . to uphold the laws of Barath . . . to preserve its customs . . . to protect the country and its people . . .

"I solemnly swear so to do."

Over and over, the same words. Between each vow, Galthi dipped a thumb into a little bowl of scented oil and drew it across Shara's forehead.

At last, all the words had been said, all the rituals performed. No more pieces of fabric draped over his shoulders or objects pressed into his hands. No more oil, no more prayers.

Only the crown.

Galthi held it within Shara's line of sight, his hands still and sure. Three layers of some dark, nearly blue metal had been fashioned into a miniature Barath—gracefully cresting waves washing against the gentle rise of hills and the jagged peaks of mountains. Two metal discs, one gold and one silver, marked the sun and moon, and the tiny silhouette of a bird soared over one of the islands.

"Iliath Aven Adani, son of Isith and Losel, you have pledged your life in service of Barath and its people. May the Guide's blessing come upon you, and may he lead you on his Path through your reign."

With no hesitation, no warning, no anything, he settled the crown upon Shara's head.

A rippling hush swallowed the room. Galthi reached out a hand and helped him to his feet. With a steadying breath, he turned to face the room and nearly jumped when Galthi cried, "Hail His Majesty, King Iliath!"

The room echoed the words, solemnly at first but soon with more cheerful abandon, until as one they erupted into applause to rival any storm of sky or sea.

Shara had finally managed a daunted smile when the window behind him exploded.

Chapter 24

The Shattered Throne

Glass rained through the air. Shara threw his arms over his head, and the world spun in a blur of fabric, startled screams, and the eerie song of glass on stone.

Then silence. Hundreds of wide eyes stared. Guards hastened up the aisles. Galthi stepped protectively toward him.

"Your Maj—"

Something small and dark sailed between them. It clattered to the ground and rolled toward the throne, shrieking with a high, thin—

The throne exploded in a spray of shrapnel.

Shara reeled back, tripped, fell. His skull slammed against the stone amidst broken glass and the remains of the throne. The world went dull, then erupted. Shrieks and shouts, the angry bellowing of chair legs dragging over the floor, the thunder of footfalls, more explosions. Barks of pistol-fire stabbed at his ears, and a soft hiss filled the room like a den of snakes.

A pair of hands seized his shoulders and pulled him to his feet. "Your Majesty!" Galthi's wide eyes trailed to Shara's shoulder, where a jagged piece of wood protruded like a tree growing up from a lake of blood.

Pulse racing, Shara yanked it out with a grunt and buried the alvithi traits trying to burst through his skin in response to the pain and threat. "I'm fine."

Fine. He'd been listening to Korith far too long if he could say such—

Korith.

He spun, searching. People bolted for whichever exit was nearest, tripping over chairs and knocking them aside as they scrambled to be the first to safety. Princess Nashai disappeared within her entourage, one arm wrapped protectively around Lady Masar's shoulders. Thick, billowing smoke enveloped it all, stinging his eyes and nose.

Flashes of red uniforms filled his hazing vision. A woman grabbed his arm, and a swarm of guards ushered him across the dais toward a door ahead. Through the barrier and the smoke, Shara glimpsed Malothi, her blue coat swirling like a patch of calm sky as she tried to keep the stampeding crowd in some semblance of order.

His eyes snagged on Korith, and he staggered, dragging his guard to a halt. His cave-brother strode across the room, determined gaze fixed on something Shara couldn't see. *Not the attacker. Korith, don't—*

Movement pulled his attention from Korith. A black-clothed shape pushed in the wrong direction, weaving strangely, melting into the smoke and reemerging. A familiar voice shouted angrily. A flash of blue, another crack of gunfire.

Malothi crumpled to the floor at the attacker's feet.

"No!" Shara shoved against his protective wall, snarling with fury. "Let me—"

The attacker's head lifted; the fabric obscuring her—his?—face had come loose, and—

Shara flinched, slamming his eyes shut with a gasp of pain. But no, he had to see. He pried his eyes back open, but with every second they stung worse, refusing to focus properly.

Everything disappeared into a white stone corridor and the blood-red uniforms of the guards dragging him to safety. He threw them off, spun—and collided with the just-closed door. Staggering back, he hit a pair of hands that gripped his arms and guided him, none too gently, down the hall.

More doors, more paintings, more guards, everything flashing past. Whatever had held him together in the throne room began to splinter. Each noise raked his ears like claws. The coronation garments rubbed against his skin, and blood and smoke and sweat burned his nostrils.

Senses scraped raw, he closed his eyes and let the guards lead him.

Their pace eventually slowed, and he found himself in a large room bustling with people who maneuvered through rows of simple cots, their arms full of bowls and bundles of fabric. The stinging scents of medicines and blood mingled in the air. Shara's throat closed, and he stumbled back into the hall.

Tishel caught his arm. "Your Majesty, you're injured."

Injured? He glanced down at his bloodied coat.

"Oh. Right."

With a poorly concealed roll of her eyes, Tishel escorted him to a cot and scowled until he sat. A young doctor began pushing the layered coronation garments carefully aside, and Shara jolted—he'd forgotten his injury because it had already begun healing. As the doctor bared his shoulder, he forced it to tear itself back open, hissing in pain and frustration.

Molting fragile humans.

Motion and noise crowded the edges of his senses. Doctors called to their assistants, and Tishel reeled off orders to her guards. Though Shara did not care to listen, he heard enough to know that the attack had ended. Guards were searching for the would-be assassin, keeping watch over Nashai and her entourage, and ensuring that all the coronation guests made it safely from the palace.

All but Malothi. Malothi and . . .

His nails bit into his palms, and the sting shoved a sudden idea to the front of his mind. "Captain."

Tishel detached herself from the activity in the hall and came to stand at his side.

He lowered his voice, though the doctor was busy mixing some sort of sharp-smelling liquid. "Can you send Lord Aman a message with wind? Find out if he's all right?"

Pity flashed in her eyes. "Lieutenant Mereth invented that. He's the only one who's managed to do it properly so far. I'm sorry, Your Majesty." She hesitated. "I'm sure he's fine."

She stepped away, and Shara sagged.

"I'm afraid this will hurt, Your Majesty." The doctor lifted a cloth soaked in the liquid.

He closed his eyes, growling through clenched teeth though he hardly felt the sting. The moment the doctor finished tying his bandage, he leapt to his feet. He didn't want to be here when they brought in other injured people. When they brought in Malothi.

"Your Majesty." Tishel stepped away from a pair of guards and watched Shara as he adjusted his clothing, her expression unreadable. "If you'll come with us, please."

He followed her down yet another corridor, marvelling in a detached corner of his mind at how consistently everyone was calling him Your Majesty. And just when he'd finally started responding promptly to Your Highness . . .

Tishel bowed him onto a balcony overlooking the city, and he squinted into a grey world. Early spring foliage hung heavy with rain, and dark streaks lined the palace walls as though the whole place were bleeding with its king. Cold seeped through him. A natural cold. Not a reminder that he'd nearly been killed, that Malothi was dead, that others might be as well.

Tishel prodded him in the back. "Wave."

"What?"

"They need to see you're alive and well. Rumors will have already begun to fly."

Flanked by the two guards, he stepped into the chill of spring rain and lifted a hand. A vast crowd waited beneath hoods and umbrellas and celebratory banners, and raucous cheers swept up to meet him.

He stood in the rain for several minutes while Tishel held hushed conversations and received reports of new developments. At the word *body*, Shara shoved the voices firmly away and strained to hear individual shouts from the crowd, as if he were actually their king and had resolved to learn all their problems one by one. Despite the rain, a glider dove past the balcony, and one of the guards raised his pistol and shouted a warning. Shara shrank back, heart thundering, ears ringing . . .

The pilot banked hastily away and veered off toward the palace's signal tower, and the guard holstered his pistol with a protective look at Shara.

Shara made himself nod calmly, but heat crawled over his face. Someone had tried to kill him and might try again, yet he cowered instead at the prospect of hearing more gunfire. Gritting his teeth, he raised his hand and waved again, letting the raindrops soothe and settle him.

At last Tishel summoned him back inside, and the little group set off again. The guards hovered uncomfortably close, and all the questions Shara wanted to ask Tishel faded into the stifling silence. He paid little attention to his surroundings until the scent of sulfur and lingering haze of smoke pricked his senses.

They'd returned to the throne room.

It might have been a tomb ransacked by robbers—chairs knocked over, fans and parasols and shawls ripped and ruined, streaks of black and red across the polished floor. No sign that he'd become a false king in this room.

Every head turned as he entered: Gepar and Admiral Thosena and Lieutenant Mereth, Nashai and her advisors, Lady Masar and Captain Sothal. Around them all crowded watchful guards, Barathi and Tethamari alike.

No Korith.

"Iliath!"

Nashai made it halfway to him before Tishel and Thosena leapt in front of Shara.

"That's quite far enough, Your Highness," Thosena said. She smelled strongly of sulfur and blood, and Shara's gaze fell unbidden to her weapons.

"What is this?" Nashai's brow furrowed, and her confusion darkened into offense. "You cannot suspect *me* of—"

"I'm afraid we can."

Thosena gestured toward an alcove to their left, and Shara's throat closed. A figure in black sprawled at the foot of a table, the floor around her dark with blood. As if in a collective trance, the group moved close enough that they could make out her features. Threads of grey in her dark hair, a sharp nose and jaw, thin lips. She was neither remarkable nor familiar.

"This is the attacker?" Shara heard himself ask.

"One of them."

"One?"

Mereth cleared his throat. "Accounts suggest there were probably half a dozen all told. Possibly fewer—some had fabric over their faces, and descriptions of those who didn't have been remarkably vague. Though in such a panicked state in the midst of all that smoke, I suppose we can hardly expect accurate observations. Witnesses described both men and women, so there were at least two."

"And you dare suggest that this woman is Tethamari?" Lady Oshari somehow scowled at all the Barathi at once.

Thosena raised her hand. A pistol balanced on her index finger. "Her weapon. Tethamari made."

Oshari scoffed. "That proves nothing. Our countries are engaged in trade. You eat Tethamari grain. Why, His Majesty—"

"Be extremely careful," Tishel warned, "how you finish that sentence."

Her face colored. "I only meant—"

"That Tethamar is supplying the Secret Order of Remarkably Nondescript Revolutionaries with weapons," Thosena finished mildly.

Nashai's gasp drowned out Shara's poor attempt to turn a snort into a cough. Crouching beside the dead woman, she settled a trembling hand on her arm. "I'm afraid they are correct. She was one of our guard."

No one spoke as Nashai climbed back to her feet. The Tethamari stared blankly. Captain Sothal inched closer to Nashai. Lady Masar fidgeted, clearly waiting for someone to speak so she had something to do. Not even Thosena and Tishel seemed certain how to react.

Shara's mind spun. Iliath had invited the Tethamari here to establish peace. Was it actually possible . . . ? But why would

Nashai so readily identify the woman? Why come at all if they'd intended to kill Iliath so publicly?

"Your Highness?" Again he heard his own voice, though he had no memory of deciding to speak.

Nashai fixed her eyes on him, cool and steady. She raised her hands, and for a fearful heartbeat, Shara expected her to say something in sign language that Iliath would have understood. But she only smoothed her hair. "Please accept my sincerest apologies, Your Majesty. I accept full responsibility for my guard's actions and will make whatever recompense you require. I never would have . . ." Her voice faltered, and she shook her head. "I cannot claim that all of my people share my family's desire for peace, and I assure you that she did not act on our behalf. I came here on good faith to treat with you. Please allow me to prove that."

If she was lying, she was exceptionally good at it. The human belief that alvithi could sense lies was mere myth, but alvithi certainly detected signs of falsehood more easily than humans, and Nashai betrayed none of them.

But nobody else was alvithi. Gepar scoffed nervously, Thosena stared, and Tishel folded her arms and said, "You persist in claiming you are innocent?"

Nashai's expression hardened. "I do. And since the rest of the assailants were allowed to escape—"

"If your people are truly innocent," Tishel snapped, her voice higher than usual, "then your guards bear some of that burden. I don't recall any of them lifting a finger to help."

"Making up for your deficiencies is not their job," Lord Fethan retorted. "Trust me, Captain, if we wanted a war, you would know it plainly by now. Such trickery is not Tethamar's style."

"Those who have crossed paths with Kana Faresh would argue differently."

Lady Masar's hands faltered, but Nashai had caught enough. "You dare—"

"Enough!" Shara growled, throwing his arms out.

It hit him at last—exhaustion, uncertainty, overwhelm. He could face down their weapons and drown out the noise and cover his nose against the stench, but this . . . The coronation had done nothing. He felt no different; he *was* no different. Still just Shara. And surely not even Korith would find Shara's heart and instincts sufficient for this situation. Especially when they were telling him to run.

Or perhaps that voice was something less dependable than instinct.

In the rain-spattered window, his reflection watched him. Clothing dishevelled and damp and bloody, hair in disarray, eyes too wide, breaths too shallow. But Iliath's crown remained on his head, unmoved despite everything.

There, Korith. I noticed something positive. Something immaterial, but it was better than nothing. Korith would have said so, anyway, if he'd been here instead of . . .

Please let him be safe.

He cleared his throat. "I wish to speak with my advisors," he told Nashai, "and I'm sure you would like to confer with yours. Why don't we resume this when everyone has had a chance to . . . rest."

Judging by the twist in Nashai's lips, she knew he'd chosen a kinder word than he wanted to say. "Very well. But I would speak with His Majesty first. Privately."

Thosena started. "Absolutely not."

Nashai's smile cooled. "Very well then." She narrowed her eyes at Shara. "You are—"

"Wait." A shiver crawled up his spine at the look in her eyes, like she had a final piece to play in a game that should have ended. And he had a horrible feeling he knew what piece it was. "It's fine, Admiral. I will speak with her. Please escort the rest of our guests back to their quarters."

He held up a hand to silence her protest, dimly aware that it worked, that Korith would have told him he was doing well.

One by one they turned, all scowls and quiet grumbling. Only Lady Masar lingered, and after a brief conference with Nashai, she too shuffled away, casting protective yet fearful glances over her shoulder. A final look, and she was gone.

Shara stared past Nashai and out the window, where the rain had swelled into a storm. That was for the best—he'd been expected to parade through the city after the crowning, but surely they would cancel it, and poor weather would serve as a better excuse than an attempted assassination.

Slowly Nashai moved into the center of the room, far enough from the guards Tishel had left flanking the door.

Shara gripped the back of a still-upright chair. "Well?"

She tilted her head like a hawk surveying its next meal. "You," she said after a painfully drawn-out moment, "are not Iliath."

CHAPTER 25

JUST SHARA

Shara's mind went blank.

He'd expected the accusation; he'd had a plan, a response. . . . It was gone.

Not Iliath . . . just Shara . . . not Iliath . . .

"No," he managed, tilting his chin the way Korith had taught him while he scrambled for words. "As of minutes ago, I am *King* Iliath."

Nashai snorted, and her expression flitted through amusement before settling into disapproval. "You think you're clever, do you?"

It was a more generous word than *desperate.* "What proof do you have?"

"Let me see." She pivoted and paced through the maze of chairs. "You defer to your advisors on everything. You guard each word as though a wrong one might spell the end of Barath. You don't remember any of the signs I taught him, and you've not so much as—" Her cheeks flushed. "I've met Iliath, you know. Five years is enough to change a man, but not to transform him into a coward who questions his every thought."

Shara winced and tried to hide it with a weak smile. "So it wasn't the squirrel-dragons crawling all over me in the gardens?"

Another smile fluttered over her face. "It could have been. Or maybe . . ." She stalked forward until a mere step separated them and prodded him abruptly in the shoulder. "Maybe it's that you pulled a piece of your throne out of your body *minutes ago* and were waving your arms around without pain shortly after. Or do all Barathi heal with such miraculous speed?"

Burrs! Molting, sea-cursed humans and their slow healing.

Nashai's expression darkened. "I could declare war on Barath right now. First you accuse my people of instigating this attack—"

"I didn't—"

"—and now this breach of faith. To think I might have sailed home with an alvithi's signature on our peace treaty."

A memory, driven into hiding by everything else, now nosed its way to the front of Shara's mind. "And when you went, would you have taken the squadron hiding in the Talons with you?"

Her eyes flew wide and then narrowed, but she said nothing.

"So you don't deny it?"

Her scowl deepened, and she prodded one of the overturned chairs with her foot. At last she huffed. "It was a precaution, nothing more. As I said, I came here on good faith, but good faith only carries one so far in another's land. I doubt you know enough of our shared history to appreciate how things stand."

"I know enough. You humans carry a peace offering in one hand and a weapon in the other, and you wonder why your relations are strained. The nobles here swear oaths to their future king and make alliances behind his back. Iliath's advisors thought replacing him with *me* was preferable to civil war. Do you really want peace, Your Highness? Is that truly why you came here?"

"Yes, it is." She met his gaze, her expression hard but unwavering, fierce but sincere. Still no hints of falsehood. "But I will not see my country calumniated or deceived, and even you, whoever you are, must admit that my wariness is justified when I learn that the Barathi thought they could put an impostor on the throne and carry on as usual. Where is Iliath?"

Shara choked on laughter. "Do you think I would be here if we knew? No one wants me here, Your Highness. I'm not Barathi or even human, I have no idea what I'm doing, and you said it yourself—I'm a coward."

To his shock, her scowl faded. "That was . . . unfair of me." She twisted the signet ring on her finger. "You are not Iliath, but you agreed to take his place amidst extremely trying circumstances. There is no cowardice in that."

He ducked his head. She wouldn't say that if she knew the circumstances of his agreement. "It wasn't really . . ."

She tapped her fingers against her palm the way she often did when asking someone to repeat their words. "Pardon?"

"Never mind." He couldn't make himself thank her, but maybe Korith would be satisfied knowing he'd at least not apologized.

"Very well. So Iliath simply disappeared?"

Possible responses rolled around in Shara's mouth. How much to tell her? *Yes, he was kidnapped out of his chambers and two of his guards were killed. We have no idea who did it—it might be your uncle, by the way—or where he is.*

"Yes."

"And you have no idea where he might be?"

He rocked back on his heels. "We've eliminated the most

likely location, and Lord—er, we're investigating several others. Captain Tishel will be able to tell you more."

"Hmm." She looped her hands behind her back and stared down at her feet, humming softly. When she raised her eyes again, regret lined her face. "Unfortunately, I will not—cannot—treat with someone masquerading as a king. Now that the coronation is over, I'm returning to Tethamar immediately."

Shara's jaw dropped. "Wha—? No! You can't—"

"The real king is missing, someone from my country just tried to assassinate his replacement, and you appear to be the only person willing to entertain the possibility of my innocence in the matter—in *both* matters, I imagine. I have little incentive to remain."

She moved toward the door, and Shara dove in front of her, throwing his arms wide. How ridiculous he must look, the newly crowned monarch flailing like a child. "Wait, please. Give us a chance. A . . . a week. Stay a week."

"And give this situation time to worsen?"

"Or improve." His mind tumbled through possible arguments. He glanced at the body of the dead Tethamari, and something nudged his senses, the same sensation he felt whenever he overlooked an opponent's play in malir. But whatever it was, it wouldn't help him convince Nashai to stay. "Look, you admitted she was one of your guards, and with everyone so suspicious of you, you could end up imprisoned or punished, and—"

Nashai's perfect eyebrows shot into her hairline. "I beg your pardon?"

Shara cringed. "That's not—"

"This is supposed to convince me to stay? Threatening me with execution? Or would you like to pretend I misunderstood you and start again?"

He ground his teeth and sucked in a steadying breath.

Alanthas. Be like Alanthas. Cool demeanor. Calming voice. "I'm sorry. I didn't mean to threaten. I only meant that if you leave now, you'll look even more suspicious. But if you stay, we still have a chance at finding the truth and making peace. I'll ensure the investigation is conducted fairly and thoroughly and that the Tethamari are given the benefit of the doubt. And with luck, we'll find Iliath so you can speak to him before deciding about the treaty."

Nashai bit her lip and folded her arms, tapping out a rhythm with her finger. The rain beat against the windows. Shara held his breath.

"Please," he pressed when his lungs could bear it no longer. "This isn't Iliath's fault. Or Barath's. If the assassination attempt was the work of a few dissenters, surely Iliath's disappearance was as well."

More rain, more silence. Nashai's mouth quirked. "You're diplomatic, whoever you are; I'll grant you that. But why should I believe you can achieve any of what you offer? You have no power of your own. You promised to invite my uncle to stay in the palace, but when Lord Gepar tried to dissuade me, you refused to speak against him."

"I . . . You're right." He ducked his head before remembering she needed to see his face. "I'm nothing but a lost alvithi. I've hardly lived here a month. But there are people and places and things I care about here, and I want peace for them. I'm going to try my best to preserve it. Please . . ." He swallowed, tasting unfamiliar words on his tongue. "Please trust me."

With agonizing slowness, she unfolded her arms. "You're right. And I truly do want peace. You may have heard rumors about a marriage alliance between me and Iliath. I had . . . hoped to see that come to pass." Her cheeks flushed, but her resolve never wavered. "Very well. I will give you until the full moon."

All sense of victory fled. "That's three days!"

She nodded. "If I were here alone, I might be able to remain longer, but with my father's advisors present, I'm afraid that's all I can offer. If, after that time, we've not found any evidence that Tethamar sanctioned this attack or orchestrated Iliath's kidnapping—and I assure you that we won't—I will return home."

Somehow Shara made himself speak over the sound of his heartbeat. "And then?"

Her face became a careful mask. "My father is king; I can neither conceal what has happened here nor guarantee his response. I will do whatever I can to help discover the truth behind this attack, but I suggest you use your time wisely."

Shara's arms tried to wrap around his torso, and he forced himself to stand tall. "Very well. Three days. Thank you."

Better than nothing.

. . . thinking like Korith did not make him feel nearly as positive as he'd hoped.

Nashai surveyed him thoughtfully, then slipped a hand into her coat and extracted a small notebook and a charcoal pencil. "Your name?" she asked, holding them out to him.

The pencil knocked between his trembling fingers, and the little blank square of paper gazed up at him judgmentally.

Shara.

It looked so small in the middle of that empty space, and before he could scribble it out and replace it with *Iliath*, he thrust the notebook back at Nashai.

She mouthed his name but did not speak it, only tucked the notebook back into her gown. "Congratulations on your coronation, King Iliath."

She dipped into a small bow and departed in a swish of fabrics, leaving Shara alone with the rain.

Chapter 26

Permission and Presumption

"She knows."

Tishel scowled and kept pacing. Gepar muttered, "Of course." Shara traced the path of two raindrops chasing one another down the window. Korith was still missing, and Malothi's absence loomed over the council room. Without her, neither Tishel nor Gepar seemed willing to speak.

Shara didn't want to, either, but Nashai's words kept buzzing through his mind like a swarm of bees. Three days. The full moon. They didn't have time to delay. "It seems Iliath is different than she remembers." *A coward.* "And my wound healed."

"Healed?" Tishel pivoted.

"Our bodies heal themselves quickly. We can recover from a lot. Probably not a sword through the heart or a beheading—"

She held up a hand. "A word of advice, *Your Majesty*: in light of recent events, telling people how best to kill you is even stupider than usual."

"Right. Sorry."

She rolled her eyes and started pacing again. "You'd be sorrier if I were one of the assassins."

That was debatable. At least beheading, unlike humiliation, would be quick and painless.

Probably.

"So she knows." Gepar wove another nonexistent spell with his nervous hands. "Was that all she wanted? Did she try to blackmail you?"

"Blackmail? No. Well, not really." He steadied himself against the sill, grasping for the quickest explanation. *Three days.* "She threatened to go back to Tethamar. And strongly hinted that her father might not be happy that Barath expected her to negotiate with an impostor."

"Yes," Tishel muttered, "he'll like it as much as we like them trying to kill our king, impostor or not."

Shara squirmed and pushed off the wall; he couldn't stand still any longer.

"Then she's leaving?" Gepar asked. Did he know how hopeful he sounded?

"I convinced her to wait three days, but—"

Tishel spun so quickly she nearly collided with Shara. "You talked her into staying?"

"I— Well, yes. I tried for a week, but . . ." He shrugged. *Korith thoughts.* "But it's better than nothing. I told her we'd investigate the attack together and that Barath would give Tethamar the benefit of the doubt while we . . ." His footsteps faltered, and warmth flooded his face. Their expressions betrayed no relief, no approval. Tishel's practically bled pity. "You think I'm a fool to think it could be dissenters. To believe she and her family are innocent."

Gepar scoffed. "They're Tethamari; of course they aren't innocent! And while we're on the matter—" He turned his back to the door and the guards beyond, and his voice dropped to a hiss. "Who gave *you* the right to make any sort of agreement with her? Or have you forgotten what Lady Malothi said—and what those *innocent* people did to her?"

Shara's chest tightened, and his head ducked. He had not expected praise—he'd long since grown past believing he merited anyone's notice or pride. And yet, following Nashai out of the throne room, he'd almost been pleased with himself. He'd delayed something awful and created a chance for reconciliation.

But instead of a boar's den, he'd led everyone to neeka yet again.

No. Some fiery creature wiggled through his insides. Nashai, a neeka? The people who had come here for peace?

Or was he simply naïve?

But even if he was, that didn't change their reactions. "You don't *want* war, do you?"

They both stiffened. Guilt flashed over Tishel's face and hardened into resolve. "We want," she said with clear effort at calm, "to find Iliath and bring these attackers to justice. And speaking of which, I investigated the matter of the prisoner aboard Faresh's ship—"

"You what?" Gepar's eyes grew as round as his spectacles, then narrowed. Derision pulled at his mouth. "Taking orders from our *king*, Captain?"

"I had my reasons," she said coolly, "but we found nothing of note."

She frowned pointedly at Shara, but a softness tinged her gaze. Apology? Disappointment? Or exhaustion?

"Thank you," he said. Whatever her reasons, she'd tried. "I'll tell Korith and see if he's found any more ideas in—"

Burrs. Was it too much to hope they'd not heard that ill-begotten sentence?

"More ideas in *what*, precisely?"

Of course it was. "We, uh, found some papers in Iliath's rooms. Korith thought they might be useful, so he took them home to look through."

Tishel's jaw dropped. "That . . ." Her hands bunched into fists. "That little . . ."

"Ransacking His Majesty's rooms!" Gepar accused. "Neither you nor he had any right—"

"—going to get himself *killed*—"

"—might have stumbled on anything, secrets or incriminating information or—"

"—thinks he's going to rescue Iliath on his own—"

"All right, I understand! I'm sorry." They didn't have time for this. "So what are we going to do now? What should I do?"

Gepar smoothed his coat and rubbed a hand over his beard. "I will apprise the council of recent developments and tell them you're resting and recovering from the attack, but I fear you will have to speak with them eventually given the gravity of the situation. For now, you will return to His Majesty's rooms and stay there, and you will not make another decision without my approval. Captain, go with him. And when you've done that, perhaps see about finding our king. Or his attackers. Either would be progress at this point."

Tishel flushed. Jaw clenched, she gave a stiff bow and marched to the door, beckoning Shara with a jerk of her head.

He scowled at Gepar before he followed.

As an alvithi, Shara had always drawn comfort from being physically close to others, but royal guards were the exception. Nearly a dozen accompanied him down the hall like deadly bees hovering around a delicate flower, and when another group stopped to confer with Tishel, he did his best not to squirm in their midst.

To his relief, Tishel sent most of them elsewhere, and she and Shara set off again with the four who remained, pausing frequently for servants who broke up hushed conversations to bow and express their relief that their king was all right.

They'd almost reached the gardens when Thosena came striding toward them, straightening the cuff of one sleeve over what looked like a bandage around her wrist.

"Your Majesty. Captain." She fell in step beside them. "The Tethamari have settled in their quarters, and I—"

"Have been to the healing rooms," Shara cut in, guilty. "I'm sorry, Admiral. I didn't realize you'd been injured."

She flapped the uninjured wrist at him. "It's nothing serious. Might delay the paperwork a bit."

"Tragic," Tishel muttered, lips twitching upward.

Tishel launched into a summary of Shara's meeting with Nashai, and though Shara kept his eyes on the rain-streaked windows and trees beyond, he pricked his ears toward her. Would she tell Thosena the truth? With Malothi dead and matters in such a state . . . But Tishel wouldn't make that decision on her own, and Gepar would never approve such a step.

Either would be progress. He gritted his teeth. At least the royal guard respected their captain, and Thosena showed no concern about Tishel's lack of nobility.

They rounded the corner to Iliath's rooms, and at the end of the hall, two familiar figures leapt to their feet.

"Your Majesty!" Amesal sagged against his desk and back into his chair with a shaky laugh.

"Si!" Korith hurried forward as fast as his limping stride would allow, and before Tishel could flee, he collided with her and wrapped her in an embrace.

"Lord . . ." She stiffened, her face turning vivid red. "I'm fine, Lord Aman," she mumbled, wriggling in a rather feeble escape attempt.

Thosena propped a fist on her hip. "Isn't anyone happy to see me?"

Shara bit down a laugh, and Korith grinned at her over Tishel's shoulder. "Shall I embrace you as well, Admiral?"

She smirked. "Do you want to be covered in blood and gunpowder?"

Korith chuckled and stepped back from Tishel. His smile faded, and he chewed his lip as he shifted his weight from foot to foot, oddly subdued. "Listen, Si, can we talk?" he asked softly.

"I'm busy, my lord."

"I know. I don't mean now. But soon? There's something I need . . ." He rubbed the back of his neck. "I owe you an apology, and . . ."

Tishel started, and her eyes narrowed. "An apology," she repeated slowly, flatly.

"Yes. You know, where I admit I've been a less than amazing bro—"

"I'm busy." She spun sharply, placing her back to him and smoothing invisible wrinkles from her uniform with sudden, intense focus. Her expression had frozen, as emotionless as her voice.

Korith's face fell, but before Shara could shoot him a look of support, Thosena cleared her throat loudly. "With your permission, my king, and if Captain Tishel will pardon a suggestion, I would recommend we search the dead guard's quarters."

Fierce energy overtook Tishel's features, nearly obscuring the fact that she'd just tried to take a drink out of her pistol instead of her flask. "Absolutely. And the ship, too, once this weather has cleared—she may have left possessions on board.

We'll also want to question the remaining Tethamari guards and search their rooms. The advisors as well, if possible."

Out of the corner of his eye, Shara watched Korith open his mouth and, with visible effort, snap it shut again.

"Good." Thosena turned to Shara, expectant. Even eager? Or was he seeing things? First Nashai, hinting at war despite her avowed desire for peace. Gepar, so certain the Tethamari were guilty merely because they were Tethamari. And now Thosena and Tishel, planning searches and interrogations. Hoping for incriminating evidence?

Nashai was right. He *didn't* appreciate Barath's history with Tethamar.

"I . . ." He stopped himself from looking at Korith and nodded wearily. "Fine. Tell Nashai what you're doing. I expect she'll want to come with you or send someone."

Thosena's eyebrows shot up. "With respect—are you certain that's wise, Your Majesty?"

Shara fought the urge to squirm. "I told her we would conduct this investigation fairly," he said, though he sounded more like an apologetic child than an insistent king. "She's already threatened to go back to Tethamar, and I don't want to encourage her."

Thosena's eyebrows came back down, falling in time with her head as she bowed. "Very well, Your Majesty."

"Oh, and Admiral, I . . ." He bit his lip. He'd promised Nashai the benefit of the doubt. Telling Thosena about the squadron would only pile more suspicion onto the Tethamari. "Never mind. Thank you for your service, both of you."

They bowed in unison and strode away, already discussing their plans in low, urgent voices.

"Your Majesty?" Amesal glanced up as Shara and Korith moved toward Iliath's quarters. "I'm sorry, but guild merchants Mira and Lesar have already been by to see you, and they were"—he winced—"insistent that I let you know."

Shara tried not to groan and mostly failed. "What did they want?"

Amesal faltered, shoulders hunching as his gaze fell to the record book on the desk. "Ah . . ."

"Given that it was Mira and Lesar," Korith said mildly, twirling his cane, "they were probably fighting over who would be first to offer Barath their services supplying weapons for the upcoming war."

"We aren't going to war!" Shara snapped.

The entire hall flinched—Korith, Amesal, the two guards at the door. A grin tugged at Korith's mouth.

"Come on," Shara muttered, face boiling. He forced a smile at Amesal as the guards held open the doors. "Thank you. Please don't admit anyone else."

Especially if they want to start a war.

CHAPTER 27

THE RIGHT THING

Korith had been tailing Faresh, and he'd come to a horrible conclusion: "I don't think he was involved."

Shara yowled. He'd recounted everything that had occurred since the attack, then dissolved into a lynx in the middle of Iliath's bedroom. Since then he'd been sprawled on Korith's lap, listening with ever-tightening nerves while his cave-brother relayed what he and the Tears had discovered—and not discovered.

"I know," Korith muttered, tugging lightly on one of Shara's ear tufts. "He's certainly invested in the treaty, and it's obvious he believes you're Iliath, so killing you would get him what he wants. But after what I saw today, I don't think it's him. Whatever he's up to, it's not about Iliath. Or it is, but not in the way we thought."

Shara's ears flattened. Their best lead—their only lead—was an empty den. Three days to find Iliath, and they had to start over. Suppressing a whine, he curled into a ball and draped a massive paw over his face to block out the room, the weather, the world.

Korith smoothed his fur. "We'll find him," he insisted, but though his voice never wavered, his hand faltered over Shara's shoulders.

Not Korith, too. If even Korith lost confidence . . .

Heaving himself upright, Shara jumped to the floor and shifted. As much as he wanted to hide, it wouldn't get them anywhere. Sometimes you had to make a bad play to advance the game. He'd never been able to convince himself that the same rule applied to life, but right now, anything seemed preferable to stagnation.

Coronation clothing billowing around him, he crossed the room and climbed into the window alcove to think. The cushion sat propped where he'd left it, and he drew it to his chest and squeezed it hard. He'd felt guilty at first for rubbing his scent all over everything in Iliath's quarters, but a human wasn't likely to notice.

When the cushion had absorbed as much of Shara's nervous energy as it could, he leaned his head against the grating and pushed open the window. Cold, misty air filled his senses, driving away the last of the smoky scent still clinging—

"The attackers." His eyes widened. "Did you see any of them? Look directly at them, I mean."

"One," Korith said. "Briefly. He was . . . He had . . . Hills, I don't remember a single detail." He frowned. "Usually I'm incredible with faces. More incredible than my usual incredible, that is."

"Of course." Shara pulled the crown from his head and spun it slowly in his hands. "Was his face blurry?"

"Blurry? Through the smoke, you mean?"

"No." The pointed tips of the crown-mountains bit into his palms. "I looked at one of them, and it was so blurry it *hurt.* But when I looked away, everything else seemed normal, so it can't have been the smoke."

Korith gnawed his lip, eyes raised to the rafters in thought. "No, nothing like that," he said absently.

The contemplative silence lengthened. Shara squirmed, each soundless minute weighing heavier, until he wasn't sure why he'd spoken at all. "Never mind. I was probably mistak—"

"Wind sense."

"What?"

"If you saw something the rest of us didn't, it has to be because you're alvithi."

Korith's faith shouldn't have surprised him by now, and yet every time, it brought him up short. He frowned. "But alvithi don't have wind sense."

"No, but maybe the attackers were using it. Manipulating the air around their faces to make themselves harder to recognize." Magic sizzled through the air, and a faint blur swirled for a moment over Korith's eyes. "And since you have stronger senses, you were more strongly affected."

Shara turned the idea over in his mind. "I don't remember tasting magic during the attack, but—"

"Tasting? You can *taste* magic?" Korith sat forward, his face spreading into a grin as Shara nodded awkwardly. "That's bizarre. And amazing. We need you in the Tears after this is all over."

Shara looked away sharply. It had been an innocent suggestion free of Korith's usual underlying hints, but even so, it raked his scales the wrong way. *After this* was the dawn above a far-distant horizon, the only thing keeping him aloft while everything else spun out of control. He didn't want Korith's eagerness painting guilty clouds over his freedom.

Besides, what had Korith said about the Tears? The only people the king trusted? Shara would be disqualified on that alone.

"Why did *you* join the Tears?" he asked, digging up an appropriately distracting question. "You're so . . ."

"So?"

Shara shrugged. "Pick any positive word you like."

"Ebullient."

"Not that one. Kind? Caring. Un-spy-ish." He ducked his head. "Or perhaps that's the whole point."

Korith climbed from his chair to stand nearer the fire and tapped his cane against the stonework as if the correct combination of beats might open a secret passageway. "I've been drawing for as long as I can remember. People would sit for me and talk while I drew, and I'd nod and pretend I cared and not remember a single thing or a single person. They were all just faces." He grimaced and shook his head, but after a moment, his expression relaxed. "Then one day I finally started listening. Truly listening. I heard tragedies and triumphs and unfulfilled dreams and romances and fears and failures . . . And all those people stopped being simply models I could use to improve my art."

Shara smiled, the first real smile he'd worn since . . . he couldn't remember.

"But," Korith went on, and the tapping ceased, "you pick up a lot when you're willing to listen. Some of it you wish you hadn't heard. Sometimes you can help, but other times your only real skills are drawing and flying and resetting dislodged joints."

"That's not true." But he said it more for himself than Korith. He *needed* it to be untrue, now more than ever. Because if Korith was just like anyone else . . . like Shara . . .

"No, you're right; I'm also pretty good at talking. Most of the time." He grinned at Shara's huff. "My point is, the Tears cared, too. Suddenly I had allies. Ways to help all those people I couldn't help before." He gave Shara a knowing smile. "Until playing the gryphon felt so natural, I forgot to be anything else. Until the people I cared about became projects." His gaze flicked in the direction of the hall, and he scuffed his foot over the floor. "Even my own family."

Shara slipped from the alcove and moved to stand beside him. Together they gazed into the dwindling fire, but it offered little heat and even less inspiration. After a few minutes, the lingering warmth melted away, and Shara reluctantly closed the window and resumed toying with Iliath's crown. Such an odd way to designate a ruler—pieces of metal, melted and refined, molded and tempered and smoothed.

Perhaps a crown was a fair representation of a king after all.

Slowly, Korith stretched out a hand and brushed his fingertips over the crown. "He's even worse than I am, you know." He chuckled softly. "Just wait until you meet—" His voice faltered, and his hand withdrew.

"We'll find him," Shara said with confidence he didn't feel.

They *had* to find him.

Korith swallowed hard and drew a bracing breath. "Yes. Yes we will. All right. I'll go back to his files. There has to be something, and we need to find it soon."

Determined energy pulsed through Shara. "I'll help. Tonight, after supper." And in the meantime, he'd find something to do, somewhere to search, someone to talk to. King Iliath had to stay in this room, but Shara could be anyone, and none of them were staying here.

"Thank you. And . . ." Korith pivoted to face him directly. "Thank you for staying. I hope you don't think I've been making light of all this because of the way I've been encouraging you. I know this is difficult and uncomfortable and, well, generally terrible. And I'm sure you'd rather be anywhere other than Barath right now. So thank you."

It was fortunate the crown was solidly made, or Shara would have twisted it into a guilty knot by the time Korith finished speaking. His tongue, meanwhile, had twisted itself, and before he could push words into sound, Korith patted his shoulder and stepped toward the door.

The determined energy sputtered into doubt. "Korith." He didn't want to ask, but he had to. "Do you think they did it? Or did I do the right thing?"

Korith's hand hovered over the door handle, and he turned back slowly, lips pursed. Shara's stomach heaved.

"The Tethamari have breached faith before," Korith said after a pause. "Hills, Tethamar was born out of a Barathi civil war, so some would say they've been doing it from the beginning. I'm sorry to admit that if they are found guilty of this attack, I won't be entirely surprised. But at the same time, relations have improved since King Rhoda took the throne, and more than that, I can't see him endangering Nashai like this.

"As to whether you did the right thing . . . I don't know. But for what it's worth, *I* think you did the right thing." In the few seconds it took Shara to work out the distinction, Korith snatched the crown out of his hands and dropped it on Shara's head. "I know how much you hate it when I'm impressed, but I'm impressed."

"I—" He clamped his jaw shut before the familiar words escaped, forcing his hands to remain at his sides though they itched to reach for the crown. This time he'd not lied to Korith or doctored the story to hide his fear and make himself sound less inept. If Korith thought he'd done something right amidst all that floundering . . . "Thank you."

His cave-brother's eyebrows shot up like the sun rising over his familiar grin. "*Finally,* he accepts a compliment. I should've thrown you into unexpected solo negotiations with a foreign princess sooner."

Shara made a show of removing the crown. "I take it back. I did everything wrong and I'm sorry and you shouldn't be impressed."

But as Korith departed, the determination returned, boiling up from an unexpected warmth in the pit of his stomach.

CHAPTER 28

BLOOD AND BLACKMAIL

Shara had no desire to witness Tishel and Thosena's investigation, so he stayed as far from the Tethamari quarters as he could. Dressed in the simplest of Iliath's garments—travelling clothes, judging from the smell—he went instead to the throne room and pretended to be another servant sent to restore cleanliness and order.

The storm had moved on, and the lingering patter of rain mingled with the soft hissing of hushed voices. Shara placed himself in the center of the floor and scrubbed at a black mark from one of the smoke explosives while his senses explored the room.

Murmurs filled the air, but here in the room where the attack had happened, with guards standing watchfully at each door, nobody wanted to do more than whisper about how terrible and frightening it had all been. Nor did any scents stand out—smoke and gunpowder, the occasional sour of blood and sweat, a dozen lingering perfumes, and the mingled odors of hundreds of guests.

The body of the Tethamari guard had been moved, and

Shara wasn't the only one shooting furtive glances at the corner where she'd been lying. Swipe by swipe, he scrubbed his way toward it. With each brush of his rag over the polished stone, details tumbled through his mind. Memories of the attack, fragments of his conversations with Nashai, Tishel and Gepar, Korith.

Three days.

A coward who questions his every thought.

Who gave you the authority . . .

I think you did the right thing.

He squeezed his rag, sloshing sudsy water over the floor.

Three days . . .

The faint scent of death pulled him from his thoughts. Someone had scrubbed the corner clean—but not well enough. A little circle of dried blood stood out a few paces away, hardly distinguishable from a vein of dark red-brown in the stone. Shara crawled toward it, shoving up his already-damp sleeves and grimacing at their clammy grip around his arms.

He sat back on his heels to peel the coat off, and his gaze snagged on something ahead. His heart leapt. Not a single missed drop of blood. A trail.

Sucking in a breath, he followed it, pretending to scrub away one spot after the next. The guard at the door neither moved nor reacted as Shara drew nearer. Why he was following it, he couldn't say—there had been several injuries, after all, and many hundreds of people fleeing the room. It was a Shara sort of thing to do, chasing a pointless trail.

His hand fisted around the rag, and he kept crawling. Right now, Shara sorts of things would have to suffice.

Two more drops, and he passed the guard. His gaze skipped forward to the next few droplets, and his nose scrunched in thought. All those people stampeding into this corridor, yet this trail of blood had survived their trampling feet without any of the spots smearing. As though the blood had already been dry.

Which meant someone had left the room, injured, *before* the coronation.

Pulse quickening, he gave up all pretense of cleaning and shuffled forward, seeking the end of the trail, seeking an answer.

It's just a servant who got cut on a shattered piece of glass during the decorating process.

But what if—

"Boy!"

Shara's squawk was distinctly unhuman, but the man towering over him merely scowled.

"Sneaking away from your duties, are you?"

"I . . ." Shara gestured. "There's blood."

The man rolled his eyes. "Of course there's blood; there's blood everywhere! Now get back in the hall. We don't move out here until in there's been cleaned."

"Oh." He climbed to his feet, trying out of the corner of his eye to discern where the spots went. "Could I—"

"Now," the man barked, jabbing a finger toward the throne room. "Or I'll give everyone else this afternoon off, and you can come back here after lunch and clean this entire corridor yourself."

That was fine with Shara, but rather than provoke the man by saying so, he shot a final look at the floor and returned to the throne room.

Every time Shara sought to sneak from the room or shift and dive out a window, he felt the overseer's eyes on him. Not until the servants all filed into the kitchens did the man seem to think it safe to shift his attention elsewhere.

Despite Shara's annoyance at the wasted time, hunger kept him in the room for the meal, and he lingered in a corner with a small plate of honeyed rhubarb and grilled fish. Eagle willing, the servants would talk more openly now.

They did, but no one said anything useful. Those few who'd attended the coronation found themselves the center of attention, asked again and again to repeat their experiences. When Amesal arrived for his afternoon meal, they all converged on him, inquiring after His Majesty's health and pressing him for his rendition of the coronation story.

No matter how many times Shara willed the conversation to turn to the night Iliath had been kidnapped, it remained stubbornly on the morning's events.

"Do you think it's the same people as the last attack?" he finally asked.

The kitchen dissolved into speculation, but nobody had any insight to offer on this, either, and Shara gave up hoping that a servant had taken tea to Iliath that night and seen or heard something suspicious. Head ducked, he padded away, wedged himself behind a statue a few halls down, and shifted into Iliath. This time no one would question his presence outside the throne room.

The halls grew more refined as he left the servants' wing, the doors spaced further apart. Soft conversations floated from behind a few, and Shara quickened his pace each time lest someone emerge and seize the opportunity to fawn over His Majesty.

"—was *not* the agreement."

Shara drew up short. He knew that voice.

"It's time for the agreement to change." For all its politeness, Nashai's reply held no room for argument. "Call it a sign of good faith, Lord Gepar."

Gepar's scoff grated like claws against the door, and Shara inched closer to better hear the reply over his quickening heartbeat. "I call it blackmail."

"Blackmail?" Nashai gave a short, mirthless laugh. "You want blackmail? His Majesty's advisor is accepting bribes—how's that for blackmail?"

Footsteps scuffed against a rug. "You dare accuse *me* of accepting bribes?"

"And you dare deny it? What other motive could you have for refusing? Certainly not deference to your *king*."

A pause, and when Gepar spoke again, his voice was calm, delicate. "You know as well as I that our current ruler has nothing to do with this, nor with anything at all save making a proper show."

Shara's cheeks tingled with an uncomfortable flush, and a high ringing in his ears nearly drowned out Nashai's next words.

"Perhaps you underestimate him."

Gepar laughed dismissively. "It's difficult to underestimate someone from whom you expect nothing. The *king*, on the other hand, made clear his position on this matter, and I *do* defer to him."

Heat crawled like insects over Shara's body. *From whom you expect nothing.*

Good. He clenched his hands and nodded at the door, as if it cared about the strange stinging in his stomach or the urge to squirm that he couldn't quite suppress. *Good.* Gepar understood better than Korith or Nashai. Amidst war and assassins and abductions and politics, Shara was just Shara.

The door swung open. He leapt back, trying to shift as rapidly as possible, and nearly fell over. Nashai and Gepar started. Gepar's face turned red and pinched in displeasure; Nashai merely raised her eyebrows as her lips puckered in amusement.

"Your Majesty."

Shara gulped. "I . . ."

Before he could decide how to proceed, Nashai bowed with a polite "Good afternoon," and in a swirl of her familiar scent, she swept off down the hall alone. It seemed she, too, had escaped her guards—unless Tishel and Thosena had arrested them all.

A hand clamped on his arm and dragged him into the room. The door thundered shut, and Shara cringed and looked automatically at the window. Closed, of course.

"What are you doing?" Gepar sounded like a bad actor trying to convey fatherly concern. "I specifically told you not to leave His Majesty's rooms."

"What agreement?"

Gepar blinked. "Agreement?"

Shara hadn't meant to ask—the question had simply burst out—but now he hurried on. "Nashai said your agreement had changed. What are you—"

"That doesn't concern you," Gepar replied crisply. He spun a slow, measured circle, examining the room as though looking for more eavesdroppers, but when he faced Shara again, his expression had changed. "Her Highness wished to speak with me about an arrangement between herself and His Majesty that will be settled with the signing of the treaty."

Shara's stomach bubbled. "The marriage?"

Gepar shot him a reproving frown and muttered something about meddling as he picked lint from his sleeve. "She seems to be under the impression that it would be, as she put it, a show of good faith if I were to allow her to alter the terms of that agreement now. I did not agree."

Shara's heartbeat resumed its rapid pace. Alter the terms how? Was Nashai trying to break off the marriage? Defer it? Or—nausea swirled up his throat—move it up? If she married "Iliath" now . . .

He wrestled that thought aside. "And the bribery?"

More red blotches spread over Gepar's face, and his hands twisted. "It's a common and rather amateurish play, accusing someone of corruption when you dislike the answers they give you. She knows perfectly well that I do not possess the authority to make such a decision, even if it might appease Tethamar until Iliath is found."

"Appease how?"

"As I said, this is none of your business." He regarded Shara with narrowed eyes. "The last thing you need is another excuse to make unsanctioned agreements with our *guest* based on your pitiful knowledge of Barathi politics. Barathi anything, for that matter."

"I . . ." His head dipped, and he forced it back up, though he could think of nothing to say. The words were true, yet something that wasn't shame burned in his chest and fired in his throat. "But—"

Gepar's hand flailed inches from his nose, and he leapt back with a squawk.

"Stop staring like that," Gepar snapped. "You never blink. It's unnerving."

"Sorry." The word escaped before he could catch it, and he clenched his teeth in a silent, scolding growl. He wasn't sorry. He was . . . he didn't know. But it wasn't sorry. "I'm alvithi."

"Yes, and you should remind yourself that that's the only reason you're here."

Shara's face flooded with warmth—half embarrassment, half whatever new, unapologetic sensation had overtaken him, so wholly unfamiliar that he hadn't the faintest idea what to do about it.

"Now then." Gepar scratched his fingers through his beard. "I've spoken with the council. You're fortunate that most of them felt you took the appropriate course in convincing Nashai to stay." He sniffed. "You will need to address the people as soon as possible regarding what happened—assure them their king is well, urge them not to panic, dispel the rumors. The usual. I will write it, and you will deliver it tomorrow, and you will say *nothing* apart from what I write."

Shara nodded, but unease misted around him. What was Gepar going to write? What if—

He batted the thought away. Gepar was right—he knew practically nothing. He wasn't the king, and it didn't matter what he thought. He'd already butted in too far, and what had that gotten them?

Three more days, that's what, said Korith's voice.

Shara rolled his eyes.

"What was that?"

"Nothing." He rubbed a hand over his face and pretended to be massaging away a headache.

On second thought, he wasn't pretending.

Gepar huffed. "Very well. Now go back to His Majesty's rooms." He shoved past Shara and out into the corridor. "And for goodness's sake, *stay there* this time."

CHAPTER 29

ASHES

Shara intended to fly all the way to Korith's apartment, but when his seabird eyes caught the sunspot cart on its usual street corner, he wheeled overhead and landed in a nearby alley. Between everything he'd been through today, everything he had to tell Korith, and everything they still needed to find, they'd likely be awake all night, and nothing would keep them going like warm, honey-soaked desserts.

Humans were odd, but they excelled at comforting foods.

Shifting amidst the late-evening shadows, he brushed at Iliath's travel-worn coat and raised the hood, enveloping himself in its miniature cave. Immediately his nerves settled, and as he slipped from the alley and down the street, he piled his troubles and fears and questions into the back corner of the cave. He left only a burning energy at the front, the force that kept him moving forward.

To think that this morning, his most pressing concern had been reciting Iliath's coronation vows properly and not tripping over his ceremonial garments.

Little clusters of people dotted the street like patches of

black on a piebald pony, each humming with low, intense conversation. Over and over, the same words. *Tethamari, assassination, attack, war, king, princess, coronation, dead.* One woman claimed her sister in the south had seen a fleet of Tethamari ships pass by not hours ago, while a man declared loudly that the whole thing was a ruse to justify raising taxes. In the sunspot line, a third speaker hoped for peace, only to be rebuked by a fourth, who called Iliath weak for having entertained the idea of peace in the first place.

Shara glanced over his shoulder to see whether number four was Gepar and rubbed his temples with a sigh. Was Gepar adhering to Iliath's wishes or accepting bribes and working against the Tethamari? Was Nashai trying to preserve peace or maneuvering herself into a place of power?

He wouldn't speculate based on so little information. He ought to have pressed for more.

Tomorrow. Tomorrow, he would talk to Nashai. Tonight, he needed Korith.

A basket of sunspots in hand, he left the cart. He had every intention of eating an entire stick's worth all at once, but mounting nausea stopped him after a single bite, and he returned the stick to the heaping pile. His body tingled at the currents of fear and anger rippling through the city, his confused instincts telling him both to flee and to prepare for a battle. Both urges protested when he merely continued walking. He had to. If he looked left or right or back or even down at his own feet, he would remember all the reasons he should stop.

"... third fight in the last hour," grumbled a man in a dishevelled patrol uniform to his companion. "Thought I'd be breaking up drunken coronation celebrations."

"Or *at* one."

Shara's shoulders slumped, and he held the sunspot basket

closer and drew in a deep breath of honey-scented air. Foolish as it was, the aroma represented everything good about Barath and its people. All the reasons he had to keep going. All the reasons he would miss it when . . . when . . .

He sniffed the sunspots again—with rather more determined concentration than the task required—then paused. Sniffed once more.

A familiar odor wafted down the street, sharp and warm. The scent drew him back to the mountains, to nights telling stories and singing his people's histories amidst the thick, swirling smoke of massive bonfires.

But no one built bonfires in the middle of a city.

Something nearby was on fire.

No sooner had the thought blossomed than a glider swept past, its pilot shouting to someone below. "It's the herbary!"

Shara's insides froze.

The herbary.

Korith.

Shara pelted down the street, feet pounding against the cobblestones, each thundering step shooting painfully up his legs. An orange glow peered over the rooftops like a miniature sun, growing brighter every second. Was Korith in his apartment now, unable to escape the flames? What if he—

He buried the thought and ran faster.

Again and again he shoved past people who moved so slowly they might have been statues and leapt around others who swerved into his path at precisely the wrong moment.

He was about to shift despite the delay it would cause when he careened around a corner and nearly crashed into the crowd gathered about the building. Firelight flickered across his vision, and he shrank back with a whimper, then steeled himself and shouldered his way forward.

"Korith!"

No response, only flames and shouted orders, smoke and bodies pressing against him . . .

"Korith!"

Sweat streaming down his face, he dashed into the empty space between the crowd and the burning house. Heat seared his skin, and his body thrilled in warning. Shift. Escape.

Instead he spun, searching the onlookers. Silver hair glinted in the firelight, but no Korith. No cheerful smile, no waving cane—

"Shara!"

Na Mithel barrelled into him and wrapped him in an embrace. The rest of the family gathered around them, all safe.

"We were so worried!" She stepped back to examine him. "Are you—"

"Korith," he blurted out, shoving the basket of sunspots into her arms. "Have you seen him?"

Her wide eyes darted to the building and back. "No, we— Shara!"

He'd nearly reached the door when a woman in a uniform caught his arm. "Young man, you need to—"

"Lord Aman—is he still in there?"

The officer yanked her sweat-soaked shirt from her neck and raised her hands as though trying to calm a spooked horse. "It's all right. Everyone from the shop is safe."

"He wasn't in the shop; he's up there!"

He pointed, and when the woman looked, he ran. *Please let him not be there.* Korith was expecting him, but he might have gone out for food or drink or to buy another pillow.

The foolish thought nearly made him stumble as emotion

welled in his throat. Pushing forward, he burst into the shop, and the cries from outside were swallowed in a rush of fire.

He'd caught a single look at a blazing bouquet of flowers when a groan and the horrendous sound of splintering wood echoed overhead, and the staircase came crashing down. Shara gasped, gagging on smoke and staggering back out the door.

A pair of hands seized him. "Reckless boy! Get back and stay out of the—"

He raked his claws over his captor's hand, and whoever it was cursed and released him. Again he ran, but this time up the street, away from the house and crowd. He tore down the first alley he came to. The air stank of refuse, but it was cool and free of smoke, and he drew several heaving breaths before slamming his eyes shut to shift. His limbs crackled like lightning, and he didn't waste energy cursing his lack of toresh or counting the heartbeats. Korith needed him to focus.

Dragon tail lashing, he launched into the air, beating his wings in fierce strokes until he hovered above the city. His stomach turned—flames and smoke poured from one side of the upper floor. The building was stone, but the roof and rafters and furniture were not.

He dove, bellowing into the night, and plunged through the window. Glass and pain and blazing heat exploded around him. Smoke clawed at his throat and eyes.

Flames engulfed half the room already—an oily scent suggested Korith's visitor had used something to help it along— and what wasn't burning lay in ruins. The Guide's shrine had been knocked over, the little malir table had lost two of its legs, and the portrait wall stood bare, all of Korith's effort and care chewed up and spat out into fluttering bits of charred paper.

And in the far corner, huddled between the bed and the wardrobe, slumped Korith, one hand pressing a wad of blue fabric over his mouth and nose, the other gripping the Guide figurine. Sweat soaked his body, and a dark stain spread beneath him.

"Shara." His eyes flooded with relief and fluttered closed. A weak swirl of wind magic vanished from around him, noticeable only in its sudden defeat.

Shara bounded forward, butted his nose against Korith's chest, and leapt away with a shriek. His cave-brother's torso was drenched with blood.

Don't panic, don't panic . . .

Trying to steady his trembling body, he tilted his head so Korith could grip his horns. Inch by inch, Korith dragged himself upright, yanking on Shara's head with every shuddering cough and gasp of pain.

"Sorry," he rasped.

Nostrils burning, his head smeared with Korith's blood, Shara buried the urge to be sick and growled reassuringly. Something behind them groaned, then crashed in a spray of golden sparks. Pain spiked up his tail, and he lurched out of the way. Korith staggered forward and knocked Shara's head against the bed frame.

"Sorry." He made a sound that might have been a laugh. "Now's me . . . apologizing . . ."

Stop talking. Muscles straining, Shara heaved him the rest of the way to his feet and sank into a crouch. Korith more fell than climbed onto his back, a blood-soaked weight that didn't move even when Shara tried for a deeper breath and convulsed with hacking coughs.

The smoke had thickened so much he could hardly see, and the heat seared his eyes when he dared open them. Giving up, he squeezed them shut and let a wisp of cooler, fresher air guide him toward the window. His rear foot rolled over something hard on the ground. A pencil.

He paused, jolting with sorrow and a stupid desire to rescue everything that hadn't burned, each pillow and pencil and even the piko seeds.

His first human home.

The weight of Korith's unmoving body pressed down on him, and the thought vanished. With a final lurch toward the cooler air, he climbed onto the sill and launched himself into the night.

CHAPTER 30

KEEP FIGHTING

Silence covered the healing room like a shroud.

Korith lay motionless on a bed in the far corner, stripped to the waist, his skin pink beneath the shining layer of salve Shara had applied. With nothing else to do, Shara stared at the long, ugly gash splitting Korith's side. Despite the ministrations of the elderly doctor cleaning the wound, it still trailed blood onto the bed's ivory blankets, and no matter how intently Shara stared and prayed, the cut refused to heal itself.

He didn't know the doctor's name, so he'd dubbed her Willow for the thick, bushy hair draping around her squat frame and the brusque manner that reminded him of his willow-alvithi grandmother. She hadn't said much except to issue a few hurried instructions and chide Shara for opening the window beside the bed. She'd not told him to close it, though, much to his relief. If he had to breathe in any more smoke or blood or stringent medicines, he might be sick.

As it was, he might be sick anyway.

Eyes stinging, he gripped his cave-brother's too-warm hand before clutching again at his mother's coat. Only after settling Korith on the bed had he recognized the blue fabric. Like everything else, it stank of blood and smoke, but in a few places, Korith's scent still clung to the fibers.

It was the only thing holding him aloft.

Aloft, but alone. Alone and small, like the figurine of the Guide Korith had been clutching. It sat on the bedside table now, still and watchful and as useless as Shara. But it, at least, represented someone good and powerful.

Eagle. Please.

"Green."

He handed Willow the green salve and forced himself to watch her apply it, keeping all his concentration on the path of her gnarled fingers along the wound, the way the sticky substance mingled with Korith's blood and—

No, he didn't want to focus on Korith's blood.

He didn't want to dwell on the fire, either, but it rose in his mind, and with it, the only solution he could think of—the attacker must have known Korith had Iliath's files. What other threat could he have posed? Unless someone had discovered his secret?

But Shara couldn't begin to guess who might be threatened by learning Korith was a Tear. The files, on the other hand . . . Either there had been something in them, or the attacker had feared there might be.

But now they were gone. Burned or stolen. Korith, on the other hand, was still here, his life hovering in uncertain skies.

Throat working, Shara clenched his fists around the coat and buried his face in its folds. His chest burned, each breath drawn as if from a mile away.

"Bandages."

Willow unwrapped the first of the long, white bandages and gestured to Shara, who set aside the coat and practically leapt forward, grateful for the distraction. Layer after layer,

Korith's wound disappeared beneath the unnaturally white, too-clean strips of fabric. Sedated with alsum, Korith stirred only once, his words raspy and unintelligible.

At last Willow stepped back to survey the results, then indicated the medicines cluttering the table. "I'm going to start cleaning the air in his lungs. While I do that, I need you to mix those."

Shara faltered, the shadows of his inadequacies suddenly looming larger than ever in the dim lantern light. Willow might remind him of his grandmother, but she didn't know his history with healing. "Are you sure? I'm not very good at—that is, my brother Shomar is much better at—"

"At putting herbs in a bowl?" She raised her bushy eyebrows. "There's nothing to be *better* at. I'll tell you the measurements; you put them in there."

He swallowed, his own throat still scratchy as his body healed itself. "All right."

"Good. Start with the blackroot shavings; that dish there. Two scoops."

He'd added the first when the telltale sting of magic bit at the tip of his tongue. Willow settled a hand gently against Korith's throat and suspended the other over his face. To Shara's horror, slender streams of sooty air began rising from Korith's mouth and nose.

"That's—"

"A spoonful of the elden powder."

She pointed, and Shara hastily added the second scoop of blackroot before moving on to the pale yellow elden.

He tried not to look at Korith while they worked, but his eyes kept catching the movement of the darkened air.

"He was smart to cover his face," Willow said, nodding toward the coat and guiding a plume of pure, clean air over Korith's mouth.

Even so, Shara couldn't quell his dismay every time another stream of smoke shadowed the air, a gathering storm determined to snuff out Korith's sunlight.

Think of something else. The assassin. Hands shaking, he poured water into the bowl of herbs and stirred them carefully. Who could have known about the files?

Immediately his heart grew heavy. Tishel knew. Gepar knew. Shara had blurted it out not hours ago. The guards standing outside the room might have heard, and given Korith's method of listening through walls, there was every possibility someone else had been doing the same.

Water sloshed over the edge of the bowl. Was this his fault?

"Careful." Willow steadied his trembling hand before he dumped any more herb concoction on the floor. "Your friend needs that."

"Right," he mumbled. *Needs that, but not me.*

A whimper climbed up his throat as his eyes settled on Korith. And then it wasn't Korith but Omatha, another victim of his carelessness, his mistakes.

But Omatha was alvithi. Alvithi healing couldn't fix Korith.

Neither could Shara. He couldn't fix anything.

Teveth.

He sagged against the table. He was so tired of this feeling, this pervasive ache, like having Korith's illness in his soul instead of his body. So tired of that word. Hearing it, saying it, thinking it. Being it. Maybe if he said it aloud, Korith would sit up and correct him in that infuriatingly positive tone, and everything would be fine. Actually fine. The fine of sunspots and a cool afternoon breeze off the bay, of sunlight on his wings and Korith whooping into the air while Shara dove in a daring spiral.

A choked sob escaped into the stillness. "Is he going to be all right?"

Willow accepted the bowl of steeping herbs, and at her direction, a fine mist rose from the surface and travelled through the air to Korith, disappearing down his nose and mouth.

"I'm hopeful, but I can't say for sure," she said after a pause. "I've cleared as much soot as I can, and this"—she indicated the herb mist—"will soothe any burns and reduce swelling in his throat. He's breathing well, all things considered, and most of his burns are superficial and could have been much worse. There is still the blood loss and the possibility of poisoned air from the fire, though."

From somewhere in the middle of a vast hollow, Shara heard himself say, "Oh."

He didn't dare ask her to elaborate or guess at Korith's chances of recovery. In this case, Korith had the right idea: stubborn optimism.

"You should rest," Willow told him, moving another cloud of mist toward Korith. "Thank you for your help, but I can manage alone from here. I promise I'll do everything I can for him."

He hesitated, then shook his head. His chest constricted at the thought of remaining all night in this room, waiting in uncertainty, but if the assassin suspected Korith had survived . . . "I can't. Thank you, but I have to stay."

Willow glanced between him and Korith, her head tilted in thought. "You think they'll come and finish him."

Shara's blood went cold, and his claws shot from his fingers. "How do you—"

"No need to worry." She raised her hands, placating, and gestured to Korith. "I know wounds, that's all. That cut? These marks on his arm? He was attacked, no question. Fought back, too."

The adrenaline drained as quickly as it had come, and Shara slumped against the wall, gaze clinging to Korith while he tried not to picture the scene.

"You can stay if you want, but you should know I spent thirty years as a medic in the navy and fifteen before that as a sailor." She jerked her head toward the table, where several knives glinted amidst the supplies. "Your friend is safe with me."

Her words settled into the room's heavy silence, at once a reassurance and a dismissal. Shara's gaze strayed from the door to Korith, and isolation threatened to smother him. He might still have Gepar and Tishel, but without Korith . . .

No. Korith would be fine. Shara would come back tomorrow and find him awake and recovering and—selfish though the thought was—ready to offer advice and encouragement again.

Until then, Shara would have to make do with his heart and instincts.

He pushed himself upright. Staring down at his cave-brother, he traced the Eagle's sign over Korith's chest and gripped his hand again, squeezing hard in case Korith could feel it. *Keep fighting, you molting idiot.*

He nodded to Willow. "Thank you."

"Go and rest." She patted his arm.

He pulled the coat from the bed and slipped it on, ignoring the blood staining one sleeve. With a last look at Korith, he turned to the door, mind already churning.

He had no intention of resting.

CHAPTER 31

DIFFERENT

Halfway through the night, Shara remembered the blood trail from the throne room, driven from his thoughts by his confrontation with Gepar and everything that had happened since.

Beating his falcon wings, he shrieked with relief at having a new scent to follow and wheeled back toward the palace. His search had gotten him nowhere. He'd scoured warehouses, light towers, a few abandoned buildings, even a rocky cave. No sign of a missing prince anywhere, nor even whispers or suspicious behavior from people nearby.

What did the kidnapper want? Why had there been neither a demand for ransom nor any attempt to expose Shara as an impostor?

Why kidnap a prince but try to publicly assassinate his replacement?

Shara couldn't see how the two fit together, but at this hour, he couldn't see much of anything beyond the palace walls rising ahead, silvery grey in the moonlight.

A window near the throne room jutted outward a few

inches, and he pushed his way through the crack and hopped to the floor, his talons chittering on the slippery stone. Regaining his balance, he shifted into a cat, shoving aside the memory of the last time he'd worn this form.

The hall stretched silently into shadows, the portraits on the walls reigning over an empty domain. Iliath's family, all gone now. Just like Iliath himself. Shara kept to the wall, pausing frequently to listen. Some reckless part of him, still boiling with images of Korith's battered body, imagined a contingent of dark-clad, prince-kidnapping assassins creeping around the corner, and there he was, bursting with unprecedented toresh into dragon form to confront them. To end this.

Almost a shame he didn't eat humans . . .

At last he reached the room where the blood trail ended. When he'd taken his human form again, he settled a trembling hand on the door handle, trying to steady his heartbeat—and his expectations.

The door swung silently inward. Bulky shapes hovered at the edges of his straining vision, but though he opened the door wider, there was little light to let in. Cautiously, he moved forward, and his toes bumped into something soft on the floor. A seat cushion.

A weight settled on his chest. If this trail went cold, he'd take the cushion to Korith. The start of a new pillow collection.

Maybe there were art supplies in here, too.

Blinking his damp eyes rapidly, he took another step, and gradually he made sense of the angles and edges. Neat stacks of chairs lined the wall to his left, and a cluster of carts sat parked to the right, stripped of their heavy, decorative drapes. Beyond spread darkness and the sense of entering a vast cave, its dimensions impossible to determine. Its purpose, however, seemed clear: storage.

Shara stared into the emptiness, feeling confused, disappointed, and finally stupid.

Just a servant with a bad cut. No doubt any number of sharp objects dwelt in this room.

Chest tight, he retreated and shut the door, but his feet wouldn't move. Almost without thinking, he opened it again.

"Iliath?" His voice hissed over the objects.

No response.

Had he truly expected one? What kidnapper would lock an abducted prince in a storage closet for a week?

But he had nowhere else to look, so he hurried up the hall toward the nearest corridor, its entrance glowing a faint orange. He grabbed the first lit torch he found and turned back. Flames flickered before him, ruining his night eyes and flooding his senses with the scent of oil, the hot sting of fire, the thunder of crashing rafters, the shouts of people watching a building burn . . .

His hand tightened around the torch, and he thrust it as far from himself as he could.

Ducking into the storage room, he shut the door behind himself and moved cautiously forward, torch lifted. His instincts had been right—a massive space spread before him, packed with all manner of furniture and other accessories. Vases and platters, candlesticks and torches, chairs and desks, tablecloths and cushions and mirrors, all shifting eerily in the wavering light.

Shaking off the urge to explore, he crouched and planted a hand on the cold stone. There! A red-brown drop, another, another—then nothing. He shoved the torch closer.

"Where are you?"

He closed his eyes and trailed his fingers along the floor, over the textured stone, into the groove between two tiles. Still nothing. Nothing but—

Footsteps.

He lurched to his feet and whirled, fire raking over his face. The footsteps grew louder, and he spun silently, pulse racing, eyes searching. Something to duck behind, somewhere that would hide the torchlight.

He was sidling toward a wardrobe when the door swung open.

"Don't move."

That voice. Familiar, yet bitingly cold. "Tishel?"

Step by step, she moved into the room. Her eyes narrowed against the firelight, but the pistol aimed at his heart didn't waver. "Who's there?"

Gunfire barked in his memory. "It—it's Shara."

She inched closer, appraising him icily. The weapon didn't lower. "What was I carrying the first time we met?"

"What—"

"Answer me."

He flinched at the acid in her voice. "Flowers. Yellow ones. You said they made you sneeze."

You gave them to Korith.

She stepped more fully into the firelight, and Shara's breath caught. Dishevelled hair framed her drawn face, and dark makeup streaked messily beneath her damp eyes. With every flicker of light and shadow, she seemed to grow older, the lines in her face deeper, darker.

She looked exhausted. Empty.

Broken.

"Tishel, what—" Horror swept over him, and he gripped the wardrobe for balance. "He's not . . ."

"No." Her arm dropped as though dragged down by the weight of her pistol, and she sucked in a shuddering breath. "No, he's . . . he's too stubborn to die." The emptiness in her eyes began to blaze. "Too stubborn." She rammed the pistol into its holster. "And reckless. And *stupid*. And—"

She whirled and kicked the nearest chair, which fell to its side with a feeble clatter. Tishel stared at it, stricken, her body rigid yet trembling all over. Her ragged breaths hissed into the room.

The torch wavered in Shara's grip. "Amazing."

"What?"

"Too amazing to die," he managed thickly. "That's what he'd say."

She pressed a fist to her mouth, but it couldn't stifle her high, strangled keen. Her watery eyes unfocused, and she shook her head slowly. "He asked me to come," she whispered. "Come have dinner with him and talk, and then sift through all of those files with the two of you. For once, he wanted *my* help." Her expression broke. "And I said no."

Shara's heart wrenched, and he took a tentative step toward her.

Inch by inch, her shoulders fell from their hunch, and after a long silence, she cleared her throat and turned, smoothing her uniform in a businesslike manner. "What happened?"

Even more than her anguish, her familiar determination to bury her emotions convinced him of her sincerity. He explained it all, even his guilty fear that someone had been listening at the wall or door when he'd told her and Gepar about the files. He mentioned how the assassin's face had appeared to him at the coronation and shared Korith's wind sense theory. Tishel listened without interruption, her expression growing darker and her teeth grinding audibly.

When he finished, she merely nodded. The military captain accepting a report from a subordinate, forming her own theories, making her own plans—alone. "Thank you for saving him." Her words were almost calm.

He adjusted his grip on the torch. "Thank you for not shooting me."

Perhaps she heard his underlying question, for she gave a weak shrug. "After seeing him, I couldn't imagine . . . That is, I wasn't tired. Thought I'd search the throne room again. I saw the light beneath the door, and you . . . you looked different."

"Different?" He peered down at himself. "Oh, right."

She shook her head, firelight glinting off her spectacles. "Not like that. It's . . ." She folded her arms and pursed her lips. "Never mind. What are *you* doing here?"

Warmth crept up his neck, but he told her anyway, walking her toward the carts and pointing to where the trail stopped. Rather than scoff and tell him to go back to Iliath's rooms, she crouched and traced her fingers over the floor, shoving the carts aside one by one. Their wheels creaked out a discordant song as they rolled.

Shara squirmed. His discovery didn't deserve this much attention. "I'm probably building a dragon from a flea, but I couldn't think of anything else to do."

She pulled herself to her feet, a long, curved piece of glass in her hand. Orange light glinted along its razor edges. "Shattered vase. The rest is down there, shoved under that shelf."

". . . oh." The longer he stared, the more he deflated, but somehow he made his next words sound careless. "Just a servant with a bad cut."

Never had he been so disappointed to be right.

"Mm." Tishel set the glass on the nearest cart and eyed him shrewdly. "It was a good instinct, though, especially since we don't know where the rest of the assassins escaped to. Everything looks to be in place, but . . ." She took the torch and advanced into the room.

He watched her without following. That possibility hadn't

even occurred to him. Nothing had occurred to him—just desperation, some foolish desire to do something right.

You tried, anyway. It was a feeble Korith thought, but Korith was too busy fighting for his life to offer something better.

Tishel spent less than a minute looking for indications that someone had rushed into the room to hide, then returned and passed the torch back to Shara, a strange look in her eyes.

He'd never known her to comfort him, or anyone, but the fear that she might try sent him hastening for the door. "Well, I suppose we should go."

Instead of following, she leaned against a stack of chairs. "Go back to our rooms, lie awake in our beds, and think about how badly we're failing, you mean?"

Shara cringed, but she wasn't mocking him. Not only him, anyway. "I'm sure *you're* not failing."

A harsh laugh grated through the darkness. "You aren't Lord Aman. You don't have to lie to me about how well I'm doing and how brilliant a captain I am and how . . . how I . . ." Her voice splintered, sharp and brittle as the broken vase, and she stared at her feet. Her jaw clenched. "Lord Gepar is right."

Shara lurched as though he'd caught fire. "No he's not."

Her gaze snapped to him. "Oh no? Let's see, shall we?" She held up a hand and began counting on her fingers. "Lady Malothi is dead. Lord Aman was nearly killed. The Tethamari interrogation went nowhere except to start fights and strain relationships even more. And oh, maybe you haven't noticed, but the assassins escaped and the *real* Iliath is still missing."

"Well, yes, but . . ." If the right words lay in this room, they were as hidden as everything else. "But you're still searching, and—"

"And what?" Firelight flickered in her eyes. "It might surprise you to learn that it's nearly impossible to organize a search for someone when you're the only person who knows he's missing.

We've combed the city, I've spoken to every contact I have, yet we're no nearer to finding him now than on the night he was abducted. Hills, he could be dead too for all we know!"

"Don't," he croaked. "Don't say that."

A thread of regret twisted within Tishel's unravelling emotions. She uncapped her flask and had raised it halfway to her mouth when her hand stalled. Eyes glazing, she peered down at the glinting metal box. Once, twice, she swirled the contents, wafting the aroma of chocolate between them.

"He trusted me." Her voice was bitter and resigned, yet somehow pleading. "Everyone said Isith was a fool to have made me captain. But even with all the rumors about why he did it, Iliath didn't replace me. He trusted me. And now . . ."

It hit Shara like a dozen neeka. Her constant attempts to keep Korith away, her determined formality . . . It wasn't *Korith* she was ashamed of.

"And now," he managed past the wad of fur lodged in his throat, "you're going to prove them all wrong."

And prove yourself *wrong.*

She laughed grimly. "You remind me of Iliath sometimes, you know. When you're not dealing with politics or nobles or other things that actually matter."

"You matter."

She stiffened and stared at him through the torchlight. Shara held her gaze.

Silence swallowed the room but for the scrape of her nails over a chair's fraying upholstery and the creaking of wood when she pushed herself upright. She drew a deep breath, and with the barest glance at Shara, she crossed to the door and pulled it open. "You're not slouching."

"What?"

"That's why you look different."

The door closed behind her before he could respond.

$$
\text{CHAPTER 32}
$$

PERFUMES

Shara rolled over, squinted into early-morning twilight, and rolled the other way. For the first time, he'd managed to sleep soundly in Iliath's bed and form. Exhaustion and distress had stripped away all his discomfort, and he'd fallen asleep almost immediately, face buried in one of the squashy pillows.

Perhaps Korith had a point about pillows.

Korith.

He jolted upright, then flopped back to his stomach. Half of him needed to see Korith *now*, but the stronger half held him paralyzed and dreading what he'd find.

Memories of last night swarmed around his groggy mind, and his gaze strayed to his mother's coat, now draped over the back of a chair. Gratitude warmed his heart. Korith had probably just grabbed the first thing he could find, but he'd saved Shara's coat nevertheless. Shara prayed the coat had saved Korith in turn.

One hundred seventeen ticks of Iliath's obnoxious timekeeper later, he shoved himself out of bed. The cold air streaming through the open window bowled over him, and he drew a bracing breath before moving to the wardrobe.

He dressed without thinking, using yesterday's bandages to secure a small, rough piece of wood from the fire against his "wound." It rubbed uncomfortably as he rolled his arm, and he winced. Good. No hint of miraculous healing.

The fish and rodents he'd eaten during last night's search of the city were long past, but his nervous stomach wouldn't tolerate food right now. After a final look in the mirror, he slipped into the hall. The guards chorused a rather sleepy "Your Majesty," and one followed as Shara set off into the royal maze.

The palace still slept, blanketed in the hush of morning and streaked with pale light. He'd always preferred nights—stars ornamenting the sky, wind fluttering over his wings, drops of moonlight pooling in the mountain lakes. But morning over Barath's hills and shores had a peace of its own.

Until someone careened around a corner, slammed into him, and toppled over with a spectacular crash.

"Your Majesty!" A frightened, tea-drenched girl stared up at him from amidst the remains of the breakfast set she'd been carrying. "Your Majesty, I'm so sorry, I was— Princess Nashai, she's—that is, her quarters—I mean, I was . . ."

"Slow down." Shara pulled her to her feet. "Are you all right?"

"Yes. I'm so sorry." She brushed at her sopping skirt, cheeks reddening. "I was delivering breakfast to the princess, but when I arrived, her quarters were . . . were in ruins." Her wide eyes met his. "And she's gone!"

His insides froze. Not again.

He sprinted away, shouting "Stay and help her!" over his shoulder. It worked as well as he'd expected, and soon the guard's heavy footfalls and clattering weaponry were screaming their progress to the entire palace. It didn't matter—if they got there soon enough, Shara might be able to catch a scent and pursue it.

He wouldn't lose someone else.

And yet the halls seemed to have lengthened and grown more tortuous. Had they put the Tethamari at the other end of the palace on purpose?

Huffing, he rounded the last corner and staggered to some semblance of a dignified run as two Tethamari guards pivoted to face him.

"Your Majesty," said one rather reluctantly.

Shara was about to chew through them for letting their princess be kidnapped when a head peered through the nearest door. "Iliath?"

"*Nashai.*" Swallowing a relieved laugh, he darted forward and seized her hands, then checked his movement. Humans didn't sniff each other, and if he got any closer, she'd think he was trying something else.

Clearing her throat, she tugged her hands free and backed away a step, twisting the ring on her finger. Her expression became more formal. "Thank you for coming so quickly."

"Ah . . . sure. I mean, you're welcome." No doubt whoever she'd sent to his rooms was still on their way there. "What happened?"

She wrapped her arms around herself and adjusted her coat as though chilled. "I didn't sleep well and thought I would take a walk in your gardens. I left perhaps half an hour ago with my guards and Ter—Lady Masar. When I returned, my rooms . . . Well, come see for yourself."

The suite's design mirrored Iliath's, and they'd gone only a few paces into the outer room when the stinging stench of mingled perfumes crawled down Shara's nostrils and throat like a living creature. Gagging, he clapped a hand over his mouth and fought to keep his eyes from shutting.

First smoke, now perfume. He might never breathe freely again.

Grimacing as well, Nashai led him further inside, where Lady Masar waited with the Tethamari advisors in what remained of the room.

Shara stared, horrified. The blankets on the bed had been ripped away and slashed in a random, angry pattern. A shattered vase of flowers lay in a puddle of water at the base of an overturned table, and broken teacups spread like deadly crystals across the rug. A painting had been pulled from the wall and its frame broken, the wooden pieces sharp with splinters. Nashai's clothing littered every inch of the floor; some pieces bore the same knife marks as the bed and blankets.

"Your Majesty!" Three more Barathi guards burst through the doors. The first recoiled and coughed into her sleeve before asking, "Are you all right, my lord?"

Was *he* all right? What would the intruder have done to Nashai if she'd been here?

The idea hardened within him. "You." He pointed to the guard who had followed him from his rooms. "Go back and find the servant we ran into. Make sure she's all right and see whether she noticed anything suspicious or unusual. And be nice about it," he added awkwardly as the man departed. When no one questioned this order, he nodded at one of the new arrivals. "You, search these rooms."

"We've already done that," Nashai assured him.

"Unless you expect to find another conveniently dead Tethamari on which to pin this attack," Lord Fethan added coolly.

Shara narrowly swallowed a snarl. Would the man sound so snide if the next conveniently dead Tethamari was Nashai?

Before he could quell his anger, the clap of footsteps on stone accompanied Tishel into the room. One look assured him that Korith was still alive. A second promised death if Shara so much as breathed in a manner that hinted at their conversation in the storage room.

"What happened?"

Nashai repeated her story while Shara moved methodically around the room. His head throbbed, and he fought the temptation to shut his eyes and cover his mouth with his sleeve. Oily flowers and pines and—was that musk?

Focus. Think. But he only thought of more questions. Was this a threat? A warning? Retaliation?

He paused in the doorframe and traced his finger along the place where the lock slid into the wall. "Did you leave the doors unlocked?"

She shook her head. "Not this one. But your servants usually bring my breakfast around this time, so I left the outer one open."

Shara had not yet succumbed to the urge to kick open a door, but he could guess what it would look like. "Then someone had a key."

"Or picked the lock," Lady Oshari offered.

Nashai's brow furrowed. "Took the care to pick the lock but then did all this?"

Shara didn't dare ask what picking a lock meant. He could guess, anyway, so instead he nodded. His head pounded harder, and the urge to be sick welled up stronger than ever. Trying to maintain dignity, he gestured toward the hall. "Could we discuss this outside?"

"Where it smells better? Please."

They pooled into the hall. Free of the cloying aroma, Shara drew a deep breath, and his hope of following the trail of perfumes disappeared. Everything still stank—the corridor, the guard breezing past him, Lady Masar, his own clothing. As if someone had painted the insides of his nostrils with perfumes.

Exactly how unhuman would it be to try cleaning them out?

Probably not the best idea while surrounded by people. Especially since a small crowd had gathered as well. Some collected at the end of the hall to watch the commotion; a few ambled too-casually past, craning their necks to peer inside Nashai's rooms. And—Shara's gut clenched—there stood Faresh, slouched against the wall and studying the activity with amusement.

It took everything Shara had not to charge up and sniff him.

Instead he spun and ushered Nashai in the opposite direction, forcing himself not to look back. At the end of the hall, he shoved open a window, and he, Nashai, and Lady Masar drew a collective breath. Then another, and another.

"I apologize," Nashai said, rubbing her temples. "They were left in my room as a gift. It seems I didn't shove them far enough out of sight."

There. Nashai hated perfumes. Proof she was trustworthy.

Sweet, cool air rolled over them, and slowly Shara's head stopped pounding. Outside, a pair of squirrel-dragons chased each other in looping flight, chittering loudly in friendly challenge. Out of the corner of his eye, he glimpsed Lady Masar glancing between them and him, a shy yet awed smile on her flushed face.

Then Nashai had told her. She knew he wasn't Iliath.

It felt suddenly that the whole world was watching him. He tried to slouch and stand straight at the same time; the opposing movements sent him wobbling, and he gave up and began pacing instead, raking his hand through his tangled hair.

What now? He'd promised Nashai he'd do everything he could to preserve peace, but what *could* he do?

His feet dragged. "I'm sorry, Your Highness," he said,

trusting Lady Masar to sign his words while he paced and stared at the floor.

"For?"

"For everything. Yesterday you agreed to give me a chance, but I spent all night tracking boar and swallowing air, and now . . ." Embarrassment boiled beneath his kingly clothing as Lady Masar faltered. "Sorry, I wasn't actually — It's, uh . . ."

"Alvithi," Nashai supplied. "Which you are. There's no need to apologize for it. Nor for this."

He pivoted midstride to hide a squirm. It was like Korith had sent a replacement. "But I'm sure you're used to dealing with people who aren't floundering and overwhelmed and constantly falling out of the sky."

She smiled wryly. "My family rules Tethamar. I live surrounded by administrators and servants and guards. We are all of us floundering and overwhelmed. That doesn't make you less capable." She shot a pointed look at Lady Masar, like a scolding teacher whose student hadn't yet grasped an oft-repeated lesson. "Or less anything."

And another pivot. "That's easy for you to say."

Her snort was so unprincesslike that he grinned despite himself. "I require an interpreter in order to have a conversation with more than one person. Even with one, sometimes. I've practiced lip-reading for nearly fifteen years but still regularly ask people to repeat themselves. I came to Barath as a negotiator, and instead I'm facing assassins who may be my own people. And now someone's trying to get me to raise sail and run."

Shara's surreptitious glance down the hall revealed that Faresh was gone, so he gestured toward her quarters. "Any ideas who?"

She folded her arms and bit her lip. "If someone wanted me dead, I would be. No assassin sneaks into a room, finds it empty, and takes out their frustration on the room instead. I expect it's someone angry about yesterday, but that could be anyone in Barath. Or"—she broke into a grin—"perhaps it's Teren trying to convince me to flee to safety."

"Excuse me." Lady Masar planted her hands on her hips. "I was in the gardens with you, remember? And if I wanted you to flee to safety, I'd drug your tea and make Captain Sothal carry you."

"Again."

"Oh, let it go. There were pirates. Anyway, it wasn't me this time. Besides, you gave your word that we'd stay and help end this."

Shara's footsteps faltered, and he faced Nashai directly. "You don't have to, though," he said, little though he wanted to. "After what just happened, you don't have to stay."

She fixed him in a thoughtful gaze, twisting the signet ring on her finger around, around. "But you feel you do," she said, "though you are not Barathi, nor even human. You said you're falling out of the sky, but you keep flying all the same."

His face burned. Her tone, her expression, Lady Masar's subtly admiring gaze, like they considered him some sort of selfless, unyielding hero.

"I hope I get to meet you when this is all over," Nashai went on before he could explain the truth. "As you, that is. I expect it'll be a relief to be yourself again."

"Uh." His voice came out as a pathetic, rasping croak, and he cleared his throat and tried again. "Yes. That'll be . . . nice. Meeting you, I mean. As me." An idea sprang to mind—a chance for a different topic and for answers. "Perhaps I could come to the wedding."

"Oh, that would be lovely!" A wide smile lit her face but wavered almost immediately. "Assuming Iliath still wants . . . Assuming he's even . . ."

Lady Masar settled a hand on Nashai's arm. Shara cringed, then frowned. That flutter of surprised happiness, broken so quickly by fear and doubt. If she'd already been rethinking the marriage, surely she wouldn't be so—

His breath caught. "Your Highness, you said you put those perfumes somewhere out of sight?"

"I put them in the far corner of my dressing table. More out of reach than sight." Her eyes widened. "You think someone smashed them on purpose. Because of you."

He tilted his head up the hall. "Did you tell your advisors? About me?"

She pursed her lips. "You think they did it to make us look like victims." Her braids swished as she shook her head. "To be honest, I wouldn't be surprised if that were the case, but no, I didn't tell them. Only Teren."

Something heavy settled in his stomach, and he nodded grimly. "Then I need to visit *my* advisor."

CHAPTER 33

AGREEMENTS AND ALLIES

There was something satisfying about pounding on doors. Shara did it several times before Gepar deigned to answer. The man's eyes widened, and his hand slipped from where it had braced against the doorframe. "Your Majesty."

His voice wavered, hushed and almost reverent, and for a second, Shara forgot why he'd come and what he'd been about to say.

Gepar's expression pinched. "Oh, it's still—" His eyes snagged on the guards flanking Shara, and he dipped into a bow. Water droplets glistened in his damp hair. "That is, please come in, my king."

He bowed Shara into the room and closed the door firmly before crossing to the desk. Shara stared after him. Had he actually believed . . . ?

He shook off the alarming thought and looked around. The office might have been an overstocked bookstore. Dark-stained shelves stuffed with pristine tomes lined the walls and blocked most of the window, but the books didn't stop there. They'd spilled onto every available surface, collecting in tidy piles on tables, chairs, and nearly the entire floor.

Shara picked his way along a narrow, book-free trail and stopped before the desk, where Gepar had stationed himself like a soldier mounting a final defense against an invading army. Gesturing stiffly for Shara to sit, he began opening drawers at random. A worn carving of a dog wobbled atop the nearest stack of books as if to call attention to how little it belonged in this room.

Shara knew how it felt, and rather than sit, he drew a deep breath. His nostrils stung, and his already-pounding heart beat faster. But though he'd gone so long without a victory, this one felt hollow. Malothi dead, Korith healing, and now here sat Gepar, reeking of perfumes.

How quickly he was running out of allies.

"I expect you're here for your speech," Gepar said lightly.

Speech?

He'd forgotten it completely, and it said something about everything else bearing down on him that the idea of learning a speech and reciting it before an entire city sounded like a welcome relief.

Gepar extracted a piece of paper from beneath a stack of books and pushed it at him. Cramped, angular writing covered about half of it, full of words like *attack* and *security*, *strength* and *coronation*. "You will deliver that at noon from the north balcony. I will come fetch you shortly before that. I suggest you spend the morning learning it."

"I will."

"Good. Now if you'll excuse me, I have work to do." He gestured dismissively at the door and, without a second glance at Shara, resumed searching his drawers.

Shara didn't move. He folded the speech into a little square and tucked it into his coat, fighting the urge to strip the garment off. How could anyone work in this room? Warm, stifling air hung thick around him, sharp with the scent of Gepar's familiar soap and traces of the perfumes he'd not been able to wash away.

His hands fisted, and a different sort of heat engulfed him. "Why did you do it?"

Gepar leaned back in his chair. "Why did I do what?" he asked, each word clipped and precise. Despite the tautness of his muscles, a smug superiority tugged at his mouth and flickered in his eyes, Faresh-like.

Shara didn't have time to be intimidated. "You know what." He gripped the back of the chair as images of Nashai's ruined suite rolled over him like perfumes. "Why did you break into Nashai's rooms and destroy them? Your king wanted peace with Tethamar, and you—"

"My king." Gepar gave a high laugh and pushed to his feet. "You think you can stand there in his body and appeal to my loyalty to *my king*? You think because you look like him, I am beholden to you, duty-bound to answer your meddling questions?"

"I only—"

"I am advisor to the king! In case you've forgotten, *you* answer to *me*. I owe you no explanation, no matter how long you stand there pretending to be someone important and looking at me with that unnatural alvithi stare."

Shara's gaze dropped before he could stop it. Gritting his teeth, he pinned it back on Gepar, holding steady as long as he could. "I need to know who my allies are. And why one of them smells like perfumes."

Face sour, Gepar spun with a scoff and stared out the sliver of window not hidden behind a bookshelf.

"This is about Faresh, isn't it? You let me think the agreement you and Nashai were discussing was the marriage, but it was Faresh. Nashai wants him back, treaty or not. A sign of good faith. You said no, so she thinks he's bribing you."

Gepar whirled. "He is *not* bribing me!"

Shara stumbled back. Wild anger twisted Gepar's expression, and the venom in his voice left no room for falsehood. For a heartbeat, Shara feared he'd been wrong yet again, but then it hit him. "He's threatening you."

Gepar crumpled. His shoulders slumped and his head hung, and when he braced himself against his desk, the whole thing trembled along with its owner. "You wouldn't understand."

Heat pooled in Shara's chest. "Wouldn't understand being trampled on?"

"Wouldn't understand why—"

"I might if you explained it. I'm not as hopeless as you think, you know." His mind stalled over the unexpected words, and the next ones tumbled out without thought. "But if you prefer, I can find Tishel and Nashai, and they can explain it to me."

Gepar's glower travelled over Shara, toured the room, and landed again on Shara. After a long stillness, he pushed himself upright, desk creaking under his weight. He spent a long time straightening his garments, but at last he folded his hands and, with obvious effort at control, said, "The circumstances are none of your affair, but suffice to say that I fell into debt to Faresh. When I could no longer pay, I . . ." His throat worked. "You will recall a conversation we had at the treasury regarding duplicate receipts."

Shara's eyes flew wide. "You—"

"Yes," Gepar snapped. The veins in his hands stood out as his fingers twitched through an angry spell. "You needn't say it."

"Sorry."

He drew a raspy breath. "I took the money to Faresh, but he guessed where it had come from. He threatened to expose me unless I convinced Iliath not to send him back to Tethamar.

Yesterday, as you've guessed, I spoke to Nashai about the matter. She suggested instead that Barath could demonstrate our commitment to peace by handing Faresh over when she departs."

"So you ruined her suite in the hopes that she'd flee and forget to take Faresh?"

"I was desperate." His gaze darted about the room, part fury and part terror. "He'd already made his threat clear, but last night he . . ."

Pity rippled through Shara. Not even Gepar deserved to be toyed with by Faresh. Biting his lip, he let his gaze trail over the desk, the books, the little dog. Hissing sharply, Gepar yanked the figurine off the pile and stuffed it out of sight. As if Shara might judge him for the one thing here that made him approachable.

"Lord Gepar?" Tishel's voice sounded over the rapping of her knuckles against the door.

Gepar stiffened. "If you breathe a word of this . . . Yes, come in."

Shara swallowed a promise he wasn't sure he should make and turned to greet Tishel.

"Your Majesty." She glanced between them. "I take it you've been apprised of the situation, my lord?"

Gepar twitched.

"We've had no luck identifying or finding the invader, but we're investigating who had access to keys to that room. I also have servants cleaning the room and others helping Nashai move to new quarters. And I've set additional guards around the area. Her advisors weren't particularly pleased, but they didn't argue."

"Good." Gepar wrung his hands. "Good."

Tishel's lips parted, and her brow furrowed. She peered

questioningly at Shara, who did his best to look lost. Odd having to fake it for once.

"Well." She adjusted her spectacles. "Now that everything is mostly settled, I've informed the Tethamari that we will be searching their ship. Nashai and her advisors have insisted on coming, of course."

"Very well," Gepar said. "I will accompany you. Shara will remain here. He has a speech to learn."

He frowned at Shara, half command, half fearful anticipation. Oddly, though, Shara didn't feel like protesting. Eating breakfast, visiting Korith, and learning the speech in the stillness of the gardens sounded much more appealing than scuttling around a ship dodging Gepar's warning scowls and listening to Nashai's advisors exchange snide remarks.

"I'll go back to my rooms, then."

"His Majesty's rooms," Gepar muttered. He cast a final glance at the drawer where he'd stuffed the little dog before sweeping after Tishel.

As Shara made to follow, Gepar held out an arm to block his path. Pulling the door shut, he braced himself in front of it. His hands had stopped twitching.

"Who your allies are," he said quietly, "depends entirely on whether you keep your mouth shut and remember who *you* are. It would be most unfortunate if it were discovered that an alvithi had disposed of our king and attempted to take his place."

A chill shot up Shara's spine.

"That," Gepar growled, jabbing Shara's chest where he'd tucked the speech, "and nothing else."

Then he stepped into the hall and strode after Tishel.

CHAPTER 34

ANSWERS

To Shara's immense relief, the speech didn't contain any-thing worrisome. Nor did it take as long to learn as he'd expected, so he left the gardens and headed off to see Korith, pausing at Iliath's rooms to collect another bowl of dried fruit and the king's now-incomplete malir set. He waited while Amesal informed one of the warmongering merchants that His Majesty was unavailable, listened until the angry foot-steps faded entirely, and snuck back into the hall with a grateful smile at his secretary.

He left his guard standing outside the healing room with the two others Tishel had stationed there. He wasn't going to visit Korith while royal guards watched awkwardly from the corners.

Korith was still asleep, resting under the influence of an-other dose of alsum. Little though he wanted to be anywhere near that stench, Shara set the board on the bedside table and laid out the pieces as the Guide figurine watched.

"You first," he said quietly.

He drifted the length of the room, his mother's coat swishing around him. It probably looked odd over Iliath's royal clothing, but he didn't care. It made him feel less alone.

As he walked, he practiced the speech aloud, refusing to let either his footsteps or his voice falter. If he paused even a moment, Gepar's threat would catch up to him and drag him down into the mire. Betrayal, indignation, uncertainty—he could roll in all of those after they found Iliath.

Two days.

He tripped over nothing and caught himself against the wall, then forced his feet to move again.

But after a dozen rounds about the room, he could no longer ignore the fact that the words he was rehearsing were Gepar's as well, and the rest of their conversation sank its claws into him.

Keep your mouth shut and remember who you are.

Shara almost scoffed. How could he forget?

Giving up, he returned to Korith and removed all the game pieces from the board.

"You'd have lost anyway," he told his cave-brother, setting the board aside. "All right. This." He lifted the magician and put it in the center of the table. "This is me. This"—the prince—"is you."

He placed Prince Korith beside the magician and knocked it on its side. Might as well be accurate.

The lady became Nashai, the unicorn Lady Masar. The two soldiers were Tishel and Thosena. The black bull for Faresh, the red one for Gepar, and the butterflies for Oshari and Fethan.

Piece by piece, he positioned them at various points around the table. He clustered Tishel and Thosena together and reluctantly added Gepar. On second thought, he removed Thosena because she didn't know his secret. But did that mean Nashai and Lady Masar should join Tishel and Gepar? No, Thosena should remain. But then it was Tethamari against Barathi, the very conflict he wanted to avoid. He could organize them based on trustworthiness—it would be satisfying to knock Faresh off the table and watch Gepar teeter on the edge—but that would be guesswork and wishful thinking more than fact.

Never mind that he had a whole collection of unused pieces. The palace staff, the entirety of Barath, all of Tethamar. Lady Pareth, the two merchants, the sunspot vendor. People he'd never spoken to, with grievances he couldn't imagine.

"This," he told Korith as he swept all the pieces from the table and grabbed a slice of apple, "is an empty den."

An empty den. He snatched up the black king and set it in the center of the table. "Iliath is here in his study. You—well, me. We're coming to the gifting. He's already met with a whole herd of people today."

Tishel and Malothi had spoken to them all, but no one had remembered anything unusual about that day. Nothing to suggest a kidnapper was coming.

Mumbling to himself, he placed the two soldier pieces outside the imaginary outer door and walked the red bull toward it. Paused. The guards had been killed inside the office. Had the fight broken into the front room?

"Or did you know who it was? Someone you thought was trustworthy." Until it was too late.

He laid the guards gently on their sides and moved the bull into the study with Iliath, but again he stalled. Tishel's search of the room had identified the alsum as Iliath's. Shara supposed he couldn't blame the king for wanting relief from the headaches of rulership.

"So they knock him unconscious," he muttered, tipping the king piece over, "and find the alsum. Or maybe it's already out. Add it to the tea, soak the cloth, and hold it over his mouth. Then somehow carry him out without anyone seeing."

As if he hadn't been through this a dozen times in the last week.

He braced himself against the table and sighed. This was useless. He might as well go door to door through all of Farna, sniffing for Iliath's scent.

"Iliath." He frowned at the prone game piece. "Iliath faked his own abduction because he needed a rest."

It was as good a theory as any, not to mention an idea that became more tempting with every passing hour.

"... pick ..."

Shara leapt, knocking into the table and sending the game pieces rattling like his heartbeat. "Korith?"

"... pickles ... escaping ..." He slurred something that sounded like *wuffles* and settled back into silence.

Slowly, Shara's pulse steadied, and he let out a breathy laugh. Escaping pickles. Humans were—

Well, no. This was just Korith.

He prodded his cave-brother's arm gently. "Next time say something useful, will you? Like a name."

His reenactment of Iliath's abduction lay in shambles, as did all desire to reconstruct it or try something similar with the coronation. Seizing the fruit bowl, he resumed pacing, gnawing as enthusiastically as he liked on the sweet, leathery pieces. No one to stop him, judge him, doubt him.

A small mirror hung on the wall, and after another four turns about the room, he stopped in front of it. After a glance toward the still-closed door, he shifted away Iliath's form. The royal grandeur faded like fog clearing into daylight, and a familiar face greeted him, birch scales and horns and all. The face of someone who could look like anyone. Be everyone.

But he wasn't everyone. Just Shara.

Always just Shara.

His toes curled, and he met his reflection's eyes. "Two

days." Korith's bed loomed in the corner of the mirror's reflection, and beside it, the table and scattered malir pieces and the Guide watching it all. "What are we going to do, just-Shara?"

Just-Shara vanished. His nose lengthened, his horns darkened to pine, his eyes seemed to fill with arrogance. "Stay out of the way and try not to burr anything up."

A confident grin and white hair glinting in its owner's natural light. "We'll make better mistakes next time."

Sharp blue eyes and sea-weathered skin. "Sometimes you leave it all behind and start over."

One by one he drifted through forms, first in search of advice, then for the comfort of seeing them. Maybe someone would spark an idea or reveal an overlooked clue. The effort of shifting kept his thoughts from straying too far, and soon he'd developed a rhythm. Lethir often compared Shara's shifting to a human timekeeper, all jarring ticks and individual steps and no toresh, but now Shara relied on it, the push and pull, like a bird's steady wingbeats keeping it aloft.

The door clacked, and Shara jumped, his features blurring with the speed of his panicked shift back into Iliath. He spun to see an apologetic servant delivering a cart of clean bandages, and as soon as she'd ducked back out, he returned to the mirror with a relieved sigh and a roll of his eyes. His fastest shift ever, all for . . .

His body seized. His fastest shift, so fast his face had *blurred.*

Arms tightening around the fruit bowl, he tried the sequence again, but faster this time—as fast as he could make himself shift, until he was no longer chasing a form but fleeing his current one, no longer trying to become someone specific but simply changing what he was. His face stretched and pinched, contorted and lengthened, swirled and solidified and swirled again.

At last he staggered back and closed his aching eyes, steadying himself against the nearest bed while his mind ran on ahead.

What if it wasn't wind sense? What if—

He hurried to Korith's bedside and dropped the fruit bowl amidst the malir pieces. "Watch that, will you?"

He needed a second look in the storage closet.

Shara hurried through the corridors toward the palace courtyard, a pair of guards striding along in his wake. For once being Iliath offered some benefit—no need to explain his haste or apologize for whatever ridiculous things he did while he waited for Nashai and Tishel and the rest to complete their search of the *Rosette*. They ought to be returning soon, and he'd use the wait to pick apart his theory and decide whom to tell. Whom to trust. Because if he was right . . .

Clattering weapons and footsteps on stone met him as he emerged at the top of the stairs leading down into the sunlit courtyard. A blur of red-garbed royal guards surrounded a small group of people, all jerky movements and sharp voices as they shuffled across the courtyard. Special guests arriving for Iliath's speech?

But as the glare of sunlight faded, he saw it for what it really was: Nashai, Lady Masar, and Lord Fethan in the middle of a contingent of Barathi guards.

Not an escort. An arrest.

He plummeted down the stairs and pinned his most royal frown on the nearest guard. "What is this?"

"Iliath!" Relief filled Nashai's voice, but fury blazed in her eyes.

"What's going on?" Shara demanded.

The guard—it was Lieutenant Mereth, Shara realized through his spiking panic—coughed uncomfortably and rolled his shoulders back. "Your Majesty."

A hand clamped on Shara's arm and steered him from the group.

"Carry on, Lieutenant," Tishel snapped over her shoulder. "I'll explain matters to His Majesty. Don't stop for anyone else."

"This is a mistake!" Nashai's voice pierced through Mereth's orders and the slapping of shoes on stone. "King Iliath, I demand to speak with you at once!"

Tishel's hand spasmed on Shara's arm, stalling his attempt to turn around. "His Majesty is indisposed," she said crisply, pulling Shara through a side door. The creaking hinges drowned out the last of the courtyard chaos.

"What happened?" His voice came out more pleading than insistent, and when Tishel ignored him and continued dragging him down the hall, he cleared his throat and tried again. "Tishel, what—"

"Not now."

He craned his neck as though he could see through the walls and follow Nashai's progress—where? To the prison?

His churning stomach grew heavy. What had they found on the ship?

Had he been wrong about Nashai this whole time?

They rounded a corner and practically jogged up several flights of stairs, emerging in a deserted hallway. Shara recognized the place; the balcony where he'd deliver the speech was at the end of the corridor. Midway down the hall stood Gepar, who gestured them into a small room.

Shara didn't wait for him to shut the door. "What happened? Why did you arrest Nashai?"

"There's been a change of plans." Gepar handed him a piece of paper. "A new speech for you to deliver. Learn it quickly."

It was not much longer than the receipt Gepar had asked him to sign on his first day as Iliath. It even had lines at the bottom for signatures. And the text itself—

His whole body went cold. "You want me to declare war?"

CHAPTER 35

ILLUSION

"No." The speech fluttered in his shaking hands. He'd guessed it, but to see it on paper in those official words of state, with all of Iliath's formal titles . . . "No, I—I can't."

"You can and you will."

"No, I won't. I mean . . ." He raised his eyes and met Tishel's fierce gaze.

What if he was wrong?

His throat closed and his pulse quickened. He knew all about being wrong. What if he was *right*?

"You *won't*," Tishel repeated, voice lowering. She settled a hand on her sword and took a step toward him.

His body tried to fold itself into as small and submissive a posture as it could manage, and it twitched uncomfortably when he forced it to stand straight and unmoving. In the corner, Gepar snorted.

Teveth.

Maybe so, but he made himself speak anyway. "I think the assassin is alvithi."

She blinked. Gepar blinked. Slowly they turned to one another. Shara knew that look. He'd grown up with it—in the expressions of others and in the mirror every time he looked at himself.

No, not every time. Not the last time. "Look, everyone you talked to described someone different or didn't remember a face at all. So we thought it was a group of people. But apart from the woman who was killed, every single one of them escaped."

Color rose in Tishel's cheeks. "So?" The false carelessness in her tone didn't quite mask the emotions below.

"So what if a single person was moving through the crowd, using the explosions and confusion and smoke to hide that they were changing their appearance?" He waved his hands in front of his face, and the words tumbled faster. "That's why the attacker looked like a blur to me—my senses are sharper than yours, so I could tell something was wrong. Korith thought it was wind sense, but I think it was an alvithi constantly shifting individual little parts of their face. It makes sense!"

It did, didn't it? He'd thought so a second ago, right before Tishel had folded her arms and given him a look that sent an apology crawling up his throat.

"Is that all the proof you have? One of them was blurry in the middle of clouds of smoke? Panicking witnesses couldn't recall faces they barely glimpsed?"

Uncertainty flared, but so did the determination burning in his chest. Being right would mean nothing if he couldn't convince them. "I know it isn't much, but listen, I—"

"Don't bother." Tishel slapped a piece of paper against his chest, and something dangerously like pity flashed across her face. "We searched their ship. We found that hidden among Lady Oshari's belongings. It's—"

"A locking order." Intricately cut edges, a swirling signature, a seal. The same sort of document he'd seen on Thosena's ship all those weeks ago. The same reminder how little he actually knew, and at the worst possible moment. His free hand fisted around his mother's coat. "What does it mean?"

Not even Gepar's obvious dread that Shara would betray him could stop him from gloating. "They're distributed to Tethamari agents given special assignments. Someone writes out the task and cuts the paper in half; the agent takes the bottom half and memorizes the contents of the top. The cuts are always unique, and both the design and the memorized contents must match when the agent returns to Tethamar. Keeps out impostors and *meddling alvithi*."

"And before you point out the obvious fact that the assignment isn't written on this half and could therefore be anything," came Tishel's voice between two beats of Shara's pounding heart, "you should know that Oshari all but confessed."

Confessed.

No. "*All but* confessed?" He was clawing at clouds, but . . .

Tishel scowled. "She wouldn't say anything explicitly, but she said plenty nonetheless. Her Highness, however, was ignorant of the plot as you suspected. Either King Rhoda hoped it would ensure her safety, or he knew we'd demand answers of her after the coronation."

"And didn't trust her to lie," Gepar muttered, as though he couldn't respect anyone who wasn't capable of lying.

Shara's head swam. Confessed. The Tethamari . . . "But if Oshari confessed," he asked, still grasping, "why didn't you arrest her? She wasn't in the courtyard."

Finally Gepar's disdain moved from Shara to Tishel. "If it weren't for Oshari's confession, I might suspect our own royal guard. Iliath is abducted, not a single attacker at the coronation is captured, and now Oshari."

"She escaped?"

Tishel bristled. "The entire shipyard is searching. They'll find her."

"Not if she's alvithi," Shara pressed, though he could no longer tell whether he felt certainty or desperation. "How do you know that was the real Oshari? Tishel, I checked the storage room again. I went all the way to the back this time and found a cart covered in blood. What if someone killed that Tethamari guard and took her place before the coronation? And left her body for us to find. What if someone *wants* us to declare war?"

"The alvithi?" Doubt still laced her voice, but her expression cracked. "You're really blaming your own people?"

"No, but it could be *an* alvithi. Maybe an imarth who grew up here."

"Perhaps it's you," muttered Gepar, throwing up his hands and rolling his eyes. "This is ridiculous."

"It's no more ridiculous than the Tethamari royal family . . . what, having Iliath kidnapped, then ordering fake-Iliath's assassination?"

Tishel shook her head. "They did not so much as hint at Iliath's abduction. Difficult as it is to believe, I expect the two are unrelated."

Gepar scoffed. "Give them a few days in prison and I'm sure they'll remember where he is. In the meantime"—he jabbed a finger at Shara—"you are going to sign that for Iliath, and then you're going to go out there and deliver it."

His whole body trembled, but not his voice. "No, I'm not. Not until we know the truth."

"The truth?" Gepar snatched the speech from his hands. "The truth is you're drunk on power. *His* power. Hoping we won't find him, are you? Hoping you'll get his position and his future wife and—"

"I never wanted any of this! I'm tired of being stuck as someone I'm not! But this doesn't make sense, and I'm not going to declare war just so you"—he jabbed a finger at Gepar—"can preserve your reputation and you"—Tishel—"can feel better about yourself!"

He was cringing before the last words escaped, but it was too late. Tishel had frozen, and her pale face flooded with color. Her hand settled on her sword hilt, the tendons standing out, and she drew a long, shuddering breath.

Shara did the same. "Tish—"

The flutter of paper sliced through the one apology he did need to make. Gepar set the speech on the table in the corner and, with a savage flourish, signed on the first line. Then the second.

Shara gritted his teeth. "No peace treaty, no *arrangement*." And plenty of experience forging Iliath's signature.

"Precisely." He extended the stylus to Tishel, no waver in his movements now. "Captain."

Her burning gaze fell to the paper, but she didn't move or speak or even blink. Shara held his breath.

But Gepar had run out of patience, and with a final signature, he straightened and marched to the door.

Shara dove for the speech as he passed. "You can't—"

"It seems His Majesty is still recovering from the shocking attempt on his life and will need a representative to deliver this in his stead. Captain, keep this brat from interfering—I trust you are at least competent enough for *that*."

The door clacked quietly on his departure like polite applause after the sky had promised thunder. Shara stared, too shocked to move, until a sound from behind him cut into the stillness.

He whirled around. "Tishel, I'm sor—"

"Do you remember what we told you when this all

started?" she seethed. "You are *not* Iliath. You're not here to have an opinion. You are certainly not here to stand in our way or pass judgment on our actions. Now"—she gestured out the window—"get out."

His breath hitched, and his heart plummeted like a falcon mid-dive. "What?"

"You said it yourself: you never wanted this. You told Lord Aman that when it was all over, you'd be gone. Well, we never wanted you, and I'm declaring it over. Your assistance is no longer needed. Fly back to Iliath's rooms, gather your things, and go." She swallowed hard. "You've done enough."

The world spun as the words echoed between them. Sucking in a breath, Shara stared at the window and the land beyond, not truly seeing any of it, only waiting for something to fill the sudden, gaping hollow in his chest where emotion should have been. "But I—"

"But *what*?" Sunlight threw her shadow in a dramatic arc as she crossed to the door. "None of this is your business, nor your decision. You're not Barathi or Tethamari or *human*. You're a pawn who's done nothing but get in the way and cause us further problems. Now all of a sudden you think you know everything, but the truth is that whatever Lord Aman claimed he saw in you is just another alvithi illusion."

"That's not—" His voice cracked, high and weak. Sticky heat crawled over his body and pooled in his stinging eyes. Through a mist that seemed to dampen all sound, he saw Tishel turn to go, saw his hand shoot out of its own accord to grab the back of her coat. "That's not true."

She batted his hand away. "Oh no?"

The words hung thick in his throat but wouldn't come again.

Tishel drew her keys from her belt and strode away. "Stay here or fly away. I don't care. But don't interfere."

The door closed and the lock clicked.

CHAPTER 36

DOORS

Shara stared at the door. Sunbeams spilled through the windows and stretched across the wooden barrier, cheerily illuminating its pattern of waving lines and bulging knots.

He'd hated doors ever since that first morning aboard Thosena's ship when the lieutenant had marched him into the admiral's cabin and shut the three of them in. Warm, stale, thin air, the sounds outside as dim as the light within.

Then had come the doors of the human shops, of Korith's home, of the palace. The doors to Iliath's rooms, creating little sanctuaries for the privileged, the specially chosen.

He trailed a finger over the wood grain to the metal hinge, its surface warm in the sunlight.

Doors were meant for secrecy. Privacy. Security.

But he'd discovered other doors, too, doors that weren't physical. Yet they remained closed even more tightly than those built of wood and metal and stone.

Doors to shut out others. To prevent conversations from beginning or cut them off before they could properly end. Doors to protect wounded hearts and bar entry to hurt and pain.

Doors for safety. Doors to cower behind.

Even alvithi had those doors. And he had opened his, and it had all gone wrong.

Just another alvithi illusion.

The words hardened in his chest, and he drew a breath for what felt like the first time in an hour. Letting it out, he took a step back and gazed listlessly around the room. The windows and their decorative iron lattice blurred, then sharpened, and he moved toward them in a daze. He'd never been good at shifting into small things, but right now he'd shift into nothing if it would allow him to fit through one of those little holes.

Teveth.

Maybe Tishel was right. Maybe he was nobody after all. But surely even he could summon toresh for a moment if it meant being nobody forever.

Running his hands over the rough stone of the sill, he closed his eyes and imagined it. He'd fly out the window, soar away from Barath, and the whole world would be his. Shimmering blue above and below, frothing white waves and glittering stars, the green and brown ridges of an endless stretch of islands all beckoning to him. No doors but the one over his heart.

It rose in his mind, not so much a door as a large stone guarding a cave entrance. The dark interior welcomed him like an embrace, warm and certain, full of everything he needed. All he had to do now was crawl back inside, and the weight on his heart where the massive stone teetered between open and shut would disappear.

No, not disappear. But it would be familiar again. The weight of satisfaction with so small a world.

So small a self.

Keening softly, he slouched against the wall. His mother's coat swirled around him like the sea, and something crinkled in the pocket. More for the distraction than because he cared what it was, he pulled out the piece of paper and unfolded it. Amid creases and tears, a face stared up at him, drawn in bold, familiar strokes.

Korith's impossible Shara.

A wad of fur caught in his throat, and he tried to toss the sketch away even as his hands spasmed around it and held it tighter. Slowly, almost fearfully, he traced a finger over sketch-Shara's face.

It looked so unlike the drawing he remembered that he flipped it over and glanced at the back. Nothing. Hands and heart fluttering, he turned it over again. No laughing pride shone in that expression. No jutting chin or cocky smile. Sketch-Shara held him in a steady, level gaze, his eyes clear with quiet confidence. His chin angled only slightly upward, and his lips parted as though he might speak or laugh.

Korith hadn't drawn his soul inside Shara's body after all. Only the soul of someone who could be anyone else—and didn't need to be.

Almost without thinking, he shifted. The hands holding the sketch still trembled, but they were his own. His feet were too small in Iliath's shoes, but they remained firmly planted. His body swam in the king's ill-fitting clothing, but he stood erect anyway.

He tucked the sketch back into his pocket and slowly, awkwardly shifted again, holding the image of a squirrel-dragon in his mind so firmly that he had no attention left for the usual frustration and inadequacy. Bit by bit, he worked his way into the little form, and when the shift was finally complete, he wriggled through the lattice and leapt into the air. Loosing a chittering cry, he fluttered along the wall, seeking an open window and two familiar figures.

Tishel and Gepar had not gone far, and Shara practically

dove between them, skidding to a halt in the middle of a room nearly identical to the one he'd left. Two sharp voices cut off abruptly, the better to inject more venom into their expressions while he burst back into his human self.

"You're wrong," he said before either of them could speak.

"Oh, this should be good," Tishel muttered.

He spun to face her directly. "I don't think I know everything. I'm not sure I know anything at all. But you're right about this: I'm not a king. I'm not Korith or Alanthas or Rathen. I left my clan because all I ever did was fail. And maybe I'm completely wrong about this, too, and I'll cause you more problems and get in everyone's way again." He met her eyes. "But maybe getting in the way is what I need to do right now."

She held his gaze for an eternal heartbeat, then looked away, her scoff grating like stone.

"You simply don't quit, do you?" Gepar said.

Warmth swelled in Shara's chest, like Gepar had tried to drench a fire in water and accidentally thrown oil instead. He held out a hand. "Give me the speech."

Gepar's eyebrows took a slow, incredulous journey toward his hairline. "I beg your pardon?"

"I asked you to give me the speech. I'm not going to let you do this."

A long, stale silence passed, but at its end, Gepar held out a crumpled wad of paper. "You're aware I can simply write another?"

The paper crinkled in his fist. "You're aware I can look like your king?"

Tishel twitched, but what might have been a smirk vanished the moment he glanced her way. Unfolding the ruined speech, he eyed its contents and started. The bottom right corner had been ripped off, and with it, Tishel's signature.

"Little good it'll do you," Gepar grumbled, thrusting the

locking order at Shara before stalking away. At the door, he pivoted and swept into an exaggerated bow. "Your *Majesty*."

The latch clicked, and stillness settled over the room. Thrumming with relief and lingering panic, Shara peered cautiously at Tishel. She refused to meet his eye.

He traced his thumb over the speech's softly jagged edge. "Thank y—"

"I didn't do it for you." The words trotted out with emotionless precision, as though she'd already said them a dozen times in her head.

"I know. But you did it."

"Yes. Well. I'm at least competent enough for that." But there was no self-pity in her eyes, and her lips pressed into a thin smirk as she crossed her arms. "So, you seem to have all the ideas today. What do we do next?"

Lightning shot up his spine. Now he had to do something about everything he'd just done.

"Right. Yes. Um." He stared down at the papers in his hands so he wouldn't have to see Tishel's reaction. "Now we, uh, see if we can find Lady Oshari. And if she's alive. And maybe Nashai can tell us something about this . . . this . . ." A soundless mist enveloped him; even his heart seemed to have stopped, not daring to interrupt. "I've seen this before."

Tishel's eye rolls were uncomfortably loud for something that shouldn't have made a sound. "I waved it in your face a few minutes ago."

"No, before that." Gepar had said each locking order was unique, and Shara had no idea how much they might differ. But distinct, familiar features leapt out at him—those intricately cut overlapping feathers, that lone ink blot, the way the oblong green seal seemed to swing from the end of the last letter of the signature. "I sailed to Farna on Admiral Thosena's ship. When I visited her office, *this* paper was there."

A queasy sensation swept over him and began running circles in his stomach. There had to be a roster, a list of sailors and passengers. If they could find out who'd been on that ship . . .

He bounded past Tishel and threw open the door. "We need to visit the—"

Admiral Thosena blocked his path, her pistol drawn and pointed at his heart.

CHAPTER 37

NEVER AGAIN

No one spoke. Inch by inch, Shara retreated. Thosena shut the door behind her as she followed, never lowering her weapon. Slowly, almost casually, she reached with her free hand and drew her sword.

Magic scorched the air, and a faint barrier of wind swirled up to block her path—and, Shara prayed, her bullets. Wind shield in place, Tishel drew her own weapons.

Thosena eyed the shield, then Shara, then Tishel. Finally she flicked her pistol between Shara and the window. "Last chance to disappear, little alvithi. This doesn't concern you."

Heart beating against his ribs, he lengthened his claws and drew a slow breath. "Yes, it does. And I'm done running."

"Very well." With fierce energy, she strode to the edge of the shield.

A growl rumbled in Shara's throat, but though his hackles raised and his body ached to shift, no instinct could overpower the stinging hollow in his chest. Here stood the woman who'd let him on her ship when she could have thrown him over the side or arrested him. Who joked about paperwork and seemed to possess one of the only senses of humor in the whole palace.

"Why?" He didn't care that he sounded desperate, betrayed. "Why would you do this?"

A short, humorless laugh could not mask the gravity beneath. "Surely even you've seen what a mess Barath is. Pirates raid the northern islands, and Tethamari squadrons sail within our borders. Kana Faresh lives just beyond these walls. And all the while we fight amongst ourselves. Our own merchants bicker over who controls the rights to shipping routes and merchandise while cities sit and wait for necessary supplies. Nobles bribe navy officers to provide them with escorts." Her lip curled. "The king's advisors were so desperate to prevent a civil war over the throne that they were willing to let you pretend to be our king rather than admit that Iliath had disappeared."

"You mean admit he'd been abducted. By you."

Her eyes narrowed. "I never meant to take him. Not then, anyway. But he caught wind of my plans. After our meeting that day, he asked me to return later in the evening, and when I did, he confronted me. Accused me of poisoning his father."

Shara jolted. Plants. Iliath had been researching plants.

"And did you?" he asked, trying to sound merely interested. If Thosena hoped to lure him and Tishel out or recruit them by sharing her secrets, he'd not discourage her.

"Isith was weak and complacent. As long as Farna's sea was smooth, he didn't care what happened elsewhere. The noble houses fought for his favor, and he sat and basked in their gifts and pledges and fawning. My last report about Tethamari movements was dismissed as *too complicated*."

"So learn to write more clearly," he retorted, betrayal and false interest splintering into anger.

Her posture relaxed as she laughed, but her precise control over her weapons never faltered, and he shoved aside the temptation to take her bait and leap.

"Barath," she went on, "needs a common enemy to unite us before we tear ourselves apart from within, and Tethamar needs to be put in its place."

"And the coronation of a new ruler was guaranteed to bring a member of their royal family to Farna," Tishel ground out.

"Precisely. After that—"

"After that you framed them." The wind shield shuddered. "Shara's right about the coronation, isn't he? The guard, the storage room. And you. You *are* alvithi."

"Or imarth," Shara guessed. She'd gone after two female Tethamari, and while she'd been able to make her facial features look male at the coronation, she'd never tried to fully impersonate Iliath, not even long enough to declare war.

"Imarth, yes. My alvithi father stuck around just long enough to teach me that word." Quick as lightning, her face shifted into Tishel's, Lady Oshari's, the Tethamari guard's, and back to her own. "I taught myself the rest."

Shara bristled, and though she'd stopped shifting, he saw new faces. Iliath. Malothi. Korith. "And you used that gift to hurt and murder people to make the Tethamari look guilty so Iliath—so I would declare war."

"A careful balance," she said, as if she were explaining a recipe. "I couldn't frame them too openly or the attack would look illogical and therefore suspicious, but I needed enough evidence against them to keep tensions high and justify further investigation. After that, I was prepared to do whatever was necessary to convince Iliath of their treachery. But then things went awry and you replaced him." Her eyes glinted. "It was almost too easy, I thought. A cowardly little alvithi taking orders from Iliath's advisors, from Captain Tishel, from me."

"And he called a truce instead." Only traces of bitterness at defending Shara lingered in Tishel's voice.

"Yes, well . . ." Thosena shrugged. "You can't have everything."

Shara's blood boiled, and his claws pierced his palms. "No, just war against an innocent—"

"Innocent," she snarled. "Innocent of this act, but not of others. You have no idea what I've seen on the seas, no idea of our history with Tethamar. Iliath himself admitted it; even he doubted whether we could overcome our shared past. I knew I could manipulate that, but I wasn't prepared for your ignorant idealism and pathetic fawning over Nashai."

Shara's ears burned. So much for thinking she wanted to recruit him. "And yet she turned out to be innocent after all, so maybe I'm better off as I am."

"As nobody, you mean?"

So she did recognize him. "Yes, nobody. But you helped me anyway." Another pang shot through his heart. "I can't believe the same woman who did that would condemn her own people to war. Her crew."

Emotion rippled through her, but it wasn't regret. "Barath will suffer some losses, yes, but that is a price I am willing to pay. As for my crew . . . I've sailed these seas for most of my life and commanded this navy for over a decade. No one knows the Tethamari fleet better than I do, and no one knows better than I how to defeat them."

"So that's your goal." Tishel jolted as if emerging from a trance. "You don't want a war only to unite us. You want a war you can manipulate. End or prolong as *you* see fit."

Thosena's gaze settled heavily on Tishel, and the shield seemed to crackle in the heat of her earnest energy. "Surely I'm not alone in dreaming of change. Of hoping to eliminate certain behaviors and attitudes."

Color rose in Tishel's cheeks, but her shoulders squared and her eyes narrowed. "Behaviors and attitudes? What about *people*, Admiral? Our king! My guards, the Tethamari, Lady Malothi. *Korith.*"

Thosena's expression hardened. A calculating light flashed in her eyes, and her tone grew mocking. "Your dear, meddling brother would still be alive if he hadn't taken those files." Her attention slid to Shara. "A word of advice, *Your Majesty*: be careful what you say when there are guards outside the door."

Tishel sneered. "You mean second-rate admirals disguised as guards?"

Shara's jaw ached, but he held it shut. He'd blurted out that Korith had the files and nearly gotten his cave-brother killed—the least he could do now was protect Korith's life by not alerting Thosena to her failure.

"And Iliath?" Tishel demanded, stepping forward. "What have you done with him?"

"He's fine—for now." She gestured smugly at the locking order. "In light of your discovery of Tethamari treachery and *Lady Oshari's* convenient admission of guilt, Nashai and her entourage have been imprisoned, as you know. The ship's crew, however, have been ordered to return to Tethamar immediately."

"And why would you do that?"

Her goading smirk grew sharper, and Shara saw the alvithi in her for the first time. "Because King Iliath isn't going to arrive to deliver his promised speech. A frantic search will reveal that the Tethamari smuggled him aboard their ship. I, of course, will lead a squadron to recover him—"

"Only to arrive too late," Shara guessed, a weight settling on his pounding heart. Wind tousled his hair, and he forced himself back from the edge of the shield where her gloating words had drawn him.

"Tragic, isn't it?" She sighed dramatically. "If the monarch is killed in wartime and there is no replacement, temporary rulership passes to a council of Barath's highest-ranking military officers. Well, *noble* military officers."

Tishel's shield roiled like a storm. "And as the admiral who wins us the war and reforms Barath, you'll be perfectly placed to assume permanent rulership, is that it?"

"A gamble, I admit." She flashed a grin. "But it certainly won't hurt that Iliath will spend his dying breaths bequeathing me his signet ring—even if he doesn't remember doing it."

Warning shot through Shara, but too late: the shield swelled outward and burst. Thosena staggered, Tishel leapt, and before Shara had the presence of mind to react, the admiral hurled her sword at him. He bounded aside as Tishel and Thosena clashed. A gun fired and someone shouted, and the thrown sword hit the stone with a clang. Snarling, Shara kicked it out of reach and spun, claws raised, to see Thosena duck beneath Tishel's oncoming strike, twist with alvithi speed and grace, and bury her pistol in Tishel's exposed side.

A muffled bang rent the air, and a gale of wind sent them hurtling apart. Thosena collided with a chair, cursing in pain. Tishel hit the opposite wall and crumpled to the ground, silent and unmoving. Blood spattered around her, and her magic sizzled into nothingness.

"Tishel!"

Shara's body went cold, and terror broke like lightning across his vision. Beyond it rose a dark blur, and his mind screamed in warning as Thosena leapt. Half-blind, he raked his claws through the air and felt them slash through something warm. A snarling hiss, a glint of light, and she plunged a knife into his chest.

Howling, he staggered back and reached for the hilt, but he'd barely grasped it when Thosena collided with him. The blade twisted between them, and he screamed and flailed for it again, snapping his teeth as she tried to grab his wrist. Cursing, she threw herself forward and slammed her skull against his, and as he reeled, she seized his arm and wrenched it around.

Something cold clamped over his wrist.

The world darkened, and horror thrilled through his limp body. *No, no, no!* He had to get out of the void, had to stop her before—

She locked the second cuff and yanked the knife free.

Shara bit down another scream and staggered sideways. His legs jumbled beneath him and his knees hit the rug. He landed on his shoulder with a shuddering cry.

The air thickened around him. Blood and gunpowder and blood and death and blood . . .

I'm going to die.

His heart lurched. Maybe it wasn't too late. Thosena had locked the cuffs after she'd stabbed him. Maybe he could still—

A soft click from above stilled his fluttering heart, and a shadow blocked the cheerful sunlight streaming obliviously through the windows. He felt rather than saw Thosena crouch beside him, felt the pressure of her pistol against his chest.

"You should have run," she hissed. And fired.

Pain lanced through him, and spasms wracked his body as his healing abilities battled furiously against the binding magic. His senses flared, desperately taking in every last moment of life, every scent, every sensation—the swish of Thosena's coat, the thunder of her footsteps, the clack of the bolt in the door.

Then silence.

He rolled onto his back, sucking in breaths like someone had pressed one of Korith's pillows over his face. With agonizing effort, he brought his hands to rest on his torso and fumbled with the cuffs, unable to raise his head to look at what he was doing. Slick liquid coated the metal, and high, angry shrieks pierced his ears as his claws raked the slippery surfaces in search of the seams. If he could pry them open . . .

But the gaps were far too narrow for him to get enough grip, and even if he could, he might not have the strength. Already the pillow pressed too hard, and every motion sent an avalanche of pain cascading over him. The sun burned with unbearable warmth, its rays like razor-clawed fingers stabbing his eyes no matter how many times he tried to shut them. Beneath him, the rug seemed to have come alive, each thread crawling against his skin like a swarm of ants dutifully going about their work.

He ought to have been dead already, but his continued survival brought no hope. He could feel it. It was only a matter of time. Minutes. Less.

You should have run.

"... no." Tears trailed along his cheeks as though fleeing his dying body, but though fear pinned him beneath its weight, he was free of shame. Whether he lived or died, he'd never run again.

His mother's face flashed before his eyes, followed by Korith's, and Shara's heart strained harder than ever. Lurching back to his side, he reached toward Tishel's body, but his tingling arm went everywhere except where he wanted. He dragged himself forward, gritting his teeth, distantly aware that he was smearing blood all over his coat.

Thosena shot a hole through it, anyway.

Annoyance and misplaced priorities propelled him the next few inches, and at last he flailed his hand toward Tishel's waist. He had to find her keys.

"Shara."

He thought he'd imagined it until Tishel extended a quivering, bloodstained hand toward him.

"Tishel! You're ... I need ..." He gave up and focused on tracing his fingers along her belt, working by feel while the world spun in ever more violent loops.

There! An involuntary twitch of his trembling hand tore the snap free, and the keys clanked to the rug. Snatching them up, he saw with dismay that there were at least five . . . eight . . . he couldn't tell, everything was so blurry, so unsteady . . . After what felt like an hour, he forced his numbing fingers to close around the first one and guided it toward the cuff's keyhole . . . keyholes? Why were there three? Why were they all moving?

Metal scraped against metal, too loud.

"Shara," Tishel rasped. "Shara, you . . ."

Was her voice growing weaker, or was his connection to the world fading away? Darkness covered everything, and the ants had grown larger—one skittered over his fingers to his wrist, and when he tried to pull away, his body wouldn't respond. Not to move, not to fit the key into the lock. His only chance, slipping away more rapidly with every remaining heartbeat.

No. A weight pressed on his chest that had nothing to do with his wounds. Not now. He couldn't die now, not after everything . . .

"Shara!"

He jerked and found someone shaking him; another spasm, more searing pain through his chest. A greedy ant pulled the keys from his hand and loomed over him, but already the darkness had smothered him again.

Chapter 38

Out of Reach

Shara awoke with a violent lurch and immediately wished he'd stayed unconscious. Everything hurt, and what didn't hurt was numb, and though he could tell his body was mending itself properly now, a wound like that would take days to completely heal. How easy it would be to close his eyes and slip back into stillness, into freedom from pain and treason and war, responsibility and failure . . .

But a miasma of blood and gunpowder soured the air, driving away the last of his unconsciousness, and instead he pushed himself upright. The room spun, and he rubbed at his eyes as his shirt peeled itself from his back, sticky with half-dried blood.

"About . . . time," came a hoarse voice.

He jumped. "Tishel!"

She lay near the door, pale and breathing with effort, and as he crawled toward her, the scent of blood and tang of magic grew sharper. Tear-soaked makeup streaked black over her face, and her spectacles hung askew. She'd shoved a wad of fabric against her bloodied side—a table covering, from the looks of the bare table and shattered vase nearby.

He crouched beside her, trembling, not daring to touch her. "You're alive."

"So far." She squeezed her eyes shut and adjusted the fabric against her torso with a whimper. "Tried to . . . block with . . . wind." Another strained breath. "Didn't work as well as I'd . . ."

"Don't talk. Just . . ." Just what? She needed help, but he'd never be able to carry her all the way to the healing room, and even if he could get her on her feet, he doubted they'd make it far together. "Hold on, let me shift into something bigger so I can—"

"Don't." She reached toward him, more energy in her now. "Go save Iliath. Stop Thosena. It's already been . . . too long."

She was right—judging by the angle of the sunlight spilling across the blood-soaked floor, he'd been unconscious nearly an hour. Enough time for the Tethamari ship to have departed, or nearly so. And once it did, Thosena would "discover" their treachery and launch her own squadron—war declaration or not, she'd have to go after them, and if she required a formal document to justify her actions, she could doubtless manipulate Gepar into writing one. Or, knowing Gepar, she could simply ask.

Urgency set his heart pounding painfully, yet he hesitated. "Tishel, I—"

"Go." Her eyes narrowed, though it might have been exhaustion as much as determination. "Someone will . . . find me."

He nodded resolutely, claws biting into his palms. "I'll make sure someone does. Just . . . hold on, all right?"

She groaned. "Whatever you say, Your Majesty."

A faint smile pulled at his mouth, and he patted her shoulder gently before struggling to his feet. Aching all over, he staggered to the door. Needle-fine claws tore at his insides, twisting and gouging with every labored breath and heartbeat.

"Shara." She waited until he'd turned before continuing. "If I . . . don't . . ."

Terror spiked through him. "Don't think about that."

"If I die . . ." Her knuckles whitened around the blood-stained fabric, and another black tear slid down her cheek. "Tell my brother . . . tell him I . . ."

The rest of the message faded into unconsciousness, and her grip on the tablecloth went slack.

A shuddering breath racked Shara's body. For a moment he stood rooted, shaking madly, half of him desperate to flee and the other half unable to look away.

If I die . . .

Tearing his gaze from her eerily still form, he stumbled into the hall. As quickly as he could, he made for the balcony, leaning against the cold stone wall and gripping doorknobs for support. One breath at a time, one step at a time. Save Tishel. Rescue Iliath. Stop Thosena.

Tell my brother . . .

He pushed her words away. She'd give Korith the message herself. Thosena thought she was saving Barath, conjuring war to create unity. Shara wouldn't let that war destroy Tishel and Korith's chance for unity.

Save Tishel. Rescue Iliath. Stop Thosena.

The tasks marched through his mind as his sluggish steps whispered a prolonged hiss in the eerie silence, like a huge snake dragging itself through the underbrush. Behind him, a trail of blood marked his passage, a grim reminder of the storage room. He'd been right after all. Right about the blood trail, the attacker, the locking order.

Next time, he was going to be right about something pleasant.

Like the hall, the balcony stood empty, but it was the bay

Shara sought. Glaring sunlight reflected off the water and into his already unfocused eyes, and he forced them to stay open, searching through the blur for the *Rosette*'s distinctive green markings.

So many ships, so many sails. It appeared the Tethamari weren't the only ones leaving Barath in a hurry after everything that had happened.

"Where are you?"

He ground the heels of his hands into his eyes and blinked hard, and his vision finally came into focus.

His stomach lurched.

The military docks swarmed with the ordered chaos of unfurling sails and twining ropes and dozens of sailors all preparing for a hasty launch. Already the Barathi emblem fluttered boldly from the tallest mast of each ship, and below it, a swath of dark-red fabric. Shara didn't have to be Barathi to know what that meant.

Breathe. He gripped the balcony railing, wringing out his anger and fear on the stonework until only determination remained. Below in the courtyard, a pair of guards patrolled, and Shara nodded to himself.

Down to the courtyard, then on to the docks. "Save Tishel. Rescue Iliath. Stop the war."

At least he had a plan for the first two.

Bracing himself against the railing, he drew as deep a breath as his body would allow. With a last look at the bay, he shut his eyes to concentrate. Salty air cooled his sweat-soaked face, and seabirds' cries echoed in the wind, summoning him.

White feathers, webbed feet, a curved yellow beak, and—

Searing fire ripped through his chest. Stars exploded over his vision, then faded into encroaching darkness. The world spun, and the next thing he knew, he was on his back, teeth clenched around moans of pain, his head throbbing as it welcomed a new bruise.

"Owww."

He rolled onto his side and pressed his cheek against the cool stone, trying to concentrate on breathing instead of the knives jabbing at his nerves and the claws constricting his chest.

Slowly they released him, but when the agony had gone, a thought much worse than pain settled in its place.

I can't shift.

What was he supposed to do now?

He tottered back down the hall, his thoughts and heartbeat outrunning his feet like rabbits racing a snail. He couldn't shift, and at his current pace, he'd never make it to the docks in time. Not even sprinting the whole way would get him there before the ships launched.

He had to find Gepar. The man might be as good as a traitor, willing to declare war in order to settle his agreement with Faresh, but there was a splinter of a chance that if he knew the truth about Iliath and Thosena, he might still be willing to help. If not . . .

If not, I'll help myself.

Somehow.

Tishel lay where he'd left her, unmoving but still breathing, and he allowed himself only a momentary glance before re-dedicating his energy to making it to the staircase.

Find Gepar.

He tripped over the nonexistent plan. What did he expect Gepar to do? Even if the man was willing to help, he had no faster way of reaching the ships than Shara. Unless he had a glider, or—

His eyes widened, and a wave of energy crackled through him like lightning. The palace had a signal tower. He could tell a passing servant or guard about Tishel on his way, then send a message to the docks exposing Thosena and ordering the ships not to launch. And if that didn't work, he could at least warn the Tethamari ship about their extra passenger—and who was coming after them.

Heart pounding, he started forward again, but heavy footsteps brought him up short. A pair of guards emerged at the top of the stairs and halted at the sight of him.

Shara swayed into the wall and brushed damp hair from his sweaty forehead. Thank the Eagle. "I need your help. Iliath is in danger, and Captain Tishel needs—"

A pair of unsheathing swords hissed over the last of his words.

"Stay where you are," demanded the taller of the two, as if Shara weren't using a wall to keep himself upright.

"That's impossible," murmured her companion in a voice she probably thought Shara couldn't hear. Steel-hard eyes flicked over his form, fixing on the knife and bullet holes in Shara's blood-soaked shirt. "The admiral said she killed him."

Shara started. Killed?

"I'll have to thank her for her oversight," snarled the first woman, levelling her sword. "Means I get a chance instead."

"Wait." He lifted his hands. "There's been a mistake. I'm not who you think—"

"We know exactly who you are." Her expression darkened. "The Tethamari spy who murdered our captain."

He stumbled back, ice flooding his veins, his poor shredded heart beating faster. "No, listen, she's still alive, she needs your help!" He gestured wildly to the room behind him.

"Thosena tried to kill her, and now King Iliath is in danger. You have to—"

"We don't have to do anything you say. Now put your hands up and walk forward slowly, and we might let you live long enough to die alongside your precious princess."

Adrenaline surged through him—the threat to Nashai, the knowledge that he had only one chance, rage at Thosena for this last indignity. Snarling, he propelled himself off the wall and straight at the guards. Two startled shouts and a swipe of his claws later, and he'd barrelled past them and was clambering down the stairs, his heart screaming with every jolting step.

Curses and footfalls thundered in his wake.

CHAPTER 39

PURSUIT

Almost immediately, Shara's heart stopped screaming and started hurling obscenities at him instead.

He slipped on the bottom step and caught himself on the banister. Gunfire rang behind him, and a raptor screech tore up his throat as he hurtled down the corridor toward the south end of the palace.

Run, run, run, run!

But already his burst of energy was fading. He could never hope to outrun them and their bullets.

He had to hide. Hide, let them pass, and then sneak the rest of the way to the tower.

But hide where? As soon as he disappeared around a corner and vanished entirely, they'd start searching the rooms. And like Tishel, they probably had keys.

Tishel. Her limp form flashed in his memory, and his blood boiled. Thosena had blamed *him*. He could practically hear her weaving some tragic story about how Tishel had cornered a Tethamari agent and selflessly given her life trying to bring him down. How Thosena herself had arrived too late to save the heroic captain of the guard.

And it *would* be too late if Shara couldn't get someone to Tishel quickly.

He almost spun and tried again to convince his pursuers of the truth, but another gunshot snarled in his ears, and an explosion of stone ahead of him sent him veering down another corridor. Dark wood panels greeted him, and the jar of his feet on stone became the booming echo of each stride. Even as the shock to his legs lessened, he winced. So much for secrecy. Maybe humans built things from wood to hinder spies.

Spies.

A desperate idea leapt to the front of his mind—if he could prevent himself from collapsing long enough to get there.

"Stop!" barked one of the guards.

"Go back!" he shouted. "Tishel needs—"

The flame in his lungs swelled from a candle into a bonfire. Speaking was no use, not with a band of iron constricting his chest with every heaving breath. Shutting out the sounds of pursuit and the strain of flight, he dug into his memory for a map of the palace. The room wasn't far. To the end of this hall, down another flight of stairs, right . . . or was it left . . .

His feet slid in Iliath's overlarge shoes, and he stumbled, caught himself, pushed on. No time to pause and remove them—behind him, the voices seemed to have multiplied. He didn't dare turn around to confirm his fear. If he let their words roll over him without really listening, he could pretend they were cheering him on instead.

His next gasping breath erupted as a strangled laugh. Of all the molting awful times to think Korith thoughts.

Or maybe it was exactly the time for Korith thoughts.

He careened down the next flight of stairs. Too much speed, no control—he hit the opposite wall with a yelp and ricocheted away, but the motion kept him moving in the right direction. Windows lined the wall to his left. What if he smashed a window open to distract the guards into thinking he'd tried diving into the gardens? But he had nothing large or heavy enough, and probably not the strength to lift it.

He ran on instead, glancing repeatedly toward the gardens and the bay beyond, seeking the red streaks of war flags.

At last he reached the hall he'd been looking for and skidded around the corner. One, two, three—he bolted inside the fourth room, shut the door as quietly as possible, and sidled past a table to the fox painting hanging on the eastern wall.

"Please work, please work."

He yanked it down and pried away the wood panel beneath. Shoving the panel into the newly created hole, he scrambled in after it, then leaned over the edge and grabbed the painting. After a few trembling, scraping failures, he caught it on its wall hook.

Darkness and pain wrapped themselves around him. The energy that had kept him running and dulled the fiery knives twisting in his chest drained away abruptly. He slumped against the wall with a moan, his sweat-soaked, bloody clothing clinging to his clammy skin. Everything hurt. Was this how it felt to be Korith?

Beyond his hiding place, angry voices and banging doors rumbled like thunder. Holding his breath hurt as much as breathing, so he focused on keeping the air coming steadily and quietly as the voices grew nearer. If only they'd hurry up; whether this worked or not, he didn't have time for delay.

Breathe. Breathe and heal, heal and plan. Assuming it did work—

The door outside flew open and hit the wall, and someone barged inside. Probably for the best, because Shara couldn't recall ever having assumed that one of his plans would actually work, and his mind had gone rather fuzzy at the idea.

The room had few furnishings and offered no hiding places but the one Shara had claimed. So long as they didn't know . . . so long as they couldn't hear his hammering heart or scent his acrid fear . . .

The stomping guard drew nearer. Shara held his breath. Somewhere above him, a spider scuttled along its web, impossibly loud.

Knuckles rapped against a wall, but not his wall.

"Anything?"

Wood scraped over wood in a harsh bellow. "All of these rooms look exactly the same. What could they possibly need them all for?"

"Hiding spies, apparently," grumbled the first voice. "Come on."

Footsteps, footsteps, the clack of the door.

Silence.

Shara blew out the caged breath and tilted his head back. *Thank you, Eagle. And you too, Korith.*

He grinned at the thought of Korith hearing this story, and his taut muscles loosened. It wasn't the rush of renewed energy he needed, but it was enough. Slowly he pushed himself upright and reached for the portrait. More guards would be scouring the halls within minutes.

He had to reach that tower.

CHAPTER 40

THE SIGNAL TOWER

Shara crouched behind the plinth of a statue and waited, counting the passing footfalls like ticks on a timekeeper marking out yet another delay.

In the scant minutes he'd been sneaking through the halls and ducking into alcoves, he'd already learned to distinguish footsteps. The heavy, purposeful strides of the guards. The hasty shuffle of the servants, whose low, urgent conversations mingled with the flutter of their soft-soled shoes. The infuriating starts and stops of the nobles, who seemed incapable of gossiping and walking at the same time, though they moved quickly enough when chasing after the servants in the hopes of gathering up spilled rumors.

Shara's attempt to tell a servant about Tishel had earned him a look of alarm and time enough to utter half a sentence before the poor boy fled. Everyone was too on edge. The whole palace whispered, and always the whispers were the same. The Tethamari and Iliath, betrayal and war. It didn't matter whether Gepar or Thosena had made an official declaration—everyone believed it had happened. Had or would.

Only the guards whispered something different: Shara. A description of him, speculation as to where he might be and where he'd last been sighted. And always the snarling accusation that he'd murdered their captain—never the suggestion that he'd tried and failed.

Never had Shara wanted so badly to be known as a failure.

The passing servants disappeared around the corner, and their murmuring faded away. Shara pulled himself out of his crouch with a wince and a wobble. Sneaking through the palace put considerably less strain on his body, but since he jumped at the slightest breath of wind or scrape of a tree branch against a window, it made little difference in the end. Everything still hurt.

"Come on, Shara," he whispered, gathering bunches of his mother's coat in his fists. "Keep going."

With a final glance up and down the hall, he hurried on, ducking below the windows in case someone happened to be looking up or across. He still couldn't shift, not even enough to change his hair color.

Thankfully, humans had the decency to announce their presence from three corridors away.

The tower shouldn't be far now. He'd left the wooden wing of the palace and now wove through cave-like stone halls again. As he skirted around a corner, his feet rolled uncomfortably in Iliath's shoes, and at the next statue, he unlaced them, yanked them off, and tossed them behind the plinth. The floor's chill crawled into his feet and up his body like a refreshing breath of air, and he set off again.

One door, then another. One hall, then another.

Whether moving or hiding, he focused on composing the message he would send when he reached the tower. Something that didn't sound threatening or deceitful, assuming there was a way to say *The Barathi navy is bearing down on you* without sounding threatening and *Our king is on board your ship; could you save him, please?* without sounding deceitful.

Never mind how he would convince the tower keeper to send a message to a supposed enemy, especially when the royal guard believed he was a Tethamari spy.

Save Iliath.

He ground his teeth. "I'm trying, all right? No one's cooperating."

The words had no sooner left his mouth when a new sound hit his ears, not a purposeful stride but the faint tap of boots and the sting of sharp whispers. Guards, but careful ones, and close. Too close.

He half jumped toward the nearest door before checking himself and dashing in the opposite direction. He was so near—not five dragon lengths lay between him and the next corner.

He took the turn too sharply, and his feet leapt out from beneath him. His hands and knees hit the stone, and a grunt of pain slipped between his rattling teeth.

The hissing stopped, and the footsteps stilled. Shara froze with them, palms throbbing.

". . . hear that?" someone whispered.

Slowly, deliberately, he tilted his head to better listen, and his heart nearly erupted a second time—the corner of his coat trailed back around the corner, a faithless flutter of blue sitting in the dark pool of his shadow. Before he could think, he was scuttling forward.

"There!" came the hoarse voice again. "Did you see that?"

"What?"

"At the end of the— Never mind, come on!"

Abandoning it all, Shara scrambled to his feet and almost trilled with relief at the staircase waiting at the end of the hall. That had to be it.

He burst into a silent sprint, struggling to outpace the clattering footfalls behind him while some stupid voice in his head chose that moment to point out that he'd never won a race against anyone.

Shut up, he snarled at it, throwing himself at the first steps of the spiralling staircase. *I'm busy.*

He took the stairs two at a time and almost collided with a heavy door at the top. It groaned in traitorous welcome as he shoved into it and toppled, huffing and aching and dizzy, into a small room.

"I need to send a message," he blurted out, slamming the door. Only one other corridor branched off from the hall below, and if the guards weren't fooled into thinking he'd taken it, they'd be here any second.

A burly young man stared back at him, half-risen from his seat at a small table. One hand hovered over the deck of cards he'd been shuffling, and the other twitched toward his pistol. "May I—" His eyes widened.

Shara didn't care to think about how awful he must look. Drawing himself up, he cleared his throat and tried to sound official. "I need to send a message. Immediately."

The tower keeper was perhaps eighteen, and it was clear he'd never seen anything like Shara. "Oh." His gaze flicked uncertainly over Shara's unusual, ill-fitting garments. "And who're you? Um, sir?"

"I'm . . ." He made the mistake of looking out the wide, paneless window. A cluster of ships prowled through the bay like a pack of wolves. "I'm, uh, Lord . . . ko Han."

A jolt ran through the young man's body, like deference was colliding with what his eyes told him about the bedraggled and barefoot figure in front of him. "Lord ko Han."

"Yes." He almost believed his voice this time.

The young man nodded his head toward the mirror con-traption positioned near the window. "I'm, uh, very sorry, my lord, but this is a military tower. I'm authorized to send only messages delivered by the guard or signed by a superior officer. If you want to send a personal message—"

"It's not personal. Look, I—"

Heavy boots pounded on the stairs. Shara whirled and threw the bolt in the door. The tower keeper's jaw dropped.

Shara gestured out the window. "You need to signal the fleet and tell them to stop. And then tell the Tethamari—"

"Namel!" The door clattered, and someone cursed. "Namel, are you all right?"

Namel's wide eyes darted from Shara to the door and back. "Yes." His lips moved silently as if in rehearsal, but when he spoke, all he said was, "All's fine here."

Beyond the door, a deeper voice muttered, "Move over." Keys clanked.

"Please." Heart pounding, Shara inched toward the mirror device. "Please, you need to warn the Tethamari."

For all the uncertainty in his manner, Namel drew his pistol with practiced precision and stepped between Shara and his destination. "Communicating with that ship is forbidden. Admiral Thosena fears what the Tethamari might do if—"

The door leapt open. A man and a woman rushed in, barking orders as they levelled their pistols. Shara shrank back and lifted his hands, animal panic roiling through him. Phantom shots raked at his ears.

"Don't move!"

They closed in, and though he didn't dare try to run, he could still speak. "Namel, please. Stop Thosena. And tell the Tethamari"—the first guard seized him and wrenched his arms behind his back—"tell them Iliath is on board their ship!"

"As if they don't already know," sneered the guard who

wasn't cuffing Shara's wrists.

"They don't!" He threw a last, desperate glance at Namel as the swirling void engulfed him. "Listen, Captain Tishel is still alive, and Admiral Thosena isn't who you—"

A hand clapped over his mouth, and the guards dragged him from the room.

CHAPTER 41

WAITING FOR PERMISSION

Shara's captors marched him through the halls with a military efficiency he'd have appreciated under other circumstances. The world swirled about him, diving in and out of focus, fading and brightening like an indecisive sunset. The footsteps he'd listened to so attentively had ceased—now servants and nobles alike paused to gawk and whisper as he staggered past. He ignored them, less by choice than the necessity of keeping all his focus on walking and breathing and not passing into darkness. He hadn't rescued Iliath yet. He still didn't know whether Tishel had been found. He had to keep trying. Even if trying, for the moment, meant merely staying conscious.

Within minutes, they'd arrived at a familiar but unexpected location: the Tethamari guest quarters, a room several doors down from Nashai's now-ruined suite.

Had it truly been only this morning that he'd worried about perfumes?

"Found him, sir." The woman's voice boomed in Shara's ear, but he hardly had the energy to flinch.

Lieutenant Mereth pivoted as they approached, his usually smiling face hard. He fixed faintly red eyes on Shara, and they narrowed. Anger flickered to confusion. "This is the spy?"

A spark of hope coursed through Shara's heavy limbs. Mereth had seen him once in his own form, the night of Iliath's abduction. "No, I'm—"

Another hand pressed over his mouth, and this time he bit it. Cursing, the guard yanked her hand away and shoved Shara at her companion.

Shara seized the opportunity. "Lieutenant, please, you—"

The guard wrenched on his arms, twisting his words into a yowl.

"That's enough." Mereth scowled at all three of them. "Take those off and put him with the others. We'll deal with them after this is over."

Shara stilled as the guard reached reluctantly for his keys; he could feign docility long enough to have his abilities freed.

Energy, purpose, and relief spilled over him like a waterfall, but before he could summon it all and weave it into another protest, the guard pulled open the outer door and shoved him inside. He tripped over the upturned edge of the rug, stumbled into the desk, and pushed himself off of it and back around. The door slammed in his face.

Molting doors. *Not this time.*

"Lieutenant Mereth!" He rammed his fist against it. "I need to see Lord Gepar! Tishel is alive! Admiral Thosena is a traitor! She put Iliath on that ship herself! She's going to kill him! You need to stop the fleet! And warn the Tethamari!"

"Be quiet!" barked someone who wasn't Mereth.

He shouted every rendition of those words he could think of, and when nothing happened, he started repeating himself, punctuating each phrase with another round of pounding. Still nothing happened.

No one was listening.

Stay out of the way, Shara.

"No." His hand hung suspended before the door, then clunked against it in defeat. "No, I . . ."

"Ahem."

Shara whirled. Nobody outside was listening, but four people stood clustered in the doorway to the study, all staring at him as if he'd gone mad.

"Your Highness!" He took a hurried step toward Nashai.

Captain Sothal took one to match, and Shara faltered. Right. He wasn't Iliath anymore. It was too late to hide his bare feet and the bloodstains marring his coat and shirt, but he smoothed his hair and tried for some semblance of dignity.

It didn't work. Lord Fethan looked him up and down with disdain. "Who are you?"

"Never mind that." Half-dragging Lady Masar, Nashai pushed past Sothal and planted herself in front of Shara. "What's this about Iliath?"

Shara had related only part of the story, with a few significant details left out, when the door creaked open. Lieutenant Mereth stuck his head in and gestured to Shara, who hurried into the hall, Lord Fethan's disgruntled mutters snaking after him.

"Lieutenant, listen, Captain Tishel—"

"She's been taken to the healing room," Mereth said. Shara swayed into the wall with a trembling sigh, and Mereth's expression softened. "She's alive, though unconscious, and therefore she can neither confirm nor contradict your story." He gestured to the man at his side. "Lord Gepar, however, has assured me that you are not the person we're looking for."

Shara gaped. In spite of all his shouting and demanding to see Gepar, he'd never expected Gepar to respond. And judging by Gepar's pinched expression, he was already regretting his decision to do so. Gripping Shara's arm, he pulled him down the corridor, shooting furtive glances over his shoulder until they were well out of hearing range.

"What have you been doing?" he whispered at last, rather shrilly. "When Lieutenant Mereth said they'd captured the man who . . . Not even *you* . . . And Admiral Thosena said the Tethamari have—" His eyes widened. "Wait, then they have the real Iliath?"

"Yes." Shara stopped beside the window where he, Nashai, and Lady Masar had gathered earlier in the day, drawing an odd comfort from its familiarity and the cool air spilling through it. "Thosena kidnapped him and smuggled him aboard the Tethamari ship."

Gepar puffed a disbelieving breath. "That's absurd. She just went after them. Why would she put him there in the first place if she planned to rescue him?"

"She doesn't. She— No, wait." He swivelled and beckoned Lieutenant Mereth, who raised his eyebrows but came trotting toward them.

Gepar twitched. "Are you certain you should be bringing others into our confidence?"

"He needs to hear this too." And Shara needed more allies.

Pacing despite his exhaustion, he gave them the briefest summary he could manage. Every time his thoughts wandered, he snatched them back—he had to concentrate on what he was saying and on presenting it clearly. Not even Nashai had seemed convinced of his story, and if he couldn't convince anyone, he would be very alone indeed.

"She nearly killed Tishel." With trembling fingers, he pulled aside his shirt to reveal the two oozing wounds. "And me."

Gepar's gaze darted away, his face paling as he lifted a hand to cover his mouth.

Mereth swore, but though the muscles in his jaw strained, his eyes narrowed in doubt. Slowly they trailed to Shara's wounds, and he chewed his lip a moment before turning to Gepar. "You're certain this . . . man is trustworthy, my lord?"

Squirrel-dragons gnawed at Shara's insides.

Gepar levelled a hard look at Shara. "He is many things," he said slowly, and his expression changed—not softer or kinder, but less like he was regarding a burr in his paw. "But not a liar. Nor a murderer." His hands twirled. "At the very least, not with a pistol."

Knowing Gepar, he probably thought alvithi ate humans, too, but he could have his false beliefs if they meant he'd declare Shara innocent. Whether he would help was another matter.

Mereth folded his arms and nodded curtly. "I'll have someone signal our ships. And the Tethamari. If what you say is true, it'll do little good, but it's worth trying."

He bowed to them both and loped away, calling ahead to one of the guards standing outside the door.

"Well, that's . . ." Gepar said, inching away from Shara. "That's that. Why don't you—"

"We need to go after them."

He blurted it out like he'd been planning it all along. Maybe he had, somewhere in the far corner of his mind where he knew the truth. The Tethamari would never trust a message from Barath, and the Barathi squadron would never reverse course so long as Thosena was at its head.

"Go after them? On what ship?" Gepar flicked a hand at the window. "Merchant sailors will be scattered throughout the city, and it would take far too long to gather enough people to crew a ship and prepare it for launch. And the only navy ships Thosena left behind are docked for repair. Besides, couldn't you . . ."

He lifted his eyebrows meaningfully, and Shara shook his head. "I can't. I'm still healing."

"Oh." For the first time, he looked disappointed that Shara couldn't do something alvithi. "Well then, I'm afraid—"

"Look." Shara stepped toward him, and Gepar winced. "I'm going to do everything I can to rescue Iliath before Thosena kills him. Now, I know you don't care—"

"I never said—" Gepar sputtered. "That is to say, I certainly didn't mean . . . But what do you expect to do? You're . . ." His head tilted and his eyes narrowed, like if he stared just right, he might be able to convince himself he was looking at Iliath— or at least someone other than Shara.

"I know. But—" An idea bolted through him. "Faresh! Faresh has a ship."

Gepar's eyes went as round as his spectacles, and he backed himself into the wall like he expected Faresh to come stalking down the hall at the mere mention of his name. "Absolutely not. He's completely untrustworthy, as you perfectly well know."

"Of course he is. But he has a ship. And a crew. It's right out there, ready to sail. And it's small and fast and actually has a chance of catching the *Rosette*. So we borrow it."

It was a horrible idea, but then again, Korith *had* told him to make better mistakes.

"No. We are not . . . If you go to him, he'll know I . . ." His hands twitched a warding spell while horror and anger tugged at his features. "I forbid it."

I forbid it.

Not until those words did Shara realize he'd been waiting for permission. Seeking someone else's support, hoping for confirmation that he wasn't about to jump off another ledge with no hope of sprouting wings, no Lethir to catch him, and a king's life in the balance.

All this time running through the halls, trying to find Gepar. But Gepar wasn't going to jump with him, nor even cheer him over the edge.

"Fine." He cupped a hand gently around the pocket containing Korith's sketch. "Then I'll go myself. Lieutenant Mer—"

"*No.*" Gepar gripped his wrist in a quivering shackle. "You *can't*. If anything goes wrong . . . If Faresh suspects . . . My son . . ."

The floor rocked beneath him. "Your *son?*"

Gepar dropped his wrist and wrapped his arms around himself. "Faresh has my son. The prisoner he mentioned the night you and Lord Aman were there . . ." His shoulders slumped, and he gave a low moan. "He said he needed insurance. That he didn't believe my concern for my reputation was enough motivation. So they took him, too. He's just a boy, and I . . . I wasn't even there to stop them."

The words buzzed in Shara's ears like angry bees swarming up from the sudden hollow where his determination and plans and senses had been.

"Last night he contacted me again. He suggested . . ." He shuddered. "I can't risk it. There's no telling what Faresh might do if he thinks he won't get what he wants. He could flee Barath entirely, and then I might never get him back. I'm sorry, Shara, but between my king and my son . . ." He shook his head hopelessly, not bothering to put on false calm when Mereth halted beside them.

"Messages are being delivered," the lieutenant reported breathlessly. "What next?"

Shara clenched his fists as red blotches flashed across his vision. He knew exactly *what next*, and he hated it. But it would work.

"We're going to borrow Kana Faresh's ship," he told Mereth, glancing down the hall to the Tethamari's room and back at Gepar. He couldn't fault the man for his choice—but maybe it didn't have to be a choice. "All we need is the right bribe."

Chapter 42

Persuasion

"You're going to *what*?" Nashai's eyebrows hit her hairline and had nowhere else to go, and Shara hadn't even reached the most disagreeable part of the plan.

"It's the fastest option." His skin prickled under the heat of so many stares, but he couldn't afford to waste energy pacing—if he convinced them to go along with this, he'd need all his remaining strength to carry it out.

"Trusting Faresh and his crew?" Lord Fethan had worn a sour expression ever since Shara's return, but it twisted into something darker now. "You're mad."

"Not *trusting*." Shara clawed at the air, seeking a better phrase. "Working alongside. Temporarily." And regrettably.

Fethan snorted. "As if that improves the situation in the slightest. Are you aware what that man is capable of, *Lord* ko Han?"

Shara kept his gaze from Gepar, who sat at the desk in the corner, scribbling furiously on a fresh sheet of paper. "Yes, I am. If you have a better idea, I'd love to hear it. Otherwise, we need your help, and quickly."

"A better idea? Here's one." Fethan pushed past Lady Masar and jabbed a finger into Shara's chest, narrowly missing the bullet wound. "Rescue your king on your own. If what you've said is true, your admiral is responsible for this entire fiasco. She's already murdered one member of our delegation and has quite possibly done the same to Lady Oshari. It is most certainly not our duty to solve Barath's problems—especially since you have, if you'll recall, unjustly imprisoned us here."

"And you're going to stay unjustly imprisoned if Thosena isn't stopped, because if she wins, Iliath dies, and Tethamar will take the blame for it." Shara tried to fold his arms over his chest and winced. "I don't know what'll happen then, but I don't expect it'll be good for you and your country."

Fethan turned to Nashai, but she was scrutinizing Shara. She'd been doing a lot of that since his reappearance—frowning as Lady Masar related the conversation, exchanging glances with Lady Masar herself, frowning again.

"He's right, Lord Fethan," she said. "If we can help prevent Iliath's murder, stop a war, and exonerate Tethamar all at once, then we ought to give them any help they require. So what do you need from me, Lord ko Han?"

Shara knew better than to take deep breaths, but he did it anyway. "We're going to give Faresh what he wants. He lets us use his ship and crew, and you agree to let him stay in Barath indefinitely."

Lady Masar's fingers seemed to wince over the statement, and Nashai's lips bunched as though she might spit.

Fethan crossed his arms. "That's—"

Nashai raised a hand, and the room fell silent. Shara stopped breathing, just in case. Only Gepar's quill continued its steady scratching.

"Surely we could commandeer the ship?" Captain Sothal

cut in from the shadowed corner beside the door. "In Teth-amar, the military can make use of any civilian ship in certain circumstances. Isn't it the same here?"

Shara swallowed a growl. He'd known they would ask all these questions, but each one gave Thosena and her squadron that much more time and delayed his own rescue effort that much longer. Never mind that he didn't know the answer.

Again his ignorance crashed over him. It would take only one question he couldn't sidestep, one misspoken statement, and they'd know that Lord ko Han was merely Shara.

He stomped down the uncertainty and lifted his chin. Just-Shara might not be well-versed—or any versed—in maritime laws, but he knew he had to rescue Iliath. That was all that mattered right now.

"Lieutenant Mereth is rounding up members of the guard who have sailing experience, so if we have to take the ship by force, that's what we'll do." He didn't want to think about it. "But we need as much speed as possible, and from what I've heard, Faresh's crew is both extremely loyal and extremely dangerous. I'd rather give them all a reason to cooperate."

And he wanted Faresh to have no claim whatsoever on Gepar's son.

The scrape of a chair interrupted the ensuing silence, and Gepar slapped his hand onto the paper. "Finished. All it needs is your signature, Your Highness."

All eyes settled on Nashai, who shifted her weight and frowned at nothing in particular. Lady Masar drifted to her side, and they launched into a conference with sharp, swooping fingers and a lot of pointing at Shara.

Drawing another too-deep breath, he twisted a handful of his coat and pretended to be fascinated by a painting on the wall. Its simple red and yellow lines couldn't hold his attention, though, and his thoughts drifted to the fox painting he'd hidden behind. But the painting made him think of Korith and the fox of Iliath. Anxious all over again, he turned back to watch Nashai.

She'd finished with Lady Masar, and now Fethan stepped forward. "Your Highness, I must strongly advise you against signing this. You were specifically instructed by your father to bring Faresh home."

"Your advice and objection are noted, but I was also instructed to negotiate peace with a man who might be murdered in our name in order to ensure that peace never happens." She hesitated only a second before accepting the quill from Gepar. Humming softly, she trailed her fingers over the feathers. "If this is the price we have to pay, so be it. We can set aside our pride and my family's rivalries long enough to save Tethamar, don't you think?"

"But," Fethan pressed, "we don't even know if this boy is who he says he is." He scowled down at Shara, who had not truly appreciated Iliath's height until that moment. "What if he's an agent of Faresh and is trying to take advantage of the situation? For all we know, he's invented this entire story."

"Oh, I'm quite certain he isn't an agent of my uncle," Nashai answered. "Whether he is who he claims to be is another matter."

Her eyes met Shara's, and his hand slipped into his coat pocket and closed around the sketch. It was wrinkled and blood-spattered and torn, but at the same time, still whole. Rather like the real Shara.

A faint smile played at her lips, and she sat at the desk and nodded at him to sit beside her. Her head tilted toward his as she fiddled with the stylus, and her voice lowered. "I'd say you're doing rather well for being . . . what was it? Floundering and overwhelmed and falling out of the sky?"

Shara's heart might have fluttered if it hadn't still had a

hole in it. "Thank you. I'm sorry we're not meeting in"—he gestured at the document—"better circumstances."

Her mouth twisted. "I don't like it, but if it's the best option we have . . ." Hand steady, she scrawled a looping signature along the bottom of the paper and pressed her signet ring into a pool of green wax. The paper crackled as she fanned it through the air and blew on the ink, then handed it to him. "He's your problem now. Do me a favor and find a way to wipe the smug grin off his face someday."

CHAPTER 43

BARGAINS AND BRIBES

"Well." Smirking gleefully, Faresh held the document up to the light as though searching for secret messages.

Shara swallowed both a snarl and the urge to jump into the sea and swim away. Everything about Faresh set him on edge, including the fact that the man obviously knew they were in a hurry and had every intention of taking his accursed time getting to the point.

We ought to have taken the ship.

Mereth had collected several dozen members of the palace guard, all with rudimentary sailing knowledge. Now they bustled around the ship making preparations while Faresh's crew stood idle, watching without protest.

His heart sank lower. If he'd gone straight to Mereth and explained Thosena's treachery, the lieutenant could have collected more trustworthy people, enough to make up for—or face down—any of Faresh's crew who proved uncooperative. Shara could have avoided arguing with Gepar and Fethan. He wouldn't be standing here now while Faresh pretended to read the entire document one word per minute.

He clenched his hands and steadied his breathing. He was running again—running into the past to explore what he should have done, running along roads he hadn't taken to see where they might have led. But he'd done what he'd done. Now he had to make it work.

"Well," Faresh repeated. "I must say, this seems like a very fair agreement."

Shara, Gepar, Mereth, and Sothal hissed out a collective sigh like a four-headed snake.

Shara struggled to smile politely through his nerves and ship-induced nausea. "Good. Then—"

"Ah." Faresh held up a hand and bestowed his smug smile on Shara. "I said it seems fair. But I'm sure you'll understand if I would prefer to take a closer look at this signature and seal before I agree to come between my dear family's ship and the Barathi navy, even for so noble a cause."

Shara cringed. They hadn't told Faresh why they wanted to follow Thosena and the Tethamari, but based on those words and the glint in his eyes, he already knew.

"It shouldn't take long," Faresh went on. "Half an hour, perhaps?" He drew close to Shara with that smooth predator's grace and gave him a cool smile. "You don't mind, do you, little lord?"

The sea breeze crackled with snickers as Faresh sauntered away and leaned lazily against the nearest mast. Shara's phantom hackles rose, and his whole body throbbed with the urge to shift.

"We should have brought Nashai after all," he muttered.

"Then he'd be demanding Iliath's signature as well," Mereth returned, his jaw clenched. "You know he doesn't actually care if it's legitimate."

Nor did he care if Iliath died, though Shara couldn't imagine Faresh would be any better off with a military council or

Thosena ruling Barath. Perhaps he simply wanted revenge for what Iliath had planned to do with him.

Dragging his bare toes over the warm wood of the deck, he glanced askance at Gepar, who showed no sign of having heard any of the conversation. His eyes had been darting about the ship ever since their arrival and continued to do so now. No need to guess what he hoped to see—and no reason to expect any aid from him so long as Faresh held his son prisoner.

Before Shara could decide on his next step, Mereth's people began hauling on one of the ropes, unfurling the first sail. With every heave, the canvas spread wider, and in the shadows creeping across the deck, Faresh's crew stirred. Their hands drifted to their weapons, and though nobody moved, a dozen silent battles raged suddenly across the ship as crew and guard locked gazes.

Slowly, Faresh looked up from the document. His eyes narrowed, and he seemed to be reassessing Shara. "Planning to steal my ship, are you? I have it on excellent authority that Iliath made no formal declaration of war before his tragic abduction, which means you and your military have no legal claim on this vessel."

Burrs. He did know about Iliath, then—*and* he knew the law.

Still at a loss, Shara opted for as cool a stare as he could manage. Smirking, Faresh slid lower against the mast, exuding more control and authority than ever despite his worsening posture. He made a show of lifting the document to continue studying it, and as he moved, his scarf caught a shaft of sunlight. The familiar black fabric rippled with veins of gold.

Another eddy of alvithi power washed over Shara's skin. Gritting his teeth, he leaned toward Mereth. "Take Lord Gepar and go below. Gepar will know why."

The lieutenant's brow creased, but he nodded and whispered a quick word to Gepar. The two hurried away, Mereth striding purposefully, Gepar scurrying like a mouse. Several of Faresh's crew startled as they breezed past, but no one moved to stop them—except Faresh, who shoved off the mast and stalked across the deck. Without thinking, Shara jumped in his path, and when Faresh tried to slide past him, he held out his arm and moved again.

Eyebrows lifting, Faresh stepped forward until he and Shara were chest to chest. The sole of his boot pressed down on Shara's bare toes. "Shall I have you removed from my ship, boy?"

The boot crushed harder, and Shara winced. What had he been thinking, vowing never to run away again? Sometimes running was the smart thing to do. Like when you were facing a Tethamari royal who was about to order his crew to throw you into the sea.

Breathe, Shara. He'd faced Thosena, after all, and—

She shot you and you nearly died.

. . . well, at least Faresh didn't have a weapon.

But the crew had weapons, and Faresh had their loyalty, and once again, Shara had nothing but a risky, half-formed idea and no one to carry it out but himself.

He met Faresh's eyes. "I was going to ask you the same thing."

Faresh's jaw dropped, and he tossed his head back and laughed. "Remove me from my own ship? For what, precisely? Inconveniencing you in the middle of your little rescue mission?"

The crew sniggered again. Did Faresh pay them extra for that?

Shara nodded toward the stairs as the second sail descended with a feeble flutter, rather like his heart. "For kidnapping. And refusing to release the boy after Lord Gepar paid his debt."

Surprise flickered over Faresh's face, then shifted, quick as an alvithi, to smugness. "Oh," he breathed, tilting his head closer, his wine-laced words meant only for Shara. "I see. You think poor Lord Gepar and his brat are the victims here, is that it? I suppose he conveniently forgot to mention that he robbed the treasury to pay that debt, did he?"

Shara stared, unblinking. More than anything, this lack of reaction seemed to give Faresh pause.

"He didn't have to mention it," Shara said, choosing his words carefully. His hand balled around the sketch again, and he lifted his chin a little higher and tried to summon some of sketch-Shara's poise. "Money from the royal treasury—did you really think King Iliath didn't know?"

Every muscle throbbed as he waited, praying the danger-ous gamble would pay off. He had no idea what other crimes Faresh had committed and no idea what, if anything, Iliath could learn from putting money from the treasury into the man's hands.

But Faresh knew. And judging from the paling of his face, the subtle baring of his teeth, the shifts in his weight, there was more than enough to send him cowering into his cave.

Footsteps clattered on the stairs, and Mereth emerged from below, controlled fury darkening his expression. Gepar fol-lowed, leading his son, who clung to him with one hand and clutched a small dog figurine in the other. The boy glanced toward Faresh with both a child's fear and a noble's indigna-tion, and Shara gasped—it was the servant boy he'd startled when disguised as Darai.

As the crew leered at Gepar and his son, Faresh swung back to scowl at Shara. One long, hard look.

Shara held his breath. If Faresh could imagine all the things Iliath might know about him, surely he could also imagine everything he might gain—or avoid—by saving the king's life.

"My lord?" the real Darai called.

Eyes still trained on Shara, Faresh folded his arms, and just when the silence had stretched too long for anything good to come of it, the corner of his mouth quirked upward. "Prepare the ship!"

CHAPTER 44

THE CHASE

Shara was going to be sick, though that could have been because he hadn't breathed recently.

His chest ached, and he forced himself to draw air into his lungs, but his eyes never left the *Rosette*. It bobbed on the waves ahead, its fluttering green pennants visible beyond the mass of white sails and blood-red banners that decorated Thosena's squadron. And if Shara could see the Tethamari, that meant they could see Faresh's ship, and that meant—

"Nothing." The woman in the dragon's perch didn't look particularly apologetic, though she'd finally stopped smirking every time she thought Shara wasn't watching.

Hope rushed out of him like smoke from a puff mushroom. He steadied himself against the rail and tried to appear calm and lordly and like someone who didn't keep forgetting how to breathe. "Hail them again."

She rolled her eyes and shook her head. "It's no use. They're about to pass around the cliff." She waved her arm toward the mountainous island ahead. "We'll have to wait until we've rounded the island too."

This time she wasn't just being difficult—as Shara turned his squinting, watery eyes into the blasting sea wind, the lone Tethamari ship disappeared around the cliff. The Barathi squadron would soon follow.

His attempt at a nod wrenched a muscle in his too-stiff neck. "Very well."

There was nothing for it but to keep sailing.

Fortunately, the *Accomplice* moved with the grace and speed of a sea dragon, whether by design or by the wind and water sense flooding the air with the sting of magic. Sothal had assured him that even with the same magic, Thosena's bulky, heavily armed ships would make less headway; likewise, the *Rosette* had been built for comfort, not speed.

Yet with every wave they crested, every lurch forward, the voices in his head bickered more loudly.

We're going to make it.

We're not.

We're going to save him.

He's going to die.

"He's not." He gripped the railing, alvithi power bubbling beneath his skin and patterning mismatched scales on the backs of his hands. By now he could have done a superficial shift—changed his eye color or lengthened his hair—but nothing would grant him more speed or power, nor lessen his anxiety.

He slouched against the rail and dared a backward glance over his hunched shoulders. Eagle be praised, Faresh had disappeared into his quarters without so much as an offer of hospitality—not that Shara would have accepted. The crew tended to their duties without him, diligently following whatever orders Darai shouted over the thunder of wind and sea. Commands Shara didn't understand, words as meaningless as Korith's attempt to explain chamber pots.

A grin stole over his face, and he buried it quickly as Sothal glided over. Mereth followed, wobbling like a day-old cub determined to keep up with an oblivious parent.

"Not much for sailing either, my lord?" Mereth asked Shara, seizing the rail in a white-knuckled grip.

"I prefer flying." He tried to rake his fingers through his hair and snagged them in tangles. "And I'm not really a lord, you know."

No more pretending—not about what he was, nor about what he wasn't. With Gepar and his son safely in Farna, Shara was formally in charge here. Mereth and Sothal deserved to know, albeit belatedly, the depth of the mess they'd burrowed into.

Mereth glanced back toward Farna. "And I'm not supposed to be in charge of the guard. Yet here we are, faking our way through while we try not to get sick and lose our dignity in front of our esteemed Tethamari allies." He jerked his head at Sothal, whose mouth pitched into a smirk. "So, what's our plan?"

"Don't let Iliath die."

"Good." Mereth rapped his knuckles on the rail. "Simple. I like it."

Shara flushed even in the cold sea air. "We'll hail them again as soon as we can, but after so many messages and not a single reply, I'm afraid they're ignoring us."

"If a Barathi squadron *and* Kana Faresh were chasing me, I'd be ignoring us, too," Mereth offered, cupping his hand above his eyes to peer toward the cliffs.

"Unless they're not responding because they're looking for Iliath?" He glanced hopefully at Sothal.

The guard captain's weathered face screwed up in doubt. "Commander Albrith would suspect a trap, especially now."

"In that case, pray we reach them before Thosena does.

And if we don't . . ." He drew a long breath. The Barathi ships had likewise ignored their messages. There was little doubt what would happen when all the ships finally met. "Then we fight our way on board and find Iliath first."

Sothal nodded resolutely, and Mereth scowled and gripped the hilt of his sword. "She nearly killed my captain and is going after my king. I could use a fight right about now."

Shara stared into the churning water, less easy with the odds than his companions were. Six ships full of trained Barathi navy against Nashai's demoralized crew, Mereth's handful of royal guards, and whichever of Faresh's people wanted an excuse to join a fight.

And the three of them, of course. A Barathi lieutenant, the Tethamari captain of the guard, and an alvithi with a fraction of his abilities.

Not enough. But it would have to be. *He* would have to be.

"My lord!" The woman in the dragon's perch leaned over the rail and swept her arm south.

Shara jerked upright, and his pulse began to race. They'd rounded the cliffs. "Good. Hail them—"

His voice faltered. She wasn't pointing at the mountains. Beyond the Barathi squadron and the lone Tethamari ship rose another swarm of hulking shapes flying bright green banners, all of them bearing down on the advancing Barathi.

Sothal's eyes widened. "That's our—"

A streak of something dark darted from the lead Tethamari ship, and a resounding boom cut through the air as water erupted like a barrier in front of Thosena's squadron.

Elation and horror swept like a kick into Shara's legs. The battle was balanced now—but also more inevitable than ever.

"Did you mean what you said about fighting, Lieutenant Mereth?" he asked weakly, clutching the rail.

Mereth gave him a sharp smile. "Of course."

"Good." He locked eyes with Faresh's formerly smirking crew member and jabbed a finger toward the *Rosette.* "Whatever you have to do, get us to that ship!"

"Belay that!" boomed Shara's least favorite voice. "Not so fast, Lord ko Han."

Shara whirled, a growl crouched in his throat. What now? "Lord Faresh?"

"I do believe," Faresh purred, a sharp sneer cutting at his mouth, "that the terms of our agreement specified that I and my crew would . . . how did you put it?" He slipped a finger beneath Shara's chin and forced it upward. "Get you to the Barathi squadron. Am I correct?"

"I don't remember," Shara retorted, skin crawling. "Maybe if you gave me time to think about it. Half an hour, perhaps?"

Faresh snorted appreciatively and shoved Shara's chin away, then brushed his fingers on the black-gold scarf, lips pinched in distaste. "You think you're awfully clever, don't you?"

"No." Shara brushed his sleeve over his chin in return. "Just stalling."

Behind him, Mereth coughed out a poorly disguised snicker.

Folding his hands behind his back, Faresh glided past and surveyed the scene as the *Accomplice* arced around the Barathi ships and cut its way toward the *Rosette.* Another black shape whipped through the air and exploded into the water. Another deafening boom.

Trust the humans to build themselves ship-sized pistols.

"Well, given that you don't recall," Faresh went on in his silken voice, "it seems only reasonable that we defer to my memory instead. And according to my memory, I agreed to transport you to the squadron. As you can see, we've arrived, and I'm certain you'll agree that it's quite unreasonable for me to endanger myself and my crew in order to enter a battle in which I have no stake."

"No stake?" The words burst out before Shara could stop them.

But of course Faresh had spoken the truth. He would benefit from war no less than Thosena would. Possibly more. And now that he'd been formally pardoned by Tethamar—now that *Shara* had convinced Nashai to pardon him—he was probably safe to travel between the two countries, profiting off both with little concern for the welfare of either.

. . . when this was all over, Shara was going to have a long talk with Korith about his mistake-making outlook on life.

"So what do you expect us to do?" he asked, gesturing toward the swarm of ships. Stalling hadn't worked for long, but they'd drawn dangerously close to the battle, and he had no intention of letting Faresh sail past. "Swim?"

Why hadn't he learned to fly a glider?

Faresh flashed a feral grin, his glee so sickeningly palpable that Shara nearly choked on it. Patting Shara's arm like a concerned parent, he nodded to a nearby crew member, and his gaze flicked to something further down the ship. "Amusing as that would be, little lord, I think I can offer a better alternative."

CHAPTER 45

THE SEARCH

The only thing worse than ships was little ships.

Arms aching from the climb, Shara toppled over the *Rosette*'s railing and into the middle of a battle, and for a ridiculous moment, he considered leaping back over the side and dropping into the dinghy that, seconds ago, he'd been so desperate to escape.

Go back to a roiling sea tossing him carelessly amid seventeen wooden monsters that wanted to crush him, or stay here surrounded by soldiers and sailors fighting a meaningless battle with biting swords and barking pistols?

Neither. Why wasn't neither an option?

Sothal and the rest of the guard spilled onto the deck beside him, and the choice was made whether he liked it or not.

"You know your jobs!" Sothal shouted. "Go!"

They charged into the fighting, and Shara scanned the chaos for Mereth and the other half of their group, who had climbed up from the opposite side. The battle spread before him like a horrible drama, and in the swirl of furious choreography, there was no telling whether Mereth and the rest had made their cue.

But someone else had: Thosena's ship loomed at the other side of the *Rosette*, dwarfing the Tethamari vessel with its bulk and flooding it with sailors.

A heavy weight shoved into Shara, and he hit the deck as something exploded above him.

"Pay attention!" Sothal hauled him back to his feet.

His croaking laugh disappeared into the song of steel and the echo of cannon fire. "To *what*?"

"To everything!"

Easy for him to say. Shara's senses churned, overflowing like a cup full of tea to which someone had added those wretched piko seeds, then honey, then milk, then whiskey, and finally a few handfuls of grass and a spoonful of pond scum for good measure.

The urge to be sick overwhelmed him, and despite Sothal's warning, he closed his eyes and sucked in a slow breath; after an eternal pause, he let it out.

The next time he decided to grow a spine, it was going to be over something simple like asking Lady Masar to teach him sign language and telling her he thought she was pretty.

An entirely inappropriate grin skittered over his face. Mind clearer, he breathed again, this time through his nose. Gunpowder, sweat, blood, human, sea spray. As he'd suspected, scenting Iliath amidst the battle would be impossible unless they walked right past the room where he was held. But waiting for Thosena to come aboard and following her through the battle would be too risky. And if she was already here—

"Lord ko Han!" Mereth skidded to a halt beside them, chest heaving, his uniform in disarray. "Captain. Did you all make it?"

Shara had no desire to relive the harrowing journey, so he simply nodded. "You?"

"Barely. Sergeant Pir took a bullet to the arm, but she'll be fine—just grazed." He ignored Shara's shudder, and a sharp-toothed smirk pulled at his mouth. "Tragically, Faresh's dinghy is in pieces."

Shara's expression twisted to match Mereth's as he imagined the little boat being crushed between the *Myriad* and *Rosette*.

Then it was time to focus. He couldn't dwell on Faresh or Thosena. Only on what he and his allies could do. Pushing out his claws, he nodded at the group. "All right, let's g—"

"Sothal!" A woman careened toward them, fierce eyes narrowing at Shara and Mereth. "What are you doing?"

"Trying to stop a war, Commander Albrith. Listen, is King Iliath here?"

Her jaw dropped. "Then it's true?"

"So we're told." He jerked his head at Shara.

"Well, honest Barathi. First time for everything, I suppose."

Mereth jerked forward. Sothal caught his shoulder, and they exchanged a glare that seemed to satisfy some long-established need for rivalry.

Sothal turned back to Albrith. "We're going to search the ship. See what you can do about stopping the battle."

"Stopping . . ." She glanced over her shoulder and frowned. "No guarantees, Captain, but—"

"Wait." Sothal pointed to a familiar silver-haired woman leaping onto the ship, her sword already out and arcing toward the nearest threat.

Bile rose in Shara's throat.

Beside him, Mereth drew his own sword. "I'll distract her. Find Iliath."

Sothal threw out an arm. "This isn't the time for revenge."

"It isn't revenge. You fight her, it's a war. I fight her, it's a statement. Between me and Albrith, maybe some of them will stand down. Now go."

Before anyone could argue, Mereth darted across the deck, weaving with surprising grace toward Thosena as the ship rocked violently to one side.

Shara forced himself not to watch, but he heard the first clash.

Shara stumbled along the edge of the ship toward the staircase, ducking as he ran and dodging ropes and crates and pairs of fighters with glinting blades. His feet slipped on the slick wood, and he tripped, grabbed for the rail, and heaved himself forward. A span of rough wood rammed splinters through his palms.

If I survive this, I'm never getting on a ship again.

Another thundering crash echoed somewhere in the distance, and his gaze snapped toward the sea. Frothing water, cannon smoke, torn canvas—and there was the *Accomplice*, disappearing around the cliff while its sails fluttered a cocky farewell.

"And good riddance." Molting, sea-cursed—

Two combatants lurched into the rail in front of him, snarling like a pair of neeka. Hardly thinking, Shara pounced. He knocked the man's sword from his hand and kicked his legs out from under him, then dove at the woman with a deep-throated growl. Eyes wide, she staggered back, and as she flailed for balance, he wrestled her weapon away as well. Before either could recover, he tossed both swords over the edge and hurried on.

Sothal stood a few leaps ahead, watching. He raised an eyebrow. Shara raised one back.

At the head of the staircase, they skirted a prone, unmoving figure and clambered down into the ship. The sounds of the battle faded along with the light and blood-scented air. Shara sniffed again, but no Iliath. Nobody else, either, though distant scuffles and shouts of "Iliath!" indicated that some of Mereth's guard had made it to the lower level—and that others were meeting resistance.

"You take the port," Sothal said, sheathing his sword and striding off into the dimness.

"The what?"

Sothal pivoted. Stared.

"Look, I'm new to ships."

His expression flattened, and he lifted a hand and pointed an exaggerated finger at the other side of the ship. "That side."

"Right." Shara ducked off toward his assigned half.

"Technically, it's the lef—"

"No one cares!"

"Tell that to the crew."

Shara bit down a retort and strained his ears; perhaps Iliath would respond to the sounds of their bickering.

No pounding, no muffled shouting, no frantic scraping or clinking of shackles.

"Iliath?"

Still nothing.

It was like searching the *Accomplice* all over again, but as a human instead of a cat and with no need to be silent. He squinted into one shadowed corner after the next. Shoved aside hammocks and flipped them over for no reason except to be thorough. Prodded at the crew's rucksacks. Dodged pillars that loomed like unfriendly sailors at the edges of his vision but solidified the moment he spun and raised his claws. With every uneven step he took and every pile of rope he uncoiled, the battle above raged more loudly. Only the anxious voices in his head could rival it, mocking him with whispers of failure.

Teveth.

"Iliath!" Dropping to his knees to peer beneath a table, he cupped his hands and shouted again. Louder than the battle; louder than the voices.

"He's probably unconscious."

"Lucky him."

Mishala's horns, what did anyone need with this many crates? He knocked on them like they were locked doors and kicked them aside when no one responded. From the not-port side came the scrapes and thuds of Sothal doing the same, punctuated by curses and the occasional grumbled commentary on Barathi.

Reaching the opposite end of the ship at long last, Shara reviewed his achievements: a stitch in his side and a strong desire to sleep for a week. "Where could he be? Where haven't we looked?"

"I'll check below. Maybe the guard found him and didn't bother telling us."

Sothal's footsteps pounded a steady, calming beat on the stairs, and Shara slumped against the nearest post and wiped at his damp forehead. What were the odds the guard had actually found Iliath? And if not, what did he try next?

A curse and a metallic clang sounded beneath his feet. Shara leapt for the stairs, but he'd gone down only one when a female voice said, "Sorry, sorry. Thought you were—"

"It's fine, Sergeant."

Sothal and Sergeant Pir appeared at the bottom of the stairs, and Shara craned his neck to better see them. "Anything?"

"He's not down here," Pir said, shaking her head wearily and rubbing at her bandaged arm. "We're still looking, but . . ." She gnawed her lip and ventured, "Is it possible they did get our message, killed him, and threw him over? Or found him and put him in a boat and sent him to safety?"

"No. Albrith wouldn't lie." Sothal gestured up the stairs. "If what Lord ko Han says is true, he's here."

They both raised their eyes to Shara, and cold washed over him. *If what Lord ko Han says is true* . . . Could he have gotten something wrong? Could Thosena have lied about the whole thing? But then why would she be here, fighting on the deck like everyone else?

He stared frantically around the ship. *Eagle, what are we missing?* How many places could there be to hide an abducted prince? Or maybe Iliath would simply climb from a hammock they'd overlooked, complaining of an ache in his back and grumbling that Thosena had not put him somewhere more—

"Wait, where does Nashai sleep?"

Sothal's eyes flew wide. "The royal cabin."

He charged up the stairs and back the way they'd come, Shara stumbling after him and cursing the ship's never-ending pitching. On the main deck, the battle roiled like the sea, and though Commander Albrith's voice cut through the din as she shouted orders to stand down, no one listened.

Mercifully, the cabin sat just to the right of the stairs, tucked beneath the upper deck and guarded by elegantly carved wooden doors. Shara crouched in a corner beneath the overhang, and Sothal reached into his coat and withdrew a key. He shoved it into Shara's hands and planted himself before the door.

"I'll stay here. Knock some sense into anyone who comes by."

The key slid smoothly into the lock, and Shara toppled into the cabin and slammed the door behind him. For the first time ever, being shut in a room came as a blessing. Pressing himself against the cool wood, he let his head loll back and breathed in a moment of silence.

His nostrils flared.

Iliath was here.

Chapter 46

King Iliath

"Iliath?"

No response, but he didn't need one. The king's scent pulled him across the handsome room to the bed wedged into the far corner, its blankets drawn neat and smooth as if mocking the chaos outside.

Sunlight streamed through a row of windows set into the back wall and pooled on the floor like a cheerful rug. Sinking to his knees in its midst, hardly daring to breathe, Shara leaned over and pushed aside the draping blankets.

There beneath the bed sprawled a familiar white-haired man, his hands bound, his eyes closed.

Elation had barely taken hold when a tendril of something sour stabbed at his nostrils. Not the sweat and dirt of a week without a wash, but something sharper. And not alsum this time, either.

"No, no, don't be dead."

Heart hammering, Shara dragged Iliath into the sunlight. He bent over the limp form, brushing the king's hair from his eerily familiar face before settling a trembling hand against his neck. A steady pulse tapped a reassuring message against his fingers.

He blew out a relieved laugh. Not dead. Not poisoned. Drugged—ensuring he'd put up no fight when Thosena arrived to "rescue" him.

"Iliath?" He gave the king a gentle shake, and a shiver passed over his skin and wrapped him in a strange mist of detachment, almost numbness. It was like staring into a mirror and seeing your reflection move while you remained still. "King Iliath?"

Did Iliath know he was king now? Would he be angry when he learned they'd held the coronation without him? Never mind the whole part where they'd replaced him with an alvithi.

Shara shoved the bizarre thoughts and sensations away and prodded the king again, but all he got was a quiet moan.

His insides pitched along with the ship. So much for Iliath storming onto the deck, quelling the fighting with a single look, and implicating Thosena before Barathi and Tethamari alike. Even if Shara managed to wake him, he'd probably be too dazed and ill to walk, let alone accuse an admiral of treason. And dragging the still-unconscious king outside would only confirm Thosena's accusation that the Tethamari had abducted him.

A horrible crash resounded against the door, followed by a heavy thump and a voice Shara had prayed not to hear. Thosena, ordering Sothal to move.

Mereth.

Swallowing the thought, he shoved to his feet and spun in a slow circle. Bed, bureau, table, windows . . . What were the odds this room had a hidden door, a way out the back and—

And straight down into the sea?

Right. Ship.

Another sickening crunch, but though the door heaved, it neither splintered nor burst open. Sothal snarled something that would have earned him a tail-slap from Shara's father, and at the base of the door, flashes of light and shadow tracked the dance of two pairs of shuffling feet.

He turned back to Iliath, and something beyond the window caught his eye. Another dinghy, this one hanging from some sort of supports, ready in case the cabin's occupants needed an escape.

"Straight down into the sea."

He bent and rolled Iliath over, and after some awkward struggle, he unbound the king's hands and peeled the coat from his body. Then his shoes. At last he crossed to the windows and shoved one open.

"Sorry, Your Majesty."

He heaved Iliath into his arms and half dragged him across the room, increasing his speed with each new curse from beyond the door, each new creaking strain of hinges and locks. Ribcage grinding into the sill, he maneuvered the king through the window and into the dinghy; Iliath fell the last of the distance, head striking the bottom of the boat with a dull thud. Shara winced. At least Iliath was unconscious, though he'd have the bruises to commemorate yet another indignity.

Huffing with exertion, Shara shed his mother's coat, tucked it into the dinghy with the king, and pulled the window shut. He tugged on Iliath's coat, then his shoes.

And now the shift.

It was less a shift than a sculpt, each step of the process in need of guidance, each feature attended to individually, all of it built around a still-healing heart that had to remain untouched and unaltered. Eyes squeezed shut, he moved into that ticking rhythm, all his concentration fixed on becoming Iliath one piece at a time. Like directing his body through the process of breathing despite having done it without thought all his life.

But he hadn't. Shifting had never been thoughtless, never toresh. This was just another shift. A Shara shift, and though his people might scoff and shake their heads, the far corner of his mind whispered that none of them could have done this.

Something rammed the side of the ship. Shara staggered. He hit the far wall and collapsed to his hands and knees, hardly feeling the pain through the sizzle in his straining limbs and his fixation on Iliath's form. His white hair, his green eyes, the proud tilt of his chin that seemed built into his body, the graceful curve of his fingers. Each inch of height physically stretched him; each additional bit of muscle threatened to erupt through his skin. His heart raced, afraid to be forgotten.

Iliath.

A splintering sound echoed as if through a long tunnel, and somehow it snapped the last of the shift into place. Panting and trembling, royal clothing clinging to his clammy skin, Shara hoisted himself back to his feet. He didn't need a mirror to know that he was Iliath once again.

No. I look like Iliath.

He didn't need more than that.

With a final smoothing of the coat and a brush at his hair, he crept to the side of the doors, unbolted them, and waited.

CHAPTER 47

ISHARA KO HAN

The doors burst open, and Thosena barrelled into the room shouting "Your Majesty!" as if she truly cared.

The act lasted but a moment. She called "Keep searching!" to whoever was outside and shut the doors behind her.

Shara leapt.

He'd drawn the knife from her hip before she realized he was upon her, and as her eyes widened in shock, he spun the weapon and plunged it into his own shoulder, making no effort to stifle his scream.

"Your—" Thosena tried to back away, but Shara held her firm.

"Help!" he cried, throwing himself backward into the doors. His body throbbed, but he did it again, scrambling for the doorknob with one hand and clinging to a seething Thosena with the other. A frantic twist, and the righthand door opened. He pitched sideways and let himself fall through, dragging Thosena with him.

Her weight crashed on top of him, and the wind rushed

from his lungs on a gasp of pain. He tightened his hold, writhing and shouting for aid.

Thosena strained against his grip. "You little—"

He slammed his forehead into hers. She cursed and jerked back, and he dug his fingers into her arm as stars danced over his vision. Fear knotted in his gut—the battle raged on, fierce as ever. No pause, no shouts of surprise. No Sothal or Mereth.

"Help!" With every passing second, the struggle was less a ruse. Thosena too had alvithi blood, and Shara wouldn't be able to hold her long. "Traitor! Someone hel—"

She wrenched on the knife, and his cry cut off in another raw scream.

"No you don't," she snarled.

Tears blurred his already swimming vision, and a whimper bubbled in his throat. Someone *had* to have noticed. If they didn't—

"Your Majesty!"

The voice and thundering footsteps broke over him like dawn after a nightmare. His body went limp, and Thosena leapt to her feet—and stumbled into the hands of two approaching figures.

A third stepped tentatively forward, his expression part awe and part horror. "Your . . . Your Majesty."

Shara let the sailor pull him to his feet and nearly collapsed against the poor man with a lurch that involved no acting at all. Across the deck, the sounds of battle began to fade, rippling outward from the sudden appearance of the battered Barathi king.

He'd done it.

Now for the difficult part.

"This is absurd." Thosena jerked against her captors as they stripped off her weapons. "Release me."

"So you can attack the king again?" Coated with blood and

clutching his twisted left arm, Mereth sidled forward, pain and relief mingled with anger in his expression. Throwing a look of deep loathing at Thosena, he crouched beside a figure sprawled on the deck amid streaks of blood. Sothal stirred and moaned as Mereth helped him sit up.

Thosena glowered. "I—"

Her voice faltered; she seemed to have planned no defense for this situation. Quiet murmurs rose from the onlookers, and weapons hissed as they were wiped clean and sheathed. Others in the crowd kept their weapons out, exchanging frowns either of mistrust for their enemies or concern for their admiral or king.

Drawing himself up, Shara pulled the knife from his shoulder. Cringing at the pain and his stupidly overdramatic flourish, he tossed it at Thosena's feet. "You *what*, precisely?" he asked over its ringing clatter. "Or will you tell me that's not your knife, that it wasn't you aiming at my heart just now?"

The murmurs and expressions darkened. As sailors whispered to one another, Shara jerked the cabin door closed, disguising the movement as a jolt of pain.

"Your Majesty." The sailor who'd helped him up inched closer, looking both hopeful and terrified that Shara might lean against him.

"I'm fine." Movement beyond the ship caught his eye, and he jolted for real this time. "Signal the other ships to cease fighting. This battle is over."

The sailor hesitated, glanced once between his king and his admiral, and hurried away. No one else moved.

Shara locked eyes with Thosena, and another pang of regret cut through his resolution. Her jokes about paperwork, her easy manner . . . How much of it had been an act? How long had she planned this, believing the carnage strewn around them to be a price worth paying?

"Well, Your Majesty?" Her lip curled in a snarl.

Korith's lessons ringing in his ears, he lifted his chin. Still uncomfortable. It probably always would be—and something about that thought, about the fact that it didn't bother him, made the posture easier to maintain.

The guards frowned warily when he ordered them to release her, but they did as commanded and retreated a few short paces. Shara stepped forward and raised his voice.

"Admiral Thosena, you attacked and abducted me, drugged me, smuggled me aboard this ship, and just now you tried to murder me." He rubbed at the still-burning knife wound. "All with the intent, I assume, of placing the blame on our Tethamari allies and turning this battle into the first of a war. Do you have anything to say?"

Thosena's back and shoulders sloped in supplication, but her head remained level and her eyes glinted. "I have only a request, Your Majesty."

"Oh?"

She nodded at the royal quarters. "Send someone to search the cabin. I believe there is evidence which will... *shift* the blame elsewhere." Her eyes bored into him, and when she spoke next, the sneering words were for him alone. "An alvithi impersonating our king and accusing an admiral of murder and warmongering. What will they think of that, I wonder?"

Icy insects crawled up his spine. This was not Faresh, circling his prey and convinced of his utter superiority. Thosena faced him as an equal, daring him to meet her challenge while knowing full well that he wasn't Iliath.

In a flash of memory, he was crouched on a beach in a storm, where a grinning Korith announced with unwavering certainty that next time, Shara would rescue him as a sea dragon.

The same urge to flee shot through him. He let it seize his limbs, let its chill soak him like rain—and amid its swirling storm, he slowly raised a hand and waved the nearest royal guard toward the cabin. The fear's hold broke, and he met Thosena's eyes. "Let's find out."

Her face slackened, then hardened into stone. Shara turned toward the doors, a flock of seabirds spinning circles in his stomach, and waited.

The world waited with him, still and silent apart from the sloshing of the sea and the soft flutter of sails and banners. No more ringing swords, thundering cannons, shouting sailors. Even the ship rocked gently, too tired to spite him any longer—or else it simply knew that he couldn't handle more nausea right now.

A grunt. Metallic creaking. The scrape of chair legs on the wooden floor. Shara's stomach-birds wheeled faster. What if Thosena's drugs had worn off and all the noise woke Iliath? What if he called for help or sat up in the dinghy and caught the guard's attention through the window?

Long, agonizing moments passed, but at last the guard reemerged. "Nothing, Your Majesty." She ruffled a hand through her windblown hair and glanced between Shara and Thosena. "I checked all the drawers, the cabinets, under the bed, even picked up the mattress. Unless we're looking for Her Highness's hairbrush, I don't think there's anything there."

Shara nearly swayed with relief, but somehow he maintained his royal demeanor. "Well, Admiral?"

She glowered, but she had no response.

"Thank you," Shara said to the guard. He gestured at the cuffs clipped to her belt. "If I might?"

Thosena's expression darkened as the woman handed the cuffs to Shara, but she offered no resistance when he fastened the first one over the torn sleeve of her jacket. Her narrowed eyes watched him in anger . . . but also something else. "Who are you?"

He stepped closer, bringing them nearly chest to chest, and lowered his chin to regard her directly. "My name is Ishara," he said quietly. "I'm a teveth of Clan Han. Did your father teach you that word, Admiral? Teveth?" He searched her face. "It means my wings are still growing, but I fly all the same. It means I claw myself back up when I fall. It means I don't run. Not from the storm. Not from you." Korith's grinning face flashed before his eyes, and his throat tightened. "And never from myself."

The second cuff gave a resolute *click*, and Shara stumbled back, elated yet suddenly exhausted. The sailors grasped Thosena's arms again and marched her toward the hold. Shara watched their descent as if through a spring mist, staring until the rustling movements across the deck finally pulled him back into everything that remained.

"Captain Sothal." He pivoted slowly. "Commander Albrith?"

The two Tethamari made their way forward, Sothal supported by Mereth.

"Please accept my apology for the actions of my admiral and everything that has resulted from them. I know it's hardly sufficient given what's happened, but I hope to prove my sincere desire for peace with more than words. If you wish to press on to Tethamar, I understand." He swallowed a ball of nerves. "But I hope that you will instead return with us to Farna. Her Highness and I will lay this to rest once and for all."

He extended his hand. Sothal clasped it immediately, and though Albrith's handshake was stiff, she shook nonetheless. As they and Mereth began barking orders at those well enough to still manage a ship, Shara slipped into the cabin and locked the door behind him.

The real king was waiting, and the least Shara could do before curling up in a sunbeam and sleeping forever was ensure that Iliath did not wake up in that dinghy.

CHAPTER 48

MORE SHARA

The next time someone made Shara king, he was going to outlaw healing rooms.

Well, no. That would be horrible. But perhaps he'd change the configuration of the beds, which seemed to jump into his path no matter where he paced.

And while he was at it, he'd get rid of the stench. And the oppressive silence, too, which was leaving him little to do but think about all the ways his impending audience with Iliath could go wrong.

He almost wished he and Korith hadn't stopped to visit the still-sleeping Tishel on their way to Iliath's rooms, but Korith could twist any route through the palace into a detour past his sister, and Shara could pace here as easily as he could outside the king's study.

At the far end of the room, he pivoted sharply and nearly collided with yet another bed. With a feline hiss, he leapt out of its way.

"All right there, furball?" From his place beside Tishel's bed, Korith gave a quiet laugh that sputtered into a cough, and

Shara changed course to hurry toward him. "I'm fine," Korith chuckled, waving him off. "But you need to calm down. You know they can smell fear." He gestured around the room at the empty beds.

Shara rolled his eyes, but his muscles loosened. "I know." Smiling sheepishly, he raked a hand through his hair and over his horns. "I know."

He wove the rest of the way to Korith. After giving the sleeping Tishel a soft pat on the shoulder, he fell against the wall, blowing out a breath and inhaling deeply. Korith's scent mingled with the tang of burn salve, but he no longer reeked of smoke and alsum, and Shara battled down the urge to shift into something small and curl up in the afternoon sunlight spilling over Korith's shoulders. Iliath would never know where he'd disappeared to.

The moment of calm faded, and tension coiled through his limbs again. Perhaps all this waiting to meet Iliath had not been wise. Shara had spoken with him, of course—he'd revived the king on the *Rosette* and explained enough that Iliath wouldn't accidentally reveal the true circumstances of his kidnapping. But the remaining explanations had been left to others. Korith, Nashai, and Gepar had spent most of the past few days locked away with the king, each telling what they knew of the previous week's events. All of them had thought it best that Shara not formally meet the king until Iliath had accepted the news that "we, uh, replaced him," as Korith had said with an awkward shrug.

But now the time had come, and not even Korith's presence and the hope of Tishel awakening made the waiting any easier.

Fiddling with his shirt—Korith had gifted him Barathi garments and politely neglected to comment when Shara removed most of the shirt's back and added his mother's coat to the ensemble—he shifted his weight from foot to foot. The floor's chill seeped into his toes, and the rough stone of the wall scraped over the leaves and twigs along his spine.

The sensations should have been reassuring, but he only fidgeted worse. Should he have dressed more human? Looked more human?

At his side, Korith bent forward, careful of his wound, and swiped Tishel's flask off the bedside table. Shara shoved aside the doubts and focused on the sleeping figure.

Willow had been as honest about Tishel's chances of recovery as she'd been about Korith's, but her hope had shone through, as well as her admiration—Tishel's wind shield had been more effective than she'd believed. Several days had proved Willow's optimism well-founded, but though Tishel was now waking regularly, neither Shara nor Korith had yet witnessed it, and every hour Korith fretted more and said less.

Korith turned the flask over and over in his hands, and the faint sound of sloshing liquid filled the otherwise quiet room. Sunlight reflected off the polished metal, sending streaks of light flickering over the wall and wisps of chocolate scent wafting between them with each—

"Do you think she's avoiding me?" Korith asked.

Shara started, his half-formed words of comfort stalled by the unexpected question. "What?"

"Do you think she just . . . pretends to sleep every time I come?"

A pang shot through his chest. He'd not delivered Tishel's unfinished message—she'd survived, after all, and he hadn't wanted to put the wrong words in her mouth. But he doubted the right words had had anything to do with avoiding Korith.

"No," he said earnestly. "No, of course not. They said she asked about you when she first woke up, remember?"

"That doesn't mean . . ." He swallowed hard and rolled the flask faster, until Shara worried his shaking, blistered hands would drop it. "I wanted to set things right between us. But every time I asked to talk to her, she said she was busy. And she was, I suppose, but... But what if she—" His knuckles whitened, and he shoved abruptly off the wall and gave a jerky shrug as he grabbed his cane. "But you're probably right. Anyway, we should go. Don't want you to be late."

Shara stepped into his path. "Korith, she's healing. She's not avoiding you. Trust me. I'm alvithi. I'd know if she were awake." He shook his head dramatically, then snatched a wilting flower out of the vase on Tishel's bedside table and ate it for good measure.

A small smile tugged at Korith's lips. A few more turns of the flask, and the expression widened somewhat. "I'm not sure I believe you, but you gave yourself a compliment, so I'll take it."

"Oh, be quiet."

"No, really, if I'd known I could balance us out by wallowing in doubt, I'd have done it a long time ago."

"You're hilarious."

"Or was it because I nearly died? Because I could do that a couple times a month if you need—"

Snickering, he ducked Shara's swat—then yelped in surprise and lurched into the table, arm clutching his wounded side. The table legs dragged over the floor with a loud bark, and the vase wobbled dangerously. The cane and flask both slipped from Korith's hands and hit the stone in a loud clatter.

Tishel groaned, and her eyes fluttered open.

"Si!" Korith hurried around the bed, nearly tripping over the fallen flask. "You're awake!"

Shara's heart swelled. "About time."

She squinted against the sunlight and tilted her head away from its morning cheer, only to stiffen when her gaze came into focus on her visitors. Her face colored as she took in

Korith, then twitched in surprise at Shara. For long seconds, her eyes travelled back and forth between them, refusing to settle, but finally she frowned at Shara.

"Have you always been half tree?"

He laughed. "Yes, I have."

"Oh." Cautiously she drew her arms from beneath her blanket and plucked her spectacles from the bedside table. She slid them on and surveyed him again. "That explains a lot."

The remark was so like Tishel that he grinned despite having no idea what she meant.

Across the bed, Korith showed no sign of having heard the exchange. His intense gaze had stalled somewhere near Tishel's chin, and his trembling hands twirled a flask he no longer carried. "How are you feeling?" he asked softly.

"Awful," she said to the rafters, which seemed to be as close to Korith's face as she could make herself look. She pressed a palm gingerly against her torso, and a bit of steel sharpened her expression. "But less dead than Thosena hoped. Nothing keeps you alive like spite."

A soft, almost frantic laugh broke from Korith, and though Tishel glanced at him for only half a breath, his face spread into a wavering smile. "It's not spite. You're . . ." He swallowed so visibly that Shara's own throat closed in sympathy. "You're too amazing to die."

Tishel flushed, scoffed, looked anywhere but at Korith. Her attention paused on Shara before settling on the bed Korith had been placed in after the fire. She clenched her jaw and looked away, daring another half-glance at Korith. "Yes, well," she said stiffly, her face growing even redder, "maybe it's a family trait."

Korith's face lit up. Shara chirruped.

With obvious effort at ignoring them both, Tishel drew a bracing breath and pushed herself upright. Immediately she fell back, her sharp gasp deepening into a frustrated huff.

Korith reached out. "Can I—"

"I don't need your help," she growled.

He flinched back, and by the time regret flashed over Tishel's face, he'd already pivoted to stare at the wall. "Right. Of course. Sorry."

Tishel's hands balled around her blanket. "I'm—"

"No, it's fine." His voice came out high and thin. "I was . . . Never mind. We should go."

He rattled off something about Shara visiting Iliath and himself going to see the Mithels, his tone so painfully casual that the errands sounded like excuses even to Shara. With a forced smile at Tishel, he snatched up his cane and hurried for the door, shoulders hunching. Chest tight, Shara followed.

"Lord—" Tishel's voice caught. "Korith."

Korith staggered to a halt. Inch by inch, his shoulders lowered, but he didn't turn. Stuck halfway between the bed and the door, Shara could only glance from one sibling to the other, as invisible as if he were a whole tree.

Tishel stared at Korith's back, one foot twitching visibly beneath her blanket. "I'm going to be extremely bored, stuck here like this. Perhaps you would . . . come back. If you have time."

Korith whirled around. "Of course," he croaked, voice splintering. A smile spread over his face, and with unsteady footsteps, he made his way back to her bed. "Of course. We can talk. Or play malir. Or drink chocolate. Or . . . or sit and do nothing. It'll be amazing."

She rolled her eyes. "We can expand your vocabulary."

"Sure." Korith grinned. "Whatever you want. Just us. No gryphons."

Tishel frowned at Shara, who smiled and shrugged. Korith could explain if he chose, assuming he had any more complete sentences left in him.

Unperturbed, she nodded. "All right. Good. I . . ." She fidgeted with her shirt, then released it abruptly and resumed staring at the ceiling. "Good luck with the king, Shara."

She said nothing else to Korith, but from the look on his face, he didn't care.

Leaving Tishel to rest, they made their way toward Iliath's rooms. With every step, Korith's smile grew wider and his gait more buoyant, until Shara feared rain might start falling out of the cloudless sky just to counteract Korith's cheer. But no rain fell and no clouds formed, and Shara had nothing to do but bask in the sunlight, startle passing servants, and absorb Korith's good mood.

"So," he observed after several hallways, grinning, "now that that's settled, you have only Lady Bethen to worry about."

Korith's face turned bright red. "One thing at a time, furball," he chuckled, shoving gently into Shara.

But the rest of the way down the hall, he alternated between glancing over his shoulder and composing lunch invitations under his breath.

By the time they arrived at Iliath's rooms, Shara had startled one too many passersby, and it was no longer amusing.

He and Korith were bowed into Iliath's outer office by two frowning guards and a wide-eyed Amesal, and Shara immediately began pacing. The lack of hospital beds did not make his progress any easier—he couldn't see a single thing while images kept flashing across his vision. The people in the halls. Amesal and the guards. Tishel.

He passed in front of the mirror and paused almost automatically to check that his horns were straight, and the childish old habit sent his nerves flaring like lightning.

What if Iliath didn't let him stay? The thought had not occurred until now, when all those reactions cascaded into him at once, reminding him how alvithi he was.

Yes, Thosena could have achieved her goal without her imarth abilities, but her actions had made all too clear the threat that an alvithi among humans could pose. Shara wasn't foolish or suddenly overconfident enough to ignore the truth: He'd impersonated the king. He could do it again.

Suddenly his straight horns seemed more an indictment than a recommendation.

"Shara?" Korith appeared beside him in the mirror, soft concern in his eyes.

"Do you think he'll let me stay?" he blurted out, tearing his gaze from his reflection.

Korith's brow creased. "What?"

"I want to stay. I know I said . . ." They hadn't ever talked about his resolution to leave, and now that it could very well become reality—a royally decreed reality—he needed Korith to know the truth. "But what if Iliath . . ."

His fears tumbled out of him while he paced the bed-free office, Iliath's study door looming in the corner of his vision like a gaping maw preparing to devour him. Korith listened in silence, and Shara was preparing to give him permission to be as overoptimistic and gryphony as possible when the inner door opened and Princess Nashai emerged, her eyes alight and an armful of papers clutched to her chest. Lady Masar followed, hiding behind her hair.

They started in unison, and Shara wilted further.

But immediately Nashai's expression shifted into delight. "Shara."

The cheer in her voice brought a smile to his face despite everything, and he bowed, trying not to squirm or otherwise destroy her first impression of his true form. "Your Highness. I hope the negotiations are going well?"

There'd been plenty of uncertainty about the treaty even after Iliath's recovery—longstanding prejudice did not die because of a single joint rescue effort, and Shara had overheard more than one grumbled conversation in the past few days, some among the Barathi, others among the Tethamari.

But Nashai and Iliath were still trying. And if the humans could see past old prejudices and misconceptions, perhaps there was hope for Barath's lone alvithi, too.

Nashai nodded resolutely, fingers working the edges of the papers. "I do believe there's hope yet for this treaty, thanks to you."

Thanks to you. Old denials and self-deprecations warred with a new urge to cherish the compliment. "I'm glad. I heard Lord Fethan wanted you to return to Tethamar."

Nashai and Lady Masar shared an expression that was somehow both smug and embarrassed.

"He did indeed," Nashai said. "Poor Teren had to sign a number of words she pretends not to know."

Lady Masar turned pink, and Korith shifted a snort into a cough.

Shara winced. "Was it that bad?"

She smirked. "It was nothing I couldn't manage. And excellent practice for negotiating with Iliath." Shara's face must have done something horrible, for her smile softened. "You needn't worry—he's in a fine mood, and very eager to meet you."

By the time Shara remembered he could shift away a blush, it was too late, and there was no alvithi cure for nausea. "That's, uh. That's good."

Unless Iliath was simply eager to get rid of him. Or behead him.

Did humans behead people, or was that idle rumor?

Nashai hefted the papers into one arm and tucked a stray braid behind her ear. "You're still coming to dinner, yes? I'm so looking forward to speaking with you at greater length."

His face warmed. Between his nerves and Tishel's awakening, he'd all but forgotten her invitation. "Yes, of course."

"Wonderful." She nodded at her papers, then the outer door. "Well, if you'll excuse me, I have a great deal to think about already. Lord Fethan will be furious at some of the terms Iliath suggested, but it isn't negotiating unless someone's furious, right?"

"Oh. Um, sure."

He shook her proffered hand, and she bid him farewell and disappeared out the door. Lady Masar lingered on the threshold, chewing her lip as another deep blush spread over her cheeks. Shara squirmed—had he actually thought telling her she was pretty would be easier than rescuing Iliath?

Had he actually thought she'd want to hear that from *him*?

"Teren?" came Nashai's voice.

She jumped and half disappeared out the door before sticking her head back through. "I like your horns. They're really bushy."

The door slammed in Shara's flushed face.

Over the patter of his heartbeat came her rapidly tapping footsteps, then a shriek of dismay. "'Really *bushy*'? What was I *thinking*?"

Korith's laughter billowed through the room like a swirl of brisk wind promising a refreshing spring rain. "There, see?" He gave one of Shara's horns an affectionate tug. "So long as Iliath is as enamored as Lady Masar, you have nothing to worry about."

"Oh, shut up." He batted Korith's hand away, but he couldn't quell a smile, and the squirrel-dragons in his stomach started to settle. Lady Masar wasn't bothered—far from it. Nashai had supported him before, and her opinion hadn't changed. Tishel had wished him luck. Even Korith, he recalled, had at first feared that true-form Shara might eat him.

His taut muscles uncoiled, and the looming jaws before him shifted back into a simple study door. He hadn't come all this way to start hiding and apologizing again. He would meet Iliath as himself—all of himself.

Breathe. "I can do this."

"Yes. Yes you can." Korith patted his shoulder. "And don't worry—I may be watching my gryphoning more carefully, but I'll still be around when you need me. Now, however, is not one of those times."

He gave Shara's horns another tug, and a single yellow leaf fluttered to the ground between them. Shara nudged it with his toe and felt himself smile, and when heat spread through his face, he didn't bother shifting it away. "More Shara?"

"More Shara." Korith spun him around and shoved him toward the door. "Good luck."

CHAPTER 49

TEVETH

King Iliath was a lot more intimidating when he wasn't unconscious.

He stood beside the window, his posture straight and regal, his hair combed and tied in a sort of artful disarray. An emerald coat set off his sharp eyes, nearly distracting from the dark shadows beneath them.

It was utterly disconcerting staring at the man who'd been his reflection for a week, but even more disconcerting were the little differences: a faint pockmark above Iliath's left eye, a bit of sharpness to his nose, a somewhat softer curve to his jawline. If the king moved, Shara would undoubtedly notice additional—

The king.

Cursing himself, he dipped his head and dropped to his knee, flourishing his mother's coat as Korith had taught him. "Your Majesty."

Soft laughter floated above him. "I don't imagine you've bowed to many people this last week."

The lingering tension in Shara's muscles loosened a fraction. Iliath didn't *sound* furious or threatened. "No, Your Majesty."

He rose from the bow, and he and Iliath spent an awkward moment pretending not to be assessing one another. Though the king's gaze never wavered, his fingers twitched at his sides, bunching handfuls of his coat into emerald knots. A nervous habit?

He couldn't possibly be nervous?

As if in imitation, Shara found his fingers playing at his own coat. He'd washed away the blood and patched it as best he could, and though it was a bit bedraggled still, a bit out of place overtop his modified Barathi garments, it felt right. What was Shara, after all, if not a bedraggled, unusual blend of alvithi and Barathi?

"I must admit," Iliath said at length, "that after everything I've heard, you're not what I expected."

Diplomatic—there was no telling whether he'd intended it as a compliment or a slight.

Even so, warmth crawled up Shara's neck. "And what did you expect, Your Majesty?"

Iliath broke into a smile. "A dragon."

Shara couldn't quell a grin, though only his feet saw it at first. "I could be a dragon," he said when he'd forced his head back up, "but our conversation would be rather one-sided."

Was that too bold? How had he spent a week being a king and not learned how to talk to one?

But Iliath merely laughed and gestured to the table beside the fireplace. An overlarge bowl of fruit peeked out from amid piles of notes and open books, and the king nodded to it when they'd taken their places. "They seem to believe abduction has increased my appetite. Please, help yourself."

Shara took an apple and feigned innocence.

"Now then." Iliath folded his hands on top of a book. "If you would, I wish to hear this story from you."

It spilled from him like rain, soft at first, but soon steady and strong. Every failure and embarrassment, every triumph and trial. Soon he'd leapt to his feet and begun striding about the room, waving his hands like Gepar while his coat fanned out around him. Details he'd have omitted a week ago now flowed into the story almost without reserve. All the pieces of himself swirled together, both the ones he'd left too long in the midday sun and the ones he'd buried in the darkest corner of his cave.

When he finished, Iliath leaned back in his chair and gazed up at him in a kind of quiet awe. "I was mistaken," he said after a long pause. "You are most certainly a dragon."

Shara's feet got another embarrassed smile.

Rising from the chair, Iliath gestured him toward the door. Swallowing a fresh wave of nerves, Shara slipped after him and settled into step at his side, smiling at a slack-jawed Amesal as they left Iliath's rooms. The two guards followed them watchfully.

They passed through the halls in silence and descended the stairs to the gardens. Shara drew a long breath, taking in the blossoming flowers and awakening greenery as though meeting old friends after a long winter apart. Cool air breezed over him, dancing through his horns and rustling the leaves trailing down his back.

The guards frowned in unison when Iliath waved them away, but they retreated nonetheless. Chuckling wryly, Iliath led Shara to the far end of the miniature wilderness and leaned against the stone barrier, his face to the wind coming off the sea. In the sunlight, the shadows beneath his eyes stood out more starkly, yet the ordeal seemed to weigh less heavily upon his shoulders.

For long minutes, they stood there together. Iliath's fingers twitched against the stone, and Shara wrapped himself in his coat's folds and shifted scales off and onto his arms. It felt as though he'd strained a muscle and needed to gradually begin using it again, easing it back to its former condition.

Without warning, Iliath spun to face him, but when he opened his mouth, no sound emerged. Snapping it shut, he turned back to the bay and cleared his throat. "I've spent two days attempting to craft a proper way to thank you for everything you've done, and I have nothing. So I hope you will accept a simple, honest thank you." He bowed deeply. "I am grateful beyond words, Ishara."

If Shara could have shifted into a puddle, he would have. A big, boiling puddle of alvithi. "I . . ." He laughed. "I'd like to say it was my pleasure, but the truth is, most of the time it was downright unpleasant."

Iliath's mouth pitched into a knowing smile. "That's something of a relief, to be honest."

Shara's stomach twisted, and he braced himself against the wall. There it was, and yet he couldn't make himself broach the subject, so he only added, "But it was my honor, Your Majesty."

A rush of wind leapt up from the sea and swirled around them, and they both distracted themselves righting their garments and smoothing their hair. Shara closed his eyes and imagined riding the current to some far island, Korith on his back. Not to escape, but simply to fly.

"And what will you do now?" Iliath seemed to read his thoughts.

His claws shot out, and he gripped at the stone, grounding himself in the sensation. "I want to attend Lady Malothi's funeral. After that . . ."

He owed it to the clan to return, to address what had happened at the hunt. And he owed them a proper farewell. But even after everything that had happened, the thought of facing them made him want to be ill. Perhaps Korith would come if he asked.

Korith Aman meeting an entire clan of alvithi. He nearly laughed.

"Once I've fully healed, I need to go back to my people."

Iliath's expression closed. "Yes. Of course."

Disappointment feathered the king's words, giving Shara the courage to say the rest. "Ultimately, though, I'd like to remain in Farna. But if you'd prefer I leave Barath—"

"Absolutely not." Despite his firm tone, Iliath's body relaxed, and his fingers stopped twitching. "Nashai and I have an agreement: if you leave Barath, she may invite you to the Tethamari court. And I'm not starting our alliance with *that*, let alone our marriage."

A competitive glint sparkled in his eyes, and Shara could not think of a single appropriate response to the announcement that Iliath and Nashai were having an amicable argument over who got to keep him. "Then the marriage—"

He bit his tongue. That was none of his business.

But Iliath didn't seem bothered. "We're still negotiating, and after everything that's transpired, there is more to discuss than ever. But I am hopeful, yes." An awkward grin flitted over his face, and with an overloud cough, he straightened and regarded Shara again. "More to the point, however . . . If you truly do wish to remain in Barath, then I would like to offer you a place in *my* court."

"A—what?" Would the guards come running if he shifted out bigger ears?

Iliath's gaze became serious, searching. A bit sad. "Admiral Thosena will face justice for her actions, but I cannot deny that she was right about many things. Barath is an economic disaster. When my nobles aren't showing false devotion, they're squabbling with one another or making alliances of their own that cause more harm than good. Faresh hasn't been seen since the day of the battle, and pirates will continue to threaten the north as well." He sighed and ran a hand through his hair. "My father left me a country full of knots, I'm afraid, and I was always too cowardly to question him. I need people I can trust to help me set things right."

Shara was still appreciating why Korith respected Iliath so much when the last statement bowled into him like Rathen. "And you think I . . ."

Iliath studied him keenly. "It has not escaped my notice that while you pretended to be me, one of the four people who knew the truth died, and two others nearly did as well." Anger flashed in his eyes. "Some might call me a fool to trust you. I spent a week in the hold of a rotting ship, at the mercy of a trusted officer who betrayed me. One of my advisors was stealing from the treasury. Perhaps I've not learned my lesson."

Shara held his breath.

"And yet you had every opportunity to take my place, and instead you went searching for me and uncovered Thosena's treachery. She left you for dead, and you came after me. You stopped a war few others cared to prevent. Even I . . ." He stiffened. "For all my talk of peace, I am not proud to admit that I would likely have done precisely what she wanted in the wake of the coronation."

A flock of seabirds soared overhead, and Iliath watched them with a sort of determined distraction. When at last they'd disappeared over the water, some of his tension had faded.

"Given what you've experienced and everything I've said, I understand if such a role is not to your liking. And I will gratefully reward you in whatever manner you wish. But you are unlike anyone in my court, Ishara, and I *would* be a fool to ignore the value in that."

A rueful grin tugged at Shara's mouth. He'd been ignoring it for years.

But now. Now Iliath wanted him to join the Barathi court. And not only join it, but act within it. Like Korith or Malothi or Tishel. He gripped the wall, lightheaded. It was like that day in the bookstore all over again.

But while part of him still searched the horizon for a nice cave on a secluded island, the rest looked down into the city and thrummed with a sense of possibility.

Besides, he could visit a secluded island any time he wanted.

"Your Majesty, I'm honored." He drew a steadying breath. "I would be proud to aid you in any way I can." Another pause, this time to ensure his next words were born of fact rather than doubt. "But I still know little of Barath and life among humans, and I'll need to learn—"

"Oh, yes, of course." Iliath's face lit. "I'll see that you are tutored in everything you need to know and assisted in developing those skills and inclinations you already possess. You have the instincts and tenacity, not to mention your unique perspective. Anything else can be taught, though it will be a great deal of learning, and of course—" His cheeks flushed, and he glanced toward the sea with an embarrassed laugh. "I've never rewarded someone before. I feel I'm doing a rather terrible job of it."

Shara chuckled. "By offering the opportunity to learn and grow and help build something better?"

"Even so, I expect I ought to have mentioned the estate first."

Trailing a foot through the cool grass, Shara bit down a reply. He could find another time to decline an estate and inform Iliath that he'd spent his first month in Barath sleeping as a lynx at the end of Korith's bed.

"So." Iliath looped his hands behind his back, but even that did not obscure the finger twitching. "You accept, then?"

His heart swelled, whole again in more ways than one, and a shiver spread over his scales. "I do, yes."

Smiling broadly, Iliath launched into an enthusiastic description of all the things Shara could learn, the books he should read, the people who would teach him.

Turning to gaze out over the water, Shara let the words roll over him like the salty wind. Tutors and books and lessons in being Barathi. At this rate, he'd be teveth forever.

Slipping a hand into his pocket, he brushed his fingers against Korith's sketch and smiled.

There were worse things to be.

Acknowledgements

It is a truth universally acknowledged, that a writer who has completed a novel, must be in want of the words necessary to thank everyone who helped her do it.

deep breath

First and foremost, huge thanks to you, the reader, for supporting a debut author and her floofy shapeshifter sidekick. Whether you're someone I've known for years or someone I'll never meet, I'm so excited that you wanted to spend time in my imaginary world.

Massive thank-yous to my beta and sensitivity readers: Julie, Anna, Jameson, Olivia, Michele, Claire, Sarah, Lauren, Grace, Selina, Michelle, and Deborah. Reading a book draft is a huge commitment, and I'm so grateful that you stuck with mine. TWK would not be the book it is without your edits, critiques, enthusiasm, suggestions, and copious marginal emoji. Thanks also to Shannyn and RJ for chatting with me about EDS and chronic pain and to Libby for suggesting more character arc for Korith.

Much dark chocolate to my alpha reader, Laura, who saw the first and worst of Shara and wouldn't let me light his story on fire no matter how many times I wanted to.

Endless appreciation to Comet Coffee, Zingerman's Deli, The Java House, and Global Infusion for supplying coffee, chai, pastries, and writing atmosphere.

Eternal gratitude to my writing groups, the Sparkly Space Wrimos and the Creative Retreaters (we need a real name, y'all). You listened to me whine, gave me feedback on my zillions of map drafts instead of running away screaming, enthused over all my snippets, worked through story problems with me, answered my n00bish business questions, and wrote Hamilton parodies for our characters to sing on karaoke night.

Shout-out to the FBI agent stuck monitoring me after my writing research put me on a watchlist. I'd love to meet you at a book signing someday!

Many batches of Chex Mix to my family for supporting me and my fantasy-nerd endeavors and for nodding and smiling when I ramble about my imaginary friends. (And apologies to my dad for the lack of submarines in this book. I'll see what I can do in the next one!)

And finally, to my Eagle and Guide. For all the grace, inspiration, and aid I never even thought to ask for—thank you. You rock.

ABOUT THE AUTHOR

K.T. Ivanrest wanted to be a cat or a horse when she grew up, but after failing to metamorphose into either, she began writing stories about them instead. Soon the horses became unicorns and the cats sprouted wings, and once the dragons arrived, there was no turning back. When ~~procrastinating~~ not writing, she can be found sewing, bookbinding, baking, and dreaming about the beach. She has a PhD in Classical Studies, which will come in handy when aliens finally make contact and it turns out they speak Latin.

www.ingramcontent.com/pod-product-compliance
Lightning Source LLC
Chambersburg PA
CBHW031303210726

48287CB00005B/1398